SPARROWHAWK

JACK FRAKE

Book One in the Sparrowhawk Series

A novel by

EDWARD CLINE

MacAdam/Cage Publishing
155 Sansome Street, Suite 550
San Francisco, CA 94104
www.macadamcage.com

Library of Congress Cataloging-in-Publication Data

Cline, Edward, 1946 —
Sparrowhawk—Jack Frake : a novel / by Edward Cline.
p. cm. — (Sparrowhawk ; bk. 1)
ISBN: 1-931561-00-1 (alk. paper)
1-931561-21-4 (PBK)
1. United States—History—Colonial period, ca. 1600-1775—Fiction.
2. Great Britain—History—george II, 1727-1760—Fiction.
3. Immigrants—Fiction. 4. Smugglers—Fiction. 5. Boys—Fiction.
I. Title. II. Title: Jack Frake.
PS3553.L544S63 2001
813'.54—dc21 2001044181

Manufactured in the United States of America.

10 9 8 7 6 5 4 3 2 1

Book design by Dorothy Carico Smith.

Cover painting "Shipping Off the South Coast of England"
by Charles Brooking, 1723–1759

SPARROWHAWK

JACK FRAKE

Book One in the Sparrowhawk Series

A novel by

EDWARD CLINE

MacAdam/Cage

The special province of drama *"is to create… action… which springs from the past but is directed toward the future and is always great with things to come."*

— Aristotle, *On Drama*

CONTENTS

1744

Chapter 1: The Map

IT IS WHEN THE FOG CLEARS, AND THE MOON AND THE STARS ARE BRILLIANT, and the white sails of faraway ships on an invisible horizon are sharp and almost luminescent as they glide past on their grand, unknown errands, that a boy of ten may take stock of himself and of the world he knows. This is a quiet, precious time; he knows that the world is not so much focused on him, as he on it, through a special lens in his inchoate soul. The brevity and suddenness of this moment, which strikes without warning such souls as do not submit to the intrusive humdrum of their daily lives, signals its own importance, for its incandescent violence must make one passionately certain that one is a worthy crucible.

Jack Frake was a boy of ten, and tonight he was such a crucible.

The wind that gusted around him in the cubbyhole of rocks, on the edge of a cliff high over the shore below, surged through the coarse material of his clothing and chilled him so that he shivered. But the uncontrollable spasms in his knees and shoulders made him aware only that this same wind drove the distant sails and lifted their pennants and banners to snap proudly in the cold air.

The charge that ignited the moment for him was a map, the first he had ever seen. He had learned some hours ago that he lived in Cornwall, and that his secret cubbyhole sat precisely on the southern edge of a great island, England. Where before he had been aware only of the hills, fields and cliffs on the one side, and the ocean on the other, now he held in his mind an abstraction, and it was drawn from a part of the world he knew. Beyond that tiny realm lay the thrilling, unexplored empire of the island. The island itself was big enough for his ambition; he had the crazy notion that he could run along the path of its outline from the point where he sat and return to it days later from the opposite direction, not to impress himself with the magnitude of the island, but to prove his joyful possession of it.

The map belonged to Robert Parmley, rector of the parish of St. Gwynn-by-Godolphin, whose church was a five-mile walk from Jack Frake's home in Trelowe. The parson, once a rising authority on antiquities, was now a lonely, shunned old man whose indiscreet, risqué remarks decades ago on the private life of a prelate of the Church of England had been forgotten by both the prelate and the parson, but whose gravity was such that he had been condemned to permanent assignment in this spiritually bovine parish. Here he preached to sparsely attended services, helped the poor, infirm, and old when he could, and collected a few worn coppers, aside from tithes, from villagers and cottagers who could spare the time or the care to put their children under his tutelage.

From Jack Frake's locally notorious parents he had exacted only a promise from them to appear regularly in church once a month. The promise was not kept — the parson suspected that Cephas and Huldah Frake merely wanted to be rid of the boy for a while — but Jack Frake was the brightest youth he had ever undertaken to introduce to the rudiments of reading, writing and ciphering, and so he was reluctant to ban the boy from the converted stable which served as a schoolhouse in the back of the rectory.

This afternoon the boy had done remarkably well in reading passages from Ecclesiastes, in copying words onto his slate as Parmley dictated them to his seven pupils, and in exercises in two-digit subtraction. He felt a curiously clean duty — something verging on a desire — to reward him. Jack Frake's progress had been relentless, while the other boys had to be re-drilled in the subjects over and over again. And so, when he had dismissed the six other boys for the day, Parmley pulled out from his makeshift desk a great book of maps. The book had been sent to him, many years before, by his brother, a successful printer and cartographer in London.

He had put the book there weeks since, knowing that the reward was inevitable. Cephas Frake was now laboring for the union of workhouses of St. Gwynn-by-Godolphin, Gwynnford, Clegg, and Squillante parishes. The boy knew that Parmley had arranged for his father to work through the parish, yet the father would not tell his son where he was laboring on any given day. The boy had asked the parson, bluntly, in private, a number of times over the past year, why his father was so secretive, but Parmley could offer no explanation that would not exacerbate the boy's unhappy domestic situation. Cephas Frake, he knew, was ashamed that his circumstances were so desperate that he was forced to plead pauperism in order to feed his family.

Parmley propped the book up against others on his desk, and let the map dangle as he stood by it. Jack Frake gripped the edges of his bench and stared at the colored phenomenon. The parson pointed with his finger to a cream-colored shape that resembled a ragged leg of mutton. "This is our land," he said, "our *island*. England." His finger moved to rest on one tiny area at the very bottom of the mutton leg close to a vast expanse of green. "And here we are. England is composed of numerous counties. We reside here, in *Cornwall*. A very lonely, but somewhat attractive county it is. This is the English Channel." The finger then moved to rest on one of the innumerable, tiny, finely printed names that filled the space. "And here is where we live, in the parish of St. Gwynn-by-Godolphin. Godolphin, as you must know, is the name of the quite modest river that flows through Pendyn Valley to Gwynnford and the Channel — and was, coincidentally, the name of the late Queen Anne's unfortunate lord treasurer. Our — *your* ancestors long ago gave it that name because some fishermen reported having seen dolphins frolicking in the estuary there. *The river that goes to the dolphins.* Do you see?"

Jack Frake nodded.

"And even longer ago, a monk named Gwynn lived in a hut somewhere near the river. He was a holy man, recognized by our church, the Anglican Church, who helped travelers cross the river. Thus, Gwynnford, a town perhaps a century older than our own St. Gwynn. Being directly on the Channel, the town is some miles removed from St. Gwynn's original domicile. Gwynnford has seen better days," he added with disapproval, thinking of the taverns and sailors' hostelries that lined the little port's main street, and of the good-natured but unpleasant rough-housing he had received there at the hands of some its *habitués*.

Jack Frake glanced up, expecting more.

Parmley felt an inner glow, and smiled. "Here is your home," he continued, moving his finger west along the coast. "Trelowe. *Its* etymology is deceptively obvious, yet more than likely spurious. Perhaps it was so called after the stunted oaks that grow near your commons, but there are other, equally convincing apocryphal explanations. And to the east of St. Gwynn, the villages of Pondwrinkle and Clegg. South and east of us, Gwynnford. North of Trelowe, the village of Squillante. Ah, and here is Treethick! A great forest once stood in its fields. The farmers, I hear, still break their ploughs on the ancient stumps that are still in the soil. And close by it, Marvel." He paused. "It is said that Marvel is the secret headquarters of that scoundrel, Augustus Skelly." Parmley paused again to frown at the boy. "Have you ever seen smugglers, Mr. Frake?"

The boy shook his head. It was true. He had only heard of the smugglers. They were phantoms who moved in the night, as mysterious and frightening as the fantastic creatures his mother threatened him with if he did not obey. He had heard his parents and other adults in Trelowe talk in whispers among themselves about Augustus Skelly. Skelly and his men, they said, hanged customs officers and informers, and kidnapped children whom they fed to sea monsters so that the monsters would not molest the gang's smuggling boats. But, as with the ogres and goblins in his mother's arsenal of terror, he had never seen a Skelly man.

"And here," continued the parson, pointing with his finger, "is Stanyard-on-Pendyn — Pendyn being the pretty little brook that feeds the Godolphin — ten miles west of Trelowe." Parmley searched the boy's face for signs of recognition. There was a tin mine in Stanyard, owned by a man who had a labor agreement with the union workhouses. Cephas Frake, he knew, was often sent there to load and push ore carts. "The ancient Romans, a people mightier than we, had a fort there, the ruins of which may still be seen. They, too, mined tin."

Parmley paused in remembrance of something that pleased him, and took a large penny from his coat. He held it up. "Bronze, my boy. Part copper, part tin. Some of this coin may have come from those very mines." He turned it over and showed the reverse to the boy. "Do you recognize her?"

Jack Frake nodded. On the reverse was the profile of a seated woman holding a spear in one hand, her other arm resting on an upright shield. She wore a great helmet with a curving crest.

"Do you think Britannia was a creation of His Majesty's Mint?"

Jack Frake shrugged.

"Britannia is as old as the Romans," continued the parson, unmindful of the fact that the content of his discourse had begun to range far beyond the boy's knowledge and perhaps even his interest. But the boy was an attentive listener, and the parson was lonely for a receptive audience, and so he went on. "She first appeared on their coins during the reign of Antoninus Pius, in the second century. Our version here was modeled by Frances Stewart, the Duchess of Richmond, almost a century past. She must have been a noble, lovely lady. The pose and the style, however, are undeniably Greek in inspiration. Yet I had my own name for Britannia, when I was a young man at Oxford. I dubbed her 'The Auditing Athena.' Athena! The Romans called her Minerva. The goddess of wisdom and power. Does she not look like she is listening, weighing, and judging what she hears? I thought it appropriate that we should choose her as our symbol." Parmley stopped for a moment, looking more abstractly pensive. "Wisdom and power, my boy," he sighed. "The two notions are not antithetical, as some aver. It depends on one's dictionary. Today, of course, they are in mutual disrepute: wisdom, because it reveals our failings and makes us jealous of it; and power, because it dispenses with the need for wisdom, and offers instead the spice of avarice. This is true all over, but especially in our England, in this anxious year of 1744. We, above all other nations, should know better, for are we not envied for our vaunted liberties?" Parmley studied his penny for a moment, then put it away. "But — I digress. That is the purpose of a symbol, to remind a man of his first meaning. To remind a nation, too. Someday, I hope, England will remember hers." The parson glanced at the map, and sadly tapped it with his hand. He studied the boy, and wondered if any portion of his reverie had found a home in the young mind. "Names, Mr. Frake, are not casual. If ever you must choose a name or symbol for something important, think on it most earnestly."

Jack Frake stood and approached the map. He put a tentative, wondering finger on the edge of the island and traced the coast of Cornwall. Then he stepped back to his bench and sat down.

The parson, however, was through for the day. He refolded the map, and slammed the book shut. "You may go now, Mr. Frake. When you return next week, I may show you what lies beyond the Channel." He paused with a shadow of a grin. "I may show you a *globe*."

He then received his own and quite unexpected reward. Jack Frake, who rarely volunteered a word more than what was required, and who Parmley, in spite of his affection for him, had concluded was the most introverted, ungrateful boy he had ever had in the schoolhouse, smiled up at him and said, "Thank you, sir," then jumped up and ran out the door into the chill afternoon.

Chapter 2: The Cottage

WHAT NORMALLY TOOK HIM TWO HOURS TO WALK, TODAY TOOK THREE. Jack Frake was neither eager to go home, nor anxious to get there before dusk. He set off mechanically from St. Gwynn-by-Godolphin on the country road that meandered through the fields, pastures and meadows that lay between the two villages, his mind and energy happily preoccupied. He was hungry, but the prospect of the bowl of gruel his mother would fix for him neither enticed nor repelled him. He was deaf to the pleadings of his stomach.

His thoughts did not include his home, which was a one-room cottage on the edge of Trelowe's commons, half a mile from the cliff and the Channel; or his bed, which was a pallet of straw on the dirt floor in a corner of the cottage, between the fireplace and the woodbin; or his parents, whom he regarded as looming nemeses to his life.

Nor did his thoughts dwell on the risk of encountering highwaymen or kidnappers. He had nothing a highwayman could want, unless it were the crudely repaired shells of leather that were his shoes, or the patched and re-patched rags that were his trousers, shirt and jacket. And the peril of being taken by a gang of kidnappers to be sold ultimately as a servant to gentlemen in the colonies — wherever they were — was faintly intriguing to him, even alluring.

His parents used that threat, too, in addition to the ogres and goblins.

"We could get a guinea for you, boy," his father would say gruffly when he was in an especially foul mood. "So you mind your own nose and keep your mouth shut, or it's off to the colonies with you!" His father disliked him, almost as though he were not his own son, but a special guest of his mother's; his mother was indifferently tolerant of him, as though he were a penance she had accepted and worked into the daily drudgery of her life.

He understood these relationships as little as he did the one which existed between his parents. They argued often, and even fought with fists, pans and stoneware, drawing him, when they noticed him standing by as a spectator, into their bloody donnybrooks, whose points of contention were beneath his ken or care. What he witnessed between his parents was not what he imagined ought to be love and marriage. Reason, which his young mind was striving to enthrone in all matters that came under his purview, dictated that they should part and go their own ways. But their continued, embittered union defied reason and all his efforts to understand it. Jack Frake did not hate his parents. He simply was too young to grasp the role of enmity in the lives of adults such as Cephas and Huldah Frake. The word *inertia* was not yet in his vocabulary, but an unlabeled notion of it existed in his mind and it seemed to be the basis of his parents' marriage. And he himself was a hostage to it by the unanswerable triumvirate of custom, law, and his youth.

At home, his life in and around the cottage was centered on the chores of feeding the chickens and pigs, milking the cow and a pair of ewes, and acting as a human scarecrow in their field to chase away birds, weasels and other pests — which included many species of rodents and also poaching squatters — and the wandering flocks of sheep and herds of cattle of the more prosperous denizens of Trelowe. The Frake family was not prosperous. They scratched together a living by bartering milk and produce from their field with other farmers and cottagers, as their ancestors had done for generations. Coin was a welcome but infrequent guest in their household. There were no books or newspapers in the cottage, not even a Bible; the boy's introduction to letters began with the labels on liquor bottles and the trademarks on farm and kitchen implements and would have ended there, but for the intervention of Parson Parmley. Play was a forgotten pastime; Jack Frake was put to work a few years after he had learned to walk. He had never seen a toy and would neither recognize one nor immediately grasp its function. Privacy was a luxury he had to steal from the time allotted to his chores. He would roam the meadows and surrounding villages near him only at the price of a beating or the denial of dinner, and usually both; it was a price he gladly suffered. His discovery of and frequent retreats to his cherished cubbyhole had cost him more bruises and hunger than he cared to remember.

Cephas Frake inherited from his father the copyhold to a neat cottage and a productive half-acre of the commons. Lacking, though, both his father's instinct for neighborliness and his knack for discreetly exploiting loopholes in England's semi-feudal agricultural practices, he soon found himself working blindly and futilely against the tribulations of his time. He was industrious, and occasionally innovative, but as he spent no time reflecting on the possible causes of his interminable race with poverty, his industry and infrequent flickers of thought got him little. He was incapable of imagining any other way of life — except, perhaps, on a bountiful royal pension which would spare him all purpose and effort. But while Cephas Frake had a bottomless capacity for effort, he had no purpose, and there was no one to instruct him in the importance of their dual role in a man's life. Sober, he was a boisterous, convivial drone in whose soul no solemn flame had ever burned. Drunk, he was a clamorous juggernaut, and either offensively familiar or violently morose, depending on whether he was celebrating a trite advantage or soaking his sorrows. So he pitched himself against the tribulations, cursed the necessity of his struggle, and remained blithely and gracelessly ingenuous, never to learn that the things he struggled against were meaner, crasser and more insensitive than he.

Jack Frake was six when his father and mother began to offer food and drink outside their cottage to travelers who used the road that was a shortcut on the journey between Plymouth in Devon and Falmouth to the west, and to the west coast of Cornwall. His father even went to the trouble of painting a crude sign, picturing a crossed knife and fork over a glass, which he hung over the cottage door. Jack Frake was given the task of fetching fodder and water for the travelers' mounts, and earned what was to him a fortune in pennies for sweating them down with a thick brush. Once, a carriage-and-four stopped at the cottage, and he saw for the first time a liveried coachman, a gentleman and a lady, and a boy his own age in silks, velvet and a white wig. The other boy did not speak to him, and stared at him with condescending curiosity. Jack Frake did not notice the condescension, but returned the stare with a critical glance of his own. He did not know where the people came from, nor where they went, but the family, the carriage, and the other boy were his first clues to another kind of existence, elsewhere.

After two months, a county sheriff rode into the yard and threatened his father with the exorbitant fine of two guineas for operating an establishment without a victualler's license. Cephas Frake was too much of a cynic to question the necessity of a license, and too dull-witted even to think of offering the sheriff a bribe. In peevish obedience, he found his ladder, took down the sign, and chopped it to pieces in front of the still-mounted, astonished sheriff. Then he lay down his ax, and stood facing the man, waiting. The sheriff frowned, uttered another warning, and rode away, his head shaking in time with the swish of his mount's tail.

Jack Frake was also astonished at his father's behavior. Cephas Frake noticed the boy studying him. "There's crows in our corn, boy!" he growled. "Wipe that look off your face and shoo 'em!"

Two miserable years later, in the summer after the corn, beans and other crops had been sown and the wheat was beginning to come up, Cephas Frake grew more possessive of his common plot, and got into fights with villagers whose livestock trampled his garden. Then he had an idea. He would build a fence around his plot. Some of the village men had fences around their gardens. His would simply be bigger. When he told his wife his plan, she merely looked doubtful and shrugged. When he told his son, he was answered with a silent expression of awed respect, something new and unsettling to him. He was not certain that he cared for what the boy's expression implied, but he playfully mussed the boy's flaxen hair and said, "Let's do it, boy."

Together they labored for days, hauling stones from the surrounding fields in a barrow, and erecting piles of them at intervals around the plot. They took longer trips together to collect driftwood from the beach and timbers from abandoned hovels, and used the wood to connect each pile to the next. And then they laughed together when, after the waist-high fence was finished, they stood at its gate to watch the sheep and cattle on the other side of the fence stand dumbly immobile at the obstacle in their path, and then shuffle away. "'Tis a thing of beauty, that fence," remarked Cephas Frake with a chuckle.

On his own, Cephas Frake had invented the practice of enclosure without ever having heard of the phenomenon, which was then imperceptibly changing the country's rural landscape to the detriment of countless squatters, cottagers and marginal farmers, but to the advantage of the bustling manufacturing cities, which got more and better food. The commons was a major impediment to the spread of enclosure, a carcass of feudalism doomed ultimately to be removed.

Too, he had never heard of socialism — no one then had — which was what the 'commons' was a form of, as it allowed villagers and cottagers like the Frakes equal rights to timber, grazing pasture, turf and fish in the land ringing a village. Villagers and farmers could erect fences around their gardens or small plots, but only by consensus. Cephas Frake had not asked anyone's opinion, permission or advice concerning the enclosure of land which was not even nominally his, but the village's.

One afternoon, about a week after the fence was finished, the sheriff and the constable of Trelowe arrived at the cottage with a noisy mob of villagers, cottagers and squatters in tow. The sheriff, by His Majesty's authority, directed the mob to dismantle the fence, and fined Frake a guinea and a half for "theft of commons land."

Cephas Frake was shocked, first by his lapse of memory, and then by the swiftness of the retribution. He removed his hat and stepped forward. "But it's our food, sir," he said, a note of meek apology in his words. He spoke in a loud, deferential voice, addressing not so much the sheriff as the mob, hoping it had some power over the sheriff. Some of the men in the mob fed their families with the produce that came from his plot. He assumed that this counted for something. "And it's some of them men's livestock that eat it, and what they don't eat, they mash underfoot so we can't."

"Granted," said the sheriff. "But your offense is fivefold. You neglected to apply for commons leave to erect a fence or a hedge. You gleaned an excess of stone and wood beyond reasonable need, and so deprive your neighbors of their right to those materials. You raise turnips and clover without commons leave. You have assaulted or abused the persons of your neighbors for exercising their pasture rights. Finally, you enclose more than what has been deemed necessary by a committee of your peers for your own and the village's sustenance. All these omissions and commissions constitute theft of land or theft of custom, in violation of the estovers of Trelowe. No formal litigation in court is necessary, as your guilt in these matters is beyond doubt and appeal. You are so charged, and so punished. It is as simple as that." Without further word, he turned in his saddle and said to the mob, "Proceed."

Cephas Frake opened his mouth to protest again, but the sheriff had turned his mount and was riding across the yard to supervise the fence's demolition.

This time it was Frake and his wife who stood by dumbly as the villagers waded self-righteously into their task, and watched them knock down the stone piles and begin to build a bonfire of the wood in the middle of the garden. Jack Frake, however, was roused to a fury that transcended even that which he felt when his father belted him for neglecting his chores. He picked up a hoe and ran to attack the villagers who were building the bonfire. The villagers ducked the swings of his hoe, and laughed, not at him, but at Cephas Frake. But then the boy's hoe struck one of the men in the head, leaving a gash under one ear. The constable rode up and whacked the boy on the side of the face with the flat of his short sword, knocking him down.

"Do that again, young Frake," said the constable to the boy as he lay on the ground, "and you and your worthless father will be charged with obstructing His Majesty's justice, and to Newgate or Bristol you'll both go!" He paused to smile maliciously at the anger in the boy's eyes. "Or maybe it's the army you'd like to march with? They's always in need of drummer boys."

Neither Cephas Frake nor his wife moved to interfere. The boy got up and ran out of the field to the coast and his cubbyhole on the cliff.

When he returned hours later, the garden was a ruin, the stones were strewn all over the commons, and smoke rose from the smoldering remains of the bonfire. His parents were inside the cottage, at the table, drinking mugs of gin. His father pushed a dirty tin of the liquid into his hands. "They took our tillin' tools in lieu of the guinea and a half, boy. We'll have to work the soil with an ax and a poker." When the boy said nothing, Frake looked away from his scrutiny. There was something lurking in the boy's stare that was antipodal to what he had seen days before. "Drink up, boy," he muttered. "Gin's the only shoulder we got to cry on."

His mother chuckled. "Have a swig of it, lad. It'll put you to sleep and let you forget it all."

"Why didn't you fight those men?" asked Jack Frake. He put down the tin.

"What?" scoffed Cephas Frake. "And get killed or go to jail? What for?"

"Your rights as an Englishman," said Jack Frake, repeating a phrase he had heard some of the village men utter with reverence.

"Hah! My rights! Stow it, boy! You's talkin' over your head!"

"You got twenty guineas to spare us, Jack?" asked his mother with mockery. "If you got them, you can buy us some time at Inns Court and a barrister to boot!"

"If they needed the stones and the wood, why did they burn the wood and just scatter the stones?"

"Because we forgot our place, and that's the law's way of remindin' us of it!" snarled his father. "Don't harp on it, boy. It's rattlin' me. We done wrong, so we's just got to live with it and leave it."

"They had no right to do that," insisted the boy.

"Yes, they did!" countered his father. "And you had no right to take a hoe to 'em! You struck a particular good friend of mine. You shamed me, and I'm ashamed of you. They'll be talkin' about me 'til the moon turns green!"

"Why didn't you try to stop them?" repeated the boy. "It was *our* fence!"

"It *weren't* our fence!" said Frake. "They's was stones from the commons, and no one said we could use 'em that way or any way!"

"You're a coward," blurted Jack Frake.

His father turned and walloped him with a backhand that sent the boy clear across the room to tumble to the floor. "Don't you tell me my nose!" shouted Cephas Frake, rising and shaking a finger at the boy as if it held a whip. "Any more sass from you, and your mother's goin' to have to plant you in the garden! You hear?"

The boy did not reply, dared not reply. The look on his father's face told him that he had touched something that lay immersed beneath the gin-warped anger: the will to murder. So he bit his lip and pushed himself back to rest against the woodbin, and glanced away, so that his father could not see the look on his own.

Huldah Frake shrieked in laughter at the stunned look on her son's face. "Serves you right for tryin' to be the man your father ain't either!"

Cephas Frake whirled to his wife, then took a swipe at her, and another fight was on.

The indignation the boy felt over the sheriff's and villagers' actions soured into implacable contempt for his parents. Not many days later he saw his father carousing drunkenly in the village with some of the men who had helped to destroy the fence. And as time went by, his father would be absent for long periods, returning with a bag of food or a few shillings in his pocket. The boy could not be sure, by listening from his pallet to his parents' nocturnal conversations, whether his father was poaching on neighboring commons, or begging in other villages. Sometimes Cephas Frake would return with a face bruised or bloodied. And during these absences, the boy's mother would send him away from his chores when local men stopped by. One of them, a man named Leith, a cousin of the constable of Trelowe, came more often than most. These stealthy visits resulted in more beatings for Jack Frake, now by his mother, to ensure the boy's silence about her callers.

Cephas Frake, despairing of feeding himself and his family, at last submitted to the ignominious alternative of going to the parish workhouse. With the connivance of the rector of St. Gwynn, he passed himself off to the parish union governor as a landless pauper. Robert Parmley, who preferred to have boys as pupils in his classroom than as wards of the workhouse laboring, in chains and fetters, over cloth, metal and wood, agreed to take the boy under tutelage three times a week, at no charge. And so Cephas Frake went to use his muscles in the tin mines, china-fields and slate quarries in the area, and Jack Frake suddenly found himself in school.

That had been a year ago.

None of his past was present in his mind now. His thoughts on the journey from St. Gwynn to his cubbyhole were simply the unconscious enjoyment of himself and his surroundings, each step and thought adding a fraction to the intricate calculation whose final answer was the moment. The moment had seized him and, for a while, wiped out all recollection of his past. He sensed, too, but only vaguely, that it was important for him to mark this moment, for when he next remembered it, it would be with happy, selfish reverence or with the bitter regret of loss, depending on the justice he earned for himself as a man. But to a boy of ten, the reality of manhood is eons into the future, and so the fleeting insight was shorter than a footnote. It did not govern the elated, excited peace he felt in himself, and with which, from the throne of his cubbyhole, without gesture or ceremony, he blessed himself and the world.

Chapter 3: The Cubbyhole

HIS CUBBYHOLE WAS A PUNCTURE IN THE SHEER DOWNWARD SWEEP OF granite to the beach two hundred feet below, vacated by material ejected millennia ago and since ground to sand by the surf. It was not visible from atop the cliff, and hardly noticeable from the Channel. Jack Frake discovered it one day when he plopped to his stomach at the edge to watch the fall of a stone he dropped from his hand. Its roof was the ground he lay on. There was no way into it but to shimmy over and drop to the edge of the demi-cave's floor; no way out but to grip the edge of the roof and heave oneself up, taking care not to look down or to think of the space in back of or below one. Jack Frake wanted it, and claimed it, his single-minded greed overruling the paralyzing screams of fear in his mind and muscles as he mastered its ingress and egress that first time. After a while, he forgot the fear and felt that the hole was no more formidable than a fence.

He had expected to find a bigger hole, perhaps even a giant cavern, but there was just room enough for one sitting man, or one stooping boy. Sea gulls and other birds had built nests in it; he chucked them out and no more nests were built. When the wind was still, he could hear the tread of horses and the voices of passersby on the road that ran along the cliff side above. And sitting alone, his mind found the time to acquire perspective and horizon. The cubbyhole was a greater reprieve from his parents and the cottage than was his pallet of straw. There, in the darkness, the trials of the day and his mundane surroundings triggered an almost instant lapse into sleep; here, he could remain awake, and think, and dream, even though the hole was often dark or enclosed in damp, thick fog, and the pounding surf below was relentless in its effort to lull him into a mental haze as gray as the fog.

Tonight, the wind was strong and blew against the cliff from the south. On it came a thick fog that erased the sea, the sky, and the sails. The coming of the fog was a sign that he should start home. He had never spent a night here; it was too cold even in the summer. This was April, and there was still a chance of snow. Jack Frake leaned forward and hugged his knees to stop them from shaking.

As he did so, he saw a faint light far out beyond the surf. It was a lantern on an invisible ship. It swayed in the wind and with the barely audible creaking of the vessel as it rode the waves. The water was deep enough to accommodate a merchantman or even a first-rate warship, but only to within two hundred yards of the beach. Up until a few moments ago, the cliff walls were visible in the moonlight; even the most negligent watch could not have helped but see them. Gwynnford was three miles up the coast, but no Gwynnford pilot or tidesman would ever steer a ship into port over such a wide arc, so close to the cliffs, regardless of the roughness of the seas.

Jack Frake knew that the ship was coming on for only one of two reasons: it was lost, and would soon run aground on the shelf that rose abruptly in the water; or it was not lost, and was skirting the cliffs for a mysterious purpose. He rested his chin on his knees, and strained his eyes to discern the shape and size of the ship.

Then there was a footfall above him, and some pebbles dropped onto the edge of the cave floor. He jerked back and looked up at the roof.

"It's the *Sparrowhawk*, all right," said a voice. "I can smell the tobo from here."

"Signal her to Gwynnford," commanded another voice. "If it is she, she'll put in there, and then we'll see."

"Why wouldn't it be she? Who else would come to this point?"

"A revenue sloop looking for us. Pannell's the new customs whip now. He'd hang Ramshaw by his heels from the crow's nest to get our lay, and I can't say as I'd blame Ramshaw for squealing then. So signal Gwynnford, and we'll look her over there."

The aura of another light appeared above the hole, then flashed on and off in a series. After a moment, the lantern in the fog answered in kind. Voices came from that direction now, clear but indistinct, and the sound of sails being tacked. The ship slowed, stopped, and began to retreat deeper into the fog.

Jack Frake got carefully onto his hands and knees and poked his head out of the hole to look up.

A man stood directly over him, a tall man in a greatcoat and tricorn. The toe of one boot protruded over the edge of the roof; the boy had merely to raise a hand to touch it. Near the man stood another who held the lantern, which blotted out his own face but lit that of the first. The face of the man wearing the tricorn was a stern, clean-shaven, hard face, more forbidding than the sides of the cliff. The mouth was tight and grim, the nose almost triangular, the eyes black marbles of purpose.

The lantern light shifted a little, and Jack Frake saw the glint of inlaid silver on the grips of a pair of pistols that were jammed into the man's wide belt. He ducked back, and the heel of one of his hands rolled on a small stone and catapulted it over the edge.

"What's that?" asked the other voice sharply. The lantern light was extinguished.

Jack Frake heard the reply — the cocking of a pistol.

Moments passed. The boy remained stock-still, knowing that the two men above were doing the same. He watched the ship's lantern recede into the fog and finally disappear.

"Just a rabbit," said the other voice. "Can't be anything else. There's no place for anyone to hide up here."

After another moment, the boy heard the pistol being uncocked. "Let's get back to the cart," said the commanding voice. "She'll be in Gwynnford in an hour."

The protruding boot jerked away and Jack Frake listened to the diminishing footsteps. But in the wind he could not hear the rattle of a cart. He waited a long moment, then hoisted himself up out of the hole. In the pitch-black distance he could see another lantern moving away on the road, and hear the clop of a pair of horses and the sound of wheels rolling over dirt.

Only three kinds of men carried pistols along the coast, or anywhere else: King's men, smugglers, and highwaymen. The King's men were also called customs men, excise men, and tax collectors. He had seen them only half a dozen times, passing by the cottage or through Trelowe on horseback. No one greeted them, and they greeted no one. They were despised, but deferred to. The deference was paid grudgingly; or, what was worse, obsequiously, which, to a King's man, was much more suspicious courtesy. They were feared, not because of the pistols they carried, but because they represented the King or Parliament, whose reach was longer than a mere ball of lead. They could ruin a man in a minute, at the height of his career, in the abyss of his desperation, or over the course of a lifetime. At this time, more than half the price of any finished good purchased in England represented a tax, indeed several taxes. Jack Frake, whose family lived chiefly on barter, did not yet understand how this contributed to his family's and neighbors' straits. He knew only that the King's men had power, and that few men trifled with them.

Those who did — the smugglers — were also feared and deferred to. But the fear and deference were of another species. For Jack Frake, who could judge only on hearsay, it was difficult to determine who were the pursued and who were the pursuers, who were the law-abiders and who were the law-breakers, who were the good and who were the bad. On one hand, the King's men were said to be agents of the law, and the law was derived from the people — according to something called the Constitution. The Constitution existed to secure men's lives, liberty, property, and freedom to trade, and its laws punished murderers, thieves, cheats, and other miscreants.

On the other hand, he had heard the King's men called these very things, while the smugglers were lauded as saviors or heroes. Twice, while on errands for his father in Trelowe, he had overheard the name of Augustus Skelly spoken with fond respect. To a boy who preferred to judge men and things for himself, it was a moral conundrum.

He stood watching the lantern as it was swallowed by the gray, chilling sheets of fog blowing in off of the sea, fighting a desire to follow it to Gwynnford. It was late, the men had pistols, and hunger had caught up with him. He glanced up at the sky. The stars had disappeared completely, and the moon had been turned into a yellow blur. He started for the path home he knew so well, a path worn by his many trips to this spot. The sole danger he might encounter now was a pack of wild dogs.

A light was on in the cottage, and a horse stood tethered to a stone just outside the door. He recognized the horse. It belonged to Isham Leith, cousin of Jasper Dent, constable of Trelowe.

Isham Leith was a tall, gangling man who was half-owner of the only public house in Trelowe, the other owner being his brother, Peter. He wore clothes no other villager could afford, and seemed always to have coin to lavish on his whims. He stopped by at times to pick up milk, eggs, and vegetables, in exchange for meat, coffee, tea or liquor. When he called on the cottage during Cephas Frake's absences and Huldah shooed Jack away outside, he would bring with him a jug of rum or gin, and was always careful to take the empty vessel with him when he left.

Cephas Frake suspected only that Leith had incited the villagers to take action against him over the fence, but could imagine no other motive other than his refusal once to loan him the use of his ax. Huldah Frake agreed with him with uncharacteristic brevity, and if her son was present when the subject came up, threw the boy a wicked look of warning. The daughter of the village tanner, she had married Frake to get away from the smell of her deceased father's shop and the repellent attentions of her disfigured, drooling half-brother. At the age of twenty-seven, she was still regarded as a handsome woman, and had once had dreams of being a lady's maid in London. This feeble but still practical ambition was suffocated and forgotten in the course of her marriage to Frake, during which the contempt she allowed to grow for herself eventually was extended promiscuously to all men and women. Isham Leith treated her son oddly on his surreptitious visits, sometimes giving him a penny or a farthing and a hale slap on the back, other times cursing him and swatting him with his riding crop. His mother was a neutral, bemused observer of this behavior.

Jack Frake listened at the single lamp-lit window and heard Leith murmur something to his mother, who giggled in answer with liquor-slurred words. He turned and went to the small stable where the cow and ewes were kept at night, buried himself in a mound of straw, and went to sleep.

Chapter 4: The Spirits

TWO MORNINGS LATER, LONG BEFORE SUNRISE, CEPHAS FRAKE LEFT THE cottage, as usual, without a word to either his wife or son. That afternoon a clerk from the slate quarry rode into the yard in a sulky to inform Huldah Frake that her husband had been killed in an accident. A sheet of stone had come loose and had fallen onto a group of laborers. Frake was one of four who died.

He was buried in the Trelowe chapel cemetery, next to his father, in a grave marked with a plain headstone. His name and dates of birth and death were chiseled into the tablet by the village mason, who donated the stone. Headstones were not cheap and were beyond the means of most of the villagers. They thought this was a major sacrifice on Huldah Frake's part, a testament of her love for her departed husband. In fact, she had blackmailed the mason, to whom she had once granted certain favors, and who lived in chronic fear of his notoriously shrewish wife.

Small changes soon began to occur in the cottage. Leith called much more often, and both he and Huldah Frake became kinder to the boy. Jack Frake neither missed his father nor mourned his passing, but he almost preferred his pouting silence to the hollow, chummy friendliness of Isham Leith. His mother was strangely solicitous of the snugness of his clothing and the fullness of his belly. Twice she had even asked him what Parson Parmley had taught him; she listened attentively, but for some reason Jack

Frake did not think she heard a thing he said.

This new attention included treating him to a precious tin of tea when the parson dropped by, one afternoon a week later, to offer his condolences and help.

"You've a bright lad here, Madam," said Parmley that day. "He's sharp and he remembers everything. He'll make something of himself, given half a chance. I'm going to see what I can do about that. There's a small boarding school in Falmouth, the Chrysalis Academy — what a precious name, that! — that takes in boys of... well... humble means and genealogy, mostly boys from county parishes. It is not a gentleman's school, of course, but it has a better capacity to dress his mind than I have here. It will mean asking the bishop to advance a small sum out of charity funds, but St. Gwynn has never sent a boy to school anywhere, and I can see every reason why the bishop would approve of the idea. In my letters to him, I have praised young Jack here to heaven."

Huldah Frake sat forward with an angry frown. "But — I need Jack here to help me work the crops, and keep the place up."

Parmley shrugged. "You know that I have some influence with the workhouse staff, Madam. I can arrange to have some help sent to you."

Jack Frake sat forward and stared eagerly at his mother. "Please, Mum! I want to go to this school!" It was the first time he had ever pleaded for anything from his mother. He did not know what else to say.

Huldah Frake gave her son one kind of poisonous look, and the parson another. "Huh! If he goes to this school, he'd come back with airs, thinkin' he's too good for me and his chores!"

Parmley looked perplexed. This was not the reaction he had expected. "But, Madam, that is not necessarily true. Good students — and Jack here is one — rarely shirk their family obligations." It sounded false and contrived, but he had been prepared for resistance from the boy, not from the mother, and was at a loss for words.

"What's in it for you?" asked Huldah Frake, after a moment. "Why are you so interested in my Jack?"

"I must assure you, Madam, that there is nothing in this proposal for myself, except, perhaps the satisfaction of seeing a young, promising life properly launched. There is strength in this boy, and it ought to be complemented with knowledge. I have visited the Chrysalis Academy, and appraised its curriculum and its students. Its curriculum is meaty and well-rounded, and the students happy and well-behaved. As for chores, each student is assigned a task contributing to the maintenance of its building and grounds, and is severely reprimanded if he does not adequately perform it. I dare say Jack would return home after terms a much more industrious worker."

Huldah Frake stood up and planted her hands on her hips. "*I* can teach him anythin' he needs to know, and I'll box his ears if he don't do his bit around here! Huh! You ain't offerin' him nothin' but fancified schoolin'! *I'll* raise him myself, proper like, thank you very much!"

Something more than the violence of the mother's protests made Parmley uneasy, and he decided it would be unwise to press her further on the matter. He rose from the table. "Then I shall take my leave, Madam. I am truly sorry that you seem so hostile to your son's moral and mental improvement." But he was not willing to concede defeat, and wished the woman to know that this was not the end of the matter. Her manner provoked defiance. "I shall persevere in my efforts to widen Jack's opportunities. This may mean having to resort to extraordinary measures. I trust that your affection for him is but misguided, and I beg you to reconsider your present stand. Good day to you both." Then, with a brief bow, he left the cottage.

Huldah Frake waited until his dogcart was a distance down the road. "You're not goin' to his church tomorrow." She turned to find the boy staring at her. "Don't you give me no looks! Your father ain't here to wallop you, but I am!"

"He wasn't my real father, was he?" asked the boy.

"*What*? You little — !" Huldah Frake flew from the window and knocked the tin of tea from his grip with one hand and smacked him on the face with the other. "You mind your filthy mouth, Jack Frake, or I'll send you packin' like I did that parson!" She paused in sudden realization. "Did *he* say that about me?"

"No," said the boy. "I heard you and Leith talking the other night. But Parson Parmley married you and Father, so he must have guessed why, too."

"Smart little bugger, you are!" Huldah Frake folded her arms and studied her son for a moment. "We'll talk about this later! You get to the coop and gather some eggs! Leith'll be by soon to take 'em to town!"

Jack Frake obeyed. But at the door he turned and delivered another surprising statement to his mother. "Don't ever strike me again," he said. "Or I *will* leave."

There was a gale that night when Isham Leith rode to the cottage.

Jack Frake did not hear him arrive. He lay on his pallet, half-asleep from physical exhaustion and from the strain of the new tension between him and his mother. The exhaustion stemmed from the running fight he had all afternoon with a squatter's son who, like a dumb animal, kept sneaking into the garden to poach beans and corn. After a series of bare-knuckles bouts and wrestling matches, Jack Frake settled the matter with a well-aimed stone that struck the other boy in the head, sending him bawling across the moor.

His mother had not said another word to him after Parmley's visit. Something in her brooding manner told him that a decision had been made. She had served him his day's-end gruel too dutifully, almost as though he were one of the pigs or chickens, not caring if he ate it or not. He was thankful for the gale. The howling wind and patter of rain on the walls and roof of the cottage lulled him into a nervous sleep.

Isham Leith shook the raindrops from his hat and coat and hung the sodden articles on a peg near the fireplace. He quickly bussed Huldah Frake, then sat down at the table. He removed a black glass flask of rum from his frock, took a swig from it, then set it on the table. "All right, what's all this hush-and-hurry about Jack?"

"Sssh!" cautioned Huldah Frake, putting a finger to her lips. "You'll wake him!"

Leith glanced at the figure on the pallet at the side of the fireplace, then took the candlestick from the table and went to study the boy more closely. He came back and sat down again. "You're sure he's not lyin' doggo?" he asked in a half-whisper.

"He's out," the woman assured him. "I got him to cut the wood we got yesterday, and then he had a busy day in the field."

"All right. What's up?"

"Leith, we got to do it soon."

"Do what?"

Huldah Frake gulped and lowered her eyes. "The *spirits*."

"You mean — ?"

The woman nodded. "It's got to be soon."

Leith shook his head. "I can't push 'em, Huldy. I 'splained it all to you. We got to do it coy-like, so we can get top guinea and no one 'round here is wise to it."

Huldah Frake sat on a stool opposite him. "*Listen*. The parson came today. He's keen to send Jack to a ragged school down in Falmouth. You'd think Jack was his own son, the way he went on! I bollixed him — don't think he ever got the tongue I gave him! — but he swore he'd be back."

Leith looked disgusted. "So tell him to oomph off! You don't need his bloody charity!"

"I said that. I said just that."

"Nobody'll look at you wrong for wantin' to keep him. He's *your* son, and you got to have extra hands for the work here. *You* got first claim on him, not the bloody parish!" Leith's voice had risen from a whisper to a near-shout.

"Keep your voice down!" exclaimed Huldah Frake. "Do I got to draw a picture for you? Parmley's got the power, Leith. He's threatened to take Jack, through the workhouse. He can do it. I can't keep this place for long without a man, and they'll take him — *and me* — because all our kin are dead and they'll call us paupers!"

Leith waved his hands. "*You* look, Huldy! It's dodgy right now, and nobody'd try it! There's revenue men and soldiers all over the place! Gwynnford's like an ants nest with 'em, and there're even a few in Trelowe. They're lookin' for Skelly, who's supposed to be in these parts tonight, and then I hear there's somethin' up again with the Scots. They think the Young Pretender'll land hereabouts with an army from France, just like he was goin' to a while back. They're stoppin' everyone, askin' questions and searchin' 'em for papers. *I* got stopped twice today! No, Huldy, it's damn dodgy!"

The woman's face had grown stonier as Leith spoke. When he was finished, she said, "He's gettin' too smart, Leith. I'm losin' him." She paused, then added, "He can read and write now, and he'd fetch a good price even if you pushed them, wouldn't he?'

Again Leith shook his head. "We *got* to play the prince, woman, or it ain't no good!"

Huldah Frake helped herself to the black flask. Then her whispered words softened. "Better somethin' than nothin', luv. We might lose him anyways. Know what he said today?"

"What?"

"He said he'd leave the next time I smacked him!"

"Did he now?" chuckled Leith. "Uppity little bugger!"

"He's been actin' airy for a time now. That damn Parmley's hexed him somehow. I believe he'd really bolt, and then we'd lose those guineas we need, Leith. We won't have the coin to set up shop, and your cousin won't bother gettin' us that public house license. You'll be stuck with your lazy brother, and I'll be in the workhouse."

Leith was silent for a long time. Then he sighed. "All right," he growled. "I'll fix it. For tomorrow." He looked at the woman. "But they won't come *here* and bundle him off. These fellows is professionals. They can sly the law blindfolded if they's careful. He's got to be snatched far away from Trelowe. They even got a billet on a merchantman that's unshippin' cargo in Gwynnford, and that's sailin' for Virginia in a week after takin' on goods in Plymouth."

"How would the... spirits... do it?"

"Gentle, like. They'll just talk him out of his wits, that's all. Feed him a fantasy. They got indenture papers they can fix any way they please." Leith paused and looked thoughtful. "But they got to have a story ready, so he don't start screamin' or makin' a row."

Huldah Frake glanced once at her sleeping son. "I'll let him go to the church tomorrow. And then they could meet him on the road and say they're from Parmley and they're takin' him to this school in Falmouth."

Leith hummed in tentative agreement. "What's its name?"

Huldah Frake searched her memory. "Christ of Leeds."

Leith scoffed. "Funny name for a school. Never knew Christ worked magic in Leeds. Don't recall the Bible ever mentionin' his settin' foot in England at all."

"That's what Parmley said its name was. Christ of Leeds Academy." Huldah Frake clenched a fist behind her back. She was not certain that it was right or wrong. It was the nearest she could recall the name. But she was desperate and dared not show any doubt.

"All right," said Leith. "I'll tell 'em they're to be gentlemen come from Parson Parmley to escort him personally to Christ of Leeds Academy in Falmouth." But he frowned again. "But do he *want* to go to this school?"

"He wants to, Leith. He begged me to let him."

Leith emitted a low chortle. "Maybe you're right, Huldy. The parson's rattled his noodle. Imagine *wantin'* to go to school! It ain't a normal aspiration! Next thing you know he'll be expectin' you to knit him shirts of Flanders lace and pen 'Observations from a Correspondent' to the *Cornish Gazette*, and lookin' down his nose at you if you can't! Be nervy to have 'round. Or even *embarrassin'*!" He paused, then slapped some coins — six pennies and two farthings — onto the tabletop. "There's what I got for your eggs, Huldy. Some officers snapped 'em right up. Business is always good when the redcoats is in town. Wish they'd put up a barracks here. They might, you know, since My-Darlin'-Charley's still aimin' to give George-His-Nabs the heave-ho. Wonder how much the Frenchies are into him for? They say Marshall Saxe's the best general on the Continent, and he was all set to march on London. Say, I ain't goin' back out in that rain 'til it lets up! Here, luv, help me out of my boots… "

Huldah Frake knelt and tugged off one of his muddy boots. "That's what I like about you, Leith. You got gumption, and you know things, and you can read, too."

"Sure I can read," said Leith. He assumed an air of smug superiority, and added, "But I don't never let it go to my head."

Jack Frake rolled over on his pallet of straw, away from the fire and the candlelight across the room.

* * *

"But you said I wasn't to go."

"Well, I changed my mind," said Huldah Frake late the next morning. "I can change my mind, can't I? The parson came by last night, when you was asleep. We talked about you goin' to this school and we fixed it up."

"He came here in the storm?" asked Jack Frake, trying to keep the doubt out of his words.

"Yes, he did," said his mother. "That's how much he thinks of you, he'd risk his health in that storm just to do right by you." She looked at her son once, and saw a peculiarly empty expression on his face. Then she continued to scrub the table fiercely with a wet rag. "You start at this school in a week, and some gentlemen from the school might even come by to take you there, and on a ship, too. That'll be fun, won't it? You won't be so… far away. Might even come down to see you."

The boy stood watching his mother. He did not know whether to hate her or despise her; he knew the distinction between the two judgments. But he could feel nothing, not even an echo of the choking trauma of betrayal he felt last night. Had there not been a gale, he would have left the cottage while she and Leith slept. This morning, as he went about his chores, he removed what few things he wanted or would need, and hid them in some bushes beyond the garden. He made these preparations as coldly, ruthlessly and unfeelingly as he knew his mother had discussed his fate with Leith.

He asked, "How will you mind the garden? Some new squatters'll help themselves to everything, if it isn't watched."

"I'll manage, Jack. Don't you worry. Now get along. You don't want to hold up Parson Parmley." Huldah Frake steeled herself, then broke away from her task long enough to dart over to him and bend to kiss him on the forehead. The boy remained still, his senses alert for some lingering pause in the act, some confession of reluctance. But he did not feel it. She returned to the wooden bucket of water he had drawn from the well for her, and stooped over it to wring out the rag, her back to him.

"Off with you, Jack," she said, standing to fiddle with the rag and stare at the opposite wall. "And don't dawdle along the way. And don't let him keep you so late, like he did last time. Be back before dark, or I'll beat the sauce out of you and you'll — " When she turned to him again, the cottage door was open to the sun and a cloud-flecked sky.

Chapter 5: The Globe

FOR A WHILE, HE WAS FRIGHTENED. THE FEAR IN HIS BEING — A FEAR triggered by the dreadful, featureless void that now lay before him — used every argument in its repertoire in a frantic effort to placate his conviction and send him back, humbled, to the familiarity of his home. He could choose to believe that the words he heard last night had not been spoken; or that he had not heard them; or that he *had* heard them, but only through the garbling filter of a fitful dream; or that neither the words nor their utterers had meant anything at all, and he was being vain to presume that he had been their subject.

But the words *were* spoken — for otherwise they would not have so violently seared his thoughts — and in his mind their reality wore a merciless supremacy that stood fast against the assault. At last, failing to find a breach in his conviction, and unable to shake the courage of his commitment to that supremacy, the arguments broke off their attack and melted into the mists of irrelevancy.

The emptiness no longer daunted him, once this crisis was over. He was free to fill that space with his own actions, his own purposes, and his own pennants. His glance swept over the horizon from east to west, registering the wonderful enormousness of the world before him and the magnitude of the step he had taken into it. His flight from home was not so much a rash, desperate act as it was the final, inevitable seal on his separation. He felt the radiant wholeness of himself. From that moment on, he was beyond reclamation by any conventional persuasion. Before him now lay the adventure of his own life.

The afternoon sun warmed the cubbyhole and began to dry it out. Jack Frake was not in it, but sitting on its roof, legs dangled over the edge. A cloth sack containing his things lay beside him. In it were his "Sunday" shirt, distinguished from the one he wore on weekdays by two extra brass buttons and artfully concealed patches; a pair of socks; a tin cup; two ears of corn and a pouch of peas and beans; a marble he had acquired in a trade with a village boy for a wooden button from his coat; and a handful of pennies and farthings, the ones he earned long ago and had managed to hide from his parents after the others were appropriated for the household.

He picked up his sack and swung it over his shoulder. Parson Parmley's map remained to be explored, and his globe to be seen. He started walking down the road to St. Gwynn.

A troop of dragoons caught up with him and trotted past him. Their horses were the healthiest, most powerful he had ever seen. The soldiers were armed with sabers, and pistols and had muskets slung over their redcoated backs. The captain eyed him severely but did not stop to question him.

Jack Frake hiked through Trelowe, and through a smaller cluster of cottages that had no name. On the top of a hill, he stopped and crouched behind a bush. Below, the dragoons had halted at the fork in the roads to St. Gwynn and Gwynnford. He saw the captain talking with one of three men who waited with a dogcart by the nearly leveled ruin of an ancient church. The man gesturing to the road leading to Gwynnford was Isham Leith.

When the dragoons moved on, Jack Frake left the road and cut through the moor to St. Gwynn. He supposed that Leith had a story ready to explain his presence, and was there to identify Jack and collect the price previously settled on with the two strangers. Other than this mental notation, Leith no longer concerned him.

When he reached the church in St. Gwynn, he stashed his bundle behind the rectory stable and went inside. He was late. Parson Parmley was already leading the other boys through a writing exercise. He gave a reproving look as his tardy pupil took a slate and a piece of chalk from the desk and sat on one of the benches.

Two hours later the parson dismissed his class. Jack Frake waited until the other boys had gone, then approached him. "Sir," he asked, "if I wanted to go to this school, could I go by myself?"

Parmley studied the earnest face for a moment. There was something new and indefinable in it. He had not expected to see the boy today. "Good heavens, no," he sighed. "There are expenses, you know, and you would need your mother's permission in any event. Otherwise, there would be... well... difficulties. Your mother must first be declared a pauper, and you, yourself, as well, and I don't believe you would wish that to happen. I don't expect that ever to happen, though, if the things I hear are true." He paused and sat down in his chair. He put a hand on the boy's shoulder. "I'm sorry, Mr. Frake, more than you can know."

"What things?"

"Have I heard? Well, this is merely rumor, idle talk volunteered — to *me*, of all souls! — in malice and disaffection, that your mother is considering marrying a man of dubious means by the name of Leith. If this be true, that, and her demonstrated antipathy to your attendance at the Academy — which shook me to the core, mind you — would combine to erase all likelihood of your going there. I doubt even that you would be allowed to continue coming here for instruction." Parmley paused. "Indeed, I am surprised to see you here now." His expression invited an explanation.

But none came. Jack Frake was silent. Parmley came a little closer to identifying the change in the boy. Here, he thought, was someone who was in command of his own mind. The parson's sense of helplessness about the boy's fate oddly diminished, as did his sadness. "Is there anything else, Mr. Frake?"

"You promised to show me a globe."

"Ah, yes! So I did! And so I shall!" The parson smiled and rose. "It's in the rectory, in my study." He paused. "Is there something else you think I should know?"

"No, sir."

"Very well. Follow me."

It had clouded over since Jack Frake detoured over the moor. An eastern wind whipped the trails of smoke from St. Gwynn's squat chimneys, and the air had turned moist with the promise of more rain. The rectory sat on the side of a hill, away from the main road and apart from the village of St. Gwynn. It was no larger than one of the town's cottages, but its lines were sharper and its washed walls more fastidious. It boasted five lead-paned windows and a small wood fence that sheltered the strip of grass in front.

"Sir," ventured the boy after they had traversed the yard separating the rectory from the stable, "what is a spirit?"

Parmley stopped just short of the front door of his rectory and turned to him. "A spirit? Why do you ask?"

"I heard men in the village talk about them." This was true. He had heard men in the village talk about spirits.

Parmley's sense of unease returned. "To be spirited," he answered, "is to vanish, like magic, with neither trace nor clue to the deed, as though evil spirits had snatched one from the realm of the living, from the earth itself. Those who kidnap children, and even grown men and women, and sell them into slavery, are called *spirits*." He paused. "The notion of spirits is strictly of rural origin, born in superstition. The men who pose as spirits are quite corporeal, I assure you, and deserve more scurrilous appellations than I am at liberty to utter. But their guile, secrecy and occasional successes stir the shoals of ignorant, untutored minds. They are a disappearing ilk, though. One shouldn't worry about them." He was beginning to know the boy's mind, and was certain that he would not have asked the question if the subject had not been forcibly imposed upon his thoughts for some unknown reason. He frowned down at the boy. "You don't believe in *vaporous* spirits, do you, Mr. Frake?"

"No, sir," said the boy. "Not in any."

"Why not?"

"If they existed, nothing would make sense."

Parmley chuckled uneasily. He was tempted to overwhelm the boy with the rudiments of the theological proofs of the only Spirit that mattered, but a strange reluctance checked him, a reluctance composed in part of his devotion to the necessity of God, and in part of his devotion to the boy's mental chasteness. It was the first time in his long, studiously casuistic life that the notion of spiritual purity had presented itself as a paradox. The antilogy troubled him; he could not yet resolve it or even think clearly about it, but he knew that he alone was its author. He stood speechless for a moment, then limited himself to remarking, "You're a philosopher, Mr. Frake. Truly."

He took the boy inside the rectory. It was divided into rooms — a novelty to Jack Frake. There was a kitchen, a bedroom, and a study. They were small rooms, but each seemed to be a separate world to him. There was furniture, and pictures on the wall, and in the study, shelves of books rendered inaccessible by the bric-a-brac of a bachelor scholar.

And a globe. It sat on Parmley's desk, a small blue, gold and ochre orb of metal resting in a cradle of polished teakwood. Next to it stood a tall silver candlestick. Behind the desk and a tall leather chair, was a window that looked out on St. Gwynn and the Channel beyond.

Jack Frake tore forward past the parson, recognizing the globe without ever having seen its like before. He rested his hands on its surface, each palm over a continent, and looked for England. He found the mutton leg; it was one of the smallest islands. He thought that if it were dropped into one of the oceans, it would be lost forever. Through the window, in a break in the cottages, he could see the Channel; in his mind he was imagining the distance from St. Gwynn to the Cape of Good Hope. He turned his head and flashed a grin of discovery and gratitude at the parson, then glanced back down at the globe and rolled it in the cradle.

Parmley, watching the boy from the door, was suddenly overcome with an emotion. How many men in past ages, he asked himself, had been punished, and tortured, and even put to death for having been so happily, frankly impetuous in their thinking of the world in the same manner as the boy was thinking now? The boy's joy was natural, and unsullied by any knowledge of what transpired in the world. He did not think that such knowledge would ever spoil it. It seemed to be so normal a manner for anyone to look at anything.

This thought was followed by another, equally stunning one: he was glad that the boy had not heard very many of his sermons on piety, humility, charity and deference to the wisdom of the Almighty. God and Jack Frake seemed antithetical; the one rendered the other utterly superfluous. Parmley leaned against the doorframe, drained by the power of the contrast and by the implications of this crisis of faith. He felt shame, and also a desire to apologize to the boy for having subjected his person to absurdities.

There was a knock on the rectory door. Angry at the interruption, Parmley whirled around and strode to answer it. He opened it, ready to vent his distracted passion on the caller. He saw a tall, bony, slovenly looking man standing there, who removed his tricorn and worried its brim nervously with the fingers of both hands. A saddled horse stood tethered to a post of the fence. Just up the dirt road were two more men sitting in a dogcart, watching and waiting with too casual an interest.

"What is it?" demanded Parmley, one hand on the edge of the door, the other on the frame.

"Reverend Parmley?" asked the man with hesitancy. He had expected a more affable greeting from a man of the cloth.

"Yes?"

"Pleased to make your acquaintance, and beggin' your pardon, sir," said the man with a slight nod and a toothy grin. "My name is Leith. Isham Leith. I own, well, some property in Trelowe."

Parmley frowned. "And?"

"Huldah Frake — of course, you know her — she sent her son Jack here for schoolin' a while ago, and I'm just inquirin' if he came."

Parmley had never before lied in his life, and he lied now, brazenly, without calculation or conscious decision. "He's come and gone, sir."

"Gone? Well, we've — *I've* just come from the Trelowe road, and I didn't see him, so I — "

Before Leith could finish, there was a crash of glass from the back of the house. Parmley turned and rushed to the study. The window was broken. He went to it and looked out, just in time to see Jack Frake disappear behind the rear of the stable. The globe and its cradle lay broken on the ground a few feet away from the window in a spread of shattered glass and bent panels.

Isham Leith had followed the parson into the study, and growled over his shoulder, "You spoke too soon, Reverend." He snorted scornfully, then began to sweep the parson out of his way with an arm, so he could jump out of the window to pursue the boy.

But Parmley would not be budged. He put a hand on Leith's chest and pushed him away. "No, sir!" he exclaimed in a voice he reserved for his most booming sermons. "I spoke too late, it would seem! You and your spirit friends may leave now! Your victim has fled! God save him, and God damn you!"

Leith, shocked by both the vehement authority and the apparent revelation of his purposes, backed halfway across the study to escape them and the shaking fists of the parson. "What do you mean? What'd the tyke tell you 'bout me?"

"*He* told me nothing! But I can guess why *you're* so concerned about him! I *know* who those men are outside! Do you think that because I am childless, I cannot interpret a child's coy questions?"

Leith's soul cringed under the drilling point of Parmley's ferocious glance. His was one of the superstitious minds of which the parson had spoken; he ascribed mystical powers to moral men and felt that his soul and motives were completely bared to Parmley's scrutiny. "*Spirit* friends, eh? What else'd he say — ?" He shut his mouth, even though he knew that he had blundered and said too much.

"It's a hanging offense, Mr. Leith!" said Parmley, shaking a finger. "My advice to you is to leave St. Gwynn and never set foot in this town again, or I'll have our constable clap you in irons!"

Leith bridled at the admonishment, and squinted contemptuously at the parson. "I'll step where I please, you withered, dodderin' old fool!" He took a taunting step forward to assert his claim.

Parmley stepped closer and raised his hand to push Leith away. Leith, stung by the defiance and also propelled by the vision of an ineluctable solution to his entrapment, exclaimed "You cockalorum!" and snatched at the first thing within his reach — a candlestick — and lashed out. The sharp metal of the base struck the parson in the neck and severed an artery. Parmley gasped, clutched at the break, and collapsed onto the bare floor.

Leith stepped back again, and watched with horrified fascination as the parson's blood spurted, trickled, oozed, and finally stopped. It ran from the side of his neck to form a pool that fed the neat canals of the joints of the floorboards. The parson's eyes remained fixed on the ceiling as life drained out of him. After a while, his chest stopped heaving.

Leith glanced out of the broken window and saw a tiny figure move rapidly across the moor, then dip over a hillock and vanish.

He looked at the candlestick in his hand — its base was smeared with blood — and began to toss it away when he saw that it was made of silver. He grinned madly, then barked a single laugh of triumph when he surveyed the contents of the study. Brandishing the candlestick, he shouted out the window, "You ain't cheatin' me, you little bugger!" Then he quickly ransacked the room.

Moments later, wide-eyed with fear but propelled by success, he emerged from the rectory carrying a valise stuffed with silver plate. In it also was a small chest — which he had found hidden behind some books — that contained paper notes and coin, including twelve golden guineas. This was the treasury of the parish of St. Gwynn. He closed the door gently behind him and looked around. No one was about but the two men in the dogcart, who had driven into the rectory yard.

"What's up, Leith?" asked one of them, watching him with caution.

"What was all that racket?"

Leith waved a hand and hooked the handles of the valise over the horn of his saddle. "Pack it in, gents!" he exclaimed. "The kid's done a Turpin on us!"

"What took you so long?" asked the other man, eyeing the valise and then the rectory with suspicion. "What's that you got there?"

Leith swung into his saddle, then reached into his coat and produced a pocket pistol. He cocked it and pointed it at the second man. "Never mind what anythin'! Our business is over!" He chuckled at their gaping mouths. "In case you get the scruples," he added, "you know me, but I know you, so that makes us square! Don't get no ideas about collectin' a bounty!"

"Don't want no trouble, Leith," said the first man, who glanced at his partner with a panicked expression. He picked up the reins and coaxed the horse through a hasty turnabout, and the two men left as quickly as the dogcart would allow them.

Isham Leith galloped past them out of St. Gwynn. West of the town he left the road and took the same shortcut across the moor that Jack Frake had taken earlier in the day. It had begun to rain lightly, but the wind drove the drops into his face and he slowed his horse to a trot. The raindrops began to cool his face, and also his mind.

On top of a hillock he stopped, and sat to watch the dogcart a mile away inching toward him along the road to Trelowe. The "spirits" — whose names were Oyston and Lapworth — had taken a room above his tavern, and would stop there to collect their baggage before leaving, no doubt in a hurry. An idea grew in his mind as the men in the distance approached. The murder of Parson Parmley would cause an uproar all along the coast, and would subside only when the parties responsible for it were brought to justice. Parties, he thought. One of them also carried a pocket pistol, the other a knife. He saw a way of letting two murders wipe out one. He had tasted murder, and found it troubled him not a whit.

He opened the valise and put a hand inside to feel the candlesticks and plate. His palm lingered covetously on the cool hard metal. He sighed, then swore. Much of the loot would have to be sacrificed. But enough would be left over. More than enough.

The boy, he was certain, could know nothing of what had happened. He could be dealt with, too, if he returned home. The little bugger *knew*, he thought. Chances were that he wouldn't be back, but if he dared come back, he couldn't prove a thing. Leith tapped the neck of the horse with his riding crop and moved on.

There remained the task of inventing a story for Huldah Frake, and for his cousin, Jasper Dent, and for anyone else who might express curiosity, a story that would completely exonerate him from any association with Parmley, Oyston and Lapworth. It ought to be easy, he thought. More difficult would be explaining the money, once he decided to spend it.

Chapter 6: The Sea Siren

GWYNNFORD WAS MEASURABLY MORE COSMOPOLITAN THAN EITHER ST. Gwynn or Trelowe; it gazed outward by necessity and could not afford the luxury of insulation. It sat nestled at the mouth of the Godolphin in a broad break of the cliff line. It boasted six public houses, including two cozy inns which were better known for their amenities for traveling gentlefolk than for their stocks of liquor or raucous milieux; a Norman-style church, called St. Brea's, which could seat ninety, but rarely did; a miscellany of neat and well-stocked shops; a rope-works; an ironmonger and smithy; a coffeehouse; a bowling green; the parish union workhouse, which occupied a former linen-works on the outskirts of town; a wholesaler's warehouse; and a customs house. It exported rope, iron moldings, granite, slate, salt, fish, and local agricultural produce to the rest of England, and sometimes to the Continent, and imported as much of the world as its wherewithal and the customs collector would allow. Its gabled roofs were overshadowed by the square tower of the church and by the masts of ships anchored in the jetty-protected harbor, which could accommodate four merchantmen and a fleet of smaller fishing vessels. Gwynnford's lighters were owned by rival families who competed fiercely for the right to load and unload the merchantmen. The streets during any season bustled with activity. It was a snug, prosperous town, friendly to all who sought gainful employment and hostile to any who mistook it for beggars' turf.

Hiram Trott, proprietor of the Sea Siren public house on Jetty Street, the main thoroughfare, bristled on occasion when he recalled how he came upon his new scullion, but counted his lucky stars nonetheless. Also, because he was penny-particular, he counted the contents of his coin box. He could chuckle at the memory, once he disallowed the minor upheaval it had caused.

A week ago he was intercepted, on one of his endless trips between the kitchen and the victuals pantry in the backyard of the establishment, by a hatless, rain-soaked imp who stepped out of the darkness directly into his path. Before he could reach for the butcher's knife tucked securely between his apron and ample stomach, the imp had stared up at him and asked, "Sir, would you employ me?"

"You gave me a fright!" he bellowed at the intruder. Trott was a stocky man of six feet, and he loomed over the boy and scowled down at him. The creature was most likely a pauper — he had hired a few of that ilk in the past, much to his grief, for they had been thieves — but this one somehow did not exude their air of artful earnestness. "Employ *you*? What for?"

"Because the boy you have now lets the soldiers steal your plate and cutlery. He even sees them break your candles in half and light what's left so you don't notice, but never tells you. Your spit isn't turned enough, so your meats and fish are burned on one side and not done on the other. Your serving wench talks too much to your dishonest patrons and the ones who don't buy much, and ignores the honest ones. Your floor isn't swept clean, so rats and mice come out and eat the scraps and leave droppings — "

"Ho!" exclaimed Trott. "Where's your leave to say a bit of that? I ain't never seen you at one of my tables!"

"I watched from the window," said the boy.

Everything he said was true, and more, thought Trott. The staff so accused, however, happened to be his son and daughter. Since his wife had died a year ago, there had been no one to watch over his progeny; he commanded more respect from his regulars than from his offspring. He could toss two soldiers out the door at one time and was impervious to anyone's fist, yet his children did not fear him. He had let them work on their own terms; good help or bad was hard to find on any terms. Custom had never been better, yet his profits were inexplicably slipping. And here was someone willing to work. It was the first instance that anyone — himself included — had offered so frank a critique of his trade's deficiencies and a desire to correct them.

"Where's your home, lad?"

"Clegg," answered the boy.

"And your parents?"

"Dead."

Trott hummed in doubt of the truth of this statement. Clegg was a mining and market town, and this boy wore farm clothes. But it was none of his concern. "And so you've hoofed your way to this great metropolis to make your fortune! Is that it?"

"No, sir. I mean to go to London."

Trott hummed in doubt again, then scowled. "All right, you! I'll pay you a shilling a week, and maybe a few pence more if custom is extra good. Room is the woodbin on dry nights and under the steps on wet. Board is your pick of the leftovers and sherry to warm your gizzards. Filching gets you a beating or the boot." He paused. "What's your name?"

"Jack Frake."

"All right, Mr. Jack Frake, formerly of Clegg," chuckled Trott, "it's also understood you got no supervisory status here. You got observations or notions, you see me."

"Yes, sir."

"If that's square with you, you can start now. Get inside and put on an apron. Find a broom and sweep the floor, then come to me."

"Yes, sir." The boy turned and dashed inside.

Jack Frake launched into his job with an energy that astounded Trott, who had almost forgotten how spruce a tavern his place once was. The floor was swept, and stayed swept. The meat and fish were turned in the fireplace, and Trott began to experience again the pleasure of patrons' compliments. The dishes were washed thoroughly, and plate and cutlery stopped disappearing, for they were collected almost the instant a patron had finished his meal. The boy had the knack of espying pilferers among the patrons, and kept a sharp eye on those most likely to clip his employer's candles. This scrutiny deterred his suspects, and earned him threats of beatings from some of the soldiers. His efficient attention to patrons compelled Clarissa, Trott's daughter, to become a fairer and busier waitress; he established an uneasy truce with her, even though she began accruing more farthings and pennies in gratuities than before. He helped Trott and his itinerant cook prepare the vegetables, scale and bone the fish, and slaughter the poultry. He had two fights in the backyard with Bob, the son, who was one year older; the first over the fact that Jack Frake was a stranger and Bob wanted to assert his tenure; the second because he caught Bob stealing his possessions, which he had cached under the steps that led to the tavern's let rooms. He won both fights.

He worked hard, harder than his parents had ever driven him to work, barely conscious of the world beyond the inn's front door. Yet there was never a time that he thought, "Oh, Lord, give me back my yesterday." He slept soundly at night under the steps; Trott had relented during the first week and allowed him to bed down under them on a mattress of straw and burlap. It was his task to wake at first light to start the fires in the fireplace and the stew-stove in the kitchen. At nights, on his mattress, he could feel the dying heat from the great fireplace playing on his face, and before his mind winked out, it glowed with the riot of new sights, sounds and words he encountered during the day and evening.

He had fled when he heard Leith's insinuating voice at the door of the rectory; he did not think that the parson was a match for the man. Also, he feared, not the parson, but his loyalty to the law. So he had run more from the parson than from Leith, even though he felt a fondness for the man. He had never before felt an attachment to anyone, and it bothered him that he had not been able to say good-bye. As he went about his chores in the inn, questions buzzed in his restless mind. Were Leith and his mother searching for him? How would Parson Parmley have replied to his assertion that he did not believe in any spirits, including the one around whom the rector's life revolved? How long was a voyage from Falmouth to London? Where were the colonies?

Two things marred Jack Frake's perception of Gwynnford: the presence of the soldiers, and the workhouse.

At any time when its doors were open, at least one fourth of the Sea Siren's patrons were redcoats at leisure from their duties. Their meager and often late pay did not allow them much relief from the regimental kitchen, so they drank endless tankards of gin, rum, and ale. When not accompanied by a sergeant, they became rowdy; if officers were present, only sergeants and corporals on good behavior ventured in. Jack Frake learned that the butcher's knife Hiram Trott carried but never seemed to use was supplemented by a cudgel hidden in the other side of his apron. He saw it employed once on a half-drunk merchant seaman who refused to pay his bill, claiming that the fricassee he had consumed was mostly "Channel chicken" — sea gull. Trott grew livid at the charge; he was a better chef than an innkeeper, and his bill of fare attracted gentlemen and ladies staying at other inns. He felled the sailor with a practiced tap of the cudgel, and deposited him outside. He was bigger and sturdier than any of the soldiers, and none of them risked his wrath.

The soldiers were there because Gwynnford was one of several possible landing sites on the south coast for an invasion by a French army loaned by Louis XV to Charles Edward Phillip Casmir Stuart, the Young Pretender to the throne of England. An invasion fleet had actually been assembled in March near Brest, and the Channel fleet under Admiral Norris was about to give its warships battle, when a two-day gale dispersed the French and smashed Marshall Maurice de Saxe's army transports in Dunkirk. Following this episode, in fact, the French king had had about enough of trying to unsettle British politics by using the Stuarts to unseat the Hanovers and establish a sovereign amenable to French policies, and his support of Charles Edward's further schemes was lukewarm to the point of discouragement. But some powers in London were taking chances neither on the rumored exhaustion of Louis XV's resources nor on the Young Pretender's frustrated ambitions, and ordered the army to invest selected Channel ports as a precaution. Gwynnford was one of these ports.

Jack Frake concluded, on the strength of chat among officers overheard in the Sea Siren, that the soldiers were necessary, and so he grudgingly accepted their presence. The regiment was from the Midlands; its privates and corporals were homesick, lonely, and perhaps even apprehensive of the invasion. Their occasionally arrogant, besotted behavior was a small price to pay for the country's protection. He did not yet grasp that the army was composed largely of the swarf and dross of his country's society — of wanted criminals and sentenced ones, of the unemployed and the unemployables, of the dispossessed and the uprooted.

Hiram Trott, and other tradesmen in Gwynnford, he observed, perhaps felt the same way, but it was clear to him also that they regarded the money spent by the soldiers as one way of getting back some of their excise money. The redcoats, he noted, were charged a little more for their liquid and solid fare than were Gwynnford regulars.

The parish union workhouse intrigued him in an unsettling way. Late in the afternoon on his fourth day with Trott, he accompanied his employer on a cart to the wholesaler's depot to collect firewood and coal. They passed the workhouse, a long, two-story brick building enclosed by a high brick wall. Through the iron bars of its gates, which were guarded by a man in a blue coat carrying a polished black cudgel, Jack Frake saw children of various ages and a few adults loitering in a flagstoned yard. Many of them wore iron neck collars beneath their sallow faces; others were chained together in pairs, threes and fours.

"Who are *they*?" he exclaimed, his astonishment bursting through his usual reserve.

"Lost souls," replied Trott. "Orphans. Paupers. Thieves. Some, I've heard, have even killed. They get rounded up and put in there — and many places like it in our fair land."

"What do they do?"

Trott shrugged. "They work. They sort and cut firewood. They fashion the stocks of our army's muskets. They carve buttons. They sew canvas. For a while, they even poured lead for musket balls in a little building, but the fire got away from them and the shop burned down with twelve mites in it about six years ago. And they're sent out to work in mines and shopworks and fields. They do everything. Anybody that needs hands to do something cheap but got none to do it, gets them, and nearly free. Army contractors, mostly. And navy. The grown-ups' quarters are just beyond. Can't see it from here."

"Do they ever leave?"

"When they're big and shrewd enough, they climb the wall. Or if somebody takes a liking to some of them and hires them. Mostly they become criminals, and get transported to the colonies, or hanged."

Jack Frake could reach no conclusion about the justice of the workhouse. On one hand, the children he saw in the yard might have starved to death, or died of disease or exposure, had they not been apprehended and made to live there. On the other hand, their chains and fetters and the guard with the cudgel were elements that did not fit his concept of benevolent salvation. After all, he himself was an orphan and a pauper, in a manner of speaking, yet here he was, free and determined to make his way on his own resources. He now understood his mother's and Parmley's abhorrence of the workhouse, and his late father's shame. There was something cruel in such charity.

The Sea Siren had four lodging rooms, tended to exclusively by Clarissa. Two rooms were let to a major and two captains; they were gentlemen and their purses seemed always filled with silver. But one lodger earned the special deference of Trott and his progeny, a brusque, dark, ugly little man who invariably appeared in a black tricorn and a gray coat. His frock, waistcoat, trousers and boots were always immaculate. He had come three weeks ago, shortly before the soldiers. He said little, and chatted with no one. After he finished his meals, he would sit for hours at his corner table with his pipe, and listen. When darkness fell, he vanished. From Bob, who was now on speaking terms with him, Jack Frake learned that this was Henoch Pannell, Commissioner Extraordinary of His Majesty's Revenue. "He's here to trap Skelly," whispered Bob. "He's got men lodged in all the other inns and they're all ears for news of smugglers. They got mounts and they ride the coast at night, lookin' for Skelly." Three times during his first week, Jack Frake had been awakened in the middle of the night by Pannell pounding on the front door to be let back in.

There was another silent man, who lodged in the fourth room alone. He wore a brown tricorn and a brown cape. Hiram Trott knew only that his name was Mr. Blair, a merchant's agent who seemed to have much time on his hands, and that he was mute, though not deaf. He communicated with Trott and his staff with slips of paper, on which he wrote with a sliver of black chalk. He was a tall, lean man who often spent his hours, also with a pipe, at a corner table across the room from Pannell, reading books, the only ones Jack Frake saw in Gwynnford. They were small books, most of them written by someone named Shakespeare. Bob and Clarissa could barely read, did not like serving the man, and so it fell to Jack Frake to bring him his meals and drink. He seemed pleased to learn that the boy could read his notes, and gave him generous gratuities. His mien differed from Parson Parmley's; as the rector's smile had been kindly and wistful, Mr. Blair's was hearty and contagious. Once in a while, Jack Frake noticed Blair studying him with a curious intensity.

By the end of his first week, Jack Frake was enamored of the smoky hubbub of the Sea Siren, and even proud of his contribution to it. To him it represented a microcosm of the world beyond. But in the beginning of his second week an overheard conversation checked his almost monomaniacal devotion to his job. "Imagine that! Snuffin' a parson!" "What some men won't do! Took all the silver, even the church chest!" "Books and vestments and papers were throwed all over, and a window broken for malice! It's sacrilege, I say!" "It was the vestry-clerk who found 'im, lyin' in a pool of 'is own blood, on Sunday mornin', with people waitin' at the church door for services!" "The last one to see 'im alive was the widow who cooked for 'im that morning, just before 'e 'ad the boys over for lessons." "Fool! It were the boys who seen 'im last!" "Fool again! It were the killers!" "Justice wasn't long in coming. The scoundrels who did it had a falling-out over their gains, and killed each other." "The one stabbed the other, and the other shot the one." "Oyston and Lapworth? Seems I heard they was in a spirits ring in Devon that the sheriff there smashed some Easters ago." "They was found near Trelowe, close by the constable's place, by the constable himself!" "He was out shootin' bird with his cousin, and there they was, in a clump of trees. They was lodgin' in the public up there." "That's the Leith brothers' place. It was the older one who was with the constable, weren't it?" "That's right. Isham. He's a nervy bloke." "All the loot was there, in the parson's own valise, even the candlestick the constable says they did him with." "No, no, not all of the loot was found, I hear. Some of the plate hasn't been accounted for, and they never found the chest. This Jasper Dent says they lost it from the cart fleeing the rectory, or a pauper found the bodies first and made off with what he could carry." "Vicar Heskett here sent Sexton Cullis up to St. Gwynn when they got the news. Neighbors say he was in tears when he saw the carnage." "Old Parmley? Didn't he lodge here once? I recollect some salts havin' merry with him one night." "Well, I says the Lord works mighty fast when he's avengin' one of his own."

Leith, thought Jack Frake. Isham Leith killed Parmley — or all three of them had a hand in it — and then Leith killed *them*. He was at first tempted to upbraid himself for not having stayed with Parmley that afternoon. Only now did the words, "He's come and gone, sir," surface in his memory, spoken a moment before he took the globe and hurled it at the window. But if he had stayed — if the parson had not so impressed him with his reluctant devotion to the letter of the law — what then? He would have had to go with Leith and submit to an unknown fate.

But as he went about his chores, another thought — and it was not so much a thought as it was the stamina of a past one — reminded him that in that moment, hurling the globe was an act of resolve to govern his own life and never to leave it to the mercies or vagaries of others' purposes, benign or otherwise.

Still, he felt enough affection for the parson to want to do something about his murder. Yet there was nothing he could do that would not jeopardize his freedom. The mere suggestion of his knowledge of Leith and the two men would link him to Parmley; it would be his word against Leith's. The memory of the workhouse yard sat in his mind.

It took him two days to sort out these matters in his own mind. Hiram Trott noticed the difference in the energy of his scullion. He decided that the boy had proved himself, and he would give him the afternoon off, rather than admonish him for slacking. Before he went, Trott took him into the kitchen, out of his son's sight. He said, "Hold out your hand, lad."

Jack Frake obeyed.

Trott dropped two pennies into the open palm. "Buy yourself some sweets, or whatever you fancy, and be back before dusk. We'll be getting busy again then."

"Thank you, sir."

Trott then reached behind some parcels on a shelf and produced a weather-beaten black tricorn. He slapped it on the boy's head. "Not quite a fit," he remarked, "but you'll grow into it."

Jack Frake took it off and examined it as though it were made of gold. He glanced up at Trott, his eyes questioning the motive behind the gift.

Trott wanted to, but could not quite make himself explain that the hat once belonged to a second, younger son, who would now be Jack Frake's age. Two years ago the boy was fishing on the furthermost point of the jetty when he was washed away by a wave in a sudden squall. The hat, which the boy had taken off and weighted under a rock, was all that Trott was able to find. Instead, he said, "Respectable boys wear hats in this town, lad. You're an asset here, and I don't want the constable or the vicar hauling you off to the workhouse because the rest of you looks unrespectable. Get along, now."

And so, on that cold, blustery afternoon he wandered through the town he had not had time to explore. He watched the soldiers drill on a field, and exchanged wary glances with the drummer boy. He saw other children filing into the church for schooling. He stopped beneath the window of one of Gwynnford's more prosperous-looking houses when he heard a forte-piano being played, and listened to a melody that fascinated him with the pure harmony of its contemplative logic. He went into the shops and saw a dazzling assortment of things for sale. He watched lighters loaded with bundles and crates ply between the anchored merchantmen and the embankment, taking from one pile for the trip out, and adding to another from the trip back. And far out on the horizon he saw a warship, its great red ensign and pennants broadcasting its approach. Jack Frake turned and squinted to read the names on the sterns of the merchantmen. None were named *Sparrowhawk*.

And on his way back to the Sea Siren, he had an idea of what he could do for Parson Parmley.

Chapter 7: The Impostor

HIRAM TROTT SOON REGRETTED HAVING GIVEN HIS SCULLION A FEW hours' leisure, for half an hour after the boy left, business increased threefold and his cook and his offspring could barely keep up with it. The crews of two of the anchored merchantmen had finished their shipping and unshipping chores and had been released for shore time. Three carriages of gentlemen and ladies on a tour of the coast had stopped in town; he had to send Clarissa for some sheets to spread over their tables, for the gentlemen refused to allow their companions to soil their elbows on the stained planks. The paymaster of the Midlands regiment had arrived, and so more soldiers were filling up his tables. Henoch Pannell had gathered his men from the other inns and sat with them at one large table for dinner.

And then a tidesman had rushed in an hour ago and whispered to him the news that a battleship had been sighted and appeared to be making straight for Gwynnford. This news made Trott jittery. It could mean extra business; or it could mean press-gangs.

Jack Frake, when he returned, grinned and tipped his hat to Mr. Blair at his corner table, then ran to the kitchen to remove his hat and coat and don an apron. He had never before seen the Sea Siren so jammed with patrons, but even though every second of his time and attention seemed to be consumed by his job, he managed at some point to stop at Blair's table.

"Sir, would you write a note for me?"

Blair frowned, closed the book he was reading, put it down, and nodded.

Jack Frake rapidly explained his problem and its solution. Blair listened, and the nature of his frown changed from one of curiosity to one of concern and understanding. "If you'd just write something short, I can give it to the vicar here, tonight, after we've closed."

Blair smiled and nodded again, but Jack Frake did not think that the man had given him his full attention. His eyes had wandered now and then to glance at other patrons across the room — at Henoch Pannell, and at a tall, older gentleman and his two companions, whose coach-and-four stood just outside the inn's doors.

Blair took out his flat brass box and opened it to remove a slip of paper. With his black chalk he wrote: *Come back in ten minutes. Bring a bowl of pudding.* Jack Frake bent and read it.

"Thank you, sir," he said, and darted away to resume his duties.

In ten minutes he returned with the pudding and a new tankard of ale. Blair gave him another slip of paper, which read: *Sir: Isham Leith of Trelowe murdered Parmley. Capt. Venable of the dragoons asked him for directions on the Trelowe road by the old chapel on the 16th. The two men with him were Oyston and Lapworth. May justice be done. Yours, One Who Knows the Truth.*

Jack Frake breathed a sigh of relief. It said more than he had expected it to say. Blair even knew the captain's name. He smiled in thanks at Blair, then folded the paper up and tucked it inside his shirt. "The ale's on the house, sir." Hiram Trott called for him and again he rushed away.

Two hours later, the Sea Siren had grown even more crowded. Hiram Trott had sent for the tailor and his wife, who had a lute and could sing songs, and promised them a half-guinea if they could keep the place packed until midnight. Neither he nor his staff could stop to listen to the pair, who sang love songs, sea songs, bawdy songs and ballads. The patrons often joined in, and two tables were moved aside for those who wished to dance. The crowd was in a good mood. The officers and gentlemen drank toasts to their ladies. The soldiers cried "God save the King!" with every new round of drinks, alternating between that, "God sit on the shoulders of the great Duke of Cumberland!" and other toasts of a more suggestive nature. Hiram Trott unconsciously wrung his hands, pleased with the windfall business and hoping that no trouble would erupt.

Jack Frake was at the fireplace, shoveling exploded embers back into the roaring fire, when it happened. The front doors opened, and a navy lieutenant and a press-gang stood on the threshold.

All noise, singing and conversation ended, and everyone turned to glare at the newcomers. They knew that the lieutenant and his men were not here to eat or drink. Trott laid his cudgel and knife aside, for if he were tempted to use them, he could just as easily be impressed or jailed as anyone collared by the gang. Tradesmen were not immune to the appetite of His Majesty's navy.

The lieutenant, a slim young man of twenty-two, returned the hostile glare with an imperious gaze. In addition to his sword, he carried a mahogany cane. In back of him were seven men in bluejackets. Each of them carried a short, crude cudgel. The lieutenant's was not the only press-gang in town. Through the open door the patrons could hear the cries and running footfalls of others at work on Jetty Street and in its alleys, sounds which the hubbub had drowned out.

Jack Frake, shovel in hand, wandered over and stood near Mr. Blair.

The lieutenant smiled, then snorted. "Is this any way to greet His Majesty's navy?"

A voice in back of Jack Frake answered, "As long as it practices slavery! Your rhyme, sir!"

The crowd shifted uneasily in its various seats, and a few chuckles were heard.

"Who said that?" demanded the officer.

No one volunteered a reply.

"Very well," said the lieutenant. "You all look legitimate — and unsuitable for service on one of His Majesty's finest. Or most of you do. My apologies to the ladies," he added with a brief but correct tip of his hat. "We won't be long." His head turned and surveyed the crowd, his glance pausing on two or three merchant sailors who cringed in their seats, and coming finally to rest on Mr. Blair. With a gesture of his cane, the lieutenant led his gang inside and approached the corner table. He smiled with wicked pleasure at the man. With a downward stroke of his cane, he tapped the book out of Blair's hands, and with an upward stroke knocked the clay pipe out of his mouth. The pipe fell to the floor and shattered.

"Now here's a capable-looking fellow. Hands don't need roughening, they've seen rope-work. And he seems hearty enough. Keen eyes, too, eyes that could put a round through a French gun-port every time, eh, Bosun? Gunnery will be pleased." The lieutenant paused. "Seize him."

Jack Frake stepped forward. “He can’t talk, sir.”

The lieutenant glanced down at the boy. “What was that, whelp?”

“He can’t talk. His tongue’s dead.”

The bosun at the officer’s side laughed. “He don’t have to say a thing, son! He just got to take orders and look sharp!”

Another seaman said, “He won’t get no crow’s nest duty, that’s for sure!”

“Seize him,” repeated the lieutenant with impatience.

The bosun stepped over and grabbed Blair’s shoulder. Jack Frake swung the shovel and struck his outstretched arm. Blood splattered from the exposed wrist. The shovel next dug into one of the man’s knees, and the man bent with a howl of pain. The gang laughed, but the lieutenant angrily pushed the injured man into the chair opposite Blair and turned to the boy.

Instinctively, Jack Frake — with thought of nothing but that it was necessary for him to oppose the menace, and not even aware that he was emulating a stance he had seen the drilling soldiers adopt earlier in the day — threw one foot back and thrust the blade of the shovel forward with both hands, prepared to meet the assault.

This answer to his punitive prerogative only maddened the officer, whose eyes became bright round ovals of rage and his mouth pursed in contorted, unutterable wrath. He raised his cane high in the air. Jack Frake winced at the fury he saw looming over him, but bit his lip and braced himself, determined to strike at least one blow before the officer thrashed him, as he knew the man had the power and the will to do.

Hiram Trott shut his eyes and gritted his teeth, as though he were about to be struck himself. His son Bob stared at Jack Frake with open-mouthed astonishment, and two tankards of ale slipped from his tray to clatter unnoticed to the floor. The inn’s patrons watched in paralyzed fascination; none of them dared to interfere, not even the touring gentlemen, whose social status was at least equal to that of the officer’s and made them exempt from impressment. A few of the merchant seamen took advantage of the crisis to duck out the front door. And one red-coated sergeant watched the boy with a hint of admiration in his face.

Before the officer could bring down his cane, Blair rose and put a hand on his forearm. He said quietly, in a thick Scots accent, his face an inch from the officer’s, “Leave off the *bairn*, sir, or I’ll break it!”

The lieutenant did not know what to do or say. The man who could not speak, had spoken, and had his wrist — his sacrosanct, untouchable wrist — in a grip that seemed as strong as a wet jury mast knot. His men did not move to separate the two; he was a new officer on their ship and they wanted to see what else he could do besides give orders. Blair seemed to know that he would not be interfered with. He smiled amiably at the officer, his eyes sparkling with unmistakable challenge.

The lieutenant let go of his cane and the Scotsman's grip loosened. The officer then threw off the hold on his wrist with a contemptuous jerk and swept his hand down to the hilt of his sword.

"Stop."

One of the patrons stepped out of the breathless crowd, an older man in a plain tricorn and a magnificent white wig, wearing a cape of heavy gray silk with a fur collar. His gray, deep, intelligent eyes were fixed not on the lieutenant, but on Blair, and they glittered with triumph. His face was rough-hewn, but placid and restrained.

The lieutenant glowered at him. "Stay out of this, sir. This is navy business." He turned to face Blair again and drew his blade out half its length.

"I say, *stop*," insisted the stranger.

"Who's to stop him?" sneered one of the seamen.

A voice in back of the stranger said, "Rear Admiral Sir Francis Edward Harle."

The officer paused in his action. Jack Frake lowered his shovel, and discovered that his throat was dry and that he could hear his pounding heart. The stranger reached up, undid a hook, and shook off his cape, which one of his companions caught and folded over his arm. He indeed wore the uniform of a rear admiral. Its brilliant blues and yellows seemed to light up the room as no number of candles could. The press-gang stepped back, and the crowd, now completely on its feet, inched forward. The lieutenant blinked, blushed, let his sword fall back into its sheath, and stood at attention.

He said, "I humbly beg your pardon, milord."

"'Sir' will do," said Harle. He nodded at Blair. "This man interests me, Lieutenant...?"

"Lieutenant Timothy Farbrace, of His Majesty's ship of the line *Rover*, sir."

"Captain Weekes, is it?" queried the admiral congenially.

"Yes, sir."

"A fine man, Weekes. A fine ship, the *Rover*. I recommended Captain Weekes myself, you know."

The lieutenant replied, "We have the honor of serving under him, sir, and thank you."

"Just in from convoy duty, Mr. Farbrace?"

"Yes, sir." The lieutenant saw a look of expectancy on the admiral's face, and went on. "We took a prize just two days' sail from Land's End, the *Durand*, a privateer foolish enough to try to pounce on one of the slower merchantmen. We raked her with a single cannonade, and picked off half her crew with small arms before boarding her. We suffered only a broken spar or two, and a jib, which we repaired at sea. And one gun of ours was knocked out. The *Durand* has been towed to Plymouth, where she'll be refitted." The lieutenant paused. "She was originally the *Gallant*, sir, one of our own, captured by the Spanish some years ago."

"Well done, Mr. Farbrace," said the admiral. He glanced at the press-gang. "No doubt you lost crew in the engagement?"

"Yes, sir. That is why we are on this, er, recruiting mission, sir, to keep up a full complement. Captain Weekes took a ball in the leg, but he's recovering. I'm sure he would be honored by a visit from the Admiralty, sir."

Admiral Harle shook his head. "I must decline your invitation, Mr. Farbrace, as I am on urgent business here. Just passing through on tour of the ports in this vicinity. Wee Charley has agents planted in the most unlikely places. But please give Captain Weekes my sincerest regards." He paused, and nodded at Blair. "This man interests me. With your permission, I should like to interrogate him." The lieutenant's permission was not necessary, but Harle did not want to further humiliate him.

"Of course, sir."

"I believe *I* have first claim on this man, Sir Francis!" interjected a figure that shouldered its way through the crowd.

Admiral Harle turned to the speaker, a squat, ugly man who stood squinting greedily at Blair. "And you are… ?"

"Henoch Pannell, Commissioner Extraordinary of His Majesty's Revenue." Pannell paused to bow perfunctorily. "I have a letter of authority, signed by Mr. Pelham himself, to seize any person who I suspect is an associate of Augustus Skelly, or who can give me information leading to his arrest and trial." Henry Pelham was first lord of the treasury, and *de facto* prime minister.

"Skelly?" replied the admiral. "The smuggler?"

"And murderer, and deserter, and outlaw — "

"And I'm delighted to make your acquaintance, also, Mr. Pannell," said the admiral with a chuckle. "I too have a warrant from Mr. Pelham giving me authority to seize any person whom I suspect to be an agent of Charles Edward Stuart, or a French agent, or an agent of the Associators, or anyone having Jacobite connections or sympathies." He smiled with charming but pointed benevolence at Pannell. "Somewhat broader a mandate than your own, you must admit." Harle sighed. "But don't envy me, Mr. Pannell. My colleagues in the Admiralty seem to think I possess the power of Jesus, and have instructed me to ensnare and route the alien money-changers in our midst." He stepped closer to Blair's table and picked up his book. "Ah! I thought I recognized this from across the room! *Les Lettres persane*, by Charles-Louis Secondat, Baron de la Brède et de Montesquieu. A Dutch printing, too. Not of English manufacture. How treasonable," he remarked with alacrity. He flipped through a few pages, and gently put the book back. "You read French, sir. Can you speak it?"

"A little, sir," replied Blair. "What tradesman can't speak a little of it? We've had so much commerce with the French lately."

"No doubt you refer to our commerce of lead and iron." Harle turned to Pannell. "And, he's a wit, too, Mr. Pannell. Very tart... very quick... very interesting... " he added, more to himself than to his rival.

"May I point out, Sir Francis," said Pannell, "that it is not likely that this man has any Jacobite connections or sympathies. I have reason to believe that this person is Rory O'Such, Skelly's chief lieutenant. His information — properly extracted — could reveal the exact location of the gang's headquarters."

"What *is* your name, sir?" asked the admiral of Blair.

"Matthew Blair," said the man with a brief bow of his head. "I am a representative of the Bristol firm of Reddick and Eppes, iron fabricators. I am awaiting a shipment of Massachusetts pig, which is to be cast into moulds for the manufacture of various naval supplies for the Portsmouth docks, per agreement with my firm and the ironmonger in this town, Mr. Gill. The pig was purchased by our agent in Boston."

"Have you documents to prove your association with Messrs. Reddick and Eppes?"

"Yes, sir. They are in my room. I have been lodging here, awaiting the shipment."

"He's lying!" said a stout man who pushed his way to the front of the circle of spectators. "*I'm* Gill, and I never heard of this man or Reddick or Eppes!"

Henoch Pannell barked once in jubilant laughter. "Thank you, Mr.

Gill! You see, Sir Francis, this man may also match the description of Rory O'Such given to me by people in these parts. I wish to detain him and collect those witnesses."

Blair smiled at Pannell. "If you had suspicions about me, Mr. Pannell, why did you not act sooner?"

"Because you did not speak, sir, and you sat in shadow, and I was biding my time for my own official reasons."

"A rather fanciful explanation for poor industry," remarked Blair.

"His verve is well matched to his riposte. Certainly not the humor of a mere smuggler, Mr. Pannell," said Harle to the Commissioner, who was not sure whether the admiral was patronizing him or conversing with him. "Listen to that brogue — and what a tale it told!" said Harle with some amusement. "What do you think? Scots-Irish? It would account for the outlandish name you claim is his real one. I'll wager his grandfather was an Ulster Scot in debt to Cromwell."

"Whatever his antecedents, Sir Francis, he must be a Skelly man. I've trod every stone on this coast looking for a trace of the gang. They're very crafty and have the citizens of this region so affrighted that it's been difficult to find a man or woman brave enough to speak." As he sensed an indifference to his efforts, Pannell added, "Skelly's depredations rob His Majesty's government of much-needed revenue. I'm sure the Admiralty can appreciate that."

Harle shrugged. "It is widely known that expenditures on revenue collection of the kind in which you are presently engaged mostly exceed the revenue collected."

Pannell stiffened and stood his ground. "I am not responsible for that paradox, Sir Francis. I am merely performing my duty."

"Ah, duty!" exclaimed the admiral. "We have been at war a month, Mr. Pannell. In addition to the Scottish element, you must know that a number of Irish renegades, slavers and privateers operate out of France, and some were no doubt intimately linked with Louis's plans to force the Young Pretender on England. These privateers prey on our shipping and deprive us of much more revenue than you could ever dream of recovering."

"Perhaps, Sir Francis."

"And you must be aware of the fact that in times of war, military concerns supersede domestic, and that is where your duty consequently lies."

"I am *not* aware of that, Sir Francis. It would be an interesting matter to submit to Mr. Pelham and Mr. Pitt, don't you think?"

"No doubt. However, as that is not a practical alternative at the moment, may I suggest that we repair to a more private circumstance to argue our points and interview our subject properly?"

"The undersheriff and bailiff are in Falmouth at Quarter Sessions, Sir Francis. But the constable is home and has a jail back of his house. His wife is a fair cook and can fix you what you could not finish here."

"Excellent idea, Mr. Pannell." Harle turned to the officer. "Mr. Farbrace, would you and your worthies be so kind as to escort us and the prisoner to the constable's home? Mr. Pannell here will show us the way."

"My pleasure, sir," said the officer. He waited until the admiral had donned his cape again, then he glanced at Jack Frake. "But what of this scullion dog, sir? He assaulted one of my party, and that's a civil offense. I would be satisfied with impressment. We lost a powder monkey taking the *Durand*, and he looks limber enough."

Harle studied Jack Frake for a moment, and smiled at him. "Good work, lad. Some day you may want to defend your country with the same vigor." He turned to the officer. "No, Mr. Farbrace," said the admiral, shaking his head. "We owe a debt of thanks to the boy for having provoked Mr. Blair into revealing himself to us. 'Twas a noble gesture on both their parts, wouldn't you say? Leave him be. If your man wishes to pay his anger, let it be to the French or Spanish, before they do him worse than this boy could."

"Yes, sir."

"Cuff the prisoner for Mr. Pannell's ease of mind, and let us be on our way."

The lieutenant turned and nodded to a seaman, who produced handcuffs. Blair held out his wrists and the cuffs were snapped on. "Find a physician in this town and have him see to Jones," said Farbrace, glancing at the injured bosun. Then he picked up his cane and faced Blair. "After you, sir."

"You're a lucky man, Mr. Farbrace," remarked Blair.

"If you're not indefinitely detained by Sir Francis or Mr. Pannell, we'll see what you have to say about my luck." Farbrace's sight fell on the book on his prisoner's table. With his cane he swept it off, then kicked it down the aisle. "Foreign trash!"

The bosun followed the group out with a limp. Before he got to the door, he turned and glared at Jack Frake. "Don't let me catch you out-a-doors, scullion," he growled, "or you might find yerself at sea without a keel!"

When the inn's doors closed behind them, the Sea Siren's patrons resumed their revelry. Jack Frake stood with some amazement as the men and women picked up songs and conversations where they had been left off, as though nothing of dire importance had occurred, as though the wind had blown open the doors and caused confusion and temporary discomfort. Some patrons stared at him with curious looks. He turned and gathered together Blair's book, brass box, and shards of pipe to put them with his own things. The book's spine was broken by the lieutenant's boot. Still, he treated it as though it were a valuable object.

The army sergeant rose and ambled over to him, frowned, and with a slight bow, handed him a shilling. Jack Frake studied the man's face, which bore the healed furrow of a musket ball on his forehead and a saber scar on one cheek. "Take it, son," said the man, "and you don't have to sign up, either. Them tars call us dogs, too." The sergeant winked at him, then strode out of the inn.

Hiram Trott waved him into the kitchen and scolded the boy. "That was a foolhardy thing to do, damn you! You don't never tell a press-gang its business! And particularly not an officer!"

"I told him a fact," stated the boy.

"Well, the fact didn't sit well with him, did it? And it wasn't a *fact*, was it? Blair's some kind of impostor, and he's been having us on all this while!" Trott glared down at Jack Frake. "If it weren't for his lordship the admiral, your head would be broke and they'd be rowing you out to the *Rover*! And they could've taken *me* as well, damn you! The navy ain't got so many cooks they wouldn't have no use for me!"

"They'd no right to kidnap him, or me, or anyone."

Trott threw up his hands. Underneath his automatic assumption of the boy's ignorance, lay a kernel of resentment of his innocence. "Kidnap? They got the right and the law to do it, and there ain't no use arguing about it! If you don't like it, go introduce a bill in Parliament!"

"Will they let him go?"

"You heard the officer, lad! If he ain't who his lordship or Pannell is looking for, off he goes to sea! The gang got first dab on him. And that officer'll want to break him now." Trott frowned. "Now get back to work! We're lucky that gent didn't get to tumble with that officer. I got broken furniture the last time the gangs were here."

It was a lesson most men do not learn at all; or if they do learn it, forget under the pressures, burdens or lures of the banal distractions of life. To Jack Frake, it did not matter which a mob took first, with or without his consent: a man's fence, or his physical body. A fence, after all, had a purpose, and would not exist but for one's body having built it; it was, in a sense, an extension of it. Did it matter if one's body were left free to erect fences, only to have them seized at any time, for any reason? How could one go on erecting fences, or producing anything, if that likelihood always hovered in the air? How could one tolerate the likelihood, or submit to it as though it were a mere cold?

He did not dwell on the subject of the seizure of one's person; it was, to him, so self-evident an evil that it did not merit elaborate analysis.

It was hours later, after the inn was closed for the night and the Trotts had retired upstairs, that Jack Frake posed these issues and questions to himself. He sat on a stool in front of the fireplace, alone in the room. He was supposed to have let the fire die out, but he added a few pieces of wood to it, because he was restless, and wanted to think.

There was something extra in the make-up of grown men that allowed them to live with the evil he had witnessed this evening... or something missing, as though it, too, had been seized in some mysterious way. And there was inside himself something he did not share with any of them, perhaps because he had not allowed it to be seized. At first he felt a pang of loneliness and the prospect of a kind of exile from normal association with his fellow human beings. But this was followed by a gripping, steely sense of loneness — not solitude, but a distinctive grasp of his existence — the kind which eventually breeds the conscious conviction that whatever the difference between one's self and others, one would never allow one's self to be taken away, or diluted, or tamed.

The light of the flames, friendly, animate companions to his thoughts, danced over the grave lines of his young face. He turned his hands over and examined them. They were *his* hands, hands that had taken up a weapon to combat an injustice. He did not think it was so remarkable a thing to have done; that is, his deed this evening was not their sole glory. He was sure there was more to himself than that. Someday, he knew, he would be able to express what it was.

He pondered the fate of the mysterious Mr. Blair. He could think of no explanation for the man's behavior, either this evening or over the course of the last week and a half. But he was the second man to come to his defense at mortal jeopardy to himself. For reasons he could not yet identify, he had felt a fellowship with the man even before Blair confronted the officer.

It was quiet in the Sea Siren, and quiet outside. Jack Frake put on his jacket and hat, went out through the kitchen door, and strode around the inn to Jetty Street. The street was lit by cressets, one to a block. At the far end, one stood near the entrance to St. Brea's Church, whose tower was invisible in the night. Small, wet bits of cold fell gently on his face and melted, and he realized that it was snowing. He thought he saw some movement in the deep blackness farther down the street, but he could not be sure. Bob had told him this evening that the press-gangs would be busy until they were satisfied with the number and kinds of men they seized; wise men, whatever their station, would stay indoors until the warship departed for its home port.

A mad idea occurred to Jack Frake: he could accomplish two acts of justice tonight — deliver his note about Isham Leith to the vicar of St. Brea's, and perhaps rescue Blair from the constable's jail.

The first task was easy enough. He located the rectory in back of the church. It was more sumptuous than Parson Parmley's, built of cut stone. All its lights were out but one. He went to the front door, took out his note, and slipped it under the carved oaken portal. On the door was a brass knocker. He reached up, took hold of it, and banged it three times. Then he turned and ran.

He knew the location of the constable's house, on a side street close to the ironmonger's, next door to the milliner's shop. He darted across Jetty Street, then ran two blocks up, and turned a corner. He stopped in his tracks when he saw a mass of figures gathered beneath the extinguished cresset that stood in front of the constable's house. Even as he noticed it, the mass turned and moved in his direction.

A press-gang.

He turned again and ran across Jetty into the shadows, then up the cobblestone sidewalk in the direction of the Sea Siren. As he passed an alley, a man careened out of it and knocked him flat on his back. The man yelled in desperate panic, but did not stop to see what he had collided with. Even as he got back onto his feet, Jack Frake could hear his retreating footsteps down Jetty.

A hand reached out and lifted him up by his jacket collar, then threw him against the wall of the building.

"Powder monkey!" exclaimed a voice.

When his sight had recovered, Jack Frake looked up and recognized Bosun Jones. Behind him stood three other sailors from the press-gang, one of whom carried a flambeau. The man leered down at him and chuckled. A white rag was wrapped around his injured wrist, and his hand held a short iron bar, the end of which he tapped loudly in his other palm.

"I warned you not to let me catch you out-a-doors, you little bastard!" said Jones. "That's the second recruit you cost us! You ain't got no shovel now, and no bloody admiral to save your hide!" Without warning, he struck one of the boy's knees with the bar. Stunned by the pain, Jack Frake fell back on the wall and slid down its length. Before he could raise his head, the bar swished through the air again and struck him above the ear.

Before he lost consciousness, he imagined he heard the cocking of several pistols, and a voice saying, "Hands up, gents, or you each get a third eye!"

Chapter 8: The Skelly Men

"WHAT ARE WE IN IT FOR, ANYWAY?"

"Well, it's like this: Frederick of Prussia claims Silesia because of hereditary alliances and secret agreements and natural rights, and because he says it was purchased by a Hohenzollern a long time ago, only Silesia happens to be Queen Maria Theresa's of Bohemia and Hungary and Austria, because she became Holy Roman Empress — or rather her husband, the Grand Duke Francis Stephen of Tuscany, became Holy Roman Emperor — "

Another voice interjected, "It's Maria Theresa that's writing the scenes in that palace, I'll wager you on that."

" — And all this because Charles of Austria and Frederick William of Prussia winked out within a week of each other about four years ago. But Charles Albert of Bavaria, who's also calling himself Emperor, and Philip of Spain and Augustus of Poland, who think *they* ought to be Emperor, too, are claiming the crown, because of last female or male descendants or some such, so they've all declared war on Austria and sided with Frederick of Prussia."

"I was wonderin' where he got to."

"Now, Louis of France has sided with Frederick, for many reasons, to be sure, but *any* to oppose us would suit him."

"That Louis! Seems he's ruled by love and hate: love of petticoats and hatred of us."

"He's ruining France with those passions."

"More to our gain."

"Mudlark! An increase in taxes to fight the bloody French is no gain for anyone!"

"Our gain, I says! We'll have more to row in from the merchantmen!"

"And I say there'll be less of it to row in!"

"Who's his latest tart?"

"Madame Jeanne Antionette Poisson, Marquise de Pompadour."

"So you might say she's *poison* to Louis's purposes?"

"What a cheap crack! You ought to be dunked!"

"This Frederick: Is he the dead one or the live one?"

"The live one, silly. I hear he reads philosophy and composes music and writes verse."

"His father used to beat people with his cane if they didn't look dignified enough. A real cracker, that one."

"All those German royals are crackers! You'd think they recruited them from Bedlam. And here we got a pair of them lording it at Windsor!"

"Why are we siding with the old biddy?"

"Lud! Why, to oppose France and Louis, too. After all, Louis backed Young Charley last month. That broke a treaty. He should've served notice on the whole lot of Stuarts. And because Pelham and Pitt don't want to see Frederick become too powerful. And there you have it. Couldn't be simpler."

"Maria Theresa? She's no old biddy, from what I hear. Quite an eyeful, they says."

"How many men we got to defend our shores?"

"Not more than ten thousand, I've heard. Probably fewer."

"And when they send some of them over to get their arses kicked by Frederick and Saxe, there'll be fewer to deal with the Tartans, you'll see. Word is there's trouble brewin' in the Highlands."

"Who's to lead them in this arse-kickin'?"

"They say Cumberland the Uncouth himself, George's favorite son."

"Oh, God! Double kicks!"

"That's slander! He's an able man! He proved that at Dettingen!"

"You mean he shared the King's luck at Dettingen! If the French hoof weren't so eager to give our lads the quick shave, and waited until Noailles could kick George's arse, we'd be paying royal ransoms for the King and his bloody favorite! It was all luck, I tell you."

"The King led the countercharge himself, and his son commanded the First Guards, which was in the thick of it."

"Thousands drowned in the Main River, they says, runnin' from old George."

"*I* say the Duke'll sweep Saxe and Frederick and all the rest of 'em right off the field and into the river, just like his father did at Dettingen!"

"Says you! A guinea on Frederick *or* Saxe inside of a year, and Cumberland sailin' back with his tails pinned to his ears!"

"You're on! Here, any other takers!"

The conversation disintegrated into a babble of competing voices, and thereafter Jack Frake paid it little attention. The exchange about Maria Theresa and Frederick and the war was typical of the talk he heard in the Sea Siren, as much of it as he was able to catch while hurrying about his job.

"Quiet down, lads, or you'll wake the boy."

The sound of *that* voice caused Jack Frake's body to stiffen and his eyes to open. The first thing he saw was the roof of a cave. The next thing was Mr. Blair's face. The man stared down at him from where he sat on a stool. Blair smiled. There was something different about his face; it was paler in the light of the torches and lanterns that were fixed to the limestone walls; the eyebrows were not as thick and the moles on his cheeks were gone.

Then he heard a creak of leather and noticed another man near the straw mattress on which he lay, and glanced up. He had black marbles for eyes, a stern, rugged face, and a tight, grim mouth. He stood looking down at Jack with a trace of detached amusement, his long greatcoat open, his fists planted on his hips. The light reflected off the inlaid silver in the grips of a pair of pistols tucked into his belt. The man's eyes narrowed in response to Jack Frake's scrutiny, as though he knew what the boy was thinking. "Curtain," he said.

Blair rose and fixed a curtain of burlap over the entrance of what Jack Frake now realized was an alcove in a larger cave. The light dimmed, then returned as Blair lit a lantern, which he hung on another peg in the stone wall. He sat down again. "How's your head, Jack?" he asked.

Jack Frake sat up on the mattress. He felt a slight throbbing on the left side of his skull. He put a hand to it and located a swelling beneath his hair. "Almost better," he answered.

"Thanks to a generous portion of Dover's powder. You're still in pain — that bosun whacked you hard — but the opium and Indian root take off the edge. You'll feel nothing in a day or two."

"What happened? Where am I?"

"My, er, friends rescued me from Constable Skeats's quarters. Then we rescued you, collected your things and mine from the inn, and brought you here. You've been flickering in and out for almost a day now."

"I was coming to see you."

"To see me?"

"I thought I could do something to get you out."

"Thanks again," chuckled Blair. "The Admiral and his aides had retired to their inn hours earlier, and Commissioner Pannell and his men went to see some ladies to celebrate my capture. They didn't get much from me except an incredible elaboration of my Boston-Bristol story, and I suppose that tired them. As time went on I imagine the questioning would've become much less cordial. We trussed up Mr. Skeats and his wife and left them a shilling for their trouble." Blair glanced up to his companion, who remained silent. "As we came out on Jetty, we saw the press-gang cornering you. Didn't look like fair odds, so we decided to even them up."

"Was there a fight?"

"No, thank the Lord. Bosun Jones and his gang were too stunned. We left them in the alley gagged and bound together in knots I'll bet they never heard of. For good measure, I whacked Jones once or twice in your name. Don't think he'll bully another scullion any time soon who's got so many uncles and cousins."

Jack Frake stared at Blair for a moment, and remembered what else was missing from the man. "You don't have that funny tongue."

"My Scot's brogue?" chuckled Blair. "A mere theatrical illusion, but Admiral Harle and the entire company of the inn were a commendable audience."

"What's your real name?"

The silent man raised a finger, silencing Blair, then jerked his head, and the two went out past the curtain. Jack Frake noticed that all his belongings were heaped on the cave floor near the mattress. As he took an inventory of his possessions, he could hear a whispered discussion taking place beyond the curtain above the murmur of dozens of other voices.

The men returned a moment later. The friendliness of Blair's face was tempered now by a seriousness that matched the silent man's. He sat on his stool and looked at Jack Frake as a man looks at a man. "You'll get an answer to that question and others I'm sure you're bound to ask, but you're to know there'll be but one of two consequences: You'll be turned out of here, or you'll be staying. If you're turned out, we'll blindfold you and put you on a country road and you'll be on your own. If you stay, you'll take the pledge. It'll be your decision."

Blair paused. "You can't go back to the Sea Siren. That bosun will want to kill you now, and that Lieutenant Farbrace hasn't forgotten you, either, and the *Rover* will be at anchor at Gwynnford for a few days before pushing off to Spithead or Portsmouth. Did you deliver that note to the vicar? I take it that's why you were out."

Jack Frake nodded.

"So there's another reason why you can't go back. Vicar Heskett and this Parmley of yours were friends, I hear, and so he'll pester Skeats and Sheriff Prebble until they do something about it. If the best thing happens and this Isham Leith is arrested on the captain's evidence, you'll be found somehow — you're a missing mother's son and a stranger in Gwynnford — and hauled in as a witness. Remember: Venable saw *you* on that road, too. Your mother'll be questioned as an accomplice, whether she had anything to do with the murder or not. And if Leith is questioned but talks himself out of charges, he'll come looking for you. And there you are." With another glance at the silent man, Blair added, "I'm telling you all this just to lay out the full course. My friend here says you can stay a day or two until your head's clear again, ignorant of our names." Blair paused, then exclaimed, "Bosh! This is useless! How can he know to think hard when there's nothing for him to think on?"

"He knows our faces," growled the silent man. But after a moment he said, "All right. Tell him your name."

Blair rose and doffed his hat. "Rory O'Such. Also Jack Darling, Methuselah Redmagne, and Vivian Crisp, and now Matthew Blair — it all depends on which town I happen to be passing through. At your service."

Jack Frake blinked. "What name were you born with?" he asked, astounded by the number of names.

"Unfortunately, John Smith. All my efforts to imbue that name with dreadful connotations and romantic allure have failed miserably. Thus, my civil list of preferred *nominae*."

"Why?"

"To elude capture, to confound the sheriffs and the riding officers of the law, to charm the ladies, but, above all, to entertain myself."

A stone of thrilling fear seemed to fall from his heart to the pit of his stomach. Jack Frake turned to face the second man. "And you?"

The man's eyes narrowed. "Osbert Augustus Magnus Skelly," he said.

"Margrave of Cornwall," added Smith with respectful irony.

"Why so many names?"

"My parents thought if they gave me great names, I would become a great man."

"It seems you've fulfilled their designs," remarked Smith.

"They would doubt that, were they still alive," answered Skelly. He bent down and put his hands on his knees to scowl at the boy. "You *know* who I am, don't you, lad?"

"Yes, sir. The great smuggler."

Skelly jerked back to his full height, as though insulted. "I'm that, by one set of mouths. By another, I'm villainous scum, fit only to be flogged and hanged without benefit of clergy." He grinned. "What do *you* think?"

Jack Frake shrugged. "I don't know you, so I can't judge."

Skelly's mouth cracked in the suggestion of a smile. "Well, here's someone who's master of his own eyes."

"So I said," remarked Smith.

"Interview!" said Skelly, turning to his associate. "Feed your scullion, and I'll talk to him after I've settled accounts." He turned and went through the curtain.

"He wants to talk to you," said Smith. "Come on. You can wash some of that sleep off your face, and have some stew. You'll need a full stomach to think hard, and Skelly will give you plenty to think about."

Jack Frake rose, put on his jacket, and followed Smith through the curtain.

Chapter 9: The Caves

SMUGGLING WAS A MAJOR ENTERPRISE IN EIGHTEENTH CENTURY ENGLAND, a phenomenon created, aided and abetted by a complex array of import and consumption taxes, imposed by a government that wished to promote prosperity and to tax it, too. The import or customs duties were designed to nurture the growth of English industry by adding to the cost of private purchases of foreign-made goods which the government rather wished to be made at home for domestic purchase and export; "consumption" or excise taxes were levied on both English and foreign-made goods for the purpose of raising revenue. It was a matter of robbing Peter to pay Paul who was obliged to pay the Piper; only the Piper seemed to prosper, though his pockets, too, were in fact empty. One major consequence of this policy was to stunt what little prosperity and material progress managed to occur under the combined weights of royal, aristocratic, and government entitlements and preferments, the endless wars, disastrous financial schemes, and rife corruption.

It also encouraged crime and the corruption of both the taxers and the taxed; as much or more energy was diverted to evading the taxes as was invested in producing things that could be taxed. The evasion attracted men of moral character and the criminally inclined alike, who, knowing nothing throughout their lives but an irrecusable injustice, accepted it as the norm. The first group broke the law from necessity; the second broke it as opportunity. The system drew men who would surrender, meekly and guiltily, in the face of a revenue man's rain-soaked pistol. It drew brutal, indiscriminate killers whose gangs controlled whole towns and whose suppression required the employment of the army. And it drew men, fewer, perhaps, who were neither meek nor brutal, but who were dedicated, in crime, to preserving something no one could yet name. It was to them that outlawry owed its romance. These few men seemed to be the most determined and the most menacing smugglers of all. They broke the law by fiery, clench-fisted choice.

The judicial system, though modern in method and the most advanced in Europe, was rooted in large part in the precepts of the medieval period. A man could be hanged for murder, and also for stealing a length of waste silk fabric from his employer or an armful of discarded wood chips from a shipyard. A woman could be hanged for picking a few shillings from another's pocket, or for harboring a man who had stolen a sack of coal or vegetables. On one hand, life and property were revered and protected by an eclectic criteria that recognized no measurement of loss, theft or destruction. On the other, the government and the Crown treated them both as chattel.

* * *

The chamber in which Jack Frake awoke was a nook in one of several caves honeycombing a clot of low, barren hills near the market town of Marvel, some three miles north of the coast. The hills lay on the fringes of the estate of a country squire named Villers who had died in bankruptcy ten years before. The estate, which consisted of an unoccupied mansion and one hundred acres, had been the subject of contested ownership among three of the squire's surviving brothers, two neighboring propertied gentlemen who, upon Villers' death, produced deeds and receipts alleging ancient claims to portions of the estate, and the squire's numerous creditors.

While the courts deliberated, the mansion fell into desuetude and decay, and the pastures, gardens and tillage reverted to wilderness. There was no one to notice the smoke that occasionally blew from one or two of the hills, no one to hear, when the wind was right, a faint neighing of a horse, a tantalizing strum of a lute, or a ghostly crescendo of laughter. Poachers and farmers suspected that the mansion was haunted by Villers's ancestors, many of whom were slain or executed during the Civil War.

Townsmen were certain that the estate was inhabited by the Skelly gang and by spirits who granted the gang sanctuary in their netherworld in exchange for homage to pagan idols.

Neither the late squire, nor his brothers, nor the poachers, nor the townsfolk of Marvel knew of the existence of the caves, for the hills were surrounded by thick, thorny brush, impassable except by fire or ax. The squire's former tenant farmers, who now paid their rents to the court, had not thought it worth the effort to clear the brush to get to the hills, as there seemed to be nothing on them but rock and grass, of which they had a surfeit in their own pastures.

Before Skelly, the first men to use the caves were Roman officials and legionnaires, who hid their families in them from marauding Celts allied with the rebellious Iceni. After them, Britons hid in them from marauding Danes. Now they were the refuge of desperate Englishmen hiding from marauding Englishmen.

The caves were ideal for habitation. There were fissures and chimneys in the rock through which prevailing winds circulated air. An underground spring carried water from lower depths to pools in two of the caverns. The floors were flat and the walls almost plumb. There were three entrances to the labyrinth, protected by the brush and invisible to the undiscerning eye. Each entrance was reached by a serpentine path which forked into several others, which were dead-ends, and the entrances were camouflaged to look like dead-ends. The paths wound through a forest and eventually connected with the King's highway south of Marvel.

The caves were divided into three sections. One housed the gang. Another contained its inventory of contraband. The third served as a stable for the gang's mounts and as a shelter for its livestock, which consisted of chickens, pigs and goats. Gang members took turns tending to these accomplices in crime.

Commissioner Hennoch Pannell and his predecessors knew that the Skelly gang operated out of the vicinity of Marvel. Squads of dragoons drafted into Revenue service had scoured the pathways, copses and coverts around the hills but found little beyond poachers' traps, stray sheep and cattle, and encamped paupers. Pannell had even searched the Villers house once, and for a time had a watch set on it. But there were no signs of life to be found. Pannell, a London man with some cosmopolitan pretensions, cursed the superstitions of the region and the reticence of the local inhabitants. He turned his search elsewhere.

* * *

There were twenty men in Skelly's gang, every one of them wanted for various crimes against the Crown. None was a common criminal. Each had committed some action that defied authority: one, a former shopkeeper, had refused to pay a hearth and window tax; one, a former cattle driver, had struck a parish tithesman and stole back the cattle the churchman took from him in lieu of money; one had delivered an impromptu, slanderous tirade against Parliament and a corrupt minister and his clique; one had written and distributed scandalous verse about King George and his two sons, William Augustus, Duke of Cumberland, and Frederick Louis, the Prince of Wales and Duke of Cornwall; one had knowingly sold contraband tea, silk and bread; one, a former London Customs House inspector, had shown mercy to a merchant who pleaded he'd be ruined if he paid the duties on his impounded shipment of French lace, and was charged with theft of Crown revenue; one was a former butcher's apprentice whose employer was driven to highway robbery when the City trebled his stall fee; one was a former highwayman, famous for his wit and gallantry, who had offered to rob Skelly himself as he strode into Fowey, and was persuaded instead to join the gang.

Throughout Cornwall, Devon, Dorset and Somerset, the four counties that lay between the Bristol and English Channels, it was known that the Skelly gang was not simply another band of criminals, and its reputation and esteem varied from group to group. The common people revered Skelly and his gang for their derring-do and mockery of the authorities. The middle class was divided between those who openly blessed the gang for the goods it sold to their merchants and shops *sans* all taxes, and those who, with surreptitious prudence, also purchased the same goods, but were nonetheless envious of the gang's moral mettle. The landed gentry and aristocracy chuckled, over their breakfasts, at the newspaper accounts of the gang's exploits, but in their church pews exuded concern for the gang's example for defying order and established society. And customs and excise enforcement officials simply cursed the gang and their duty to ensnare it; there was neither glory nor profit in assured humiliation.

Osbert Augustus Magnus Skelly interviewed prospective members of his gang in the dining hall of his hideout and headquarters. It was the biggest cavity of the caverns. Its severe gray walls were decorated with some of the souvenirs of the gang's exploits. On it were fixed a red Customs

Service Revenue jack and a rowing boat's black backboard, emblazoned with the King's Arms, both trophies of a race between the pursuing boat and Skelly's contraband-laden galley in a wild, high tide surf near a Dorset beach; the patrol boat smashed against some rocks, broke up, and all aboard it either drowned or were dashed against the rocks and killed. There were a dozen hats hanging from pegs, their former owners excise men who had arrested one or another of Skelly's men, only to be arrested by Skelly, disarmed and relieved of their prisoners, and taken blindfolded to another county, stripped naked, and set free on a country road, their bare wrists handcuffed behind their bare backs. There was a collection of weapons: muskets, pistols, swords, and halberds, all taken from men who had guarded Customs warehouses raided by Skelly to recover seized contraband for which he had already paid.

And there was a pair of buckled shoes, set apart from the other mementos, on an otherwise bare wall.

The dining table, of shellacked oak, was thirty feet long, and was built from the planking of the deck of a revenue sloop that ran aground when its captain ordered it too close to the beach to better observe some suspicious men. Over it, suspended from a gilt-iron chain, was a silver chandelier of twenty candles, and down its length were silver and copper candlesticks. Mugs, glasses, tankards, plates, dice and packs of cards littered the top. There was even a book, and some newspapers.

In a corner of this hall was the kitchen, whose fireplace took advantage of a chimney-like fissure in the rock. Close by was a pool. Blair-Smith took a bucket, dipped it into the water, and gave it to Jack Frake. "Wash up, Jack. I'll see if I can scrape some stew for you from the bottom of the pot."

Later, still alone in the hall with Blair-Smith, Jack Frake sat at one end of the table, eating his stew and sipping a mug of ale in between glances at his surroundings. Blair-Smith sat placidly on the bench close by, reading a copy of the London *Gazetteer*, a Whig newspaper, and smoking a pipe.

But Jack Frake was full of questions. "Why were you pretending to be someone else at the inn?" he asked. "I mean, why were you there, when Mr. Pannell was searching for you?"

"We were keeping an eye on *him*, lad. We've been looking over his shoulder, so to speak, ever since he arrived in these parts months ago. He and his men have snared a few smugglers, but no one from our gang. He hasn't made a move without our knowing about it. When he left on his nocturnal patrols, I slipped out through my window in your inn and was right behind him."

"How did Mr. Skelly know you were arrested?"

"*Mr.* Skelly?" chuckled Smith. "That'll tickle him. I wasn't the only Skelly man there, young Jack. When Farbrace cuffed me, word got out to Skelly, and he planned my bail. In fact, we knew the *Rover* was heading for Gwynnford before the town did."

"Why did you let them arrest you?"

"It wasn't a matter of choice," answered Smith, snapping the paper. "It was a matter of by whom. I was going to be arrested, there was no arguing about that. But I knew why Admiral Harle was there — we'd got word he was on the road, looking for French agents and spies, and apprising invasion points. Now I can't speak French, but I can imitate a Scot, and you might have noticed there aren't many Scotsmen in Gwynnford. So it was a Scot he got. The Admiral was the least grim of my possible fates. If Pannell or that lieutenant had got his hands on me, well, that would've been the end of my illustrious career. I'd planned to speak, but you beat me to it with your shovel."

"Why did you pretend to have a dead tongue?"

"To avoid having to answer so many questions," replied Smith, snapping his paper again. "Eat your stew, or I *will* turn mute."

Jack Frake spooned a few mouthfuls. "Where are all the men I heard talking?"

"Being paid."

"You look different."

"In my former life, I was an actor."

"What's an actor?"

"An actor is a person who entertains others by being someone else. Sometimes he is paid with money; other times, with rotten fruit. He usually plies his trade in a theater." Smith relented and explained the theater to the boy, and offered to show him the make-up kit he had retrieved from his room at the Sea Siren.

After a few more mouthfuls of stew, Jack Frake asked, "What may I call you?"

"Me? Why, Smith, of course." Smith noted the look of disappointment on his auditor's face. "It is my real name. You may consult the parish register of St. John's in Wapping, if you doubt it."

"May I call you Redmagne?"

"Even though I haven't a single lock of red hair?"

"Yes. I think that ought to be your real name. Mesula Redmagne."

"*Methuselah*," corrected Smith. "All right. Redmagne I am." The newly named smuggler turned his attention back to the *Gazetteer*, now not entirely displeased with the boy's incessant curiosity.

"Did the *Sparrowhawk* go to Gwynnford?"

Redmagne frowned and dropped the paper. "What do you know about that?" he asked sharply.

Jack Frake explained.

"She hove to a mile or so west of Gwynnford," said Redmagne, looking at the boy with new interest. "And there we unshipped her."

* * *

Skelly stood before the boy, his arms folded, much as Parson Parmley had in his classroom. His two pistols winked flashes under the chandelier, and now Jack Frake saw that he had buckled on a sword. There was an earnestness in the man's face which Jack Frake could not identify. He felt ennobled by the expression, though, for he knew that the man was regarding him as a man, as Redmagne-Smith had earlier.

"I invite you to enlist in my gang," said Skelly. "I say *gang*, for that is what we are. I don't trouble myself with sophisticated nomenclature. This *is* a gang. Not a club. Not a society. Not an association. We are outside the law, however wrong that law may be. So, know this: If we are caught and tried and convicted, we shall pay the law's price.

"I am the leader of this gang. I founded it. I direct it. I set its rules. You may not stay unless you subscribe to every one of them. And the rules are these: We don't steal, and we don't accept or trade in stolen goods. We don't trade with our country's enemies, whoever they might be at any given time. We don't employ, use or help murderers, burglars, highwaymen, footpads, or their like. We don't give them a grin or a nod or a wink. To me the cut-throats and robbers are no different from the ones who take the King's coin and carry the King's warrant to do the same things to people. They just do it quicker than the King's men, that's all. We make no distinction among them. Is that clear?"

"Yes, sir."

"Folks cook up legends about me and my men, but they also make heroes of the thieves and their ilk, like Dick Turpin or Edward Bonner. That's because they see folks being robbed whom they don't like. They'd sing a different ballad if they were the ones being chivvied or held-up. It's as if their rags gave them a right to hate anyone who didn't wear rags. Me? I'd dress like the King if I didn't think it would attract attention.

"Next rule: We don't associate with secret societies or other gangs or aid them in any way. There's plenty of them around. That's not made us popular with the other gangs, but it's saved us the bother of betrayal and being mixed up in the bad sort's troubles. There are a lot of decent men who smuggle, and a lot who aren't. We don't have the time to read letters of reference.

"Next rule: If you enlist in my gang, you'll *work*. This is a business I run here. I make money selling to townsfolk the goods I buy from merchantmen. You're to see yourself as my employee. You'll get prize rates, the same as a Navy or privateer crew when it captures an enemy ship. The difference here is that you won't have to wait to collect your due. If you enlist, you'll start as our scullion. We need one. Smith here highly recommends you. You'll get a share of whatever profit we make on our goods. When I think you're ready for outside work, you'll get a bonus rate commensurate with your task. What you do with your earnings is your affair. You'll have a billet here, your own bedding and all that.

"Last rule: We're all wanted men here. Every one of us has banns posted announcing our engagement to Rebecca Rope, and no one has objected. So we live here, mostly. We don't live normal lives. Some of us have sweethearts out there, and friends and family, but none of them are to be brought to this place for any reason. There's too much chance of betrayal or slips of tongue. So if you have family, don't expect to see them for a while."

Skelly paused, then pointed to the buckled shoes on the wall. "See those?"

Jack Frake nodded.

"They were a man's by the name of Jack Strype. He was a member of this gang. He was wanted for smuggling and breaking into bonded warehouses and beating a particularly vicious customs man to death. He was with us for three years. He took the pledge. One day he disappeared, and the next week Revenue men raided my hideout near Fowey. There was a fight and men were killed on both sides. That hide-out was as perfect as this one, the Revenue men knew nothing about it, so the raid meant only one thing: an informer. We learned that Jack Strype had been arrested. We bailed him out, that is, one night we relieved the sheriff of his prisoner. We learned that he'd made a bargain with the Crown, as is allowed by law: my neck in exchange for a waiver of all outstanding charges against him, except for the murder. He was bargaining with the authorities on even that, in exchange for information about this place.

"Well, the authorities found him the next day, swinging from an oak outside of Fowey. We hanged him. Those were his shoes." Skelly paused. "We'd like to grow fond again of the name 'Jack,' my boy. It's a good name."

Skelly bent to lean on the table with both arms. His face looked as ruthless and cold as Jack Frake remembered seeing it that night on the cliff. "Do you wish to enlist in my gang?"

"Yes, sir."

"This is not a game, my boy. Or a lark. There'll be damned few sunny days in these caves or out of them."

"I know."

"Now, lad, you will answer a question, and on your answer will depend whether or not I decide to let you enlist. Is this clear?"

"Yes, sir."

"Given all my rules, why would I allow *you* to enlist in my gang?" Skelly chuckled in mischief. "Think hard, now. Remember what I said about whom I employ."

"I struck a sailor, and challenged an officer of the Navy."

Skelly stood to his full height. "And you don't think that makes you a criminal?"

"No, sir."

"Why not, if you please?"

"A man's life is his own, and the officer wanted to take his," answered Jack Frake. He glanced at Redmagne, who sat at the other end of the table.

"It's done by custom and the authority of law and His Majesty," said Skelly. "So it must be right."

Through the implacable stoniness of Skelly's expression, there twinkled a glint of humor. Jack Frake noted it but did not understand it. The boy's brow hardened. "No," he answered. It was all he could say. He did not know the law or the King's authority. But he was certain of his own rightness.

Skelly grinned a little, then turned and faced Redmagne. "You rehearsed him, did you not?"

Redmagne shook his head. "No, my friend. I didn't think I would need to."

Skelly turned to Jack Frake again. Someone coughed. The boy looked and saw some of the gang standing at the portal of the cavern, watching.

Skelly took hold of the scabbard and unsheathed his sword with a flourish. He lay the steel down on the table in front of the boy. "This belonged to a man I killed many years ago. He was a customs man, a man who seduced my wife, bribed my brothers to betray me, and stole my property in the King's name and his own. We dueled the day he came to arrest me in my own home. He had this fine sword — see? it bears the King's Arms on the guard — and I had but a paring knife. *That* I left in his gut." Skelly paused to scrutinize the boy's face. "Having second thoughts, my boy?"

"No, sir. You're not a murderer."

"No? I told you: This is not a lark! I *killed* a man! In fact, I've killed a few. If I'm caught, I'll be surely hanged. And if you're caught with me, but without a weapon, you'll be whipped, and transported, and sold to a plantation man in the colonies to work beside slaves and other convicts! And if you're caught with a weapon, you'll be hanged, too, or sentenced to a workhouse for the rest of your life! You'll be swaddled in chains from your neck to your ankles, and if you're lucky you'll die of iron fever before you grow a crooked back! But long before that, boy, you'll *beg* to be hanged!"

Skelly leaned on the table again, studying the boy's face, searching for a reaction. He saw no fear, no recoil, no diminution of interest in either him or what he had said. He saw nothing but an unswerving attentiveness. He concluded that nothing he could say would extinguish the flame of innocence he saw in the boy, nor move the rock of defiance he saw in that flame. He wondered what Jack Frake might have witnessed in his few years of life that could make him so impervious to his oft-repeated epistle of outlawry.

And — he saw a suggestion of admiration, which Skelly did not contest, mixed with a dash of hero-worship, which made him uncomfortable. Osbert Augustus Skelly was a proud man, but not vain.

On Jack Frake's part, there was a natural element in everything Skelly had said. It appealed to his young soul to remain apart from the suffocating strictures of normal life to which he had seen other grown men submit. He had not within him the capacity for the genteel regret of wistfulness. He had tasted real freedom of thought and action; resignation was a foreign sensation to the palate of his mind, a bitter substance to be spat out contemptuously. At the moment, the prospect of dying or of being sentenced to a life of servitude was unreal to him; Skelly was real, Redmagne was real, their thoughts, words and deeds were real. In a dim, as yet undefined way, he knew that he was something like these men. The thing inside him which he had sworn never to allow to be seized told him that it was right to want to be with them, to do what they did, and to reap the rewards they won and to pay the price they paid.

And he knew that Skelly was doing his best to discourage him from wanting to join the gang. It was a gang of men; so, he reasoned, something manly was demanded of him. Abruptly he rose from the bench, reached down with one hand, and gripped the pommel of Skelly's sword. He asked, more challenge in his words than query, "What is your oath, sir?"

Skelly threw an appreciative glance at Redmagne, then stood up. "All right, Mr. Jack Frake, you will take the oath." He waved a hand at the men at the portal. "There are your witnesses and colleagues. Repeat after me."

"Yes, sir."

"I pledge, upon my soul, to be always a true and mindful patriot… "

"I pledge, upon my soul, to be always a true and mindful patriot — "

"… and to obey all laws in this kingdom that secure my rights as an Englishman to life, liberty and property… "

" — and to obey all laws in this kingdom that secure my rights as an Englishman to life, liberty, and property — "

"… and to flout and oppose, with wit or weapon, at every chance… "

" — and to flout and oppose, with wit or weapon, at every chance — "

"… all those that befog, confound, or belittle them."

" — all those that befog, confound, or belittle them."

"God save the King!"

"*God save the King*," said Jack Frake.

Skelly stepped forward and thrust out his hand. "Welcome, Master Frake!"

Jack Frake let go of the pommel and reached up to clasp the man's hand. "I hope I live up to your expectations."

There was a smile on Skelly's face, but his eyes now were dark pools of solemnity.

Redmagne appeared at his colleague's side and also shook the boy's hand. "Well done, Jack," he said. "I know you'll do right by us. Tonight we'll feast to celebrate your enlistment. And tomorrow morning you'll don an apron and help clean up."

"In the meantime," said Skelly, "let me introduce you to our gang. Then Smith here will set you up a billet, and then you and I will have a frank talk about what you know about the *Sparrowhawk*."

Thus did Jack Frake begin his criminal career.

Chapter 10: The Covenant

SKELLY THRUST A HEAVY IRON CHAIN INTO JACK FRAKE'S HANDS. "TELL ME something about this chain, Mr. Frake." He sat down, unbuckled and removed his sword and scabbard, and laid them across his lap. He leaned back to wait for an answer, drumming his fingers along the length of the scabbard.

The boy stood in Skelly's quarters, a large, domed cave, more spacious than his home in Trelowe. He saw a case of books, an oaken desk and chair where the man sat, a high, slanted desk with a high stool, and a four-poster bed in a corner. There was a cabinet and a wing-table, and ten candle sconces on the walls. A framed map hung on the wall over the oaken desk; he recognized the coast of Cornwall. There were blue ribbons pinned to many points along the coast, and green ones to points inland. An ungainly looking three-legged stand stood in one space; on it a cloth covered some large, flat rectangle. The floor was smothered with a wild variety of colorful rugs.

After he had shaken hands with the rest of the gang, he was taken by Skelly through the caves and brought here. The man had asked him what he knew about the *Sparrowhawk*. Jack Frake answered as completely as he could.

"You must show me this cubbyhole of yours some time," said Skelly. "It might come in handy one day." It was then that he had picked up a length of chain from under his desk and had given it to the boy.

Jack Frake examined the chain. There were ten links to it, all coated with rust that left a dry, brownish powder on his hands. "It's not new, sir," was all he could say.

Skelly laughed. "A plain observation! I like that about you, young sir!" Then the smile disappeared. "What you are holding, Mr. Frake, is the chain that once connected a pair of leg irons. There are two links missing, one each still fastened to the irons on a man's ankles. The locks were rusted shut and could not be opened. This man, Hal Tyler, once lived near the lovely town of Sheffield. He was a simple, honest man who owned his own patch — not a commons plot, mind you — and who grew apricots and apples and strawberries and cabbages and other edibles. And — he grew tobacco, which he cleverly planted amongst his brilliant cabbages, for which he was famous in his parts. But the growing of tobacco is not permitted in our kingdom, young sir. It can be too easily sold without benefit of tax, you see. However, one autumn he needed to lay in his firewood for the winter, and the wood the town's firewood merchant was selling that year was some nasty Continental stuff that wouldn't burn properly, or if it did, burned too fast. And it was costly. So Hal Tyler took his horse and cart into the King's forest and emerged from it with a load of fine oak. He cut no trees, mind you, as tree-poachers are wont to do, but simply took up branches that lay on the ground or ones he could reach on tiptoe. And the King's warden was there at his home, waiting for him. He was charged with theft of the King's wood and with growing a forbidden commodity, and sent down to London to be tried, for these were royal matters. He was convicted, and the judge and jury showed mercy by sentencing him to life in Newgate Prison. And after three years in Newgate, Hal Tyler escaped. Newgate, I should remind you, is in London. One of the links had broken, and so he was able to walk a distance. We found him on a road near Witchampton, in Dorset, as far as he was able to beg and steal. The chain in your hands he'd wrapped around his other leg. He was starving, and in pretty bad shape from other ailments as well. He managed to tell us his story before he died. We buried him in a pretty little glen near the town.

"A tragic history, but a common one, I'm afraid. The moral of it is this: Were it not for the King's laws, we might never have made our brief but sad acquaintance with Hal Tyler! We would, I believe, be enjoying his strawberries and apricots and cabbages — and his tobacco — in our own homes, or even in Ranelagh Gardens! Give me the chain."

Jack Frake put the chain in Skelly's hands, then stepped back and wiped the rust from his palms on his breeches.

The man rattled the chain once. "An ugly sound, is it not? There is more freedom in these caves, Mr. Frake, than in our towns. And chains — these things — are a more honest form of slavery than the specious liberty enjoyed by most of our countrymen, who are chained to laws much like those which killed Mr. Tyler. You will notice something about the men here, which is that the prospect of being swaddled in chains like these frightens them less than being swaddled in chains of laws, of which there are many more links. We will submit to chains" — Skelly again rattled the ones in his hand, then said contemptuously — "but we none of us will submit to their *paper and ink* parents!" Skelly threw the chain down, and sighed. "I am not a man of letters, like your flamboyant sponsor, Mr. Frake. If I were, I perhaps could put it more clearly. Your sponsor is befuddled, too. At least he has not communicated the thing to me. It's a difficult thing to put into words, our rebellion. It's not a high-sounding cause to most men, our business of wanting to mind our own without interference or penalty, and so few of them are willing to rally to our colors. Most of those who join me discover something about themselves, and in themselves — something roused by more than mere disobedience, but which learns to glory in its unfettered state, and cannot ever be put to sleep again except by cowardice or a hangman's noose. I've not been able to say what it is. Perhaps you will, some day." Skelly chuckled. "You'll have the advantage of our example and association, and so will be able to devote more thought to it. Most of us, you may have noticed, got off to a late start. Perhaps someone has already found those words. However, in the meantime, I do know what I know, and that is the nub of it." He glanced down at the chain and kicked it back under his desk. He paused to study the boy's face. "Do you understand what I'm trying to say, Mr. Frake?"

Jack Frake nodded.

"*What*, then?"

"Even though we are chained by our outlawry, we are free men, more free than ordinary folk."

"Crudely put, but right. By my own lights, I am a patriot. We all are, here. The government tries to kill my country. I try to keep it alive. What else could I be, then, but a patriot?" Skelly smiled tiredly and put the sword in its scabbard aside on the desk-top. "Well, end of lecture, Mr. Frake. You'll get one-half of one percent of the profit realized on any consummated transaction. The rate will improve with your skills. Does that agree with you?"

Jack Frake smiled. "It agrees with me, sir, and I agree to it."

"Humph! So you say now! Wait until you see how much or how little that one-half of one percent can be! So!" exclaimed Skelly as he rose and stretched once. "Let us repair to the great hall, and see what Mr. Tuck is preparing for us for dinner! Capons, I believe, and plum pudding. I'll try to talk him into whipping up a pot of syllabub. Interesting man, our Mr. Elmo Tuck," said Skelly as he led Jack Frake from the chamber. "He was once chef for the old Earl of Danvers, who had a secret weakness for French cuisine, at which Mr. Tuck was secretly adept. However, one day Mr. Tuck, his kitchen fresh out of ingredients and condiments, innocently and without malice aforethought improvised and prepared the Earl a bowl of haggis. That's a Scots dish, you see, but he may as well have presented the Earl with a bowl of cattle fodder. The old Earl thrashed him for that alleged insult, accused him of having Jacobite sympathies — the Earl, when a young man had helped put down the '15 in Scotland — and banished him from Dorset. The Earl expired shortly after that episode, in a Weymouth inn, during a dalliance with a servant girl in his household he had brought with him. Mr. Tuck, who happened to be anonymously employed in that same inn, was found out by the Earl's sons and further accused of poisoning their father. They wished to preserve the Earl's good name by besmirching Mr. Tuck's. Mr. Tuck fled the inn only a few steps ahead of the bailiff... "

* * *

Skelly was right; life in the claustrophobic caves was no lark. Jack Frake, however, did not seem to mind the artificial regime. He was in the constant company of men who seemed to be of his own stamp. This circumstance did not cause him to relax, but to be more conscientious about his work. He could not decide whether he was motivated by a desire to earn their respect, or by a desire to grant them his. He dove into his work with the same energy and enthusiasm that he had displayed at the Sea Siren. During his first year in the caves, he rarely ventured far beyond the thickets that encircled them. He was kept busy as a scullion, as the cook's helper, as a shepherd for the livestock, as a lookout for intruders and as a scout for the gang when it moved *en masse* in and out of the caves. He grew to become possessive of the caves and their inhabitants. And he grew to covet the shillings and guineas that began to accumulate beneath his bed of straw.

Other boys might have resisted the regime and rebelled against it. Jack Frake, cherishing the privilege of living and working with a band of unusual men, submitted to it without question. He knew that he had something to learn from all of the gang-members, aside from the reasons why they were outlaws. He saw in each man a tiny reflection of himself. There was a word or phrase that identified the common denominator that united the gang. It eluded him, and seemed to elude the men, too. He saw, further, that the gang-members were truly men of good will and good cheer, but that also each one had a secret agony, which was his status as a fugitive. Paradoxically, the agony did not belie their benevolence.

The gang ate well, lived well — its living quarters were finely if eclectically appointed with contraband furniture from the Continent — and wanted for little. It went where it pleased as long as Skelly's rules were heeded. It worked as a brotherhood. Its members lived in caves, while the rest of English society lived within four walls. But each gang member grew to regard the conditions of his "free" countrymen as abnormal and could not be shaken from this conviction, even though many members spent long periods of time away from the caves with their families. The gang was knit together by the pledge; and by more: by a covenant of defiance, by a commitment to justice, by a reciprocity of respect. The gang was a kind of Freemasonry lodge, except that the pledge was its only ritual and the fugitive status of its members its only initiation.

Skelly was the moral hinge on which the rest of the gang swung. All the men deferred to his judgment, even though he was open to new ideas and suggestions. He was a touchstone for rectitude. He did not rule the gang with terror or an iron fist or blackmail. He did not seem to rule it at all; his "laws of residence" — as Redmagne humorously called them — were too obviously necessary and logical for any member to question or violate. To break any one of them was to assure mortal peril. As Redmagne came to represent a fount of wisdom and knowledge to Jack Frake, Skelly came to embody those things in action.

The dining hall served other purposes. One day it would serve as a dry bowling green, on another it was the venue for a game of skittles. But it often took on the ambiance of a coffee-house in which grave matters and light were debated. The men argued religion, politics, women, and other subjects dear to their hearts. Often they would agree on one side of a controversy and send a petition to Marvel's Parliamentary representative, or a letter to the King or a London newspaper, signed "Skelly and Company, Importers."

Each member regarded the appellation "Skelly man" as a name of honor and a mark of distinction. Years before, one of Skelly's first recruits, a Scottish merchant named Giles Kincaid, was caught, tried, and sentenced to the Falmouth gallows. From the execution cart, the rope around his neck, he proclaimed to the priest, the sheriff, the hangman and to the crowd below, "I am a Skelly man! We are all Skelly men — those of us man enough to cherish their liberty!" Piqued by this remonstrance, the sheriff ordered Kincaid's body taken down, dismembered, and its parts tossed into the Channel from the cliff of nearby Pendennis Castle. Kincaid's name and his last words were carved into the limestone wall outside of Skelly's quarters. It was his only gravestone.

Jack Frake was billeted in another niche of the caves with an older boy, Richard Claxon. Claxon was the son of a Bristol brewer and Nonconformist hanged when the Devil's Brood, a coffee-house debating society of which he was recording secretary, was raided by the authorities, and its members charged with sedition and conspiracy to kidnap the royal family. The charges were specious, based on a set of notes in the elder Claxon's hand, which was but a hypothetical question discussed by the society: Could Englishmen keep their liberty without a king or a dictator? The presiding judge and the jury ignored the context of the notes. Claxon was sentenced to death and his colleagues to imprisonment or transportation. After the sentence had been carried out, Richard Claxon assaulted the judge with a club outside his home, crippling him for life, and had begun to terrorize the jurymen when the sheriff and a bevy of constables nearly trapped him. In the Skelly gang the boy's chief task was to roam the towns and villages of that part of Cornwall to collect information on the authorities and orders from shopkeepers for goods. He was a quiet, brooding boy who kept to himself, and read his Bible. Jack Frake did not attempt to breach his reticence, and sometimes thought that his colleague had lost the power of speech.

Two men dominated Jack Frake's life in the caves. That is to say, they served as his models for different things. John Smith — now Redmagne — and Augustus Skelly.

Redmagne was the son of Caleb Smith, an influential London tobacco merchant. He was the only member of the gang who had a university education. He had spent some time at the Temple Bar, clerking for a prominent Whig barrister, with the goal of becoming a barrister himself. But an infatuation with a Covent Garden actress led to an infatuation with the theater, and he left the barrister to appear in masques and plays put on by a troupe of actors that catered to the aristocracy. His father disowned him and discontinued his allowance. But the troupe was popular and rarely idle. Smith worked as actor, playwright, and agent. He wrote many of the troupe's successful one-act satires, often on commission from noblemen who wished to embarrass their friends with oblique exposés of their affairs and scandals. The names with which he introduced himself to Jack Frake were some of the names of his characters.

In the early spring of 1733, he was commissioned to write a masque that was a thinly disguised inflammatory attack on Robert Walpole, the Whig Chancellor of the Exchequer, First Lord of the Treasury and "prime" minister, and his hotly debated excise taxes on wine and tobacco. The new levies were purportedly a first step to ending the smuggling and corruption engendered by the customs practice and intended to tighten the government's ability to collect taxes on all that it chose to tax. The proposed plan sparked riots in many cities, the burning of effigies, and the flight of many incumbents standing for re-election on a pro-excise platform from their own boroughs to avoid tar-and-feathering. Redmagne himself participated in the public opposition, delivering satirical ballads of his own composition in front of the London homes of representatives known to favor the excise, a bright red cockade that bore the words "Liberty, Property and No Excise!" pinned to his hat.

The troupe was cheerfully assured by the gentleman, who was also an earlier victim of Redmagne's pen, that the masque would be well received by the guests of another nobleman. In the party's suburban London garden, the troupe presented the piece, with Redmagne in the lead role. It was a grave miscalculation. They had been duped. The audience was composed of aristocrats and Whigs loyal to the besieged chancellor. Not long after the beginning of the masque, just as Redmagne and others were having doubts about the wisdom of their performance, the nobleman's son mounted the stage, interrupted Redmagne in the middle of a soliloquy, and challenged Redmagne to a duel in his father's name. Redmagne laughed, and with the tip of his wooden sword pushed the young gentleman off of the stage, which was only a foot above the ground. "Daff the excise, sir!" he shouted down at the prostrate figure, "and never stop a player's business again! 'Tis quite *rude*, and *not* the behavior of a gentleman!" But the young man suffered a broken neck, and died later that night. Redmagne fled.

Walpole's tax scheme was defeated that April when the chancellor withdrew it from Parliamentary consideration after months of fierce public and political opposition. Redmagne had to content himself with celebrating its demise in hiding. He still kept the red cockade that bore the words "Liberty, Property and No Excise!"

After a few years of leading a fugitive life, working in various London trades and penning verse humorously critical of Parliament and the aristocracy, he chanced to amuse an otherwise dour patron in a London ale house with a saucy ballad he had composed. The patron was Augustus Skelly.

All the gang members read and owned books; Redmagne owned a library which was crammed into his otherwise roomy niche. So it was natural that, among his other duties, and owing to his university background, it fell to him to tutor anyone who wished to pay him a penny a lesson. Jack Frake wished it, and over time received the rudiments of a gentleman's education. He was introduced to literature, to geography, to science, to astronomy, to Latin and Greek. It was from Redmagne that he learned the Latin name for Cornwall — Cornubia — and that the 'tre' in Trelowe was actually Cornish for 'homestead' and not 'tree,' as Parson Parmley once suggested.

Skelly himself was a former London merchant, the only enfranchised voter in a "rotten" borough, which, even though it had little or no population — depending on the migratory work season — was entitled to representation in Parliament. His father, who once sold miscellaneous wares from a pushcart, eventually established one of London's first in-door "emporiums," called Skelly's Select Sundries and Merchandise. The hovel in which the senior Skelly lived with his family was demolished and replaced with a mansion. Aside from a small staff of servants, the Skellys were the borough's only permanent inhabitants.

The senior Skelly elected and paid the borough's representative, a dull-witted but complaisant man named Roscoe, to sit at all Parliamentary sessions and oppose all new tax and licensing bills. He even hired a hack to write the man's speeches, which were delivered by Roscoe from the Whig benches in the House of Commons. London newspapers, prohibited at that time from auditing Parliamentary sessions, nevertheless obtained copies of Roscoe's speeches. One reported that his words "answer in kind the sonorous peals for Liberty from the steeples of minds such as Sidney and Locke. Would that our august body of talkers on the Thames echo Mr.

Roscoe's mellifluous orations with action — or perhaps with Liberty-minded lassitude — for then our ears would not be offended by the noise which regularly emanates from the Commons."

The senior Skelly died, leaving three sons; Osbert Augustus was the oldest. The two younger sons were gamblers and rakes. They were jealous of their brother's business acumen, ambition and paternal favoritism, and unhappy with the annuity their father's will provided them and which their brother would not supplement. Out of sheer malice, they made a deal with Roscoe to supply him with tea, chocolate and tobacco if he would support a Tory bill before Parliament that would add another surcharge to the importation of those very commodities. Roscoe's vote was crucial, and he wavered. The brothers contrived to borrow money from the family banker, and subsequently succeeded in bribing the representative. In the meantime, Skelly's wife of two years met a customs official at a party, and proceeded to have an affair with the man. Skelly caught them together one spring afternoon; he thrashed the customs man and disowned his wife. The customs man threatened Skelly with an investigation of the source of his emporium's stocks, many of which were contraband. Armed with evidence bought from Skelly's brothers — who were now hoping to pressure their brother into making them silent partners in the business — the customs man arrived at Skelly's mansion with the demand that he take back his wife and allow the affair to continue.

Thus the duel, and the death. Skelly also fled. Roscoe made no speeches against the new tax, and voted for it with the majority. The bank seized the mansion and the emporium. The wife committed suicide. And the brothers went to France, became involved with Jacobite intrigues in the expatriate English community in Paris, and were hired as couriers by agents of the Comte de Chavigny, French ambassador to the Hanoverian court, and English Viscount Cornbury, in a plot to overthrow Walpole and the Hanover dynasty during the Excise Crisis of 1733. When the plot was vetoed by the French and knowledge of it uncovered by agents of George II, the brothers were implicated, arrested when they tried to flee back to France, and hanged.

The name of Skelly became synonymous with treason.

Like all gangs that enjoyed self-imposed isolation, the Skelly gang relied for the necessities and luxuries of life on its members' skills and trades. From Elmo Tuck, Jack Frake learned how to cook. From Charles Ambrose, a deserter and formerly a sergeant in the Coldstream Guards, he learned how to load and fire a musket and a pistol, something of swordplay, and the basics of boxing. From Chester Plume, he learned bookkeeping and accounts. From John Finch, he learned tailoring and fashions. From Tobie Robins, he learned carpentry.

Jack Frake learned that many past members of the gang had made enough money with Skelly to buy passage on a merchantman and a new beginning in the colonies. Redmagne and Skelly were tied to England; they sought a new beginning on their own island. But they did not begrudge others their desire to depart for the colonies. These men, he learned, inevitably became part of Skelly's intricate commercial and intelligence network.

From Skelly he learned the rewards and vicissitudes of trade and business. Occasionally he was asked by the man to help him inventory the contents of the contraband cave. Every length of rope, every hogshead of tobacco, every ounce of tea and coffee, every inch of lace was measured and accounted for. Skelly allowed no discrepancies in his business. He would lecture the boy on trade and commerce, and from him the boy learned the source of wealth he saw in the towns around him.

One autumn evening Jack Frake entered Skelly's chamber to report the change in the watch on the hill above, which he usually reported to Redmagne. But Redmagne had left early that morning on business in Falmouth. The boy saw the man, pipe in mouth, sitting in front of a painting, a palette of colors in one hand and a brush in another. The painting was the covered rectangle he had noticed months ago and had only seen glimpses of before. It depicted the vista of a mass of ships anchored on a wide, busy river, in the midst of a city of domes, spires and smokestacks. Skelly added some shadow to one of the innumerable masts, then turned to the boy. "Yes, Mr. Frake?"

"I've just come to report that the midnight watch has taken his place on the hill. Redmagne is in Falmouth to meet the mail-packet from New York."

"Thank you, sir," said Skelly. He gestured to the painting with his brush. "What do you think?"

"I'd like to see it someday, whatever it is."

"That's *London*," said Skelly. He rested the tip of the brush on one of the masts. "And that's the *Pegasus*. I once owned a twenty-percent share in her. All that I left behind. Two years' work, this." He put down the pallet and brush and stood back to survey his work. He gestured again to the painting with one hand. "There is *romance* in commerce, Jack. Someday you'll see London, and on the Thames below London Bridge the masts of ships as far as the eye can see, all the way to Little Rogue Lane. I go back now and then, just to be where I ought to be, and to get my colors and perspective right for this masterpiece. If I had Mr. Hogarth's talents, I wouldn't bother with pictures of plain folk and their vices. I'd do pictures of those ships, and here's my first. It's a fine, thrilling thing to fill a house with riches, from a breeze and a hank of hemp." His face brightened. "The Bible tells us that God made the world from nothing in seven days. Well, men are gods! We make things from nothing, too! It just takes us a little while longer, that's all. We haven't his *science*, you see," he added with a satirical lift of his eyebrows. Then he frowned with concern, and said, "I fear I may have just blasphemed and offended your ears, Mr. Frake. I never bothered to ask you about your faith. Are you an Anglican, or a Dissenter, like your devout straw-mate, Mr. Claxon?"

"Neither, sir."

"Well, that certainly puts you beyond the pale, doesn't it? But if it's no matter to you, then it's none to me." Skelly paused. "You'd like to go to London some day, wouldn't you?"

"Very much, sir," said Jack Frake, looking at the painting.

"Well, the next time 'Redmagne' or I have business there, I'll see what I can do." Skelly picked up his pallet and brush again. "Now, away with you, Mr. Frake! I have some final subtleties to work into the Tower there."

Jack Frake grinned to himself as he made his way back through the tunnels to his billet for the night. He felt honored that Skelly had paused in his work to talk about it. The rest of the gang knew about their leader's pastime, but did not discuss it. Many of them thought it a useless diversion, when he could be in Falmouth courting a wealthy widow. They also knew that he still carried a cameo of the wife he had disowned. It was not a subject any of his men cared to broach.

Nor did any of them comment on Redmagne's obsession, which was a book he had been writing for years, even though they knew he was a sport with many of the ladies in Marvel and elsewhere. It was something called a novel, and its title was *Hyperborea*. Jack Frake knew little else about it. During one of his first tutorials, he noticed a great mass of papers on the man's desk and had asked about it. "It's not quite a satire," remarked Redmagne then. "Mr. Swift, in his late sanity, would not understand it. It's not quite a chronicle; Mr. Defoe would have been confounded by it. It is... a novel. I haven't quite defined it myself," he sighed with a pensive glance at the manuscript. But then his mind snapped back to his immediate task. "Enough of that, Jack. Let us return to the history of the Cinque Ports from the time of Edward Longshanks to the present, and train our thoughts on the role of *wool*. An interesting item. By the Burial in Woollen Act of 1666, it was made a felony to be laid to final rest in anything but a *wool* shroud." Redmagne paused with a mischievous grin. "A delicious premise, Jack. The subject is pregnant with comedic possibilities. That being said… "

That was all he said then about *Hyperborea*. Jack Frake was certain that he had not heard the last of it.

Chapter 11: The Career

IT WAS MISERABLE WEATHER, NOT QUITE A SQUALL, NOT QUITE A CALM SEA. Intermittent rain pelted their faces and backs. The wind was stiff enough to make the water choppy and difficult to row on. The galley dipped and bobbed, buffeted by wind and waves that opposed the boat's progress and tried to drive it back to land. The incessant movement made some of the men dizzy and churned their insides. But the galley was rowed by determined men and it made progress. White caps were visible in the dark water, and so was the foam cut by the prow of the vessel.

Though there were rags wrapped around his hands to keep them warm, and to protect them from splinters from the oar, his palms and fingers were fiery claws of pain. He could feel the strength ebbing from them with every pull on the oar. The pain and weakness crept from his hands to his wrists, then to his forearms. His back ached until he felt that it would crack like a board at the next pull on the oar. It was cold and the wind was wet with sea spray, but sweat trickled down his forehead to burn his eyes. He wanted to rest, if only for a moment.

Yet he dare not succumb to the pain and drop his oar, for if he did, it would foul the one behind or before him and break the rhythm of motion on that side of the galley, which was perfectly synchronized with that of the other side. Then the craft would veer off course and a wave could capsize it.

"Let your legs do their full half of the work, son," said one of the men when they had shoved off into the surf and attacked it with the oars. "When you pull, they should push."

Jack Frake was dressed as the other men. His hat was tied to his head with a strip of muslin. He wore a scarf around his mouth and nose to keep out the spray, which he was told could be so thick that it could drown a man intent on rowing and not on his breathing. He was soaking wet, he shivered, and he was hot. His tongue flicked in and out in involuntary answer to his labor, as though it could help him row, but he bit into it once and had to concentrate on keeping it inside. His galley was being followed by a second, commanded by Redmagne. He watched the scattered lights on the dim shore grow farther away, and would turn now and then to see the ship's lanterns sitting placidly beyond the heaving swells of dark water around him. The lights did not seem to grow nearer. This was his first time on the water, and he was naturally anxious.

He thought that each wave breaking over the prow might engulf the boat, and he thought that the efforts of eight men could count for little against the chance. Worse, all eight of them sat with their backs to the swells, so that they could not see what was coming. But the nonchalance of the men, and especially of Skelly, reassured him that waves could be conquered. The man at the tiller gave commands to pull left, to pull right, to ease up on the oars, but never to stop. Another man knelt at the prow with a swaying lantern fixed to an upright staff, not to light the way, but to let the ship's crew know the galley's progress. Skelly himself sat quietly in the middle on a chest full of money. It was a wide galley, with enough space between the two sets of oarsmen to stow what was to be unshipped from the vessel that lay ahead.

Jack Frake was eleven when he was allowed to accompany Richard Claxon on his rounds to the neighboring towns to collect information and orders. They took the longest routes back and forth to avoid highwaymen, riding officers and Revenue patrols. They led blindfolded merchants to anonymous rendezvous points to meet with Skelly to discuss business. Alone, he also traversed the countryside as a messenger for gang-members who were visiting their families, to arrange the rental of wagons and horses from farmers, and to alert tubmen — itinerant laborers and villagers — to the opportunity for work, at half a guinea a night, unshipping contraband when it was expected that a load would be too much for the gang by itself. And now he had just turned twelve and was two inches taller. Skelly judged his muscles strong enough and his wits fast enough to accompany the gang, first as a lookout on the cliffs with a pistol and a brandy-soaked bale of hay to light to warn the ships and the gang of approaching Revenue sloops at sea or patrols on land, and now as an oarsman on a galley. He had never had to ignite the hay or fire the pistol.

The ship was the merchant schooner, *Ariadne*, out of New York. They had waited a week for it to arrive at the position where it now lay, a rendezvous prearranged two months ago in a letter to its captain, Cheney, in New York, which letter was a reply to the one sent by Cheney in February, notifying Skelly of his scheduled departure. When the *Ariadne* appeared offshore this evening, Skelly signaled from the cliff that it was safe to drop anchor.

The only other English merchantman Skelly did business with was the *Sparrowhawk*, a converted third-rate frigate bought by its owners from the Navy ten years ago. Its captain and part-owner, John Ramshaw, knew Skelly from the years when he had been a legitimate merchant. The company for which Ramshaw captained the *Sparrowhawk* had no knowledge of his continued relationship with the outlaw. Like the captain of the *Ariadne*, he bought and sold contraband on his own account, dealing with other reputable smugglers but chiefly with Skelly. When a cargo was too large for the galleys or Skelly's sloop, Ramshaw or Cheney would accept payment for it at clandestine meetings such as tonight's, then deposit the cargo in a warehouse in St. Peter Port, Guernsey, for Skelly to pick up later. Guernsey and Jersey in the Channel, and the Isle of Man in the Irish Sea, were paradoxically exempt from all customs and excise levies, even though they were part of the King's dominion. Skelly rendezvoused with each of the merchantmen about three times a year.

No Skelly "run" had ever been routed or foiled by the Revenue. That was because Skelly always knew where the Revenue officers were on the date and at the time of a rendezvous with a merchantman or a landing from his own vessel. And to ensure that Pannell and his men came nowhere near a rendezvous or a landing, he would decoy them with false information. His men would spread a rumor in the taverns and inns in the port towns that a merchantman or a sloop was to anchor, say, near Tallant, when in fact it would anchor near Fennock, ten miles down the coast. To lend credibility to the rumor, he would have some of his men leave evidence of a landing at Tallant: discarded clothing, a coil of rope, a lost horseshoe, a partly doused beach campfire, a forgotten spout lantern, an empty tea or coffee chest, foot and hoofprints in the sand, and so on. Pannell and his men would come to Tallant and conclude that they had only just missed the rendezvous. The ruse worked; no other "contraband company" in the region went to such lengths to outwit the Revenue men.

Skelly's sloop, *The Hasty Hart*, was anchored in Styles, a little fishing village a mile west of Gwynnford, its ownership registered under another man's name. It was fitted out with nets, a dory, and all the other paraphernalia of the fishing trade, though none of it had ever been used since being purchased from a Dutch smuggler. Skelly had planned to use the sloop tonight to meet the *Ariadne*, but the village was unexpectedly visited by a pair of Revenue officers and a posse of dragoons, and it would have been foolhardy to set sail under their noses. Part of the gang was dispersed to the small fishing villages and towns along the coast to provide "entertainment" for any other Revenue men they found, or simply to keep a close watch on them. And part of it waited on shore with carts, pack-horses and ponies.

The blue ribbons on Skelly's map marked the secret locations of galleys owned by Skelly or ones he could rent from sympathetic owners. The green ribbons were the locations of wagons, carts and horses he could use to transport contraband from the coast. Skelly was often gone for weeks at a time with his pilot and crew on *The Hasty Hart* on journeys to Guernsey, to the Isle of Man, to ports in France and Holland. Always he would return with the hold full of tea, coffee, tobacco, brandy, wines, silks, lace, salt, and other taxable commodities. Skelly had exacted a promise from the merchants he dealt with that they would not sell any contraband he supplied them with at current, duty-inclusive prices, but to sell them *sans* all duties. This dictum contradicted the practice of most smugglers, who took advantage of the duty-inclusive prices in order to increase their profit margins. Skelly, committed to the removal of all taxes, could see no justice in that, and accepted only a mark-up for his profit. The other gangs resented Skelly's policy, but could do little to fight it. Skelly sent men out to towns to spot-check merchants to ensure that his policy was being followed. It was a unique situation even among the "contraband companies."

"Larboard oars up! Starboard oars ease up to come alongside!"

Jack Frake suddenly heard the creak of the schooner behind him and footsteps on a deck. He could not turn around now, for he was intent on emulating the man in front of him and correctly maneuvering his oar. The wind diminished and the water became calmer as the galley came alee of the *Ariadne*. Then he felt the prow bump into the ship's side. He and the men on his side worked their oars to push the galley against the hull of the schooner.

Skelly rose from the chest, looked up and doffed his hat. "Welcome home, Mr. Cheney!"

"Hallo, Mr. Skelly!" answered a voice from the deck. "Come aboard!"

Jack Frake turned in time to see a rope ladder drop from the main deck.

"Secure your oars!" shouted the tiller man. All oars turned in their pins to rest on the seats. The tiller man and the prow man threw ropes up to men waiting at two open ports on the *Ariadne*. Some of the oarsmen took out flasks of rum and drank to slake their thirst; others began packing pipes. Jack Frake, the ordeal over, loosened the scarf on his face, pivoted on his seat and lay down. He looked up and saw the furled sails on the masts that towered above him, and the pennants above them curling steadily in the wind.

A dark figure blocked his view. "I want a clerk, Mr. Frake," said Skelly. "You will accompany me to take notes of the cargo we leave with." He proffered a teakwood box that held paper and writing instruments.

His bones and muscles said no, but Jack planted his feet on the boards, stood up, and took the box. "Yes, sir." He followed the man up the rope ladder.

Once they had climbed the ladder to the deck, Skelly shook hands with Captain Cheney. "Fair crossing, I trust," said Skelly.

"Fair and quiet enough," said Cheney. "Nary a French sail on the horizon the entire voyage."

"The French have been too busy on the Continent," said Skelly. He briefly apprised Cheney of the events since November, when they had last rendezvoused. Charles Edward Stuart had landed in Scotland in July of last year and had won a succession of battles there. "They say that Cumberland the Uncouth is still searching for Wee Charlie, who we think was a fairer match for him than was Saxe." Skelly chuckled. "A few of my men lost bets on my namesake when the King called his son home after Fontenoy last year."

The captain laughed. "Fancy that! Wee Charlie gone to ground! He's routed, though?"

"Completely. He got as far as Derby before Cumberland ran him through at Culloden last month." Skelly scoffed. "If you ask my opinion, this landing of his — again courtesy of the French — was just a French ruse to get our troops out of this Succession war. They never expected Charlie to win, only to make enough fuss to panic the King. And panicked he was, as was the whole country."

"Sly French," said Cheney, "and I'll credit you the notion. Well, I suppose you've heard that Louisbourg, in Nova Scotia, has fallen to the Navy and an army of northern colonials?"

Skelly grinned. "Ramshaw brought me that old bit of news last June." The two men exchanged a few more comments. Then Cheney asked, "Where's your sloop?"

"Still in Styles. Some Revenue men rode in about an hour before we did. We'd have been hard put to explain a need to fish at this time of night, in this weather. So, we'll do it the hard way. We can safely dally here for a while. The coast is nasty enough tonight and no Revenue men will want to venture out."

"Well, come down to my cabin, have some coffee to warm your innards, and we'll trade more news! I've got tobacco for you — excellent Oronoco — and American nails, if you want them." He glanced down at Jack Frake. "New man, or a son you've sired and raised while I've been away these six months?"

"New man," chuckled Skelly, "Jack Frake. This is his first outing. Recruited him in Gwynnford after he routed a press-gang."

"Impressive work!" said Cheney. He held out his hand. "Pleased to make your acquaintance, Mr. Frake." Jack Frake shook the captain's hand. "Could have used you in New York. Gangs there snagged three of my crew a day before we weighed anchor." Cheney turned to speak to Skelly again. "We picked up some Jamaica sugar, too, if you've a mind to look at it."

"Yes, I might." Skelly put a hand on Cheney's shoulder. "A word of warning, my friend," he said. "There's a new smuggling act. It's a felony now to 'assemble' for purposes of running goods — as we do now — and of course you know your fine vessel here can be seized for hovering."

Cheney grinned with irony. "I know. But they'd have a deuced time breaking this beauty into three parts!"

"They're even thinking of fining districts whose juries don't convict known smugglers," said Skelly with a bitter sigh. "And then the 'fair-traders' among the merchants and shopkeepers have apparently bent the ears of the Customs Board. There's talk of reducing the tea duty to a shilling per pound. That will return that end of the business to the 'fair-traders' and knock the wind out of not a few gangs."

Cheney whistled in amazement. "Your colleagues on Romney Marsh will be killing each other just to make tuppence on a pound," he remarked.

Skelly nodded. "So, my advice to you is not to conclude any trades in that quarter… "

Jack Frake was only half conscious of the conversation. He was too fascinated with the masts and the complex rigging and the size of the ship. There were cannon on the deck, and nearby, a hoist over the open hold. The moon came out then, and through the ropes of the larboard shrouds he saw a long, uneven silvery band that stretched from east to west. It was the first time he had seen England from the sea.

He wandered away from Skelly and Cheney and stood alone for a time next to one of the cannon, looking at the coastline as the moon and rolling clouds played with his sight of it. With the finger of his eye he traced the length of the band, and remembered a map he had seen a long time ago. The pain and exhaustion in his body seemed to evaporate from him then, and his body and mind felt weightless. An emotion galvanized his consciousness, and on impulse, in answer to something he had once seen from a distance and now had reached, he tore off his hat to hold it high in the air in salute to the glowing triumvirate of himself, the coastline and the memory, and shouted "Huzza!"

Cheney and Skelly glanced over at the boy standing by the shrouds, peering into the windy darkness. "Is he addled," asked the captain cautiously, "or have you been working him too hard?"

Skelly smiled. "No," he answered in a quiet, speculative tone which was friendly but did not invite further questions. "What you see is a boy on the eve of becoming a man."

That night each galley made two trips between the *Ariadne* and the men waiting on shore. The carts and pack-horses carried four hogsheads of tobacco, two casks of salt, a quantity of paper and nails, and miscellaneous other goods Skelly had selected from Cheney's hold. Eight hours later the contraband was stored in the caves and some of the men left to return the carts and horses that were rented from local farmers. Jack Frake had a tankard of lamb's wool — a concoction of ale, nutmeg, and pulped roasted apples — with his meal, and fell asleep at the long table in the dining hall. His share of the value of that night's run was four guineas, six shillings and eight pence. With some of his earnings, he was able to purchase himself new breeches, shoes, a new coat, a new hat, and extra candles with which to read at night. Redmagne had loaned him a copy of Defoe's *Robinson Crusoe*.

Chapter 12: The Commissioner Extraordinary

"YOUR INFORMATION WAS TARDY, MR. LEITH."

"It were late comin' to my ears, Mr. Pannell."

It was late May. Henoch Pannell sat in a corner table in the Sea Siren with Isham Leith, mugs of ale sitting in front of them, bought by Pannell, but barely touched. No one could hear their conversation, for the inn was abuzz with the latest news from the Continent. It was rumored that the Young Pretender was still in hiding, plotting yet another uprising, and that Marshall Saxe would defeat the Austrians before the end of the year. Seamen from a merchant schooner, the *Ariadne*, waiting for their vessel to unload some cargo, fueled the noise with their own news from the colonies. French and Indians were raiding the frontier settlements in New York and the Ohio Valley in an attempt to force out the English settlers.

Pannell studied Leith, and the man squirmed under the scrutiny. Pannell did not like Leith. But then he did not like any of the informers who came to him. Most of them were motivated by greed, not conscience. This man, however, was consumed by fear, or by a greediness for his own life, which was the same thing to Pannell. Leith, he already knew, owned an inn at Trelowe, and had recently acquired a license to open another on the outskirts of the town to cater to travelers using the road between Trelowe and Falmouth. He and his brother were busy converting the cottage formerly owned by Cephas Frake into a serviceable public place, adding living space that would share the single fireplace. But the inn at Trelowe did not look so prosperous to Pannell that he believed the man could really afford the changes he was making. This observation piqued the Commissioner's interest in Leith.

Henoch Pannell made Leith's acquaintance six months ago when he stopped in Trelowe for a bite to eat. He did this deliberately, because he wanted to assess the man. The information he was able to gather from the inhabitants of this region about Skelly's — or any other smuggler's — doings and movements was worse than useless; it was deceitful. Of course, he knew that most of the plain people here defended the smugglers, for they were either their customers, or their livelihood, and so would lie about their knowledge, or deny any. Even though Leith was most likely one of the liars, the man still might be unscrupulous enough to give information. There was, after all, the matter of Parson Parmley. He could be made to give information, and he did. It had been an easy thing to accomplish, once the notion came to him.

Pannell had overheard some guarded talk about Leith around Gwynnford, which heretofore Pannell had ignored because the matter did not concern him. A shadow hung over the man and Leith was not particularly liked in the town. It was said that he might have had something to do with the murder of the rector in St. Gwynn-by-Godolphin over a year ago. But other than a note written by the son of the woman to whom he was now married, there was no evidence that he had anything to do with the crime. The only witnesses who could possibly implicate Leith were gone; the boy, Jack Frake, had been kidnapped by Skelly men in the course of releasing Rory O'Such from the constable's jail — an incident which still rankled — while Captain Venable and his dragoons had been attached to a regiment of cavalry in the Duke's army in France. Pannell had heard recent talk in the Sea Siren that the officer, once a regular customer of Hiram Trott's, was killed at the battle of Fontenoy.

He had Leith's place watched, and when Leith, his new wife, and brother were all away, went into it to search it for any kind of evidence that would convict Leith of smuggling or of consorting with smugglers, and especially anything that could possibly link him to the Parmley murder. And he had found something — besides a half dozen ankers of Dutch gin concealed in a false wall in the upper floor of the man's inn at Trelowe. He left the place as he and his men had found it.

Pannell was in no hurry, though Leith did not know this. Since his arrival in the county two years ago, he had established an exemplary record of arrests and convictions of smugglers in Cornwall and Devon, a feat surpassing his superiors' expectations. He had lost only one man killed in skirmishes with gangs; had lost no Revenue vessels; and had lost no men to desertion. In a time when allegiance and betrayal were almost synonymous, his men were unusually loyal to him. He saw to it that his men were paid, and paid a little better than other men in the Revenue Service, and that they promptly received their share of the appraised value of seized contraband, and of the posted rewards for wanted criminals they apprehended.

Henoch Pannell had a special interest in Augustus Skelly. Warren Pumphrett, deputy assistant commissioner of customs for Essex, was the official slain by Skelly twelve years ago, and had been a cousin of his on his mother's side. The Pumphretts were a well-heeled family at the time, with a great house in London on the Thames — not far from the Duke of Richmond's — and estates in Essex and Surrey. The family was even richer now. It owned a tea and spice importing concern, and had connections with men in Parliament, the Court, the East India Company and was connected, through a Pumphrett daughter's marriage to a high French official, to the French government monopoly that bought and imported English tobacco.

The Pannells were poor, kept-at-arm's-length relations, and were still so now. Pannell's own father had struggled for years as a wool-factor, cursing the export ban on wool in one breath, calling for more stringent controls in the next. But the violent death of the Pumphretts' only son had deeply affected the family. Gervase Pumphrett, the father, still offered a one hundred guinea reward for the simple arrest of Skelly, regardless of the charge or subsequent conviction. Henoch Pannell had heard from his mother that the father had bought a brace of pistols with which to shoot Skelly once he was in custody.

Henoch Pannell had never had any affection for Warren Pumphrett, nor for any of the family. During their infrequent, cool and duty-governed family reunions — his mother and aunt still had some regard for each other — Warren played cruel and often painful tricks on him. He had once gotten Henoch severely beaten with a coach-whip by both his infuriated uncle and his embarrassed father when Warren accused him of taking unseemly liberties with his sister, who had conspired with her brother to humiliate their awkward, shy, and ugly cousin. His back and buttocks still bore scars from the whipping. He had hated Warren. His motive for vengeance was wholly mercenary.

Henoch Pannell joined the Revenue Service for Essex shortly after reaching his majority, thanks to the Pumphretts' influence on the Customs Board. His career was unexceptional, unrewarding, but stable. He was given command of a Revenue sloop crewed by men indifferent to their jobs. He collected a salary and submitted costs, pursued only farmer smugglers whom it was easy to bully and apprehend, and would have been content to remain in that position, except that he knew that he could just as easily be reassigned or dismissed as a result of someone else's political influence as was his predecessor. When the appointment of Extraordinary Commissioner for Cornwall became available two years since, Pannell had campaigned for it quietly but determinedly. He got it, because no one else wanted it. It had been created almost exclusively to apprehend Skelly. His friends and enemies on the Board all thought Pannell was a fool to want the post, and not without justification; he lacked wit, imagination and initiative. And, he was as avaricious as he was lazy. These were, they admitted, inadvertent qualifications for employment in the Revenue Service; it *did* attract men of a dronish mien. They could not imagine any of their officers harrying a man like Skelly, and least of all Pannell.

But Skelly's "free-trading" activities in Cornwall were a source of hushed scandal on the Board, more so than was the county's reputation for ordinary smuggling. Skelly meant something more to the inhabitants than acting as a cornucopia of undutied goods. He was an enigma, a legend, an inspiration — a rebel, a kind of Robin Hood who robbed the Customs and excise and split the profits between himself and the poor. Nervous Board members had nightmares of him leading a march of "free-traders" on London, followed by half the countryside, setting fire to the Parliament buildings and besieging St. James's Palace. So any man who wished to tackle the problem of outwitting and jailing Skelly — no matter how dull-witted or unlikely a nemesis he might be — was given the Board's blessing. It was more a fancy than a hope which moved them to present Pannell with an extraordinary commission, exquisitely printed and weighted with the King's seal and the signature of the First Lord of the Treasury, to "take whatever lawful measures necessary to check and bring about the cessation of smuggling and free-trading in Cornwall and adjacent counties."

Henoch Pannell was a career man, sincerely dedicated to preserving the solvency of His Majesty's and Parliament's coffers. From these could come a comfortable pension and many profitable perquisites, few requiring effort or even interest. But a sensational action was needed to guarantee his future retirement. The capture and certain execution of Osbert Augustus Skelly would secure the gratitude not only of the Pumphretts, but also of the Duke of Cornwall — a son of the King — as well as that of the Board and of other powerful persons. He would be able to choose any position in the Service; Deputy Collector for London had always whetted his appetite, as had Surveyor-General of the Customs for any county (save Kent and Sussex, for these were worse centers of smuggling than Cornwall).

It had been easy to exact cooperation from Leith. There was the pair of silver candlesticks he had found elsewhere in Leith's room in Trelowe and taken away with him. Inscribed on the undersides of their bases were Parmley's brother's initials. Pannell had dropped in one evening when the man's inn was deserted, asked for a gill of brandy, and while Leith was busy with a glass and bottle, removed the items from an oilskin bag, and set them upright on his table. Leith gasped when he saw them, dropped both the bottle and glass, and collapsed onto the other bench, his head in his hands. Pannell sat down opposite him at the table, and took a pistol from his coat. "We won't discuss the gin which was found in ankers of distinctly Dutch manufacture, Mr. Leith," he said. "I know that they are Dutch, for I impounded hundreds like them in Essex. Now," he said then, tapping a candlestick with the barrel of the pistol, "one would have thought that after *these* items were taken first from Parson Parmley, then from the original and deceased thieves and murderers — Mr. Oyston and Mr. Lapworth — they would have traveled far and wide in the market for such merchandise. They might have ended by gracing the mantel of a lord in London, or the boudoir of a chevalier's mistress in Fontainebleau. Instead, here they are, *still*, and no more than a few miles from their original domicile, hidden under the floor of an untidy room in a common cloth sack, one coated with rat droppings. How did they come to be there, Mr. Leith?" He sat back on the bench, pistol still at the ready.

Leith raised his head. "I bought them in Falmouth for a song," he said with defiance.

"From whom?"

Leith pounded a fist on the table. "You had no right to search my place!" he cried.

"Perhaps not," said Pannell, shrugging and crossing his legs. "I grieve over my indiscretion. However, while the magistrate is sure to tweak my nose for my *unwarranted* action, he is sure to snap your neck." He paused to grin in surprise at his own jest, and looked at Leith to see if it had registered with him. Leith's expression indicated that he was not at the moment receptive to humor.

Pannell grunted and went on. "Moreover, Mr. Leith, I have found a witness who places you, Oyston and Lapworth at the rector's home that dreadful day. Oh, what a plum case the prosecutor will have! You alone, or you and your late partners, murdered the poor parson, and then you murdered them!" It was not true that he had found a witness, but his possession of the candlesticks lent, as he knew it would, credibility to his bluff.

"It's all a lie!" protested Leith, pounding the table again, furious with himself for having kept the candlesticks from out of all the loot he had disposed of — he had planned to sell them later if he needed to — and unnerved by Pannell, who had formerly impressed him as a slow-thinking man whom he could fool. He began to rise, but stopped when the Revenue man raised the pistol. "What witness?" demanded Leith.

"Silly question, Mr. Leith. No, that person's identity will remain a secret, until your trial." Pannell had sighed. "Or, perhaps... forever."

It took some time for Leith to absorb the meaning of the man's last words. Then his features relaxed, and he asked, "Forever?"

"Forever — if you get me good and timely information about Skelly."

Leith sat up and frowned. "Why *me*?"

"Because in the fraternity of dishonest and doubtful men in this community, I judge you to be the most worthy candidate for cooperation." He reached over with one hand and toyed with one of the candlesticks, turning it around on its base.

"I can't do it!" said Leith. "I can't spy on... *those people* or anyone else who knows 'em!"

Pannell shrugged. "Would you care to name a substitute?" He smiled. "It hardly matters to me, though it needn't be *you* that turns informer, Mr. Leith."

Leith said nothing. He sat straight, both his hands flat on the table. What Pannell was proposing was just as dangerous and risky as turning informer himself. Pannell knew that.

Pannell grimaced. "Why you, indeed! That should be obvious by now." He angrily toppled the candlestick so that it almost hit Leith's hand. "Listen to this fantastic arithmetic, Mr. Leith!" With his pistol, he knocked over the other candlestick, which rolled off the table to the floor. "There should be a truppence difference between the duty on tea at four shillings nine pence a pound, and what Mr. Rudge, the grocer in Gwynnford, charges for the same thing! But Mr. Rudge is charging, not five or six shillings, as is the custom elsewhere in the kingdom, but only *three* shillings a pound! That should represent a loss to him of at least one shilling nine pence. Mr. Rudge sells prodigious amounts of tea. His account books contradict his prosperity. They say that he paid the price reflected in the original purchaser's paid duty, not including conveyance costs from Bristol. But that cannot be, for he sells his tea — and, I might add, his coffee, his peppers, his raisins, his tobacco, his candles, his brandy, his sugar — at an unconscionable loss! He is a fat, jolly gentleman with a merry wife and three charming children, and is a respected man in that town — when, by all that is right in God's eyes, he should be in the workhouse, or at least accepting alms from the parish!"

Pannell sat back and glowered at Leith. "A similar paradox surrounds the situation of most of the merchants in this immediate vicinity. They are buying contraband, Mr. Leith. They are regularly provisioned. I know by whom. I want to know how. Who speaks for them? Who acts as their carter? Who is their middleman?" He suddenly leaned forward, raised the pistol and jammed the barrel hard against Leith's forehead. He cocked the hammer. Leith's eyes widened in paralysis as the Revenue man's bulged in anger. "Miracles occur here daily, Mr. Leith, but no one boasts of performing a single one!"

Leith could only gulp.

Pannell left the inn that evening, taking the candlesticks with him, and leaving instructions on how to contact him. They had had many meetings since then. At each one Leith told him about a planned landing of contraband. And in every instance, Pannell and his men, armed to the teeth, and once even accompanied by a party of dragoons, were too late. This had gone on for months.

Leith could not breach the code of silence about the "free-traders" in Gwynnford or any other nearby town. He had been able to report only hearsay and rumor. He had always been on the far receiving end of whatever contraband he managed to buy for his inn, and so he was not sure whether he was kept out of the circle of information by rules of the Skelly gang, or for the same reasons Pannell had approached him with his blackmail. He did not like it that Pannell had summoned him this time for a meeting here, at the Sea Siren. Customers would see them together, and would think the worst.

"You must not *wait* for information, Mr. Leith," said Pannell. "You must ferret it out. You must exhibit some discreet curiosity."

"It ain't possible to do that!" said Leith. "You'd find me stuffed down a well if I went about direct-like askin' how to talk to Skelly!" He tried to drink his ale, but could not. "Look, Mr. Pannell, sir, all I can tell you is what I hear. And all I hear is where smugglers' batmen and tubmen are supposed to gather for a landin', and I have to practically use an earhorn for that information! People stop talkin' when I'm clearin' a table or servin' 'em!"

"There was no one at Tallant last night, Mr. Leith," said Pannell. "We rode up and down the shore for miles in each direction, but all we found is what we always find, the usual leavings."

"It were Tallant, that's all I heard," pouted Leith.

"Well, it *is* tiresome, isn't it?" Pannell squinted at the man. "Next time we meet, please omit news of rendezvous. I can collect these tidbits from other places. Employ your imagination, Mr. Leith, before I am tempted to employ mine." He rose, said "Good day to you, sir," and left the Sea Siren.

Isham Leith sat quietly for a long time, thinking, and trying to remember something he had overheard one of the patrons of his own inn say and which might be important to Pannell. Or something he had seen.

A large form appeared at the edge of his vision. "Is something wrong with the ale, Mr. Leith?"

Leith glanced up. It was Hiram Trott, who studied him with a supercilious look. "What?"

"Something wrong with the ale? You and Mr. Pannell didn't hardly touch it."

"Nothin's wrong with it!" Leith lifted his tankard and took a long draught from it.

Trott glanced at the front door. "You and that Revenue chap friends?"

"No!" said Leith. His mind fumbled for an explanation. "He's makin' trouble for me over my new place that ain't even finished yet, that's all! Says he might take my license away, because he stopped at my other place last week and had some wrong beef for breakfast. Says it made him ill for two days."

"Tsk, tsk," replied Trott. "Unfortunate. That's *never* happened here." He paused. "And then he goes and treats you to an ale for all the misery you gave him! Forgiving man, I'd say."

"Awh, he's just a cockalorum, that's why! Likes to see a bigger man squirm! If he weren't a King's man, I'd show 'im his place!"

"Hmmm," replied Trott, his hands busy with his apron, "I'm sure you would. He wasn't a miser when he boarded here a while back. Always generous with his money. But then it weren't his money he was spending, was it? Moved his custom to the Saucy Maiden down the street. Sorry to see him go. Could keep a keen eye on him then." Trott smiled vaguely at Leith. "Well, enjoy your ale, Mr. Leith. Is there anything else I can get for you? A serving of beef, perhaps? Local product, mind you, none of that stringy Smithfield hoof you had the misfortune of serving Mr. Pannell."

Leith glared at the innkeeper. "I ain't got the appetite, Trott. Oomph off."

"Very well," sighed Trott. He picked up Pannell's untouched tankard and left.

Leith blinked, and turned to glance once at Trott's retreating back. An odd feeling told him that he was close to remembering something he could give to Pannell. Something he had seen.

Chapter 13: The Proclamation

EARLY ONE CHILLY, MID-OCTOBER EVENING REDMAGNE RETURNED FROM A visit to Marvel and went directly to Skelly's chamber. Skelly himself had the day before returned from a journey to Guernsey with a new stock of contraband, was busy scheduling deliveries to merchants, grocers and other tradesmen. Redmagne lay two newspapers on his friend's desk, side by side, and pointed to the items he had circled in pencil. The man put his pipe aside, adjusted his spectacles and read them. An exquisite French porcelain clock ticked away the minutes. Skelly smiled after reading one of the items, and frowned when he finished the second. Then he sat back and pushed the papers away. "Call a meeting," he said. "The men should know."

"Is everyone here?" asked Redmagne.

"Most everyone," said Skelly. "Mr. Claxon is out gathering some final information."

The meeting was held in the dining hall. Redmagne chaired it. Skelly sat near Redmagne at the head of the table and let him speak. It was some hours after the evening meal, but Skelly instructed Elmo Tuck and Jack Frake to serve the men tankards of their favorite brews from the battery of casks and ankers that lined one wall. The smoky hall was alive with half a dozen conversations. Jack Frake stood near the spit and the kettles with Elmo Tuck and waited.

Redmagne rapped the table-top with the butt of his pistol. The men ceased their talk and turned to him. He held up a newspaper, a copy of the *London Evening Auditor*. "Gentlemen," he said, "I returned not two hours ago after purchasing this publication — "

"Did you purchase it *before* or *after* calling on Dolly Fletcher?" asked one of the men. The whole hall laughed. Skelly grinned. Dolly Fletcher was the daughter of the mayor of Marvel, a staunch Whig and a spokesman for the "fair-traders" of the town. The affair between his daughter and the outlaw was known to almost everyone in the market town but the father, who thought that the charming man who sometimes sat down to tea with him was Brice Chandler, the son of a prosperous Bristol distiller.

"I shall never tell," remarked Redmagne pleasantly. "The honor of his lordship the mayor may be irreparably impugned." He laughed again with the men, then continued. "I hold here news of significant literary import," he said. "Our letter was *printed*."

The men exclaimed in surprise and delight. Weeks ago, Redmagne and the men had vigorously debated the issue of whether "God Save the King" or "Rule, Britannia" should be the country's anthem. Redmagne managed to persuade the gang, first by argument, then, accompanying himself with a lute — for Redmagne could and often did sing and entertain the gang in the evenings — by performing each of the anthems, that the one was more appropriate than the other. He then composed a letter, made several copies of it, and posted it to a number of London newspapers.

The men clamored for Redmagne to read it. He folded the paper and read: "Sir: On the occasion of the late invasion of this country by the Young Pretender, and before the folly of attempting to revive a long-expired throne, buttressed by nothing but vanity and vaporous French support, was forcefully taught the Pretender at Culloden, the correspondent was disconcerted to hear 'God Save the King' sung with fervor, first by the cast and audience at Covent Garden last year (where he was privileged to be entertained by another of Mr. Handel's splendid oratorios), then elsewhere throughout the nation. Far be it from the correspondent to discourage patriotism, but he was under the impression that Mr. James Thomson's brisk, stirring 'Rule, Britannia' had the distinction of being our anthem, and not the nutmeggishly sweet musical apotheosis of a sovereign. We may be so bold as to further point out that the words of one anthem oppose those of the other. 'Confound their politics, frustrate their knavish tricks,' is quite a distinct sentiment from 'Thee haughty tyrants ne'er shall tame,' and 'Britons will never be slaves.' It is more than idle tea-table conjecture which compels this correspondent to ask: By what politics, or by what tricks, shall Britons *not* be slaves, and at the same time *not* disturb the precious repose of the sovereign? We must own that Parliament does well enough a job of 'scattering' the liberties of Britons without the King's help! We would do well, in fact, to adopt instead an anthem for Parliament, with which that nest of 'haughty tyrants' could then smugly convene and adjourn its proceedings, and which would of necessity include the words, 'Confound their liberties, belittle their miseries'."

The men laughed and cheered when they heard the words of Skelly's pledge parodied in the letter.

Redmagne grinned, and continued. "While we confess that the lyrics of 'Rule, Britannia' ever more seem to be about a nation we hardly recognize, they and their melody are still to be preferred over the servile, fawning well-wishing to a sovereign who is as insensible to our state of liberty as we Britons are to the polish of his shoe buckles or the luster of his chamber pot. If Britons are to be free, they should reconsider the import of each anthem, and choose either a psalm of supplication, or a celebration of pride. Your most devoted servant, *Skellicus*."

Again the men cheered, and Redmagne handed the newspaper to one of the gang members to pass around. Skelly smiled and asked Tuck to serve the men another round of drinks. His visage was pleasant, but Jack Frake noted a glimmer of sadness in it.

"'Skellicus'! Everybody knows who that's supposed to be! Can you imagine the volume of hot correspondence ignited by that letter?" asked Chester Plume, the bookkeeper. "Why, the publisher might even be called to apologize in the Commons!"

"For printing someone else's letter?" asked William Ayre, the former cattle drover. He was only a few years older than Richard Claxon, and was the gang-member still confused by the number and identity of Fredericks involved in the War of the Austrian Succession.

"They'll think the publisher wrote it," explained Plume. "They'll do that, you know, just to stir up talk, and get up circulation and sales, and pretend others wrote it."

Henry Naughton, Skelly's pilot, rose and proposed a toast to Redmagne. "You never know when or where the Skelly gang will strike next!" he laughed. "At sea, on land, or on the front page!"

When the toast was completed, Redmagne held up a copy of another newspaper, the *Marvel Weekly Mercury*. His expression became serious.

The men knew that he had some sobering news to convey. He tapped the upheld paper with a finger. "On page one here you will see this large advertisement, in between the modest advertisement for Hutt's Bookstore in Falmouth — the first in any of the West Counties, I should point out — and the barely readable one for the return of six cows missing from Mr. Moore's pasture. It is the desire of His Majesty that the gentleman to my right" — he folded the newspaper and read from it "… surrender his person within forty days of the publication of this proclamation in the official *Gazette*, or within forty days of the publication of this proclamation in a public place in the vicinity of the subject's depredations, for the purpose of attainting said offender of numerous capital and civil felonies. He shall forfeit his life for the same offenses should he surrender, or is apprehended, after the expiration of the term of this proclamation. Further, any person who either harbors or aids said offender after the expiration of said term, and is himself not found guilty of other felonies, capital or civil, shall be transported for seven years… " He lowered the newspaper, and said, "That concludes the *billet-doux* from our sovereign." Then he handed it to the man nearest him. "Please read it and pass it along, Mr. Greene, so that each of you may see with your own eyes."

"You mean he's asking Mr. Skelly to turn hisself in just to be turned off?" asked William Ayre.

"Yes, Mr. Ayre, that is precisely the import of the advertisement — which, I might add, was pressed upon Mr. Carveth, the publisher of the *Mercury*, over his strenuous objections, and did not, of course, require the usual one shilling stamp tax for advertisements."

"But we already knew that," remarked another gang-member. "There's only three of us here who wouldn't be hanged: Jack, Elmo and Mr. Claxon."

"Oh, they'd be hanged," said another. "Or they'd get such a sentence that they'd wish they was hanged."

"It is a somewhat redundant but nonetheless sinister proclamation," explained Redmagne. "However, the Gazetting Act was passed by Parliament, and, while it circumscribes what few legal protections we may have in the law courts, it carries the full force of law. Trust Mr. Pannell and his magistrates to speedily employ it. If apprehended, we will be long dead before some brave lawyer champions the charge that this perfidious act is unconstitutional." Redmagne paused. "A copy of this proclamation has been posted by the bailiff on the doors of St. Brea's in Gwynnford. Skelly asked that you be advised of the development." He paused. "We are damned men now, every one of us."

His statement was answered with silence. The men knew it.

Skelly rose and addressed his men. "But — we will not grow desperate, will we? We will not stoop to the level of the Hawkhurst gang, and become brutes who taunt and torture the Revenue's informers and lackeys. We will be moved by love of liberty, not by raw, insensible malice."

The men said nothing.

"Well, gentlemen: will we? Or will we shame our likely captors with our dignity and the rightness of our cause?"

"Not without a fight," growled Charles Ambrose, the former sergeant. Other men at the table echoed his protest.

"No," agreed Skelly, "surely not without a fight! But neither with malice." He laughed. "*We* are not common criminals," he exclaimed. "It is the King and the Customs Board and Henoch Pannell who are the *desperate* men! They cannot bribe Britons to betray us, they cannot think hard enough to outwit us, and when the wind blows just a little foul and when the waves threaten to wet their woolens, they *will not* risk a bead of sweat to pursue us! So they prostitute the courts and the law to ensure our deaths. We shall not dignify these knaves with powerful hate, but spurn them with our contempt!"

This time it was Redmagne's turn to propose a toast. He asked the men to rise and take up their tankards. "We, the condemned, salute Skelly, ourselves and our liberties!"

"Aye," answered Charles Ambrose. "We *should* salute ourselves. No one else will."

* * *

Two weeks later, in early November, Jack Frake came down from his watch on the hill above the caves to report the change. The soft evening rain had turned to snow and he beat his hat against his leg to shake off the drops. He went straight to Redmagne's chamber to report the change in watch.

Redmagne, seated at his own desk, smiled strangely at him. He did not reply to the boy's report, but said, instead, "It is finished."

"What is?" asked Jack Frake.

Redmagne picked up a pile of paper from his desk and dropped it again. "*Hyperborea.*"

It was a novel based on the Greek myth of a race that worshipped Apollo and lived in a land of sunshine and plenty beyond the north wind, and related the adventures of Drury Trantham, the captain of a shipwrecked merchantman. It was Redmagne's life's work, begun after he joined the Skelly gang. It made him ashamed that he had ever written satires. In it he was trying something new in the novels of the period, a plot derived from the actions of the protagonists. He had often, in between smuggling runs, secluded himself in his chamber in the caves for days at a time to work on it, coming out only for meals.

Jack Frake saw that Redmagne was oddly affected by elation, melancholy and despair. "May I read it?" he eagerly asked the man.

"But, of course, Jack," chuckled Redmagne. "It's a wonderful story," he said to the boy, "about a land much like our own, but where there are no kings, no customs men, and no caves — no need of them, you see. I will have this published someday, somehow, but under another name, of course. Under my own the Crown would arrest the publisher, and I, like Daniel Defoe, would be honor-bound to exonerate him by surrendering myself to the authorities. But my fate would not be as sweet as Defoe's. No, Jack, not at all. No pillory for me, with the populace pelting me with flowers, as it did Defoe, instead of dead cats and stones and ordure. No, I would be hanged, and before that, forced to watch the hangman burn my book. So, I must use another name, and pay a printer to compose and bind it, and remain in these caves of anonymity."

"Why would they burn it?"

"Because, Jack, in it is a message, and the message is this: We have no need of kings, no need of a king's churchmen. And that, my boy, is a treasonable message." Redmagne rose and paced excitedly. "No kings! Can you imagine it? No kings, and so no need for all the varieties of Danegeld! It's an allegory, you see, because Hyperborea was once in thrall to another kingdom, the kingdom of Hypocrisia. But Hyperborea threw off its bondage, and became a happy land, a great land, a prosperous land. Suppose — Oh! Wild imagination! — suppose our colonies in America did such a thing? Can you imagine them nullifying their numbing bondage? Revoking their oath of loyalty to the King? Not petitioning *him* for protection from Parliament? What an outlandish miracle that would be! Perhaps too far-fetched! The parable of the loaves and fishes is much more credible a tale!" Redmagne grinned devilishly. "There are no gods in the story, Jack, except for Apollo, but he makes no actual appearance in the story, except as a statue in a temple. The book will be fortunate to be called pagan, and not atheistic. The name of God appears occasionally in some of the spicier dialogue, sometimes in jest, other times in mild profanity, but that will be up to the critics to sort out." He sat down again and chuckled in amusement.

Jack Frake asked, "Is it anything like *Gulliver's Travels*?" He had read much of Jonathan Swift's works, liking some parts of the stories, disliking others.

"A little, but much better," said Redmagne. "Swift was a bit of a crank. He did not much care for humankind. That's why he created the Yahoos and the Lilliputians and the Houyhnhnms. You remember the Houyhnhnms from the *Travels*, don't you? The race guided by nothing but reason, who knew no conflict, no war, no… stupidity. Well, *my* Hyperboreans are something like the Houyhnhnms, only much pleasanter to know, and Drury Trantham elects to stay with them — after some initial misunderstandings, of course — because he finds nothing impossible and everything wonderful about them. They live on an island in the frigid climes, but their greatness warms the earth and makes it habitable."

Jack Frake did not know the meaning of these remarks, and he smiled weakly. Redmagne did not seem happy about having finished his novel.

Redmagne observed Jack's reticence, and understood. "I am as you see me, because I am awash in melancholy, and also in this fine French wine." He picked up a glass, took a sip, then rested an affectionate hand on the top page of the manuscript. "This is the legend of Hyperborea as related by Methuselah Redmagne! Do you see here? I have put my Frake-appointed name on it! The legend with contemporaneous modifications to it. A land of abundance without labor? Well, the Greeks had their gods provide all the comforts, but we must be more realistic than that! No loaves and fishes for the Hyperboreans! My Hyperboreans labor, they create, they invent, they improvise, they think — all the things we do, Jack, and reap the full benefits and so live in a man-made paradise! Oh, Jack! I began life as a man with a knack for ditties and limericks, then became skilled at mocking useless lives, and may end it yet on a higher estate with just this one fantastic league of ink!" Redmagne's mouth became grim. "I am resolved, Jack, that while I must live in these caves, this book shall not! It shall see the light of day, forever. I have more than enough guineas for a sumptuous edition." He paused. "You have a careful handwriting, Jack. Will you help me copy it?"

"Yes," answered the boy.

"Thank you." Redmagne leaned forward in his chair. "We have no goods to run for a week. When would you like to begin?"

"Tonight, if you wish."

"Tonight? No, Jack. Tonight, I wish to be alone with my mistress." Redmagne patted the top page again. "Tomorrow would be a better time."

Jack Frake went over and looked at the page. It gave him a kind of satisfaction to see the manuscript, even though he had had nothing to do with producing it. "I have a suggestion, Redmagne."

"What?"

"Your name here. I think you should choose another."

"Oh? Why?"

"Well, wasn't your masque — *Latitia: or, the New Gorgon Unveiled* — wasn't it popular?" He had read the satires, plays and masques Redmagne had managed to save from his theatrical years.

"Popular?" laughed Redmagne. "It was our troupe's salvation! We must have performed it six times a week in various houses and courts in London. We even were invited to perform it one evening in Vauxhall Gardens. One old earl thought it too critical of civility, and threatened to have our troupe's license taken away."

"But... wasn't Methuselah Redmagne the hero?"

"Why, yes, he was."

"Someone might recognize that name and make trouble. The printer might be arrested for dealing with a wanted felon."

"Not after all these years." But Redmagne looked worried for the first time. "Jack, you've got a point." He looked at the boy. "What name would you suggest?"

Jack Frake turned and grinned. "Romney Marsh!"

Redmagne looked doubtful. Romney Marsh, in Kent, was the notorious stamping ground of some of the most violent smuggling gangs in the country. More Revenue officers had been assaulted and even killed by smugglers during skirmishes there than in any other county.

"They're real names," urged Jack Frake, "and who would think you were the author? People might think of smugglers, but no one would think of you. It would be artful coincidence. I'll wager it would sell a lot of copies!"

Redmagne chuckled. He thought the matter over, then rose and bowed. "Jack, may I have the honor of introducing Mr. Romney Marsh, author of *Hyperborea*?" Then he laughed, as heartily as Jack Frake had ever heard him laugh, and slapped his forehead once. "My lord! *Another* name!"

* * *

Over the next two weeks, Jack Frake helped Redmagne make two copies of *Hyperborea: or, the Adventures of Drury Trantham, Shipwrecked Merchant, in the Unexplored Northern Regions*. These were for the printer — provided Redmagne could find one brave enough to accept them — while the original manuscript would remain in the author's possession. Soon after the task was finished, Redmagne left for London. Jack Frake then had time to take in the novel, for the task of copying was not conducive to reading for appreciation.

And Redmagne was right: The novel was unlike any work of fiction he had read in the man's library. It was not a satire, it was not a chronology; it was not even a hybrid of the two genres. It was a story. The adventures of Drury Trantham — who he suspected was modeled in large part on Skelly — occupied his interest and free time. Drury Trantham became almost a separate person to him, an experience he had not had with any previous fictional character. The story left him happy; Drury Trantham left him confident. He was captivated by the novel, and he would turn the sheets back to his favorite episodes and read them again.

He wondered at the depth of imagination in Redmagne, who had indeed created, in his story, a land much like England, but without any of its misery. It was recognizable, yet unrecognizable at the same time, but credible. He could not reconcile these reactions, but they left him with another feeling: hope.

It was true, what Redmagne had said: There were no caves in Hyperborea, neither in fact, nor in men's souls. His mind clutched at the passages in which Trantham grasped this fact himself, for in many respects he identified with the hero. He would lie awake at night on his pallet, watching the shadows cast by Richard Claxon's candle dance on the cave ceiling, and know that Drury Trantham and other members of his shipwrecked crew were Skelly, Redmagne, and other members of the gang, released to live as they ought to have lived.

He asked Skelly if he had ever read the novel. Skelly answered gruffly, "I'll read it in its proper form — a printed book — and no sooner." But Jack Frake suspected that Skelly knew more about it than he would let on.

In a week, Redmagne returned.

"Any problems?" asked Skelly.

"None!" laughed Redmagne. He took a sheet of paper from his valise, a contract, and showed it to Skelly. "The novel will be published in May, in two duodecimo volumes, by A. Dawson and Sons, printers and booksellers, Pater-Noster Row, London."

Skelly handed back the contract. "And your 'new' name — Romney Marsh — did Mr. Dawson express any curiosity?"

"In the beginning," said Redmagne. "But it was snuffed out when I plunked a bag of guineas on his desk. He thought it was a good selling device, that name. Jack — bless his soul — was right. People will be intrigued by it, and purchase copies of the book by the gross."

"And he read the book?"

"In two nights."

"And he did not find in it anything seditious?"

"Yes — and no. He says it can be read one way or another. He will hire a Grub Street man to write an encomium proving that it is a delightful tale written by a man whose mind spins on Egyptian snuff. His very words."

"And he expressed no desire to know your actual name?"

"None. Half of Dawson's titles are authored by Anonymous."

Skelly sat down and studied his friend for a moment. "I don't need to tell you that this may prove to be more dangerous for you than running French furniture at midday on a calm sea. If this work of yours is adjudged seditious or treasonable, you will have a proclamation published all your own."

"You're forgetting the churchmen, Augustus, and charges of heresy."

Skelly rose and went to the wing table and brought back a bottle of claret and two glasses. He filled the glasses and handed one to Redmagne. "Here's to the success of your novel, Mr. Marsh. You make *my* life seem so dull."

"Dull?" laughed Redmagne. "I would not have a life, were it not for you, my friend."

Chapter 14: The Laughing Lamb

"FAIR WEATHER," SIGHED SKELLY. "THE BANE OF SMUGGLERS. PRAY for a tempest."

"*You* pray for a tempest," laughed Captain John Ramshaw. "I'll hope for a gentle southwestern breeze."

The two men sat at a table by a window in the Laughing Lamb tavern in St. Peter Port, Guernsey. The cloudless, intense July sky was only a shade less blue than the surface of the water, and at times their only demarcation was a thin, indistinct line on the horizon that was the coast of Normandy, forty miles away. A whitecap would appear now and then, or the form of a bird diving into the water, or a white sail in the distance. From the window, they could see *The Hasty Hart* anchored next to the *Sparrowhawk* in the quay. Contraband had been loaded onto the sloop the day before, and the two vessels awaited a favorable wind.

Skelly and Ramshaw were old patrons of the Laughing Lamb, whose owner, a retired "owler," had made a small fortune running wool out of England to Flanders and France. Ramshaw was as tall as Skelly, but leaner. His broad face looked as though it had survived a scalding, but this was merely the complexion of a man who had spent most of his adult life at sea. His black hair was peppered with a gray that matched his eyes. "Where is the charming Mr. O'Such?" he asked. "I was looking forward to his *bonhomie*."

"London," said Skelly, after a sip of his ale. "He wrote a book under an unusual alias and has gone there to see to some business. It's a novel, published just this May. He rushed into my chamber last week and said 'Augustus, my book is a success! It has driven the critics to a frenzy, gone into a second edition, and, best news of all, it has been paid the supreme compliment — it has been *pirated*!'"

Ramshaw laughed, as did Skelly.

"He begged me for leave from this run to see the printer," continued Skelly, "who thinks illustrations in a third edition will sell more copies and make the book more attractive than the pirated copies. The printer's had an engraver do a few plates, and wants O'Such to approve them."

"Busy life, has your Mr. O'Such," said Ramshaw. "Is it worth reading?"

"Yes," said Skelly. "And churchmen think so, too, at least enough that one or two of them have railed against it to their flocks." He laughed. "Of course, that only prods their flocks from ignorance to curiosity. Unenviable profession," he remarked. "The preacher must play the devil. To communicate the benefits of abstinence, he must dangle a delectable pippin before the eyes of a sin-starved congregation."

"Then I might get myself a copy of this book of his. Can't say I read much in the way of novels, but the crossings are long, and, who knows?" Ramshaw paused to relight his pipe.

Skelly nodded. "How soon will you sail back?"

"In a month or so. In London I'll load half my hold with the usual manufactures, then come round to Portsmouth or Falmouth for some meat and provisions. Then on up to Bristol. But that depends on how many bodies we pick up before then."

"Indentures?"

Ramshaw nodded. "Mostly. I might buy some felons, too." As a merchant captain, Ramshaw could purchase the indentures of felons and resell them in the colonies to anyone seeking cheap labor.

"That's a foul business, John," remarked Skelly darkly.

"Not so," said Ramshaw. "England gets rid of her dross, and I make a pound on each felon I take off her hands." It was an old argument between the two men, never resolved.

Ramshaw worked his pipe again, studying Skelly between puffs on the clay stem. Then he raised another matter they had also discussed many times before. "You've been beating to windward for a long time, my friend. How much longer do you think you can keep it up?" he asked.

"Until I die," said Skelly without emphasis.

"There's room for a man of your mettle in the colonies," said the captain. "In any of them. Your fortune could buy you an excellent start. You have friends in almost all the colonies. You wouldn't be alone. You could buy a plantation in Virginia or Maryland, and live easy for the rest of your days." He chuckled. "Find yourself a young widow with property and marry her! There's no lack of them over there. Might do it myself when I've tired of sailing."

"I'm too old for that kind of enterprise, John." Skelly had heard this argument before.

"Bosh! I've seen men your senior by twenty years resettle, and do well for themselves. You? I know your abilities, Augustus. If you can establish a comfortable living as a fugitive right under the Crown's nose, imagine what you could accomplish with the freedom to show your face!" Ramshaw paused. "Of course, you'd need to take a leaf from your Mr. O'Such, and adopt a new name and history."

Skelly smiled at his friend. It was neither a sad smile, nor an easy one. "If I can't show my own face, with my own name, in my own country, then I'd rather stay a fugitive."

"The colonies are your country, Augustus. They are England."

"If they are England," replied Skelly with some emotion, "then England can forgive me the death of a blackmailer, a rogue, and a thief of my happiness! She can also forgive me the effort of helping to make her the envy of Europe — so far as the material happiness of her people is concerned." Skelly nodded out the window at the two ships, and pointed his own pipe. "She can forgive what now sits in my hold there."

Ramshaw knew everything about the death of Warren Pumphrett, and also about the skirmish Skelly's gang had had with Revenue officers near Fowey years ago. He shook his head. "They won't forgive it, Augustus. Not any of it. Their nabs sit warm and rosy in Parliament and on the benches and pass their laws, and they don't know and don't care what those laws do to other men's lives. They are protected from you, but you are not protected from them." Ramshaw sighed. "That's what the Revolution was about, you know. But then they forgot what it was for, and we got our Majesties back. Now we have the privilege of electing them."

Skelly said nothing. He knew Ramshaw was right.

Ramshaw grimaced, then changed the subject. "How's that new boy of yours doing?" He had met Jack Frake in January when *The Hasty Hart* rendezvoused with the *Sparrowhawk* ten miles off the coast of Cornwall.

"Jack? Jack is most promising. Went to London with O'Such. Now there's a fellow you could argue into going to the colonies, John. *He* would do well there." Skelly laughed. "Under the tutelage of common criminals, he's becoming a man of the most upright character." He smiled fondly. "I can't claim all the credit, though. O'Such has done a lot with him. And, then again, Jack is himself."

Ramshaw grinned, then squeezed and patted Skelly's sleeve. "That's because he's a Skelly man!"

Skelly chuckled in modest acknowledgment. Ramshaw ordered another round of ale and some clams for the both of them, and they talked of other things. Then Skelly pointed with his pipe out the window. "Ah, look! The wind is up! A southeastern cloud, heading our way. Where would you place it? Over St. Malo? Or Granville?"

* * *

Isham Leith was living on luck and others' negligence. He was about to benefit from chance again, in the form of Richard Claxon's thirst and a woman's roving eye.

Even though his father had been a distiller, Claxon did not drink ale or any other kind of liquor, as this conflicted with his amended religious conviction of the sanctity of total sobriety, which lay somewhere between Unitarianism and Quakerism. At some distance beyond Squillante, where he had taken down an order from the village grocer and scheduled a nocturnal delivery, he stopped beneath a tree to shade himself from the hot July sun and to slake his thirst with the spring water he had taken from the caves. He reached for his leather-bound bottle, which he had tied to his pony's saddle. But he had not secured the knot firmly enough, and the rope slipped from his grip. The bottle fell on a rock in the road. He dismounted, shook the glass fragments from the soaked pouch, and moved on. By the time he reached Trelowe, he was desperately thirsty. He stopped at a new tavern on the road, and asked the woman there for a cup of water. The woman sullenly pointed to a well at the side of the cottage. From this he drew a bucket of water, and then gave the woman a shilling for two empty gin flasks he saw discarded on the rubbish heap nearby. These he filled with water and put into his pouch.

Richard Claxon was by now a tall, fair-haired youth of seventeen with the face of an angel. To his handsome features was added the animation and serenity of religious fervor. He was the only member of the Skelly gang who did not gamble, play games, swear or take the Almighty's name in vain. Also, taking after Redmagne, he had assumed the refined manners of a gentleman.

The woman watched Claxon, still mounted on his pony, fidget with his pouch, oblivious to her appraisal. She was fascinated by the youth's looks, and flattered by the courtesy he had paid her, which she rarely received from the men of the area. She stepped up next to his pony and engaged him in idle chatter. He pleasantly obliged, as he had time to spend until his next rendezvous.

After some desultory talk about the state of the roads, the new cheapness of tea, and the weather, the woman adjusted her *décolletage* and sighed, "It *is* hot, don't you think? And you ridin' for hours in this hot sun! You poor thing!" Her hand passed over the exposed part of her bosom, then idly came to rest on the youth's leg.

Richard Claxon's gaze was arrested by her dark eyes, which looked up at him with an intent that paralyzed him and made him self-conscious. He was unschooled in the ways of women, and utterly ignorant of sex. The woman's eyes and the touch of her light hand on his leg triggered a maelstrom of inchoate desires, images and denials, jumbled together with fragments of the most strenuous dicta from his Bible. The two storms raging in his mind and body collided and left him inert. He could only stare at the woman, who smiled at him with a wisdom that frightened him.

She said, as her fingers began a gentle tattoo on his leg, "We're lookin' for help here, my husband and me. You could board here a while and do odds and ends. Our custom's pickin' up, and you could earn an extra shillin' or two."

"I... don't know," stammered Claxon.

"Where'd you say you was goin'?"

"I... didn't say — " began Claxon. His mind raced to remember the story he had ready for strangers when it was necessary to answer their questions. "I mean... I am going to Portsmouth to seek an apprenticeship in the shipbuilding trades."

"Oh, my!" exclaimed the woman. "That's such a *long* way off! And you look so tired! Why don't you wait until my husband comes back? We can talk then. I'm sure he'd see it *my* way." Her hand became a little bolder, and began to stroke his leg. "What'd you say your name was?"

"I didn't — " began Claxon again. The tension inside him was growing unbearable. It blocked his memory now, and he snatched at the first name that came to mind, the name of a colleague in whose place he was riding today, and who had gone to wicked London. "My name... is Jack!" he blurted. "Jack Frake!"

The woman gasped, her hand darted away, and she stepped back as though he had cursed her. Her eyes were pits of anger and shock. "What name did you say?" she demanded in a low, menacing voice.

Released from the trance, and confused by the woman's reaction, Richard Claxon doffed his hat once, managed to say, "Thank you, ma'am!" then dug his heels into the sides of the pony. In seconds he was out of the yard and safely back on the road. He continued at a canter for a while, not daring to look back, then slowed to a walk. He took a watch from his coat and glanced at the dial. He breathed easier. He would be on time.

Now, Isham Leith was content, because Henoch Pannell was content. He rode out of Gwynnford on his mount, leading a pony that carried two panes of unglazed glass for the new inn. He had decided to add a window to the former cottage, and one to the addition in the back. Pannell's threat to revoke his license to open the tavern had receded with time. The new tavern was opened, and it was breaking even. His brother Peter was minding the inn in Trelowe. He felt safe, redeemed, and hopeful. He was almost tempted to whistle.

In March, by sheer chance, because a local smuggler by the name of Thomas Hackluyt and two of his friends had come to his other inn to discuss the rendezvous with a Dutch lugger the following night, and had done so with an indiscretion exacerbated by drink, Leith was able to give Pannell the time and place of the run. Hackluyt and his friends were captured by Pannell on the beach not a half mile east of Gwynnford, together with fifty ankers of brandy and eight ponies. One of Pannell's men had even managed to wound a Dutch sailor, whose lugger drifted too close to shore, with a lucky shot from his musket. The smuggler and his friends were now being tried in Falmouth, and Pannell and his men were attending the trial. The Extraordinary Commissioner was happy because Hackluyt, by his information, was responsible for perhaps a quarter of the undutied brandy consumed in the area around Gwynnford. The catch earned Pannell a glowing letter of thanks from the Surveyor-General of Customs for Cornwall. "It is most imperative," wrote the Surveyor-General in a spurt of pompous confidence, "that the Crown and its servants enjoy the duties expected on these commodities, rather than these scoundrels, who merely put these revenues to private use. And it is supremely imperative that you press your search for Augustus Skelly. If he is captured and punished, the spirit of lawlessness in this county will soon be extinguished."

Isham Leith knew nothing of the letter, of course. The only aspect of it that concerned him was Pannell's promise not to call him as a witness to Hackluyt's conversation. He knew that Pannell made this promise, not out of concern for his informant's life, but because the Revenue man was still relying on him to collect information about the Skelly gang. "Thank you, Mr. Leith," the Commissioner had said late one evening after the Hackluyt gang had been taken in chains to the Gwynnford jail to await transfer to Falmouth. "Excellent catch. I knew that you had potential. Now, if only you could help me with the Skelly gang. I would retire from this post, and leave the county to return to its former lawless state." He smiled. "I'll be out of *your* hair."

Leith convinced himself that Pannell meant it. No one stared at him when he rode into Gwynnford earlier in the morning to buy the window panes, as might have happened if anyone had suspected him of informing on Hackluyt. Even Hiram Trott, whom he passed riding out of the town in his cart, nodded in greeting to him.

An hour later, on the road back to Trelowe, he noticed a horse, a cart, and a man beneath a tree, a tree some two hundred feet from the road on the moor — the very tree where he had lured and slain Oyston and Lapworth. A fearsome, unwelcome memory froze his mind for a moment; the site rattled him and he had avoided going near it ever since that day years ago. He passed the site and cast surreptitious glances at the person sitting on a rock beneath the tree.

He frowned. It was Hiram Trott. He blinked in wonderment and rode on.

As he approached his new inn, he saw something in the distance that disturbed him. After a few moments, a youth on a pony came toward him, someone he seemed to remember and had noticed in the past, but never wondered about. He and the rider exchanged perfunctory nods.

Minutes later, as he came nearer the cottage, Huldah Leith rushed out of the yard to meet him. "Leith! That boy you passed on the road — "

Leith reined in his mount. "You mean the one I saw you handlin'?"

"What are you talkin' about? He stopped here for water, and he bought some gin bottles — "

"I *saw* you from the rise on the road yonder!" said Leith, pointing with his riding crop to the spot. The youth had crested it and was now out of sight. "I saw it all, Huldy! Is that what's to go on while I'm away?"

"Leith, I didn't — "

Leith raised his riding crop and struck his wife across the face. "I told you to mend your bitchin' ways, woman, or I'd scar that face of yours!"

Huldah Leith held a hand to the already reddening welt on her face. "You ignorant bastard!" she screamed. "That boy said his name was Jack Frake!" She had lived for years with a suspicion which she dared never name, and she wanted to know nothing about how her husband had come into the money to renovate the cottage. She did not know that he was in thrall to Henoch Pannell.

"Huh! Did he, now?"

"He did!"

"Didn't look nothin' like your bastard!"

"That's right!" said Huldah Leith, balling her hands into fists. "That ain't him, all right, but why would he use Jack's name instead of his own — unless he *knew* him?"

Leith scoffed. "He was at sixes and sevens, I'm damned sure, Huldy! The way you was coddlin' his breeches, I'm surprised he didn't say he was the Duke of Cornwall!" Leith struck his wife again with the crop.

Huldah Leith made no effort to touch her face now. "Jack's still in these parts, Leith," she warned. "He could get us in trouble. Go and stop that boy and use your crop on *him* for the truth!"

With his anger partly spent, the import of his wife's words began to sink into Leith's mind. He glared in disgust at his wife for a moment. He tethered the pony to a post. "Don't touch that glass till I'm back." Then he reined his mount around. "And we ain't finished with this, Huldy." He trotted back up the road.

He caught sight of the youth again, and followed him on the road through Trelowe. Leith gave himself time to concoct a way of dealing with the stranger, and his mind sloshed back and forth between his desire to beat the boy for dallying with his wife, and the very real matter of Jack Frake, potential witness to the murder of Parson Parmley.

The stranger rode on. A beggar appeared, coming from the direction of Gwynnford. Leith saw him say something to the stranger, who tossed him a coin. Moments later, when Leith came upon the beggar, he brandished his riding crop, and the beggar said nothing but ducked away. A mile or two beyond Trelowe, Leith stopped when he saw the stranger leave the road and cross the moor to the lone tree and Hiram Trott.

Leith dismounted, led his horse to a clump of bushes, and tied it there. Then he crept through the moor brush. In the distance, he saw the stranger shake hands with Trott. The two men then sat down together on the rock, and the youth took a large book and a pencil from the bag that was slung over his shoulder. Trott began to speak, and the youth began to write.

"I see, said the blind man!" said Leith with a chuckle under his breath. He could barely contain the joy of relief rising in him as he watched. Now he had something to tell that bastard Pannell.

Chapter 15: The Stagecoach

ONE AFTERNOON A WEEK EARLIER, WHEN JACK FRAKE RETURNED FROM the chore of grazing the gang's livestock in the Villers fields, Skelly had called him into his chamber, pointed to Redmagne, who had just returned from a trip to the Marvel post office, and said merely, "I'm relieving you of your duties so that you may accompany this literary rowdy to London and keep him out of trouble."

For a moment, Jack Frake was speechless. Then he stammered, "But — what about meeting the *Sparrowhawk* in Guernsey?"

Skelly scoffed amiably. "I've been meeting her for years without your help, Mr. Frake."

Redmagne, in his happiness, had insisted on paying Jack's fare and expenses for the journey. "It's my way of thanking you for the name, Jack," he said as they prepared to leave the caves. "Dawson reports that as many customers inquire about Romney Marsh as buy the book."

Redmagne already had a wardrobe of gentleman's clothes, and limited himself to the purchase of a silver-topped sword-cane in Falmouth. Jack Frake wore a suit of clothes he had purchased item by item over the past two years but had never thought he would have a reason to wear: a pair of new shoes with silver buckles, with a pair of spatterdashes to wear over them in the rain; a pair of green velvet breeches; a pair of white silver stockings; a fine green silk coat; a new waistcoat; a white lace-edged shirt, stock and black tie. In Falmouth, at Redmagne's urging, he bought an immaculate white pigtail wig, and a new black velvet tricorn with gold edging. At first he did not recognize himself in the tailor's mirror, once he was attired in these clothes.

In their Falmouth inn room, Jack Frake took the wig from its box, toyed with the ribbon that connected the pigtail with the nape, and made involuntary facial expressions of doubt about its value and comfort.

Redmagne noticed, and felt it necessary to restate the purpose of the wig. "You know that on every excursion beyond the caves, I assume a new name and character. Like Richard the Third, I must '... frame my face for all occasions' — though I do this to preserve my freedom, and not to wield a bloody ax. On this journey, I shall be Squire John Trigg, of Devon. You are to be my precocious nephew, Jeremy Jeamer."

Jack Frake grinned. "Those are the names of the uncle and nephew from your satire, *Sciron Revisited*," he said.

Redmagne chuckled. "Thank you for remembering one of my less illustrious efforts. As Squire Trigg and Nephew Jeamer, we are in money. At least, I am, since my imaginary but sprawling estate near Newton Abbot nets me at least two thousand pounds per annum. So we must dress the parts — and act the parts. This is to be your debut as a gentleman. Do not try to upstage me."

Jack Frake twirled the wig once on his finger. "But *must* I wear this?" he asked with a grimace.

"As a young gentleman, yes. You'll grow accustomed to it. Soon, you won't even notice it up there. And for going to Covent Garden and other places I have in mind, a wig is *de règle*."

From his valise Jack Frake took a pocket pistol, which was already loaded, and a compact box that held balls, flint, powder and wadding. He put the pistol in one ample coat pocket and the box in the other. The tiny weapon had been given him by Charles Ambrose, the deserter, before Jack Frake left the caves. "London thieves and footpads are cowards, Jack. If one accosts you, just wave that powder in his face and see him run." Redmagne also carried a brace of regular pistols in one of his valises.

They took a coastal packet from Falmouth to Plymouth, then another to Portsmouth, then a coach to Southampton. Redmagne bought fares in the coach inn yard for a flying coach to London, which would travel part of the night and stop at fewer inns en route. At the inn they met their fellow travelers. It was a formal introduction, instigated by Mr. Spencer Neaves and his wife, Winifred. Mr. Neaves was a portly, blustering man who owned a sailcloth works near Portsmouth. He saw that 'Mr. Trigg' was a gentleman of means, and forced himself on the squire. "My father started the business, and I've expanded it," he boasted at length. "Navy contracts, mostly for mizzenmasts and mainsails," he confided. "They eat so much of my product that I hardly have any left over for those damned commercial ships. The Navy pays better." Redmagne smiled vaguely at Mr. Neaves' patter and made some ambiguous remarks which the man took for compliments. Mrs. Neaves was a dour, stern-faced woman who said little and did not like Redmagne.

Next Redmagne was accosted by John Truxton, a farmer who was traveling to London to visit the Admiralty. There he hoped to convince their lordships that a contract for provisioning the Channel Fleet should be wrested from a rival and awarded to him. Redmagne shrugged in frosty indifference, and Truxton bothered him no more.

But throughout these formalities, Redmagne was distracted by a graceful young woman with a comely face and rich, brownish-red hair beneath her bonnet and cap. This was Miss Millicent Morley, a governess who was accompanying her young charge, three-year-old Etain McRae. Redmagne took the liberty of introducing himself, and in an overly proper conversation, learned that the child's parents were in London, and that the governess was taking her back home after a visit with her aunt and uncle in Southampton. Ian McRae, she said, was a new partner in a firm that supplied Virginians with the necessaries and luxuries of life. When the passengers boarded the coach, Redmagne made sure that he sat opposite the governess. John Truxton deferred to "Mr. Trigg" and made himself comfortable on the roof with the baggage. Jack Frake was squeezed in between Redmagne and Mr. Neaves, while little Etain McRae was ensconced between the governess and Winifred Neaves. As the coach rumbled out of the inn yard, Miss Morley took a small book from her bag and opened it. Redmagne saw that it was the first volume of Samuel Richardson's *Pamela*. Redmagne opened his copy of Sir Philip Sidney's *Arcadia*, while Jack Frake leafed through Brown's *Roman History*, which he regretted bringing because he was too restless with anticipation to concentrate on the gory succession of emperors.

After one hour on the jerking, bumping coach, Redmagne put aside his own book and addressed the woman who sat opposite him.

"Ah! Now there's a work that can bring a blush to any lady's cheeks!"

The governess looked up from her book, partly in annoyance, partly in surprise, but mostly from curiosity. "I have not yet blushed, sir, and I am half through this volume. Why would you expect me to?"

Redmagne smiled. "You must confess that there are in it some remarkably humid passages."

"Humid, sir? What do you mean?"

"I mean those passages which call for the busy flutter of a lady's fan to cool her brow."

The governess looked to her left, then to her right. "As you can see, Mr. Trigg, I have misplaced my fan, but my brow is still cool. Please elucidate."

Redmagne cleared his throat. "I mean having the power to arouse the passions and, at least for a lady, to cause her to wish, perhaps, that she could exchange places with the heroine."

"I am *not* a lady, sir. I am, as you know, merely employed by one." Miss Morley wrinkled her brow. "And I do not find any of the passages to which you undoubtedly refer so 'humid' nor would I wish to exchange places with the heroine in any situation I have so far read, 'humid' or not. In fact, I do not find her much of a heroine. Droll, perhaps, and at times resourceful, but not a heroine."

Redmagne smiled again. "You do not envy Pamela for being pursued by Squire Blank?"

"Not even in her most perilous moments," said the governess, shaking her head. "And I find Squire Blank to be uncommonly ordinary, as rogues go, and a man of little inner substance."

"Then why do you continue reading the work if it so displeases you?"

"I did not say that it displeases me, sir," answered the governess with patience. "I am reading it so that I may more intelligently converse with my mistress. She is continually assailing me with quotations and morals which she has culled from the novel, a copy of which rests on her toilette-table, next to her Bible."

"What devotion!" remarked Redmagne. "And a wise stratagem on your part." He paused. "It has been some years since the novel was the rage, but they say that people still gossip about Pamela almost as much as they gossip about their real friends and enemies."

Miss Morley sighed and nodded in agreement. "That is much the situation in my mistress's circle of friends — and enemies." She paused. "There is another bothersome thing about this novel," she added thoughtfully.

"And what is that?"

"The heroine, who is a servant, seems to have unlimited leave to write such long letters. Now, I did service as a maid in a large household, before I became a governess, and I can assure you, Mr. Trigg — and you may bear me out on this complaint, for you are a squire and no doubt have a servant or two — that neither I nor any other maid I came to know had so much *time* on her hands, not to mention all the shillings for the paper, ink and quills our Pamela expends!"

Redmagne chuckled. "Fair observation, Miss Morley. But it *is* a chronicle, of sorts, and the author, according to his lights, dim as I think they must be, must needs report events and cogitations somehow." He paused. "I know of a man who wrote a novel barely half the length of *Pamela*. It took him eight years to complete it, in between duties one hundred times more arduous than Pamela's. So I can sympathize with your bother — my being a squire with a servant or two."

Jack Frake glanced up at Redmagne, expecting him to mention *Hyperborea*, and how it was written. But, strangely, his friend did not.

"Thank you, Mr. Trigg. There is another thing," ventured the governess. "Regardless of what one thinks of the novel, do you not believe it has a positive moral influence on people? If it had not, people would not talk about it so much. Why, there was a time, for a while, when churchmen even read passages from it from their pulpits."

"Positive?" said Redmagne, after a moment. "I have reservations about its positive moral influence. I would say instead that the novel is popular because it answers in many people their own penchant for the common. It is insipidness dramatized." He paused. "Why do you say that Pamela is not a heroine?"

"Oh, she is a heroine in the strictest sense, in that she is the subject of the story. But in all other aspects she is, as you say, quite common, and will doubtless come to a common end, irrespective of all the verbiage the author has thought expedient to cram into her otherwise inadequate head."

Redmagne burst out laughing. Jack Frake grinned in response to Miss Morley's reply, while Mr. Neaves and his wife frowned.

"What amuses you, Mr. Trigg?" asked the governess.

"You have expressed my own summary estimate of the character — exactly!" said Redmagne. When he recovered, he asked, "What aspects *would* you say constitute a heroine, Miss Morley?"

Miss Morley paused to compose an answer. "She should be a woman who seeks in her man the practiced virtues that he professes."

"Which are… ?"

"I have not compiled an inventory, Mr. Trigg, so I could not at the moment tick them off for you."

"But," said Redmagne, "would you say this, at least, that if Richard Lovelace, the great Cavalier poet, ever encountered Pamela, he would *not* be moved to say 'I could not love thee, Dear, so much, loved I not honor more'?"

Miss Morley blushed, but held Redmagne's eyes. "Yes, Mr. Trigg, I would say that, at least, since a lady also can love honor. Someone like Pamela — of whom there are more real examples than I care to think of — could not love a man who actually placed his soul above *her* concern." A faint smile bent her mouth. "A lady could just as well say that to her man… A lady can be cavalier in character, if not in action."

Redmagne beamed at her, then said softly, "Only a *lady* could say that, Miss Morley."

A silence fell on the compartment, and seemed to make the words of the last exchange more audible. Redmagne was an arm's length and a half distant from Miss Morley, but to Jack Frake it seemed as if he were about to kiss the governess. And Miss Morley looked as though she expected to be kissed.

"Excuse me, sir!" blurted Mr. Neaves.

Jack Frake nearly jumped at the intrusive, demanding sound. Miss Morley's book fell to the floor. And Redmagne's head turned slowly, unwillingly to the source. He bent to pick up the book, and handed it to the governess.

Mr. Neaves was saying, "In my company, I will not tolerate references to treacherous Jacobites such as this Cavalier you mention! It would seem that the axing of those two instigators at Tower Hill last summer has not axed treasonable sympathies still at large in this country!"

Redmagne's eyes became slits. "Excuse me, sir," he replied, "but this country is England, where one is permitted to speak his mind, without penalty, even at the risk of offending insensitive bores."

The sailcloth maker turned in his seat to face Redmagne. "Humph! You are a squire, sir, and presumably a gentleman, but I think that you have room for improvement! I think you ought to be made to take a turn in the army! The experience would sweat out any willowy royalist notions that course through your veins!"

"Have you had the experience, sir?" asked Redmagne with wicked congeniality.

"I have done some service for the Lord Lieutenant of Hampshire. I am a captain in this county's militia."

"Oh, but surely that is not the same thing as regular army, sir! Occasional service, such as you may endure to demonstrate some alleged virtue of civic duty — " Redmagne paused and turned to address Miss Morley, " — much as I think Pamela endures the attentions of Squire Blank — " he turned again to face Mr. Neaves " — is hardly to be compared to constant service, such as our soldiers endure."

The passenger pursed his mouth and began to reply, but Redmagne continued. "I must correct you, sir, in the same manner in which you interrupted this lady and me. Englishman to Englishman, I have no royalist ether in my veins, not of any kind, neither Hanoverian nor Stuart. And as for having willowy notions sweated out of me, I daresay that I have been fighting *your* battles for nigh on fifteen years, without pension, contract, reward, or recognition, while you have wallowed in the trough of mediocrity."

The insult was unmistakable, and Mr. Neaves knew it. Redmagne brought up his cane and held it poised beneath the roof of the compartment. "Do you wish me to have the coach stopped, sir, so that we might argue the point in more spacious circumstances?"

The man stared at Redmagne, his face frozen in anger, fear and indecision. Then a sharp blow on his shin caused him to glance at his wife, who shook her head once, emphatically. The look on her face told him that she did not think he could best the gentleman in any manner of fight, and that, anyway, she did not want her journey to London delayed for any reason. Mr. Neaves turned to Redmagne. "You have the advantage of me, sir. I cannot oblige you now, as I am taking my wife to London to attend to her ill father. But you do not have my apologies."

"I have not asked for them, as I had not asked for your opinion." Redmagne turned to the governess. "My apologies to you, Miss Morley. One meets such cabbages on public conveyances."

The exchange between Redmagne and Mr. Neaves dampened conversation.

"Redmagne?" said Jack Frake after watching the rural scenery roll by during a long stretch of silence as the coach bumped over the rutted road.

"Yes... *Jeremy*," said Redmagne, looking up from his book.

"Do you remember when you led us in a toast to that government report? I mean, the one in which the Customs Board claimed that the Crown lost three million pounds of revenue on eight hundred thousand pounds of tea consumed by us last year?"

Redmagne frowned. It was a dangerous topic, and he had introduced himself as John Trigg. "Yes," he answered cautiously. "I seem to remember that. Why?"

"Well, how could they know that it was eight hundred thousand pounds? I mean, if they really had the power to collect duty on *all* the tea, maybe it would have been less than a hundred thousand pounds, because no one could have afforded to buy more of it. And all the other things, too, like the tobacco and molasses and the rest of it. They could prove the figure for the tea they collected duty on, but that's all. So it really isn't lost revenue, is it? I mean, the smugglers and free-traders really aren't robbing the *Crown* of anything, are they? And how did they get the eight hundred thousand pound figure?"

Redmagne sighed, then blinked in astonishment. That line of reasoning had never occurred to him before. He glanced with new interest at Jack Frake, who sat waiting for an answer. "You're right… Jeremy. It's a good question, and the beginning of a good answer." He grunted in astonishment again, then met the eyes of the governess, who was smiling at his astonishment. He leaned forward and said softly, "*I* taught him, you know." The governess hid her amusement by turning again to her novel, but it showed in a twinkle in her eye. Etain McRae scrutinized Jack Frake, her thoughts serious but unfathomable.

The Neaveses sniffed in disgust.

Chapter 16: The Highwaymen

THE COACH STOPPED BRIEFLY AT THE INN YARD IN BASINGSTOKE FOR A change of horses and to allow the passengers to refresh themselves and buy a basket of cold meats for the leg to Reading. The Neaveses enquired and were told that the next coach would be by in the morning. The passengers boarded the coach again in stiff silence. Redmagne had gently reprimanded Jack Frake for his *faux pas*, and no one ventured conversation.

They spent the night at the coach inn at Reading. While Jack Frake slept, Redmagne paced and smoked a pipe outside the window of the governess's room. He did not sleep much that night.

It was mid-morning the next day. The coach sped toward Ealing, just outside of London. In the strained silence, the passengers had grown accustomed to the rhythm of the horses' hooves, and became alert when, in the midst of a thick birch forest, the cadence slowed and they heard the coachman swear.

"Stand and deliver, or die!" shouted a voice.

The coach came to an abrupt halt, its wheels sliding to a stop over the dirt together with the hooves of the team. The vehicle stopped so suddenly that Jack Frake slid off his seat to the floor. They heard the coachman reply, "Don't shoot, mister! We're no trouble!"

The governess immediately clutched her charge to her, while the

Neaveses began taking money and jewelry from their persons and stashing it under their seats.

"All right, good people!" shouted a mask-muffled voice. "Out of the carriage! You won't be harmed if you offer no resistance and do as you're told!"

Redmagne glanced out his window. They were on a bend in the road that was flanked on both sides by the forest. He saw a man on a horse approach the coach with a leveled long gun. Another long gun, cocked and ready, lay slung across his saddle. The highwayman wore a long coat and a mask over his nose and mouth. Redmagne heard the coachman begin to climb down from his seat. A foot belonging to the farmer riding with the luggage appeared from above and planted itself on the sill of the window an inch from Redmagne's nose. He glanced to his right and saw a second masked rider on that side of the coach. There would be one more to the gang, he thought, covering the rear. "Jack," he said quietly, "take out your pistol and have it ready to hand to me."

"Come out, travelers!" shouted the highwayman again. "We'll shoot if you don't, and these ain't fowling pieces we carry!"

The farmer dropped to the ground, as did the coachman.

Jack Frake, still on the floor, reached into the deep pocket of his new coat and brought out the pocket pistol. Redmagne quickly opened his satchel that lay in the well beneath his seat and took out his pair of pistols. With a turn of each barrel, he readied the weapons and held them low out of sight of the highwayman. Jack Frake did the same with his pocket pistol. The boy saw the same intent look on Redmagne's face as he had observed when his friend answered Mr. Neaves.

The governess made a sound of terror, and Mrs. Neaves screamed. But before either woman could implore him not to use the pistols, Redmagne kicked the coach door open, extended one arm, and fired without warning at the first highwayman. Even through the thick blue smoke of his discharge, he could see a red spot erupt on the man's bare forehead. The man jerked back, dropped his long gun, and toppled from the saddle, one foot still caught in a stirrup. The coachman and the farmer threw themselves to the ground. Redmagne dropped the spent pistol on the seat behind him, and, clinging to the door frame, swung around to see the rear of the coach.

Jack Frake was awed by the swiftness of Redmagne's actions. It was when he saw him swing on the door frame to check the rear of the coach that Jack Frake thought to glance out the window above him. The Neaveses sat frozen in their seats, apparently more frightened by what Redmagne had done than of the highwaymen. He saw another masked rider with a brace of pistols peer from his saddle in and through the coach, then raise one of his pistols. With an urgency and an anger Jack could not stop to analyze, he rose from the floor, unlatched the door, and placed one foot on the footstep, blocking the outlaw's sight of Redmagne. The man's pistol was pointed directly at him now. Its barrel was at least five times the length of his own weapon, and gleamed ominously in the sun. The eyes between the mask and the hat glanced down at him with the same imperious arrogance he had seen in Lieutenant Farbrace a long time ago.

He had been saved once by Redmagne. But he did not think of this dilemma and decision in terms of returning the favor. Redmagne's life meant far more to him than that. He knew that he would probably die in the effort, but he raised his tiny pistol at the same time he pulled back the hammer.

As for the highwayman, he began to laugh. The pistol in the boy's grip had pathetically small power and range, and the boy stood more than five feet away, his eyes round with fear. "So be it, you little blighter!" he snorted as he pressed the trigger.

Jack Frake, pointing the pistol at the man's face, fired first.

The highwayman gasped, let go of his pistols, and clutched at his throat. He began to scream, but the scream disintegrated into a pathetic howl. The man tried to climb out of his saddle, but his legs got tangled and he tumbled to the ground.

Jack Frake saw a third horseman, who was waiting in the woods, wheel his mount around and gallop away through the brush. Jack Frake dropped from the coach step and walked cautiously over to the wounded highwayman. The man rolled back and forth on the ground, clutching his throat through the mask, blood seeping through his fingers. He made gagging sounds, like the cry of a goat that had had one of its legs broken. The sound more than the sight traumatized Jack Frake. The man tore off his soaked mask, and Jack saw that the bandit was only a boy a few years older than him. The bandit glanced up with maddened eyes and saw Jack Frake approach with the pocket pistol still clutched in his hand. He managed to get his legs under himself and stumble quickly into the woods, still gagging.

Jack Frake felt a hand on his shoulder. He turned and saw Redmagne. The man was studying him with a curious look. "That's what a ball can do to you, Jack."

"He was going to shoot you."

"Or *you*, Jack," remarked Redmagne. He put a hand on the boy's shoulder and squeezed it once in silent thanks.

Redmagne stepped away to pick up the dropped pistols. He walked back and held them out, grips first. Jack Frake put his pocket pistol away and tentatively took hold of the new ones. "These are yours, Jack. Fine pieces of Spanish work. Matching, too. Wonder who he took them from." He turned and examined the mount. "This mare has seen better years, though. We'll take her and sell her for what money she'll bring. But the saddle's new, as are the pistol cases. We'll keep the cases and sell the saddle. It'll fetch more than will the mare."

Jack Frake stared at the mount blankly.

"Come on, Jack," said Redmagne. "Climb into the saddle. We'll escort the coach as far as Ealing. Lock and case your new pistols, and reload your little one. You will guard the rear. Keep a sharp eye out for that third man."

Jack Frake obeyed. Redmagne adjusted the stirrups for him, then walked away.

The coachman and farmer were standing near the body of the first highwayman, which lay near the waiting horse. "He's dead, all right, gov-'nor," the coachman barked in satisfaction. "You gave 'im a third eye!"

Redmagne stooped down and removed the mask. "Know him, coachman?"

"I think I seen 'im at the inn on the trip out." The coachman laughed. "His road days is over!"

"Help me move him off of the road."

The three men picked up the body and deposited it in the gutter at the side of the road. Redmagne searched the body and stood up with another pistol and a bag of coins. "He won't be needing these," he said, tucking the pistol in his belt and dropping the bag into one of his frock pockets. He nodded to the horse. "Take those long guns, coachman, and keep them handy." He took out his brass box and penciled a note — *A highwayman who encountered a Skelly man* — and tucked it into one of the dead man's sleeves. Then he went and led the horse to the coach, where he reclaimed his own pistols. "When I've reloaded, coachman, we can leave. My... nephew and I will escort you as far as Ealing."

Spencer Neaves stepped down from the coach and glared at Redmagne. "Who are you, sir?" he demanded. "What is your *real* name?"

"My real name?"

"Yes," said his wife, who quickly descended and turned to the coachman. "I distinctly heard the boy there address this... gentleman by a name other than the one with which he introduced himself! It was Redman, or Redmaize, or some such, instead of John."

The coachman stared at Redmagne and stepped back. "Did you say 'Redmagne,' Mum?"

"Yes, Redmagne!" confirmed Miss Morley involuntarily.

The coachman studied Redmagne for a moment, then laughed and spoke to Mrs. Neaves. "Milady, you're safer in this man's company than if you was guarded by the King's Palace Cavalry!" He grinned at Redmagne, then winked, and climbed back up on the coach to his seat.

Jack Frake smiled. The coachman's familiarity with Redmagne's name proved the wisdom of his advice to his friend in the matter of an alias.

"I refuse to travel in this beast's company!" declared Winifred Neaves to the coachman. Mr. Neaves, shaken by Redmagne's panache, by now had little to say, and did not second his wife's motion.

"I'm afraid that's an improper wish, Madam," said Redmagne, "and, considering that my nephew and I have just now preserved your belongings and perhaps even your virtue and your life, your trepidation is keenly painful to me. Your only alternative is to walk to Ealing." He grinned. "Have no fear, Madam. We mean to get you and your husband there safely."

At a comfortable trot, Redmagne preceded the coach on the highwayman's horse, while Jack Frake followed. Redmagne said nothing else to the boy about the incident. It was an experience he would have to accept and reconcile on his own. The boy had always been prepared to fight, but until now had never had to see one immediate consequence of winning. Miles later, Jack Frake urged his mount ahead and rode up alongside Redmagne. "It might've been you that was killed," he said, "or only injured, and making those noises. I'm glad it wasn't you. I'd do it again." Redmagne nodded once. Then Jack Frake fell back to his place behind the coach.

A mile before Ealing, Redmagne asked the coachman to stop for a moment. "This is where we'll leave you, sir, and we thank you for your hospitality and discretion."

"It were my pleasure, sir!" replied the coachman with a tip of his hat.

Redmagne rode up to the window where the governess sat. He smiled down at her, then reached inside for his cane and valise, which he slung from the saddle pommel. He took out his brass writing box, and penciled something on a scrap of paper, folded it, then handed it to Miss Morley.

"My recommended reading for your next trip, milady," he said. "We *shall* meet again." The woman took the slip, but before she could open it, Redmagne bent in his saddle, took her hand, and kissed it, then on impulse took her face and kissed her softly on the lips. "Yes," he said, "we shall be meeting again... "

Miss Morley, for once, was left speechless. She clutched the slip of paper in her hand, and watched Redmagne as he rode away, oblivious to the scandalized stares of the Neaveses and the open curiosity of Etain McRae.

They waited until the stagecoach had rounded a bend a half mile down the road. Beyond the bend, over the fields and trees, they could see the spires of Ealing. Redmagne exclaimed, "Jack, I'm in love! With Miss Millicent Morley! What a primly modest name for a woman with so much... fire! I keep seeing her, with those locks of hair, not imprisoned by cap or bonnet, falling gracefully to her bare shoulders, and telling me what she thinks of Reverend Benjamin Slocock and his sermon on *Pamela*... She has a most attractive way about her... " Then he caught himself, and laughed, because the rest of what he thought about Miss Morley was not for another's ears. "Come on, Jack!" he said, pulling on his reins and spurring his mount into a field. "I know a shortcut that will take us round Ealing. London awaits!"

Chapter 17: The City

THE INTELLECTUAL POLITICAL, LITERARY AND ARTISTIC CAPITALS OF EUROPE then were London and Paris, with Vienna, Rome and Berlin acting as special satellites. It is difficult to assess which capital was the leader, and which was the follower, for in the many realms of any cultural rivalry there must be innovators and pathbreakers on the one hand, and emulators and refiners on the other. London and Paris scored mightily on both sides, to their mutual benefit, even though throughout the eighteenth century they were at war with each other more often than not. In the short intervals when the capitals were not struggling for overseas supremacy, the citizens who had been taxed to pay for the contests thronged across the Channel to trade, to tour, to learn, to observe and write, to become endeared to the other nation's charms and amenities. When gathering war clouds threatened to cut them off from home, Frenchmen and Englishmen would wistfully exchange *adieu* and Godspeeds with friends, mistresses, tailors, tutors, coffeehouse companions and favorite innkeepers.

Redmagne had a hypothesis to explain the differences between France and England. It was all his own, though he claimed no scholarly accolade for it. Jack Frake had heard it before in his tutorials in the caves. He heard it again, rephrased, in the middle of an ever-widening river on a balmy July afternoon.

They had detoured south from Ealing to Chiswick on the Thames, where they sold the highwaymen's horses and saddles to the proprietor of a leather works who regarded the asking price of ten guineas for them as something close to theft, and who therefore asked no questions. Redmagne then hired a local waterman to row him and Jack Frake to London. The waterman balked at first; his career was to ferry passengers back and forth between Chiswick and the farm country directly across the Thames, and he complained loudly about having to work against the tides the whole distance. But his arguments succumbed to two golden guineas and a promise of two more if the gentleman and his nephew were safely deposited on the Whitehall Stairs by the nearly finished Westminster Bridge. The sum represented over a quarter of his yearly income; it fueled his arms, legs and shoulders and turned him into a relentless rowing machine.

Not long into the trip down river, Redmagne posited his idea: "There's one main reason why England leads the way in politics, Jack: *Agincourt*. Can you remember why?"

"No," laughed Jack Frake, seated opposite his mentor. He was surprised that Redmagne would raise the subject now, and he was too excited about their destination to remember what had been said.

Redmagne sensed this and feigned disappointment. He raised his cane and playfully knocked the boy's hat askew. "Agincourt, Jack. But first, Runnymede in 1215, and King John's concessions to testy, abused barons who did not want to go to war again and pay for the privilege, too. Those concessions made up the Great Charter. Now, France might have produced the same phenomenon, in due time, for the same reasons. French barons could be as testy, and French monarchs as presumptuous and abusive, as any of our own. But two hundred years after Runnymede, our Henry decimated Charles's French nobility at Agincourt. There were few testy, abused barons left to challenge the monarch, and those that followed were not of the same mettle as those who perished by Henry's archers, swords and axes. France has since then been as resolutely monarchical as England has been tumultuous. That, in short, is why England, for all her egregious faults, is a better place to live, while France is a worse, even for all her magnificent virtues."

This brief lecture lodged itself somewhere in Jack Frake's half-attentive mind, and served as a prelude to his first visit to the city. Skelly had described it to him many times, as had other members of the gang. But nothing Skelly or Redmagne or the others had said about London could have prepared him for the experience.

London was the source and the primary transmission belt of the nation's virtues and faults. It was not only the capital; it ruled England in ways other nations' capitals did not. London fashions, London literature, London music, London theater, London art, and London money flowed out to other cities and towns across the island and to the colonies. This was due in part to the Crown's mercantilist policies, and in part to natural economic causes. Many of England's leading artistic and literary lights — Gainsborough and Reynolds, the painters; Garrick, the actor; Goldsmith and Johnson, the authors — journeyed to London, for that was where the power, money, patrons and audiences were. Handel could not have settled in Hull or Birmingham and composed the same oratorios and operas. The Italian craze of the period — complete with a lucrative business in smoke- and manure-cured 'Old Master' forgeries — could not have taken root in Leeds or Winchelsea. French artists and engravers could not have thrived and established a Soho in Manchester or Sheffield; these were growing manufacturing towns that did not even have representation in Parliament. London was the proving ground for nearly all endeavors that had reason, tenacity or guile to succeed.

London at this time sat almost exclusively on the 'north side' of the Thames. It began at Shadwell and the windmill-dotted Isle of Dogs, and ended abruptly some five miles up river at Millbank and the Chelsea Water Works, under the shadow of Westminster Abbey. In between lay a busy metropolis of at least half a million people. The Thames was crossed by citizens and visitors chiefly by ferry; competitive watermen vied ferociously for the business of rowing passengers between the dozens of "stairs" on the opposing banks. Until Westminster Bridge was finished three years later, only one bridge spanned the Thames, London Bridge, whose closely spaced piers turned it into a roaring, killer dam at high tide. The bridge was home to thousands in its packed, multi-storied houses; it was also an arcade of shops where penny-pinching housewives and maids could buy anything from poultry to pins. Ladies and gentlemen with golden guineas to spend shopped in the more elegant venues of the Strand or St. Paul's Churchyard, where tradesmen's goods were neatly displayed in windows.

London's most numerous edifices were churches, some three hundred of them, and their steeples punctuated the skyline. The dome of St. Paul's and the towers of the Abbey dwarfed everything else, including the diminutive Houses of Parliament, whose two bodies, the Commons and Lords, met in cramped upstairs halls. The white walls of the Tower of London were visible from miles down the river, and served as palatial confinement for a variety of Crown offenders. In addition to apartments, the Tower also contained a museum and a menagerie of exotic animals. For a small fee, one could visit the museum, gape at leopards, panthers, monkeys and even an elephant in the menagerie, or have tea with a prisoner and envy his splendid living appointments.

London was frustrating; merchantmen bringing cargo up river into the city were stopped by the barrier of London Bridge, and also by the necessity of having their cargoes cleared or dutied by the functionaries of nearby Customs House, and often had to wait for weeks in the traffic-clogged river before being able to land their cargoes at a Lawful Key or wharf. There were no docks in London and the physical task of unloading ships was done by lighters.

For all its churches, London was crime-ridden; the thieving began on the Thames, where accomplices on the merchantmen would toss dutiable goods wrapped in water-tight parcels overboard to be retrieved by 'mudlarks' on shore at low tide, and at riverside sea-coal depots whose heavers and foremen would walk off with bushels of Newcastle black. London was larcenous; enterprising thieves were not a merchant's only nuisance. Customs inspectors had unlimited power over the wealth brought into the port. For a bribe, they would clear a cargo and declare a duty paid; if they were not satisfied with the amount of a bribe, or if a merchant or captain complained or refused to resort to bribery, an inspector could threaten to "rummage" his vessel — ostensibly to search for contraband rum or other hidden goods — and order the vessel literally torn apart. Many customs inspectors also conspired with the wharfingers — owners of the legally monopolized Lawful Keys — to have cargoes condemned, landed, and auctioned in a warehouse, and split the profits. More than one merchant found himself bidding for his own goods at a government-supervised auction.

London was noisy; the incessant clop of the shod hooves of horses and the rumble of the iron-rimmed wheels of carriages, hackneys, wagons and drays rolling over its muddy cobblestone streets, competed with the cries, drums, horns, grinding stones and bells of street hawkers peddling their wares or services.

London was dirty; thousands of chimneys spewed soft coal smoke into the air, whence it fell onto trees and horses and ladies' satin gowns. When it rained or drizzled, the drops would gather soot and coat everything they touched. 'Night soil' was regularly hurled out of windows or into kennels or open sewage ditches. The city usually lay under a twilight of dreary gray. A day when Londoners could see and feel the sun and glance up at a blue sky was called "glorious."

London was lightless and suffocating, for most Londoners, even on glorious days; an exorbitant window tax on private buildings, not to be repealed for another century, drove landlords and owners of many commercial structures to shutter or block the windows of their tenants and employees.

London smelled; parish street sweepers could not keep up with the city's thousands of horses, and if a horse, other draft animal, cat, dog, or rat died, it was left in the street to decay. In parish churchyards, the poor were buried in flimsy coffins in mass graves, which were not covered over until twenty or so coffins filled the hole.

London was dangerous; although foreign visitors commented enviously on the candle- and oil-lit lamps of its streets, one could just as easily be killed for a shilling in their shadows as in the darkest alleys, and be stripped of one's clothes as well. Guides with torches or lanterns known as link boys could be hired to lead anyone traveling at night through the darker streets; often they would lead their customers directly into the hands of cut-throats. Mohocks, gangs of aristocratic toughs, terrorized neighborhoods day or night with senseless beatings and whimsical destruction of property; watchmen and constables were among their favorite sports. Gangs of footpads and teams of cut-purses and pickpockets roamed the streets and infiltrated distracted crowds with little fear of being caught; there was no police force, only frightening punishments and a feeble corps of parish-paid watchmen who trusted to luck and informants to apprehend known criminals, when they dared bother to concern themselves at all. Wigs, swords, hats, watches, fine laces and silks, and silverware could be had with a snatch and a dash, and sold minutes later in special thieves' markets. Conviction for their theft could earn one a whipping, a burned hand, the pillory, or hanging, depending on the monetary value a jury placed on the stolen property. Butlers, valets, laborers, laundresses and maids were regularly hanged on Tyburn Tree or at Newgate Prison for robbing or murdering their employers.

London was cruel; unwanted infants were either abandoned in dark alleys or on the doorsteps of the middle class or the Foundling Hospital, or murdered, usually with brandy, gin, or rum. Abandoned children who were not sentenced to a workhouse or to a trades training regimen at Bridewell

Prison very likely would grow up to be pickpockets or prostitutes by the advanced age of ten years. Beggars were everywhere; begging was a profession, employing the artifices of fake ailments and disabilities, and the real artifices of deliberately blinded or maimed children to solicit pity. Convicted highwaymen, who proudly dubbed themselves "Inspectors of His Majesty's Roads," vociferously claimed the privilege of being hanged first among a dozen or more condemned criminals taken by cart from prison to the gallows, which occurred every six weeks, usually on a Monday. Touts worked the huge crowds of spectators at these "Tyburn Fairs" and took bets on who would hang first or on how long a criminal would hang by the neck until dead; it often took as long as half an hour, as hangmen did not use trapdoors or weights. When a man or woman was pronounced dead, a tugging match over the body would frequently ensue between relatives and representatives from the College of Surgeons, who by law had first claim to the body for purposes of dissection. Men and women sentenced to the pillory, such as the one at Charing Cross, were often stoned to death in the stocks by the crowds, even though they had not received a death sentence and might have been released the next day on payment of a fine of one mark.

London was diseased; even after the Great Fire had reduced most of its vermin-ridden timber, wood and plaster buildings to ashes and moved the inhabitants to replace them with brick and stone, smallpox killed fifteen thousand people in a single year, while scarlet fever and typhus were as common as colds. The city had water mains, supplied by the pumps of three major waterworks, but its imperfectly connected, hollowed-elm conduits mixed supposedly clean Thames water with ground water and sewage from the streets. The city's three thousand coffeehouses and innumerable taverns were the only places one could safely slake one's thirst; boiled or distilled water was safer to drink, though no one then knew why. And so London was drunk.

On the other hand, London boasted over a dozen hospitals, dozens of schools, numerous colleges, over forty markets, and fairgrounds. It had opera, concerts, art galleries, Covent Garden and Drury Lane for the theater, and Ranelagh Gardens and Vauxhall Pleasure Gardens for dining, music and amusement. It had countless bookstores, printers and publishers. It was a center for silversmithing and other metal work. Danes, Dutch, Germans, Jews and Quakers all had their own quarters, chapels and fraternal associations within the city. There were chess clubs, philosophy clubs, scientific clubs and clubs for the study of antiquities. And if one grew tired of London — as Samuel Johnson claimed one could not do without tiring of life — the countryside was but an hour's hike or ride by post chaise in any direction, where one could picnic or stroll through meadows and forests.

Much of this Jack Frake already knew; none of it mattered. He was entering the city of London on one of its glorious days. By the time the waterman rowed them beneath an arch of Westminster Bridge, a long white arm of stone that languidly spanned the river, Jack Frake was in a trance of expectation. He stood on the Whitehall Stairs, valise in hand, listening to the murmur that emanated from the city before him. Redmagne, after he had paid the waterman, had to put a hand on the boy's shoulder to propel him forward.

On Whitehall Street, Redmagne signaled an idle hackney. "To the Three Swans Inn," he shouted, "on the Strand, near Burleigh Street." The coachman snapped his whip and the vehicle jerked to life as Redmagne and Jack Frake fell into their seats.

"My last legal lodging in the city," said Redmagne as they moved past Scotland Yard, "was on Dirty Lane, not far from Covent Garden. Then, after the Epping affair, I moved about as often as I held the odd job. I was even tutor to a duke's sons for a while. I happened to hand his footman one of my business cards. That footman was once in our troupe. He played Iago in *Othello* at Drury Lane, and the critics said that he was the best Iago they had ever seen. Then some obscure malady made him mute, and he wound up painting our sets. Then, the Epping affair."

Jack Frake broke his attention from the window to ask, "What name did you use *then*?"

"Peter Gammage, tutor in history, Latin, and geography. I believe I still have a card back in the caves."

"You must show me where you and Skelly met."

"At the Blue Boar, near the Corn Exchange."

"And his emporium."

"On St. Martin's Lane. I can show you where it stood. It was ultimately sold to the parish, which converted it into a hostel and workhouse. It burned down years ago."

"I would like to see where it stood."

Redmagne grinned. "All right. You'll see as much as can be seen in two days, Jack."

"Look at all the shop signs!" said the boy. "They're so big!"

"That's for the benefit of coachmen, most of whom can't read. Their illiteracy puts rather a crimp on trade names, as you'll note."

"What are all those stone posts for in front of the shops, and all along the way?"

"So that one may walk without being trampled or knocked over by coaches. They're not allowed in the footpaths, though sedan chairs are." Redmagne peered out the same window. "Actually, I've always thought those paths should be raised above the muck of the streets. Wrote a letter to *Gentlemen's Magazine* years ago suggesting just that, when I was with the troupe. Started quite a debate, though nothing came of it."

When they had unpacked their things in their room in the Three Swans, Redmagne said, "It's still light out, Jack. Dawson will still be open. Come on. We'll have dinner, then take a brisk walk to his shop."

They walked along the Strand, then up Fleet Street. Redmagne pointed out the Bank of England, the Inns of Court, and other noteworthy sights, appending a running commentary. He was not certain that his companion heard everything he said. A great carriage-and-four passed them as they approached the Fleet Bridge, and one of the footmen standing on the back of the vehicle was black, the first black man Jack Frake had ever seen. "Where did he come from?" he asked.

"Most likely his parents were brought here as slaves from Africa long before he was born, else he could not have risen to so high a station as *footman*," said Redmagne with irony. "One of our egregious faults, Jack, is the slave trade. There are ships down river, and at anchor in Bristol, crammed bilge to deck with those people, and many of them won't live long enough to be slaves once they start the crossing to the colonies. They'll die en route, and their bodies will be tossed overboard. Rival tribes in Africa round them up and sell them to the slavers. I don't know about the condition of the Negroes in the colonies, but those who live here have their own clubs and taverns, and even their own newspaper."

"Why don't they revolt, or demand their rights?"

"Why don't *we*, Jack?"

Jack Frake thought about it for a moment. Then, in affectionate mockery of his friend's style, he answered, "A good question, Redmagne — and the beginning of a good answer."

They stopped at a bookseller's shop, and Redmagne laughed when he found a pirated copy of *Hyperborea*. He bought it, and said to the proprietor, "You have impeccable taste in literature, sir."

The bookseller grinned up at him. “Thank you, sir. That’s one of our most popular titles.”

“And questionable scruples,” added Redmagne.

“Sir?”

“I shall not receive a single penny in compensation for all the copies you sell.”

The bookseller’s mouth opened. “Are you claiming to be Romney Marsh?”

“I *am* Romney Marsh.”

“Well, sir, you must admit that *anyone* could claim that.”

Redmagne quoted from memory a passage from one of the longer chapters.

The bookseller looked uncomfortable. He began to stammer something, but opened his money drawer to return Redmagne’s money. Then he stopped and regarded Redmagne with suspicion.

Redmagne laughed. “Keep the money, sir! You have some scruples, and I would not penalize you for that. Good day to you.”

When they rounded a corner of Fleet Street from the bookseller’s, Jack Frake stopped in astonishment at the sight of St. Paul’s Cathedral a few blocks away. As they came closer, he could not take his eyes off of it. It loomed above the chimneys, gabled roofs and modest steeples of the neighborhood, then soared above them, majesty in its round colonnade and dome that rendered its origins, use and purpose irrelevant. Religion, indeed, was nothing to Jack Frake; the great domed pile seemed, to him, not addressed to God, nor to the King, but to something greater than those inaccessible entities. It was an immense sight, the Cathedral, as immense as he felt about the possibilities of his life. Presumably, he thought, people worshipped in it; presumably, they held as sacred the things they worshipped. He thought that it was appropriate that so great a thing was the venue for so important an action.

“Truly a wonder of construction, Jack,” said Redmagne. “As the mass rises, the stone on each level is of a lighter weight.”

“It’s marvelous,” said the boy in a near whisper.

“That can’t be denied,” said Redmagne, glancing up at Wren’s monument to authority. “Remember, though, that it is not only a cathedral; it is also the state, toleration of Dissenters, Jews and Quakers notwithstanding.” He paused. “The lightest stone in that magnificent pile, Jack, can kill you just as easily as the heaviest — depending on the hand that pushes it.”

It was when they entered the premises of A. Dawson & Son, Printers, on Paternoster Row, that Redmagne encountered another of his country's egregious faults. Dawson saw them from the rear of the shop and rushed to meet them at the door. He took Redmagne aside and hurriedly whispered, "There is a problem, sir!"

"With the engravings?"

"No, sir. There has been talk in the newspapers about your book!" The printer took a newspaper from under his apron and pressed it in Redmagne's hands. "Sir, if you would take this and meet me in half an hour at the Graceful Garter, where we first talked, it would be, well, convenient."

Redmagne frowned, and his expression demanded an explanation.

Dawson said, "Please, sir, read the proclamation on page one! Now, please, sir, leave the premises! I beg of you, no questions now! We may be observed!"

Redmagne stared at the printer, it seemed to Jack Frake, for a very long time. It was actually only a moment, but it doused the exuberance with which they had entered the shop. Redmagne smiled, tucked the paper under an arm, and without another word, doffed his hat, and turned to walk out the door. Jack Frake followed.

Chapter 18: The Betrayal

THE GRACEFUL GARTER WAS A COFFEEHOUSE ON DISTAFF LANE, A FEW blocks away from Dawson's shop. The place was a noisy hive of printers, dealers, tradesmen and apprentices. It was bigger than the Sea Siren, and, being in the center of London, more cosmopolitan in the composition of its clientele. They went in, found a table, and after Redmagne had ordered them coffee, he unfolded the paper. It was the *London Gazette*, dated two weeks earlier. The first proclamation read:

"Whereas John Smith, of Wapping, the city of London, commonly called Rory O'Such, Toby Trist, Methuselah Redmagne, Vivian Crisp, and divers other names, author of a recent work called *Hyperborea*, was, upon the 16th day of April, 1744, on information of a credible person upon oath, by him, subscribed before James Wicker, one of His Majesty's Justices of the Peace for the County of Cornwall, arrested in Gwynnford in said county by agents of His Majesty's Treasury, under suspicion of running and carrying away uncustomed goods; then did subsequently flee said arrest while armed with firearms with the assistance of members of the notorious Skelly gang; which information was afterwards certified by James Wicker, under his hand and seal, who has laid the same before His Majesty in his Privy Council, who doth require and command that John Smith do surrender himself within the space of forty days, after the first publication of this order in the *London Gazette*... "

Redmagne handed the paper to Jack Frake. "Who knew that *name*?" he asked himself.

Jack Frake read the proclamation. "That's why that coachman knew your name! He must have read this." He paused. "What name?" he asked.

"Toby Trist."

"Drury Trantham's cabin boy?"

"Yes." Redmagne explained that no one should have known that he was the author of the novel, except someone who recognized the name of Toby Trist. "You see, Jack, the title of the masque my troupe was performing that unfortunate day was *Toby Trist: or, A Taxing Dilemma*. Trist was a picaroon, an opportunist, and a rogue who, because of some fantastic circumstances — they can only occur in satires — becomes First Lord of the Treasury for a week. Not only is he an unscrupulous, corruptible fellow who makes placemen of all his pauper friends and criminal associates, but also he hasn't bathed in ten years, and he has halitosis. Obviously a caricature of Robert Walpole." Redmagne paused. "When I went to ground after Epping's son died of a broken neck, I had no time to save all of my work. I had just enough time to stuff my bag and vacate my room. No copies of that masque survived. The troupe disbanded and my friends joined other troupes or found other employment. I had presumed the masque lost. But the Marquis is dead, and his other sons were not even at the performance. The masque was never published, and that evening's was its only performance. Someone remembered that name."

"Why did you use it again in *Hyperborea*?"

"For remembrance's sake, Jack. I wanted to mark a connection between my old life and this one, if only in the form of a minor character, as a contrast, and a continuation."

After a while, Dawson came in, spotted Redmagne, and hurried to his table and sat down. He shook his head when Redmagne offered to buy him a coffee or an ale. There was fear in his eyes; Jack Frake could not determine what was its cause. The man hunched forward and said, "I'm sorry, sir, but I've come under pressure to abandon your book." He glanced around him and continued in a lower voice. "Certain people don't like it!"

"Don't like it?" replied Redmagne. "What of it?"

"Why, even Mr. Griggs has decided to withdraw his encomium which prefaces it! In fact, he plans to have printed a pamphlet of apology and repudiation!" Mr. Dawson snorted. "And he's given the business to another printer. That's gratitude!"

"Did I misinterpret your letter, Mr. Dawson?" asked Redmagne. He took out his pipe and a twist of tobacco, slowly packed the clay bowl, and took his time lighting it.

"No, sir! You did not misinterpret it! I gave it to the postman a day before I read the... er... proclamation." Dawson paused, then asked, "Is there any truth in it, sir?"

"In the proclamation?" answered Redmagne with a smile and a puff from his pipe. "Yes, it was all a true bill. Incomplete, but true."

"Oh, God!" exclaimed the printer, pushing his chair back a little. "I've been a fool!"

Jack Frake saw now of whom the printer was afraid: Redmagne. For some reason, it made him angry.

Redmagne saw it, too, and shook his head. "My dear Mr. Dawson, I must assure you that you are in less danger from me than from the authorities." Then he casually asked, "Which certain people don't like *Hyperborea*, Mr. Dawson?"

"I don't know *which* people, sir!" said Dawson. "There is simply a general, well, sentiment about it, expressed in the most curious curiosity! Gentlemen come into my shop and ask about you, the author, in a way that lets me know in no uncertain terms that the book displeases them. Others have come in and spoiled the book, throwing an *unpurchased* copy of it on the floor and using it as, well, as a chamber pot! In *my* place! Still others have struck up conversations with me on the subject of licenses and the penalties for printing seditious-like material — without naming the book or you, sir." Dawson paused, then leaned forward even closer to whisper, "They say there is a secret, select Commons committee studying your book. They *say* — I *hear* — " he emphasized, "though it has not been reported anywhere. I have been merely a collector of hints. Nothing has been said *openly*."

"Not even in *Gentleman's Magazine*, or *London Magazine*?" asked Redmagne. These two were the only publications that successfully evaded the 1660 ban on reporting Parliamentary debates and proceedings, by employing the devices of hyperbole, allusion, and innuendo.

"By my troth, sir, not even *they* have mentioned this matter," said the printer. He looked miserable. "It's too daunting, sir!"

"And which newspapers?"

"Oh, just the government papers. You know, *The Journal*, *The Mid-Day Post*, *The Register*. They've done nothing more than make asides and passing comments of a snickering nature, burying them in items from abroad. It's clear to me that if it weren't for the war news, they'd devote more time and space to this particular subject."

"But you haven't been subpoenaed, or had your place searched?"

"No, but it could come to that if I continue printing the book — especially with illustrations!" Dawson furtively glanced around again. "Look, sir: I regret to say that the last edition of your book must be, well, the *last* edition. I *dare* not press another. You can see my position. A single torch tossed into the shop, or a gang of ruffians destroying my presses — I could be ruined! And I'd have no proof of misdemeanor against anyone." He reached into his coat, took out a small sack and plunked it on the table in front of Redmagne. "Here are the proceeds coming to you, per our contract. Please be satisfied with it."

"Keep it, Mr. Dawson," said Redmagne with contempt, shoving the sack away. "Print yourself a book on the life of St. Bruno, or of Galileo. Sign it 'Anonymous.'"

"Sir, that is unkind of you!" exclaimed Mr. Dawson. Then he sniffed and added, "Not to say vain, and presumptuous!"

"Is it? At least I can say to myself, 'Thank God for pirates!' Good day to you, sir."

Mr. Dawson, now livid, stood up and made to leave. At the last moment, he snatched up the bag of coins and walked out of the tavern.

"When there's no definition of sanity," remarked Redmagne, "even sane men can be called mad." He finished his coffee. Jack Frake noticed that his friend's hands were shaking. "Come, Jack. Let us do some detecting work, and seek out the one responsible for my literary anagnorisis."

They spent the remainder of the day visiting small theaters and old haunts in search of Redmagne's former colleagues. Finally, long after sunset, in the Orange Tree, a tavern that was an actors' rendezvous on a side street off of Longacre, Redmagne recognized William Leggate, the property master of his old troupe. And the man recognized Redmagne as he approached his corner table, for he excused himself from his party and hurriedly guided Redmagne back outside before he was halfway inside the crowded, smoke-fogged tavern. They stood just outside the shadow cast by a sputtering street lamp.

"John, what are you doing here?" he asked with urgency.

"I've come for the express purpose of *not* attending Lord Lovat's axing on Tower Hill," chuckled Redmagne. He paused and studied the anxious look on his old colleague's face. "Good evening to you, too, William," he added. "It's been ages, hasn't it?" He took Leggate's hand and shook it with emphasis.

"We haven't time to make merry or rollick through old times, John!" insisted the man. "They've been looking for you!"

"Who has?"

"Watchmen! And constables! A pair were in here not half an hour ago, and came straight to me with questions!" Leggate put a hand on Redmagne's shoulder. "John, it's known you're in London, and there's a price on your head! *Fifty* guineas for your mere arrest!"

Jack Frake said, "It must have been the Neaveses, Redmagne! They went straight to the bailiff in Ealing!"

Redmagne nodded in agreement. Leggate said, looking down at the boy, "Who's this?"

Redmagne made the introductions. "Jack, Mr. Leggate here could make a gown for Lady Yarmouth out of potato sacks, and she'd be proud to wear it to the Lord Mayor's Water Procession." He paused. "And it was Mr. Leggate who made the fatal weapon with which I poked Master Hockaday that evening, out of a barrel stave, of all things. What are you doing now, William?"

"I'm costumer for another troupe — but never mind me, John! Get out of London quick as you can! You're bound to be caught if you stay."

Redmagne was adamant. "That may be. However, I *will* have some gossip from an old friend. Is it true, what I hear? That Garrick is to marry La Violette?" he asked wistfully.

Leggate nodded impatiently. "She's made enough in the ballet to retire, and it's said her patroness is negotiating a stiff contract."

"There are holes in your shoes, William," said Redmagne, lightly tapping the objects of his scrutiny with the tip of his cane. "And your elbows are threadbare. Perhaps you should sew yourself a costume."

"I would if we could scare up more engagements, John," said Leggate with bitterness. "But the war pinched many a pocket, especially those of the higher stratum. My new troupe did a masque at the Earl of Bracken's last Tuesday, and his butler warned us to bring our own lunches!"

"Well, so much for our gossip." Redmagne frowned. "Have *you* read my book, William?"

"Yes, I have," said Leggate. "Wonderful work! I envy you for having written it. It's not your usual stuff and nonsense, brilliant as that may have been." The man relented and smiled. "If you want an epitaph for your gravestone, John, I'll suggest one here and now: 'I have gone neither to Heaven, nor to Hell, but to Hyperborea."

With a slight bow of his head, Redmagne said, "Thank you, William."

Leggate said, "It was Toby Trist who put me onto the identity of the real author. If it weren't for him, I'd never have imagined."

Redmagne glanced at Jack Frake. "What did I tell you?" Then he asked Leggate, "And who else would you think had the same recollection — and would be in a position to point a finger?"

"Adeline Cole," snapped the actor.

"There was enough acid in that reply to etch a Hogarth print, William. Why?"

"It *must* have been Adeline Cole, John!" said Leggate. "You see, she married Nicholas Hockaday — Epping's oldest son — or rather, he married her, set his sights on her one evening when she was doing pratfalls for another troupe, and away she went; she won't even speak to any of us now, her old troupers. And Nicholas Hockaday is secretary to the *Solicitor-General*! He'll be Marquis of Epping soon, for his uncle is prone with the fever and is not expected to outlive it."

"I see," sighed Redmagne. Adeline Cole, on the night of the masque, played opposite him as Idonea Lumley, mistress of a deposed Privy Council adviser. "Well," he mused, "she always envied me the last bow of an entertainment. But, then, I *was* the author of all our triumphs. And, then, I think she was furious with me because I never invited her to rehearse slap and tickle — except on the stage."

Leggate chuckled. "That's right. I remember. But she certainly rehearsed it with everyone else." He squinted into the darkness and saw a pair of men carrying staves coming in their direction. "John, go now!" he whispered. "They can't see us yet. Please go! And Godspeed!"

Redmagne turned, saw the men ambling up the street from Longacre, and then clasped Leggate's hand. "Thank you, William, for your worry, and for not asking me where I'm staying! Those fifty guineas are tempting, I know. Wait! Here!" He reached into his purse and dropped a handful of guineas into Leggate's coat pocket. "Ill-gotten gains for you, William. Don't argue! We'll meet again!"

Redmagne and Jack Frake turned and walked quickly down the street, taking care to stay in the shadows of the street lamps. They went back to the Three Swans Inn.

Chapter 19: The Tour

AT THE INN, THEY ATE A LIGHT DINNER, AND THEN RETIRED TO THEIR room. There they removed their wigs, coats and shoes. There was a single window, which Redmagne opened and moved a chair to. He looked morose. Jack Frake asked, "Will you try to see your father?"

Redmagne frowned and shook his head. "No, Jack. I tried mending things between him and me years ago. But he has a conscience to salve and a shame to erase. He would turn me in to the Crown with a speed that would make Adeline Cole blink." He chuckled. "He was so set on my going into law, and then politics. Obviously he places no value on all the jokes about lawyers and politicians."

Jack Frake leafed through his book of Roman history for a while. Redmagne said nothing, but gazed out the window. Then the boy asked, "Why does it bother you?"

"What bothers me, Jack?"

"The book, and Dawson and this actress you knew."

"Because I have been betrayed, Jack. I've known a great many injustices, but I've never before been betrayed. And what was the vehicle of that betrayal? *Hyperborea*! I've done a few things in my life of which I am proud, but that book is my proudest act. And so, there sat Adeline Cole, passing an afternoon with, to her, an amusing novel, waiting for dear Nicholas to return from the Law Court at Westminster Hall. She came upon the name of Toby Trist. 'Who's that flapper?' she asks herself. 'Why, if it isn't John Smith, up to his old tricks again! Lud! What a piece of information this is! My husband could use it and advance himself in the eyes of his gouty grace the Solicitor-General!' And so she did the deed. Well, I was right to cast her as Idonea Lumley. She betrayed Toby Trist in the masque, too." He shrugged. "Dawson? Well, I thought he would have a little more spine."

Jack Frake did not like the pain he saw in Redmagne's eyes.

Redmagne went on. "That highwayman you wounded, Jack — remember him? There is a similarity here. You see, the ball entered a part of his body, and his body and all its parts asked the question: This is a foreign thing that has invaded us. How shall we deal with it? But the body cannot deal with it. That is why men die of their wounds."

"You should not let it disturb you so, Redmagne," volunteered Jack Frake.

For the first time ever, Redmagne glared at him with anger. The boy stared back at him. He saw that his friend wanted to reply, but would not permit himself to.

Jack Frake said, "Your soul has been winded, Redmagne. But it can recover. There's no profit in being the man who could not be the author of *Hyperborea*. Be him again."

Redmagne held his glance for a while, and then looked out the window. "Forgive me for being angry with you, Jack. You're right." He lit his pipe again, and picked up one of several newspapers he had bought in a tavern on their way back to the Inn. But after a moment, he dropped it. "Listen, Jack!" he said. "It's ten o'clock. Listen to the bells marking the hour, all around the city. The parishes, whose churches don't have bells, have watchmen call out the hour. You can hear them, too. Listen; you can hear the quiet roar from under London Bridge, and the carriages rolling over its length, many on their way to Ranelagh Gardens. Listen hard enough, and you can hear people singing outside their tenements and taverns, or catch the sound of hautboys and oboes and violins of a private chamber concert." He paused. "Listen, and you can hear the whisper of Millicent Morley's nightgown as she enters little Etain McRae's bedroom to sing her a lullaby. She must know, Jack. She must have known that the Neaveses did their dirty deed, too. Would she still want a wanted man? Verily, I believe she would." He paused. "I must see her again before we leave. I'll find her."

Redmagne picked the newspaper up again. "Jack, I am resolved that we shall have one proper evening here. They will not rob us of that, at least."

He looked at his companion. "Are you willing to risk it?"

"Yes," answered Jack Frake.

Redmagne snapped the paper. "Then tomorrow we shall tour the town. The season ended in April, and many concert patrons have fled the city for the summer, but tomorrow evening Viscountess Oldham's opera company is performing a *pasticcio* of Handel's arias and choruses at the King's Theatre, Haymarket. It's a benefit for widows and wounded soldiers of the Scottish campaign, at five guineas a ticket, so we needn't worry about seats. Following that, *we* shall dine at Ranelagh." He threw the paper aside. "But tonight, we sleep."

The next day, Redmagne took Jack Frake all over the city — to London Bridge, to the Steelyard, to the Timber Yards, to the various waterworks, to the nine-story Dye Houses on the Thames. They even browsed through the bookshops in St. Paul's Churchyard. But while Redmagne was as generous with his descriptions and anecdotes as usual, their tour was soured by an undercurrent of jeopardy. They knew that they could be seized at any moment.

Redmagne visited the offices of several tobacco merchants and asked for information about Ian McRae, partner in a firm that traded with Virginia — and Millicent Morley's employer. No one had heard of him. "You might try Glasgow," quipped a junior partner in one establishment. "Those damned Scots are horning in on our business."

They next went to Cornhill, a section of the city that contained the Royal Exchange and numerous merchants' coffeehouses. In the Virginia and Maryland Coffeehouse they had to press through an especially noisy group of merchants, brokers, agents and ship captains. The place was more like a commodities exchange than a place of relaxation. A Scots trader had heard of McRae, but could not remember the names of his associates, and did not know where he lived.

Redmagne kept his promise and took Jack Frake to the site of Skelly's emporium. It was covered now with shanty hovels made of scraps and discards from the city's refuse, and lay just half a block from a prosperous street. Beggars, prostitutes, and children in rags eyed them hungrily as they stood there, and to keep them away Redmagne drew the sword from his cane as a warning. "I can't look at this without cursing the Crown, Jack. Skelly's business could have been a jewel of the city. Instead, the Crown's greed has spawned an ugly blight that has become a charge to us all. There's not a single creature in that dunghill who isn't in the almshouse racket —

and who thinks he needn't try to leave it or this dunghill, and has made poverty his career." He turned away in disgust. "Come, Jack. Enough of this. Let us go into the enemy's camp, and watch him preen himself. The Duke of Cumberland is reviewing the Horse Guards on the Parade Grounds. 'Tis a sight to see." Back on the Strand, Redmagne hailed a hackney and told him to drive to Whitehall.

From a distance, on the edge of the field, standing with a crowd of other onlookers, they watched the Duke review the mass of mounted scarlet after the Guards performed intricate maneuvers on the green expanse. As the Duke rode up and down with his aides between the ranks of the assembled cavalry, the band of the Foot Guards played The Hohen-friedberger March. Jack Frake had never heard a band before, and he watched the musicians carefully. He noticed that the drummers were black men, leopard skins crossed over their tunics and green and yellow ostrich plumes adorning their caps.

Little of this would Jack Frake be able to remember as a continuous whole. The magnitude, elegance, variety, beauty, crudity and shabbiness of all the things he saw and heard registered in specific places in his mind, and would come back to him later, unsummoned, for reasons he would grasp only after long incubation, in a flash of insight or realization.

But there was one thing he carried away from London as a distinct memory. It was a single chorus from the *pasticcio* at the King's Theatre that evening. Again, this was his first time in a theater; the magical scenery, the vibrant actors and singers, the stupendous orchestra laboring in the pit, was a beckoning confluence of elements funneled in the darkness of the vast chamber to a single elevated frame of light, all combining to hold him in awe at both his capacity to enjoy it and men's capacity to imagine it and produce it. The musical numbers followed one after another, but the one that seemed to turn his nerves to atoms and reduce his soul to a quivering aspic of gratitude was the last, "See, the conquering hero comes." A soprano led the chorus in the performance, and many in the audience joined in. The power, the lyrics, and the delivery of it invited him to adopt it as his personal anthem. He thought that this must be what was sung in St. Paul's Cathedral; at least, he associated the chorus with that edifice. When it was over, and attendants appeared to relight the candles for the departing audience, Jack Frake sniffed and was surprised to feel a tear roll down his cheek.

Redmagne noticed it, but did not comment. "It says here," he remarked, holding a candle to his program, "that the last chorus was included in *Judas Maccabaeus* in the season last year. But I attended a performance of that oratorio, and I don't remember it." He closed his program. "Oh, well. The whims of composers are a mystery, even to me."

To this, Jack Frake's reply was merely to wipe his cheek with his sleeve.

When they were outside, they lingered for a while at the entrance to watch a succession of carriages come to pick up aristocrats, merchants and other wealthy patrons, and also to wait for a hackney looking for a fare.

"Look!" said Jack Frake, pointing to the night sky. "What is it?"

Up the river, somewhere over Whitehall, the streak of a rocket burst into a star of blue, gold and red, and before its arching, falling arms faded, another star exploded, and another.

"Fireworks, Jack," said Redmagne. "Some duke or other is celebrating an event, or entertaining guests. Well, does it matter which? It's a pretty sight."

After a moment of watching the display, Jack Frake exclaimed, "Oh, Redmagne! I belong here!"

Redmagne clasped his shoulder. "So do I, Jack," he sighed. "So do I."

Ranelagh Gardens, outside the city in Chelsea, on the north side of the Thames, was an imposing round rococo building enclosed by landscaped grounds. Beneath a vast rotunda and in the center of a wide promenade was a fireplace that reached to the chandelier-hung ceiling eighty feet above. The night was warm, and so no fire had been lit. Two tiers of private boxes looked over the space, broken only by an enclosed multi-level orchestra stand. The tables around the fireplace were laid with red baize cloth and fine silver tableware; thousands of candles produced as much light as the noonday sun. Paying guests would stroll in groups or pairs on the promenade around the fireplace and the red baize tables, while musicians in the orchestra serenaded them with violins, oboes and harpsichords. It was a place to see princes and princesses, lords and ladies, and even dukes and duchesses, to be seen by them and to walk in their footsteps; perhaps to exchange nods, bows, curtsies and even frigid smiles. It was a place to gossip and to gather gossip for the next day, a place to flirt with all propriety, and to make discreet arrangements for a passionate tryst that same evening. The sparce fare of cold cuts, coffee and tea was expensive, served with grace and efficiency by an army of waiters. Redmagne ordered triple portions of everything for himself and Jack Frake. "On each of our plates, thank you," he instructed the attentive, liveried waiter, "as when we take a stroll we wish to converse with each other, and not with each other's stomachs."

They sat at a table in a box and watched the leisurely, talkative parade of guests. A bejeweled lady in the next box flirted with Redmagne, but his stare was distant. Jack Frake knew that his mind was on Millicent Morley, and that he was desperate to find some trace of her in the city before he left.

"Is this all one does?" asked Jack Frake, looking at the people with amazement.

"This is all one does," confirmed Redmagne. "It is human company of a sort, I suppose. I thought it would be more enchanting. But it is not. Now it is reminiscent of a racecourse. One may place bets on who speaks first to whom. It is an aspect of London I don't miss." Then his whole body became alert when he spied someone in the crowd. Jack Frake looked to see who it was. A family had come in and was being shown to a table near the fireplace by a splendidly attired assistant master of ceremonies. He recognized Millicent Morley, who held Etain McRae's hand as they followed the parents at a discreet distance. He smiled, and was pleased to see Redmagne beaming.

"Jack," said Redmagne, "there will be a short delay in our departure from here. We will not leave until I have a moment with her."

That moment came half an hour later, when the governess rose and took the daughter for a turn around the promenade. In the meantime, Redmagne, between snatches of conversation with Jack Frake, had taken out his brass box and penciled a missive on five pieces of paper. Into these he folded two golden guineas.

Redmagne left the box as Miss Morley and the girl passed them. Hat under arm, he followed the governess and her charge for a moment, and then strode up beside her. "Milady, you are again about to be accosted by a bandit."

Miss Morley started, first at the sound of his voice, then at sight of him. She stopped with a gasp. "It's Redmagne," said Etain McRae, pointing up at him. Then she hid behind her governess's skirts, and would crane her neck now and then for a peek at him.

Redmagne said, "Do continue walking, Miss Morley. Your employer and others will simply conclude that I am just another Ranelagh rogue."

Miss Morley obeyed. "Have you been stalking me?" she asked in a whisper.

"No," said Redmagne. "I asked about for your employer, Mr. McRae, in the city, but no one there knew him."

"He has been here only a year," said the governess, "and is only a junior partner." She paused, then said, "Oh, Mr. Trigg! I did *not* think I would see you again!"

"Have you recovered from your trip?"

"Yes, thank you. As soon as we reached Ealing, the Neaveses went to the constable there, and told them about you and your nephew. And then the constable sent a messenger to the city."

Redmagne chuckled. "I'm afraid the hue and cry was raised long before the Neaveses had the notion. The book I recommended to you may be banned. I am in danger, and cannot stay here for long." Redmagne twirled his cane. "But — what *is* your employer's address, Miss Morley?"

"Crooked Lane, by St. Michael's church, near the Monument."

"I know the street." Redmagne paused to study the governess's profile. He noticed a white ribbon peeking out from beneath her cape. "I see that you are a sympathizer, Miss Morley. Does Mr. McRae tolerate such a display of politics?"

"A sympathizer of what, Mr. Trigg?"

"Of the Jacobites, or of Lord Lovat, who is to be axed soon, I have heard." Simon Fraser, Lord Lovat of Scotland, was one of the Young Pretender's chief plotters.

Miss Morley raised her head and stared hard before her. I do not wear it for Lord Lovat or for any cause, Mr. Trigg." Her voice lowered to a near-whisper. "I wear it for you." Before Redmagne could reply, she said, "I did not thank you for the gallantry you showed yesterday. I thank you now."

"Gallantry?" asked Redmagne. "No, it was not gallantry, milady. There were two reasons why I acted so quickly. I do not like being robbed — which is why I am an outlaw."

"You admit it? That you are an outlaw?"

"Freely and with no shame." Redmagne chuckled again. "I daresay I am wealthier than your employer and all his partners combined — excluding the firm's assets, of course. There are many men like me in the country. We are outlaws, but smuggling needs capital, investors, and smart direction, too." He paused. "But, were I standing before you in the rags of an Alsatian footpad, I would admit the same as freely and without shame."

"And your second reason?"

"You, of course, though I suspect that you know that. Mind you, I would have taken the same action had we not befriended each other. But you were there, and that made my aim the truer."

He felt Jack Frake come up beside him. "Redmagne, look!"

The boy was pointing to the entrance near the orchestra far across the promenade. Standing with a group of people waiting to be seated were the Neaveses.

"Damn!" said Redmagne. He took Miss Morley's elbow and hastened her to a point in the promenade where the great column of the fireplace obstructed their view. "Milady, we must go, as you can see. Here are some verses for you." He reached into his coat and handed her the mass of folded paper. "They are not quite as stirring as Lovelace's, but I will improve with time. I promise you." He smiled down at her. "And, should you not have as many shillings to spend as did Pamela, you will find enclosed in that packet something which will enable you to purchase the adventures of a man who could *not* love her."

"*Adieu*, my cavalier," said Miss Morley, clutching the paper and holding it close to her breast. She leaned forward and kissed him lightly on the lips, then turned sharply and led her charge away. "Good-bye, Redmagne," said Etain McRae, who had managed to turn her head and wave to him.

Redmagne grinned, and swept his hat in a low bow, then led Jack Frake to a side entrance.

In the morning they stepped out of the Three Swans, valises in hand, and had a hearty breakfast at the Bedford Coffeehouse in Covent Garden. The place attracted the London literati and Redmagne pointed out some notable wits and writers to Jack Frake. "This would be my second home, if things were otherwise." He perused a newspaper, *The Morning Advocate*, and read a short item in which it was noted that "John Smith, notorious smuggler, is reported to have entered the city under the name of John Trigg, gentleman from Devon, in the company of a boy, whose true name is unknown, and is thought to be staying at one of the better inns. The Sheriff of London has offered a £50 reward to anyone who first lays hand on him in arrest. Innkeepers are advised to scrutinize suspicious-behaving travelers applying for accommodation."

"That was cutting it close," remarked Redmagne, handing the paper to Jack Frake. "Another few hours and we would have found ourselves in irons and sitting in the Fleet Prison."

He had planned to retrace their route back out of the city, but the newspaper item made him cautious. He hired another waterman to row them to Battersea, and in the village there they boarded a coach at an inn on Lavender Hill.

Two days later, they reached Marvel and the caves. Skelly, alerted by the watchman on the hill that they were coming in on the path through the brush, met them at the entrance to greet them.

"Back so soon?" he asked with a grin. "You had leave to spend a week."

Redmagne shook Skelly's hand, and then gave him his copy of the *London Gazette*. "It was a trying but satisfying trip, Augustus," he said. "But you were right. I have been marked for extinction."

Skelly glanced at the proclamation. "But you always knew that," he said.

"Yes. But not for *that* reason."

Chapter 20: The Courier

AUGUSTUS SKELLY NOTICED CHANGES IN REDMAGNE AND JACK FRAKE. He was not sure if these changes boded good or ill. He viewed them from the perspective of a leader who could do little about them.

The reason for Redmagne's change was clear, for it had been confided to him: a woman. The man had, after a series of discreet episodes over the years, met his match, and the man was happy. And miserable. Skelly knew the pain of separation from such a woman, and also a pain that he hoped Redmagne would never know: that his action years ago had probably driven his own wife to suicide. He still did not know which thing moved her to poison herself: remorse, the prospect of a shameful future, or perhaps — and he was willing to concede this last possibility — the loss of the man she had truly loved, the man he had killed. But he would never know which was true, for his wife had left no note.

He understood Redmagne's agony. The woman was not *here*; she was not in the next room, nor at the market, nor just down the lane chatting with a neighbor. She was fifty leagues away in the maw of London. Since July, in the idle times between contraband runs, Redmagne would steal away and be gone for days at a time, returning elated and desperate. His tutorials, which many in the gang paid him for, had almost ceased. His evening entertainments were also missed by the men. His desk was growing dusty. Skelly did not question him and could not stop him, for when there was no smuggling business and none to plan, his time was his own. He had broached the subject with Redmagne of eloping with the woman, of setting her up in a house in Marvel, of even going to the colonies with her. "It can be arranged with Ramshaw," he told his lieutenant one evening. "He would do it for nothing. He knows men in New York, Philadelphia, Charleston and Boston. In all the principal towns. You needn't worry about finding an occupation or trade."

Redmagne had shaken his head. "I've thought of those things, too, Augustus. But it's her father. He's a clerk for one of McRae's partners. And he owes this employer his life, for this man paid a surgeon to have her father's arm and leg set after an accident. The man is otherwise a nasty piece of goods. He'd make her father's life impossible, if she left. And she won't leave."

Jack Frake was another matter. Ever since his return from London, Skelly had watched him grow more and more restive. Not in any way that interfered with his tasks, nor in any manner that affected his character. The change lay in the way the boy now looked at things; a greater knowledge of the world showed in his eyes, and his self-assurance was more pronounced.

One day in late September, they sat together on the hill above the caves. Skelly had gone up to the watch post, a patch of grass concealed by outcroppings of rock. The leaves in the brush and trees surrounding the caves were fast turning into a palette of autumnal colors.

"I'm growing envious of Redmagne," he said to the boy. He knew the story about the highwaymen. "When will you save *my* life?"

"At the first opportunity," replied Jack Frake.

"Let's hope one doesn't present itself," said Skelly. After a moment, he said, "You ought to think on that subject he told me you raised in the coach. On government reports and mythical lost revenues. You put your finger on something that's eluded me for years. Perhaps you, too, could have a letter printed in a newspaper."

Jack Frake was silent for a moment. Skelly saw a spark of interest in his eyes, but this was not the bright eagerness he was accustomed to seeing. The boy shook his head with a pensive frown. "No, sir. Not a letter. I'd want to write a book on it."

"Another book?" chuckled Skelly. "My gang is producing so many scriveners!" Then, in a serious vein, he added, "Jack, I envy you your future. I truly do."

"I'd dedicate it to you, if I ever wrote it," said Jack Frake. "You shouldn't be living like this. You ought to be living *there*." He pointed to the vacant Villers mansion in the distance. "Or in London."

"Thank you," said Skelly. He lit his pipe, then asked, "Are you beginning to regret your shadowy life with us?"

"No, sir. I'll never regret it. I think I'll be a better man for my time with you and Redmagne and the others."

"You do us proud now. But — there are saner ways of becoming a man. And of being one. I told you in the beginning that ours is not a normal way to live."

"No, it isn't. But it's more honorable."

Skelly sighed with impatience. "'Honor' is such an empty notion nowadays. There is a better word for what you mean. The vilest rake in Parliament can claim honor. No, what moves us, Jack, is something more substantial." He smiled. "I'm sure you'll find the right word for it someday."

Jack Frake's sight was fixed on the surrounding countryside. Skelly studied his face for a moment, then asked, "Have you thought on Captain Ramshaw's proposal? You could ship out with him as a cabin boy. This time next year you could be somewhere in the colonies, starting anew. There's no future for you here, living like *this*." His pipe swept the panorama and dipped to the ground to include the caves below.

"No, sir," said the boy. "I mean, I've thought on it, but I'd rather stay. I'd like to see London again." Jack Frake was not thinking of escape, or of relief. His imagination was still dazzled by the possibilities in his life in his own home.

"Can't say I blame you," said Skelly. "I may visit London myself again, soon. And you're welcome to come with me. Well, Redmagne — blast it, Jack, you've got me calling him that, now! — he's brought a letter from Ramshaw. The *Sparrowhawk* will be laid up in Boston for a while, having her hull scraped and all new rigging strung to her. We won't see her again until next spring at the earliest. Give his offer a farthing's more thought, Jack. Promise me?"

Jack Frake looked at Skelly with alarm. "Have I displeased you somehow, sir?"

"Displeased me?" scoffed Skelly. "Huh! Quite the opposite, Jack. I value your company highly. I simply want to see you put your energy to better use." He paused. "I said I envied you your future. I didn't mean as a smuggler."

The boy smiled in gratitude. "I promise I'll think on it. About Ramshaw, I mean."

Jack Frake did not immediately find the right word, nor did he identify the last piece of a puzzle, the rivet that sealed the independence of his mind.

Until London, he had been content to remain with Skelly and the gang; indeed, prepared to remain indefinitely outside the bounds of what he observed passed for normal human existence. Skelly, Redmagne and the others — but especially Skelly and Redmagne — were his measures of all other men, including himself. Skelly he regarded as a kind of father, a model of practical wisdom and moral rectitude. Redmagne he saw as an ideal older brother, even though the man was not many years Skelly's junior.

But there comes a time in every man's life when he must make himself the measure, not of any others, but of all else. "All else" encompasses animal and inanimate matter, and so it is implied that he should command these, and not men. This is a bold but necessary step; growth and the ineluctable cementing of character require it. It is a time when character sets itself for life, and all other aspects of oneself become derivatives and extensions of it. A few men are able to reach this state of autonomous self-possession; others cease to be their measures or models. The world begins when such a man is born in this sense — to paraphrase an American poet — and the world is his to win. He reaches this state, thanks neither to divine favoritism nor to special pedigree, but because he has retained a tight grip on his original, uncorrupted, and undiminished perspective.

Far at the bottom of this scale of character, many, many more men fail utterly, do not even try to reach that threshold, and become the puppets of things as they are. To cement one's character requires one to commit oneself to one supreme, achievable thing, and these latter men wish only to indulge everything and devote themselves to the minuscule or to nothing.

Jack Frake was of the first echelon. The Whitehall Stairs were his threshold. Handel's anthem, "See, the conquering hero comes," informed him of this moment. It had been sung with heartfelt gusto by the soprano and chorus, hurled imperiously by them at the audience, and Jack Frake was a ready subject of this spiritual assault. He did not sing with others in the audience, but remained solemnly still and surrendered to the music. One does not join in a tribute to oneself.

He had seen things in London that he would not care to see every day, or ever again. He did not think he would want to live there, except on his own terms. Skelly and Redmagne belonged there, too: Skelly with his business acumen, his ability to buy and sell, his talent for juggling the wealth of the world and redistributing it in ingenious ways, to his own profit; Redmagne with his literary vision, and his need to address men of like mind, if not of like spirit. But Jack Frake had seen the devastated lot of Skelly's former emporium, and had witnessed the sabotaging of Redmagne's chances.

He was of two minds, concerning London. It was a city that granted the possible to everyone but these two men, and for that should be put to a fiercer torch than that which leveled it in the Great Fire. It was a city that could be conquered and remade so that he and Skelly and Redmagne could live in it and thrive. He hated London; he loved London. London with its various species of customs men — the beggars, the footpads, the court sycophants, the dilettantes, the yes-men — as well as the appointed ones at Customs House, was uninhabitable by the likes of him. The London that birthed and reared all the wonderful things possible only in a great city was his natural field of action.

It was October. He sat on a length of driftwood on a beach with four other men. A dozen ponies stood tethered together in back of them. They were waiting for the first galley to return from the *Ariadne* with its contraband, which they would quickly unload and secure to the sides and backs of the ponies while the galley returned for another load. It was dark, the clouds scudded past the moon, but the wind and waves were calm. He could not help but think of all the ships anchored below London Bridge in the bright sunlight, waiting to be cleared or unloaded by the lightermen.

They may act in the sunshine, he thought, because they are willing to pay a duty, or a bribe. We must move in darkness, and exile ourselves to the shadows. They may move in daylight, and reap all the benefits of liberty, without fear of arrest, under their own names, and sit in the coffeehouses and taverns and concert halls. They may plan their days and nights and lives without hindrance. We may plan only our nights, and assume other names and trades by day, when we dare. They may, and we may not — because we will not submit.

He wished with all his heart that he could want to live in London. But his knowledge of it smothered any seed of self-delusion about his chances of prospering there. The knowledge stung him to the core. But then, he thought, the price of free, unfettered movement now was slavery, or servitude. The import of Skelly's words to him that first night in the caves came to him again and again. "Chains are a more honest form of slavery than the specious liberty enjoyed by most of our countrymen."

It was a mean, trifling thing to complain about being a slave for only a fraction of one's time. He knew that this was how most men thought about the matter. To surrender that fraction granted one entree to the world. But it was a great source of solace, he also knew, to refuse that trifling fraction, for then the world was truly one's own, and nothing in it could be held hostage by any kind of customs man.

It was solace, he thought, but a disturbing kind of solace. He was not certain that he could live with it the way Skelly and Redmagne could.

When the first galley sliced through the breakers and glided ashore, he splashed into the surf with the others to help tow it in. Five minutes later the galley plunged back into the waves. Fifteen minutes later four of the ponies were laden with parcels of beaver pelts and salt.

One Sunday morning in November, while the majority of Gwynnford's respectable citizens were attending early services at St. Brea's, Hiram Trott wandered out of his bedroom to answer a knock on the kitchen door. He yawned as he ambled through the darkened tavern. He had packed Bob and Clarissa off to St. Brea's, and would dress soon to attend the second service while they prepared the tavern for the day's business. The Sea Siren had been busy until four o'clock in the morning, and the tables had not yet been cleared. Francis Autt, his new scullion, had risen long enough to start a new fire in the main fireplace, then rolled back into his blanket and straw beneath the steps.

Trott paused to glance at the prone figure. He did not like Francis Autt, who was the latest in a series of scullions that followed Jack Frake's departure. Autt was a full-grown man who had worked as a roustabout on the lighters and as a farm laborer. He came from near Trelowe, where he lived with his mother in a cottage. He could not read, could barely count, and his intelligence was as unpredictably mercurial as was his mood. He was a squat, ungainly, dirty little man. Ugly, too, thought Trott, and the long scar on his face did not improve his looks any. He had had to warn the man off Clarissa, who did not welcome his suggestive chit-chat, and had beaten him once when he caught him pocketing his daughter's gratuities.

Autt had applied for the position in late July, and had lasted. And he did the job well enough. He had a good mind to kick the man awake and set him to work clearing the tables. But the man had worked hard last night, and Trott decided to let him sleep a while longer. If he was right about the knock on the door, it was the Skelly courier come to take orders, per arrangement with the previous courier. Autt could stay where he was for the time being.

Trott opened the kitchen door and was pleased to see Jack Frake. The boy had come on this errand many times over the last three years, alternating with Richard Claxon and other members of the gang. It was safe for Jack Frake to come directly into town this Sunday morning; anyone who could recognize him was asleep or in church. "Jack Frake, my boy! Come in!" he exclaimed. Then he remembered his scullion in the next room, and put a finger to his lips. Trott waved him in and closed the door. In a whisper, he offered the boy a mug of coffee.

Jack Frake shook his head, unwrapped the scarf from around his face, and went directly to business. "It's to be west of Penlilly-by-Sea, on the night of the twelfth," he said.

"Humph! Fancy that!" exclaimed Hiram Trott. "My late wife hailed from Penlilly."

"Spread the word to the right ears."

"Oh, be sure of that, Jack. If Mr. Pannell don't hang his ears at the Sea Siren, I'll see the word goes to where he does." Trott paid a handful of trusted local men to patronize his own and other public houses — wherever Commissioner Pannell's agents happened to be — and to talk quietly, but not too quietly, about where a man might pick up some extra coins unloading contraband at night. In exchange for helping in this ruse, Trott was permitted to buy important staples for his inn for less than what other Skelly customers paid. "Meanwhile, you'll be far up the coast?"

"Or down it," replied Jack Frake with a grin. Skelly's orders to his couriers were that they were never to reveal to anyone the true location of a nocturnal landing.

"Yes, of course," sighed Hiram Trott. "Well, here are our orders. Mine, Mr. Rudge's, Mr. Cary's, and Mr. Embry's." He handed the boy several sheets of paper.

Jack Frake glanced at them. "We can get you most of it, and more than enough salt and pepper. But we're short of pommard. They say the French vineyards have had a bad year."

"Spanish will do," replied Trott placidly. "Whatever you and Mr. Skelly can manage."

Jack Frake folded the orders and put them in a leather bag slung over his shoulder. He offered a hand to his former employer. "I've got to go and take orders in Clegg," he said.

Trott playfully squeezed the boy's hand. "Clegg, is it? Seems I recall a fib you told me once about your being from Clegg," he said in mock admonishment. "And how is Mr. Claxon?"

"Down with the chilblains," said Jack Frake.

"When can we expect to see some goods?"

"Soon. We'll send word."

"I see you're still wearing that hat I gave you a while back," noted Trott, pleased. "It's looking a bit tatty, though."

"That's because I'm simply a poor boy on his way to Portsmouth to apprentice himself in the shipbuilding trades," said the boy with a laugh.

"Seems I've heard that line before, too." Trott opened the door and waved once as Jack Frake dashed back out again. He closed and barred the door, then, with a roar of a yawn, shuffled back to his own room.

Chapter 21: The Spy

AT THE SOUND OF THE FALLING LATCH ON TROTT'S DOOR, FRANCIS AUTT sat up. It was not the rap on the back door that had awakened him, nor his employer's heavy tread through the tavern; he knew that tread too well and feared it. Nor was it the hushed voices.

It was the name of Jack Frake.

Autt touched the jagged scar that ran from beneath his left ear and ended somewhere on his cheek. Jack Frake had given him that scar with a hoe, many years ago. He blinked in thought. He had heard talk around Trelowe and Gwynnford about the disappearance of Cephas Frake's son. He remembered thinking with pleasure then that the Skelly men who had taken him probably had tossed him over the cliff and into the Channel. But here he was, working with the gang! And there had been some trouble between the boy and Isham Leith, who was married to Jack Frake's mother now. Francis Autt pondered these and other related matters for the rest of the day, and so excited was he with his discovery that he dropped several dishes and, at one point, began to sweep out the main fireplace with his bare hands before he checked himself. One mishap followed another, and his mind still echoed with Trott's exasperated bellowing at him. While Francis Autt's memory was remarkable — faces, events, and even conversations stuck in his mind with the randomness and stubbornness of objects pressed into tar — his capacity to think seemed mired in the same substance.

As Henoch Pannell had resorted to blackmailing Leith to play informant, Leith was compelled to hire his own informant. Hiram Trott was the town merchants' go-between; of that, he was now certain. It was with great self-restraint that he had stopped himself from running off to tell Pannell. It was important information, but he preferred to hand the Commissioner a richer prize. However, for this purpose he was faced with two obstacles. The first was practical; he could not run his own business and also spend time watching Trott. The second was that he knew that Trott disliked him enough not to risk careless talk or behavior in his presence.

But a day following his observation of the meeting of Trott and the youth on the pony under the tree on the moor, he happened to be in the Sea Siren at the invitation of Gerald Hollings, the town brickmaster, for a few gills of ale to celebrate a minor business transaction. He made another observation; Francis Autt was stealing Clarissa's gratuities. And also sneaking quick nips from patrons' unfinished drinks.

The next day he managed to corner Autt as the latter was on an errand to the coal seller's and browbeat him into spying on Trott. He dangled the incentive of a golden guinea in front of the man's eyes, and promised to pay him as much as Trott was paying him. "You keep a sharp ear out for talk about runnin' goods, 'specially if Trott's doin' the talkin'. If you think somethin's brewin', lie doggo and see what's up. Keep your mouth shut and mind your own nose. And leave off takin' the wench's coin, or I'll box your ears if Trott don't. I'll see you every day about what you hear." He did not tell Autt the real reason for his curiosity about Trott. "I got a secret agreement with him and the freetraders," he explained, "and I just want fair dibs on the next big run. I think I'm bein' cheated. You help me learn when this big run is, and I'll make it worth your bother."

Francis Autt was of that simple ilk that could be persuaded of the truth of anything. Blatant contradictions could sit undisturbed in his mind, and he would neither know them nor be bothered by them. He did not like Leith, for the man had made sport of him in the past. But he disliked Trott more. And, as Trott knew nothing of Autt's relationship to Leith, Autt knew nothing of Leith's relationship to Pannell.

"And not a word to Trott we know each other," warned Leith, "or he'll learn all about your filchin' his daughter's coin and he'll beat you again or even throw you out. Winter's comin', remember, and you'll want a warm place and your mum'll want food on the table."

That night, after the Sea Siren had closed its doors at midnight and the

Trott family retired, Autt crept out and made his way to Trelowe. Leith was not at his first inn, and Peter Leith, the brother, nearly swatted him for disturbing his sleep. Autt ran to the new inn, the Three Ewes, down the county road. This establishment was still serving patrons. Leith frowned when he saw Autt beckon anxiously to him from the door, then excused himself from his wife and hustled the scullion back outside. "What?" he asked with irritation.

Autt whispered his news: There was to be a contraband run on the night of the twelfth, west of Penlilly-by-Sea, up the coast; Trott would see that Pannell didn't hang his ears at the Sea Siren; orders were taken from Trott, Rudge, Cary and Embry; no pommard, because the French vineyards had a bad year; Claxon was down with the chilblains; Frake was just a poor boy on his way to Portsmouth.

The information about Pannell's "ears" was wrong, of course. As nature abhors a vacuum, contradictions tend to correct themselves in excited minds. One is either aware of the correction, or one is ignorant of it. Autt was ignorant of it, and Isham Leith was no wiser for it.

At first, Leith did not gather the full import of his spy's information. Autt did not understand most of it, either. He stood shivering in the cold while Leith digested the words. Nor did he grasp Leith's growing amazement, and then his jubilation when he was told to repeat as much of Trott's and Jack Frake's conversation as he could remember. "They talked low, but I could hear every word!" he said.

Leith laughed like a man who had just won a thousand guineas on a cock-fight wager. "By God, I'm saved!" he exclaimed. Autt at first thought that Leith was crying, but the innkeeper did a mad jig in front of him and then around him, hooting and whooping with joy. Autt said, as an afterthought, "I'd like to take a hoe to that Frake boy, and see how he likes it!"

"Never mind him!" said Leith, finishing his jig with a few friendly slaps on Autt's dour face. "Francis, you're a saint! You outdid my expectations! Now — get back to Trott's before he misses you. Keep an ear open for more talk." Then he frowned, and reached into his apron and gave the man two shillings.

Autt nodded several times in thanks and pocketed the money. "Can I have a swig of gin, Mr. Leith?" he asked. "My innards is cold from the walk, and I got to go back."

"No trouble, Francis," chuckled Leith, going to the inn door. "Wait right here. Not a word to anyone about this, now! Our secret, you see! You down your gin, and off you go."

As he went about his business with his patrons, Leith's mind was preoccupied with Autt's news and how he could get it to Pannell. The Commissioner, recently returned from quarter sessions in Falmouth, was due to leave again tomorrow on Revenue business in Fowey. Everyone in Gwynnford knew the Commissioner's business; as he watched the town, the town watched him. The twelfth was tomorrow — today, realized Leith with a glance at his pocket watch — but he could hardly go and knock on Pannell's door at the Saucy Maiden at this or any hour.

Leith cursed under his breath. He would need to risk it, even if it meant waiting until dawn outside the Saucy Maiden for the man to emerge. He must intercept Pannell before he left. He was not certain how the man planned to travel — by horse, carriage or packet.

When the last patron left, Leith barred the inn door, discarded his apron, and put on his coat and hat. "I got business in Gwynnford," he said to his wife. "I'll be back by daylight." He rushed out the back door to the stable, where he quickly saddled his horse and rode off into the night on his own mission. At three in the morning, he rode into Gwynnford. He passed the Sea Siren and approached the Saucy Maiden. He saw no lights in any of its windows. He urged his mount into the alley and then back to the inn's stables. Pannell's and his agents' mounts were gone. Leith cursed his luck.

But before he could panic, he heard several sets of hooves on the cobblestones of Jetty Street. They turned off Jetty into the mud of the alley.

Henoch Pannell rode into the stable yard at the head of a posse of tired-looking men. He frowned at the sight of the waiting figure on horseback, and held up the lantern he was carrying to better see the stranger's face. He chuckled. "What brings you away from your wife's warm side this cold morning, Mr. Leith?"

"I've some news for you, sir."

Pannell scowled at the man with a sardonic lift of his eyebrows. "Penlilly, Mr. Leith?" he asked. He shook his head. "Tardy again, sir."

Leith was crestfallen with the man's foreknowledge. "There's more!" he said.

Pannell sighed. "Very well. Come up to my room. I have a private entrance here and no one will see you. I'm damp and thirsty, and refuse to talk out here." He dismounted and handed the reins of his horse to a subordinate.

In Pannell's room, the Commissioner lit a number of candles and poured himself and Leith drams of rum. He fell back into an armchair and planted his heels on a footrest. "Hard business, this night-riding. It nets but a few lonely law-breaking souls. Tonight, for example, we actually caught a man running wool out of the country. But, we let him go. Put a torch to his stash of wool, right there on the beach. His entire shearing for the season. He won't try that again!" The Commissioner chuckled. "You should have seen the Dutchman hovering off the shore! Didn't know what to make of that signal, I tell you! Then we saw his sail disappear." Pannell dropped his head wearily on the back of the chair. "And tomorrow, I take a holiday from this business. Personal report to the Surveyor General in Fowey. Leave by mail packet after breakfast. Why do I tell you this? Well, you're here, and why not? Everyone will know tomorrow anyway."

Pannell finished his rum, then warmed his palms over the candle sputtering on a side table next to him. "Now, Mr. Leith. About Penlilly. What did I tell you about false alarms?"

"You mean, you're not goin' to Penlilly?" asked Leith. "It's the Skelly gang!"

Pannell shrugged. "What for? We'll find nothing but the residue of a run. These Skelly men are specters, Mr. Leith. Why, I'll wager that when Skelly's at last put in irons, he'll somehow manage to walk through the prison walls!"

"But — "

"No, no, Mr. Leith," said Pannell, waving a hand in dismissal. "I appreciate your devotion in having ridden all this way to tell me, but we're not going to bother with Penlilly."

"Hiram Trott!" blurted Leith. "He's the go-between for Skelly here!"

"Oh?" sniffed Pannell. "Well, I've always suspected him. But it's so difficult to catch him at it." He paused, then grinned. "Who was your informant? His scullion, Autt, I'll wager."

Leith nodded, disgusted with the precision of the Commissioner's guesses.

"Thank you for the intelligence regarding Mr. Trott. But why should I place any importance on the rest of it?"

"Because, because," began Leith, and then he bent low and almost whispered, as though he did not want to hear himself say it, "because it's my wife's son who was the messenger last night. He's with the Skelly gang!"

"I see," said Pannell after a moment. "I remember him from the old days at Trott's. The little blighter who took on the Navy. Jack was his name, wasn't it?"

Leith nodded again.

After a moment, Pannell said, "Tell me as much as the scullion told you."

Leith repeated Autt's hurried message, all but for the items about the French vineyards, Claxon's chilblains, and Portsmouth.

Pannell's reaction to the information was not as jubilant as Leith's had been. Trott's tipsters had worked fast Sunday afternoon, when the taverns reopened. The Commissioner's agents in Gwynnford's public houses had already reported word of the run on the night of the twelfth, of which this was the morning. But the nature of this same information, reported by Leith, perplexed him. He asked Leith if he or his informant could repeat the exact conversation between Trott and Jack Frake. Leith said he could not, and he assured Pannell that his informant could not, either. "He's got sheep's brains, you see," explained Leith with apology, "and he gets things mixed up sometimes."

And Leith misinterpreted Pannell's silent musings. He waited for the Commissioner to go on.

Pannell smiled. He had heard the whispered talk about Leith. Rumors of smugglers and contraband runs were not the only pieces of gossip he gleaned from the town. A suspicion was forming in his mind. "Hmm," he droned. "You've no fatherly attachment to the boy?" But before Leith could respond, he waved the question aside. "Never mind that. It's none of my affair." He sighed. "Still, the information is straight from the horse's mouth. And it's early information, too. Penlilly's less than an hour's ride from here. Altogether, very curious." The missing parts of the intelligence tickled his mind. He rubbed his chilly hands together near the candle, and smiled again. "Hiram Trott," he chuckled. "It will be a pleasure to include him in the catch, if there is a catch." He studied Leith, but said nothing.

"You'll go to Penlilly?" asked Leith, hopeful.

Pannell shrugged. "I haven't decided yet." The wind blew some raindrops against the room's sole window. He nodded to it. "You'd better push off now, sir. Looks like some nasty weather's about to break." He stood up and bowed slightly to Leith. "Thank you again, Mr. Leith. Your devotion to me is most commendable. Don't think it won't have its rewards. Goodnight, sir."

Leith blinked and smiled in tentative relief. "Grateful to you, sir. Goodnight." He backed out of the room, then crept down the wooden steps outside that connected the inn stables with Pannell's room. As he went, he grunted once in amazement that the Commissioner, for the first time, had smiled at him.

In the next instant, though, his amazement was checked by the suspicion that there was something wrong with the gratitude expressed in that smile.

Chapter 22: The Trap

PENLILLY-BY-SEA WAS A COLLECTION OF FISHERMEN'S COTTAGES CLINGING precariously to a slope that was not quite sand, not quite earth. There was no central street, only a maze of time-worn footpaths between the battered cottages; there was not even a tavern, only the much-frequented home of the eldest fisherman, who was the village's principal buyer of contraband liquor.

Almost a mile west of the village was a flat stretch of beach that was a smuggler's dream. The shelf beneath the surf ran gradually out from the beach for about a hundred yards. Except during gales, there were few or no breakers for galleys and other small craft to negotiate. The beach itself rose gently to the headland above; there were no cliffs to ascend or circumvent. Ruins of an older village dotted the slope. The crumbling walls of the cottages and the salt-pocked stones of a roofless ancient chapel were virtually hidden by bramble bushes and rushes.

Pannell knew this stretch of beach well. It and others like it along the Cornwall coast were described by him in detail in a special journal he kept of likely smugglers' landing sites. But he had never caught anyone here.

In the past, he did the logical thing and came to a rendezvous point on the night of a rumored run, only to find that the Skelly gang had unshipped and toted off their contraband in daylight hours before. It did not seem to matter how early he appeared at these points; the Skelly men would always have come and gone. The phenomenon stung his sense of smartness and wit. After a two-hour rest in Gwynnford, he led his men out again into the wet darkness and rode west, hurried past Penlilly, and then doubled back beyond the county road that paralleled the coastline. It was dawn when he posted his men in the cottage ruins, and had their mounts installed out of sight in the chapel ruins. The chapel he used as an observation post, for one of its shattered high windows commanded an unobstructed view of both the beach and the slope leading to it.

On foot, by himself, he surveyed the beach, looking for evidence of a run. All he found were the decayed remains of fishing nets that had snared on tide-exposed rocks. The morning was blustery and the wind drove needles of cold rain into his face as he trudged through the sand. But he was pleased; there was no evidence that the Skelly or any other gang had ever used this beach in the past.

He went from ruin to ruin and advised his men that they might have a long wait ahead of them. There were six with him. A seventh, the youngest agent, had been given a hastily written note of apology to the Surveyor-General in Fowey to take to the captain of the mail packet this morning. Each man with him carried a musket charged with deadly double ball, a brace of pistols similarly charged, and a sword. He noted with satisfaction that none of them grumbled about their lack of sleep. This was, he knew, their first real crack at the Skelly gang. Their high morale was rooted partly in a sense of vendetta, but mostly in the prospect of sharing the proceeds of the wealth they might find in Skelly's headquarters. It was said to be fabulous.

Pannell understood this, and was also in the same high spirits. If everything went well — if it was true information he was acting on — this could be the beginning of his last collar in Cornwall.

On the road to Penlilly, he gave his men specific instructions for dealing with the Skelly gang. "We will wait until the offenders are ready to leave with their booty. Apparent success will make them cocky and careless. On my signal, we will surprise them. If they've strung together all their ponies, shoot the lead pony dead. If any one of them brandishes a firearm, shoot him. If you see any one of them giving orders, shoot him. Some of you have seen service in His Majesty's forces abroad. Treat this encounter, if it occurs, as a military one. Remember: Only one group may come out of it the victor. It *must* be us."

Thomas Fix, his lieutenant, asked, "How many are in the gang, do you think?"

"I don't know. You know we've heard talk of there being between ten to a hundred."

"Are they well-armed?" asked another agent.

"No better than we," said Pannell. He knew what was on his men's minds. Some gangs in Kent and Sussex had, in their encounters with larger posses of Revenue officers, displayed considerable military prowess. One gang had fought so skillful a rearguard action that nine Revenue men had been killed or wounded.

He gave other orders: no pipes, no fires, no cards or dice to while away the time, and no talking.

He kept two of his men in the chapel with him. They wrapped their greatcoats around their shivering bodies to warm themselves. Pannell sat on a fallen stone by the shattered Romanesque window, and set his pocket watch on the sill. In the gray dawn it read six-thirty-five.

At ten o'clock Pannell was munching on a piece of bread when a solitary figure appeared on the beach, coming from the west. It was only a pauper, who paused now and then to stoop and pick up a clam. The man passed by. At ten-twenty a sail appeared on the gray horizon and seemed to move toward the shore. Pannell glanced at his men, who were huddled together in a corner of the chapel, asleep. He picked up a pebble and tossed it at them. "Mr. Fix! Mr. Craun!" he said. "We may have company soon!" The men awoke, seized their muskets, and jumped up to join their superior at the window. "Glass, Mr. Fix!" ordered Pannell.

Fix rushed to Pannell's mount and retrieved a spyglass from a saddlebag. They watched the sail of a sloop grow larger, but never sharp enough in the haze to see it clearly. Pannell sniffed in disgust, and handed the spyglass to Fix. "Your eyes seem to be better than mine, Mr. Fix. What do you make of it?"

Fix squinted through the tube for a moment. "She's flying the ensign, all right," he commented. Then he shrugged his shoulders as the sail moved away to the west and vanished into the dawn gloom. "Might've been the mail packet, sir," he suggested.

Pannell snorted and snatched the glass from Fix's hand. "Too big to be a packet, Mr. Fix! Learn your ships!"

At ten-forty-five, a little after the drizzle had stopped, a rider appeared on the top of the slope. Pannell's tired eyes watched it with desperation, then with excitement. The rider was joined by four others. They came rapidly down the slope to the beach. Pannell sent Albert Craun to alert the men in the cottages, then raised the spyglass to watch the newcomers.

The riders dismounted and began to do odd things. One man dropped a bundle of wood on the beach leeward of a large rock just above the high-tide mark, stacked it quickly but neatly, and lit a fire. Another man reached for a pair of what looked like French china packing crates tied together over his mount's saddle, untied them and dropped them in the sand. Then he calmly kicked in the sides of the crates, and Pannell thought he could hear the breaking of the contents. Another rider untied a cluster of brandy ankers and artfully distributed them along the beach. The fourth man reached into a leather bag and tossed objects here and there into the sand, but mostly around the fire. The fifth man — actually a boy on a pony — took three of the horses and led them up and down the slope over and over again.

It was a busy group of strangers, engrossed in staging a contraband run that never occurred.

When Thomas Fix glanced at Pannell at his side, he saw that the man's broad face was a sickly red, and that it trembled with rage. Fix did not dare put into words what they were witnessing, for while he was as startled and angry at the simplicity of the ruse as was Pannell, his superior's wrath worried him more. At that moment, Craun returned, breathless and excited. "They're ready, sir!" he whispered. "Say, what kind of dodge are those fellows up to, anyway?"

Pannell did not answer. He knew what was being done, and had been done for almost five years. To him. To his predecessors. But mostly to him. His hands began to shake, and he lowered the spyglass. He shut his eyes and squeezed the ends of the glass with both hands and snapped off one end of it. Then he dropped the tube. "To our mounts!" he exclaimed, his voice a dry rasp.

Fix glanced at Craun, then ventured, "If these are Skelly men, sir, we could follow them back to their hideout, and then we could — "

Pannell jerked his head around. Fix stepped back from the fury he saw in it. "Do you think anyone could follow them across open country without being seen, Mr. Fix? Do as I say, damn your eyes!"

* * *

The five men were John Fineux, commander of the ruse and a former dancing master who had made the mistake of correcting a Peer's politics;

Aubrey Shakelady, a former Grub Street hack and pamphleteer whose limericks had offended half a dozen members of the House of Lords; William Ayre; Richard Claxon; and Jack Frake. They worked quickly and without waste of motion. They were not worried about being seen by the inhabitants of Penlilly-by-Sea, who had been advised of the ruse and rewarded for their silence with a cask of premier Dutch gin. They were concerned about the column of soldiers they had seen four miles down the county road, marching east, as the gang emerged from the moor on its way to Penlilly. Less than an hour ago they had seen the sails of *The Hasty Hart*, returning from Guernsey, beating to windward toward Portreach, another fishing village five miles east of Penlilly, and the true landing site.

Jack Frake led the horses back to the fire William Ayre had started, dropped their reins, and glanced around at the site. John Fineux was inspecting it, adding some last subtle touches to the "rendezvous." Aubrey Shakelady was trying to tease a smile from Richard Claxon with a bawdy joke. Claxon, whom Jack Frake suspected still had a fever, but who had insisted on joining in the task so that he could be paid a part of the proceeds from the actual landing, sat on his pony and stared down at Shakelady with incomprehension. Jack Frake had never been able to establish an easy rapport with the older boy, and Claxon, always lost in the pages of his Bible, had never invited anyone's friendship. Shakelady was having no better luck.

John Fineux came up to his charges. "Well, gentlemen, what do you think? Fine job, I'd say. All right, let's mount up and leave this place. Those soldiers can't be more than a mile away by now. Looked to me like they were being quick-marched." He picked up the rusty poker Ayre had left in the tent of burning wood, and stuck it upright in the center of the crackling fire. "Symmetry, my boy," he said to Ayre. "Symmetry and grace. Always strive for it." He chuckled once. "If Pannell and his crew come along soon enough," he added, tapping the top of the poker with a finger, "perhaps it will be hot enough for a certain curious hand."

The site looked as though many men had waited here for a vessel to arrive and anchor a quarter mile offshore. Burnt twists of pipe tobacco, empty rum and gin flasks, crumbs and bits of food, a dropped coin or two, a broken clay pipe, spent lantern candles, and many more little signs ringed the blazing fire and were littered for yards around it. A trail of hoof and footprints was stamped into the sand and the ground and led up the slope to the county road.

Fineux turned to his mount and put a foot in the stirrup, then paused when he heard a sound. They all froze for an instant, for it was a sound none of them had ever expected to hear. "Oh, no… " said Fineux. It was the pounding of hooves on the slope above them. Fineux glanced around once at the slope, then shouted an order. "Run, gentlemen! Split up! Get back to the caves and warn Skelly!"

Two shots were fired. Double ball struck the saddle of Fineux's mount, and as the horse reared up in panic, another struck the man in the nape of his neck. He fell to the sand and his mount bolted. For an instant, the four gang-members gaped at the bloody hole below the man's head, matted with hair and the ribbon he had used to tie it together.

Jack Frake turned and saw three horsemen riding across and down the slope from the direction of a pile of ruins. Four other men emerged from the brush. Two had stopped beneath puffs of smoke to reload their muskets. The other two halted, knelt, and were preparing to fire.

One of the men on horseback, who was in the lead, waved a pistol in the air and shouted, "Halt, in the name of the King, or be cut down!" Jack Frake recognized Henoch Pannell.

Richard Claxon, after a glance at Fineux and then at Pannell, dug his boots into the sides of his pony and began running east up the beach. One of the dismounted men took careful aim with his musket and fired. The pony whinnied and went down with a muffled scream, trapping Claxon beneath its thrashing body. William Ayre, who by this time had remounted, yelled in outrage and galloped toward Claxon to help him. Another shot boomed, and Ayre jerked from his saddle and fell heavily to the sand.

Aubrey Shakelady did not bother trying to remount, but dashed down the beach. Pannell turned his mount on the slope and galloped after him. "Halt, damn you!" he shouted. Shakelady looked back once, but continued running and splashed into the water. Pannell overtook him, and fired his pistol into the man's neck as he passed. Shakelady collapsed in the surf, face down, and did not rise again.

Jack Frake leaned in the saddle of his pony and took the iron poker from the fire. He was ready to take his chances on an escape down the beach, but stopped when he saw Pannell trot back to Richard Claxon and take a second pistol from his saddle. He did not like what he saw in the man's face, a look of perverse pleasure at the sight of the moaning youth struggling to push himself out from under the pony. He raised the poker like a sword, galloped forward, shouting and waving his weapon in the air. Pannell saw him coming, reined in by the fallen pony, and turned the barrel of the pistol in his direction. Then he smiled strangely, and turned the barrel back toward Claxon, and fired into the pony's head.

Jack Frake did not hear the hooves behind him, nor the musket balls whistling around him, and was oblivious to the Revenue men closing in a circle around him. He did not know that the second and third horsemen tried to bring him down by firing at a gallop, but had missed. One officer, Fix, came swiftly from behind and swung the stock of his spent musket at the boy's head. It connected with a sharp crack.

The encounter with the Revenue men had lasted less than a minute.

When he opened his eyes again, it was to the shock of water thrown into his face. He was lying on a pile of straw in a dark, foul-smelling room. It was a fisherman's cottage in Penlilly. Richard Claxon lay on another pallet a few feet away from him, his right leg wrapped in rags. He moaned quietly, his head rolling back and forth in the straw. Henoch Pannell and two of his men stood over them, watching and waiting. Pannell drew placidly on a pipe.

Jack Frake tried to move. His ankles and wrists were cuffed together. The back of his head ached and throbbed, but his awareness of the pain receded when he saw his predicament.

"Look at them, gentlemen," said Pannell, putting his arms behind his back, his teeth clenching the pipe. "Live Skelly men. Not very impressive now, are they?"

His men said nothing. Fix, who had been the longest with Pannell, felt it wiser not to mention that it had taken them nearly five years to capture but two of the gang. And none of the gang here, dead or alive, had been armed.

"Well, let's get this over with." Pannell turned to Jack Frake. "Get him up." Fix and Craun came over and lifted the boy to his feet. Pannell took a step closer and said, "You are Jack Frake, aren't you? It has been some time since we both occupied the same room. I recognize you from the Sea Siren. You've grown, of course. The criminal life seems to have agreed with you."

Jack Frake said nothing.

Pannell nodded to the prone figure of Richard Claxon. "And we know who he is, too. There was a Bible in his saddlebag, and his name inscribed in it. Your late friends remain nameless. What were their names, Master Frake?"

Jack Frake said nothing, but regarded the Commissioner with curiosity and fear.

Pannell frowned. "You look at me as though I were not a man, but a monster," he said. "But, a man I am, and one who is doing his job. Some men work with their hands in metal or wood. I am a man who works in law."

Jack Frake shook his head and spoke. "You surrendered your manhood when you joined the Revenue — and your humanity. So, I have nothing of consequence to say to you."

Pannell scoffed in amusement, then shook his head lightly. "A somewhat sophisticated opinion for a smuggler, that. It reflects a fairly exotic education, sir." He paused to shake out the contents of his pipe, which he tucked inside of his coat. "Well, so much for civil chatter. I will ask you this once, Master Frake, and civilly. If I need ask it again, it will not be so civilly." He took another step closer to the boy, and stood so that his face was only an inch from Jack Frake's. "*Where* is Augustus Skelly's headquarters?"

Jack Frake permitted himself to speak. He could not control his emotion. "In England, the country you betray by hunting, robbing and murdering its best citizens, as you did today!"

Pannell's hand swept up and erased the accusing face with a powerful backhand. Jack Frake was knocked off his feet and fell to the dirt floor. "*Must* I resort to the Hawkhurst gang's methods, Master Frake? Shall I take a whip to you? Shall I tie you to the underbelly of a horse and set it loose in the brambles? Beat you with a stick? Dangle you up-side-down in a well and feed you water? Or — I can improvise on Newgate methods here, Master Frake! Outside there are countless rocks. You can be tied down and some of the heaviest of them placed on your chest one by one, and left there for hours until you can't breathe! But there's no need for any of that. You and your friends have ballyragged me for too long a time. The trick must *end*, and you with it, if necessary!"

"I won't tell you a thing," said Jack Frake. "I'll die with dignity."

"Dignity?" barked Pannell. He took his riding crop from under his belt and began to beat the boy with it, the crop rising and striking with each word. "Dignity? Let's — see — how — dignified — you'll — feel — when — I — "

Fix and Craun, who neither condoned nor condemned Pannell's behavior, nevertheless winced at each blow.

"Leave him alone, sir," said Richard Claxon. The sound of his voice, a voice sweetened with gentleness and forgiveness, charged the air and dispelled its miasma of brutality. "It wasn't his fault. It was God's will. Jack isn't to blame… "

Pannell, his arm and crop poised for another blow to Jack Frake's back, stopped and stared at the other boy. He lowered his arm and stepped over to look down at the sweating, agonized face. "*What* was God's will, Mr. Claxon?"

"I know who you are," said Claxon. "You're the Commissioner of Revenue. They make jokes about you in the caves."

"Jokes? Caves? Make sense, sir!"

"God has punished me, sir. It was not your doing… my leg here. God directed your actions."

Pannell blinked once, and rose to his full height. He studied the boy's face. It was ashen white, and the eyes looked back up at him with an eerie mixture of kindness, pain and an intensity that made him uneasy. "*My* actions, Mr. Claxon?"

"I broke a man's legs, once," explained Claxon. "He was a judge. But this is His punishment for me, for taking His justice into my own unworthy hands. It is His way of revealing Himself to me… "

Pannell smiled, then glanced smugly at Jack Frake, who had managed to sit up in a corner. "God clearly is on my side, Master Frake!"

"God is your ally," confirmed Claxon.

Pannell tossed the crop away and held out a hand in back of him. "Hat, Mr. Fix!" The officer removed his tricorn and gave it to his superior. Pannell leaned down and slipped it under the boy's head. "There now, Mr. Claxon. That must be much more comfortable for you." He snapped his fingers. "Chair, Mr. Fix."

Fix found a stool and brought it over. Pannell sat down. "Now, Mr. Claxon. Let's have a serious chat here. If God directed my actions, then I must be His instrument, mustn't I?"

"Yes… "

"And if I have served as His instrument of action, then I must also be His instrument of *truth*."

"Yes," said the boy. "You could not be otherwise… "

Pannell cleared his throat before he spoke again. He felt uneasy exploiting the boy in this manner, but his greed for information hurtled him forward. "Then tell me the truth, Mr. Claxon, and earn God's complete forgiveness for your… er… crime." Pannell held his breath, then asked, "Where is Augustus Skelly's headquarters? And where is the actual landing?"

"No!" shouted Jack Frake, stumbling to his feet. "Don't say anything, Richard!"

Claxon seemed not to have heard his colleague. "Portreach," he said.

"That's his headquarters?" asked Pannell eagerly.

"No, that is where he has already landed contraband."

"And his headquarters? Where is he taking this contraband?"

"No, Richard!" shouted Jack Frake again. He tried to move toward Claxon, but the links of the cuffs tripped him and he fell again to the dirt floor. "Don't tell him!" he cried, crawling toward Claxon. "He'll kill Skelly, and Redmagne, and all your friends!"

Claxon moved his head on the tricorn so that he could see his straw-mate. "I must, Jack," he said. "He's God's instrument of truth, and my means of salvation for all my sins. I have thought of women and drink and all the other fatal distractions. I strayed, I have sinned. I confess. You must confess, too, Jack... "

Jack Frake saw a species of madness in Claxon's eyes. At another time he might have felt pity, or even fear. But here he answered with anger and contempt. "That's rubbish! He's tricking you! You're not well! Your head's afire with fever! You're — "

Pannell rose and kicked Jack Frake in the side. "How dare you pronounce such... such blasphemy!" he said. He was genuinely shocked by the boy's words. He looked at Fix and Craun. "Get him out of here." The two men picked up Jack Frake and carried him outside the cottage and shut the door behind them.

Pannell returned to his stool and grinned with benevolence. "Now, Mr. Claxon. Let's go on. Where is Skelly's headquarters? How many men does he have? Are they armed?"

He came out of the cottage five minutes later. Some village fishermen and their wives stood at a distance, watching the Revenue men loiter outside the cottage. Jack Frake was sitting on the ground, leaning against a water trough. The bodies of John Fineux, Aubrey Shakelady, and William Ayre were heaped like logs a few yards away.

Pannell smiled triumphantly, and said to Fix, as he slipped on his gloves, "Find a cart, Mr. Fix. The Claxon boy must be taken to Gwynnford and a doctor, and these dead ones must be hauled into town, too, I suppose." He locked his hands together behind his back and wandered away. His next task would be to trap the men in the caves near Marvel. He did not know how he could do this with only seven men, when there were some twenty who would be defending those caves. He would need to act soon. News of the capture of the two boys would spread quickly.

It was at that moment that he heard the beat of drums and the cadence of marching feet. He glanced up at the county road, and saw a column of soldiers approaching. Mounted officers glanced down with curiosity at the scene below. He saw artillery drawn by teams of horses, spaced between three companies of disciplined scarlet. He saw two companies of regulars, and one company of grenadiers. Pannell's eyes grew bigger with an idea that was blooming in his head.

He laughed once again, turning to his men and pointing to the column. "God clearly *is* on my side!"

Chapter 23: The Major

MAJOR ADAM LEIGH, RIDING AT THE HEAD OF THE COLUMN WITH HIS aides, had a premonition that the man galloping determinedly up the slope from the village below was bringing trouble. The rider wore the heavy gray coat of the Revenue Service, and even under the gray sky the silver Crown coat of arms on his black tricorn glinted a little.

Henoch Pannell rode up to the major and doffed his hat in salute. "Good day to you, sir! Whom have I the privilege of addressing?"

"Major Leigh, of the Middlesex Brigade. And you, sir?"

"Henoch Pannell, Commissioner Extraordinary of His Majesty's Revenue." Pannell trotted beside the frosty, wary major. "I must have a word with you, Major Leigh, and a stationary position would be a more amenable means of conversation. In private."

"We are in a bit of a rush, Mr. Pannell," said the major, not turning to the Commissioner.

"In too much of a rush to pass up a bit of glory — at the request of your King?"

The major sighed in annoyance and ordered his aide to halt the column for a rest. As the order was relayed from company to company down the column, the officer and the Commissioner wandered out of earshot of the major's aides and stopped several yards away. "All right, Mr. Pannell," said the officer, still holding the reins of his mount. "What is it?"

Pannell said, ""I've just sprung a trap and caught myself some smugglers!"

"Congratulations," drawled the major in ill-disguised unconcern. "It must have been a pleasurable experience, to judge from your demeanor."

"Oh, pleasurable it was! Shot three of the scum dead, me and my men. Got two of them alive, and one of them has given me some very important information."

Pannell watched the major, expressly indifferent to the news, reach inside his coat for a snuffbox, open it, inhale a pinch of the powder, and sneeze. Not before he had returned the delicate cameo-decorated box to his coat did he give Pannell his attention again.

Pannell was impervious to the rebuff. Instead, he glanced back at the column. "Fine looking troops you have, Major. Have any of them seen action?"

"The grenadiers were in Flanders two years ago, under another commander. The rest are recruits, mostly. Why do you ask?"

"They look fitter than most troops I see in these parts. What is your hurry?"

"We are escorting artillery to Spithead for shipment to the colonies. We must be there in three days. Then we rejoin our colonel and march to our home barracks."

"Artillery for the colonies," mused Pannell. "How long have you been marching, Major?"

"We were billeted near Falmouth. The batteries there are being dismantled. We're out of the war now, you know."

"Er... When were your men last paid, Major?"

"Three months ago. What has that to do with whatever subject you seem reluctant to bring up?"

"Only this," said Pannell. "They would be paid more frequently if the Army received its due from the Treasury. But the Army does not receive its due, because the Treasury does not receive its due from Customs — which does not receive its due from this country's commerce. Free-traders and smugglers cheat your men, Major, and the free-trader I can trap today and extinguish is none other than Augustus Skelly!"

"I appreciate the logic, Mr. Pannell, but what has it to do with me?"

Pannell assumed his own air of frost. "This is a most urgent matter, Major. Quite simply, I am authorized to draft you in the service of His Majesty's Revenue. I require your assistance to help me capture Skelly."

Pannell reached inside his coat and pulled out a document he was never without. It was his commission, signed by the King and the prime minister and bearing both their seals. He held out the cream-colored sheaf of paper to the officer. "It will cost you but a day's delay." He paused, then added with mocking drollery, "We're out of the war now, you know."

The major's jaw became rigid, but he took the document. He unfolded and read it, then handed it back to Pannell. "I can't go chasing after smugglers and owlers, Mr. Pannell, not even one as notorious as Skelly. My orders are to get this ordnance to Spithead. Besides, I must also account for every musket ball, ounce of powder, and inch of boot leather I expend."

"I'll write a letter that will exonerate you of any charges of adventurism, Major, and account for all your ordnance and more. I, too, carry a commission, from Pelham himself, as you saw." Pannell smiled. "Your country and King will be more grateful than you can now imagine. This is no little favor I ask of you, and my gratitude — not to mention the King's — will be commensurate, I can assure you."

Pannell did not wink at him, but the major got the impression that he had. "You present one with a difficult decision, sir," said the officer, angry that he had been trapped by this man.

"Doing one's duty when it arises should not ever be a difficult decision to make, sir."

The major grimaced. "All right. Where are your rascals? And how many of them are there?"

"Near Marvel," said Pannell breezily. "The whole gang is there. No more than twenty, I'd say. Probably just now returning from a contraband run near Portreach." He nodded to the column of soldiers, and barked a laugh. "They won't be expecting anything like this!" He added, "I see there is an ordnance wagon, and that your pieces are field-ready, Major. We'll need them."

The major allowed himself a slight smile. "It's a bother, but the gun crews could use some practice."

* * *

"They should have been back hours ago," said Redmagne.

"They were told to join us at Portreach when they were finished," said Skelly.

Skelly had planned to accompany Henry Naughton, the pilot of *The*

Hasty Hart, on the sloop's return trip to Styles. But he had changed his mind and boarded the last galley that carried what remained of the contraband he brought from Guernsey. His men were busy now unloading the five borrowed carts and relieving the fifteen ponies of their burdens. It was three o'clock in the afternoon. Skelly stood outside one of the two eastern entrances to the caves, watching his men lug crates and sacks of goods inside. Chester Plume, the bookkeeper, was in the storage cavern, making a record of the goods and supervising their stowing.

"Send someone to Penlilly to see what's awry," said Skelly.

"I'll go," said Redmagne.

Skelly shook his head. "No. Hopfius doesn't know you. He's tight-lipped and won't believe you're with me. Send Tobie Robins. He repaired the rudder of his fishing ketch last month." Robins was by trade a carpenter. Hopfius was the village leader.

"All right," said Redmagne. He went to find Robins.

Robins returned to the caves three hours later, long after the borrowed carts and ponies had been returned and just as the men were finishing dinner. His mount was in a lather and Robins was exhausted from the ride. Skelly took him to his quarters. Redmagne joined them. "Well?" asked Skelly.

"They're dead, sir!" stammered the man. "Except for Jack and Richard! And soldiers are out there — !"

Skelly frowned and gave the man the mug of coffee he had brought with him. "Have a swig, son, and catch your breath."

Robins gulped down the mug's contents, then reported everything he had learned. "Hopfius didn't see the fight," he concluded. "I mean, there couldn't have been a fight, because Fineux and the rest didn't even have swords."

"And only Jack and Richard were alive?"

"Yes, sir."

"One or both of them talked," remarked Redmagne.

Robins said, "Hopfius says it was Richard. He helped put him on a cart with Fineux and the others, and he said Richard was raving and spouting the Bible and all. He said Jack looked like he'd been beaten. But Pannell was alone with Richard for a while." He paused. "Then the soldiers came up the road. Half a regiment, he said, regulars and grenadiers. They was hauling guns. The Revenue men went with them. I passed them on my way back, just two miles from here. I had to go around them!"

"All right, Tobie," said Skelly at length. "Go and get something to eat before Mr. Tuck chucks the pot."

Robins left. Skelly said to Redmagne, "Let's take a look outside."

At the eastern entrance, they peered into the darkness and saw lights where none had been before. They thought they caught the sound of voices on the drift of the wind, overlapping a strange rumbling.

"When do you think they'll attack?" asked Redmagne.

"Tomorrow morning, at first light, after they've rested," said Skelly.

"They've got guns."

Skelly shrugged. "The Army has been recalling all the ordnance that was used to fortify the port towns down here. But I don't think Pannell has any special influence with the Army, other than its supplying him with dragoons, when they can be spared from Kent or Sussex. He's simply having a run of good luck."

"Could these caves withstand a siege?"

"Very likely. If we were military men, we could make the best of it," said Skelly with a sigh. "But, we are not military men, and a siege, with or without artillery, isn't going to make a difference in the end. We could be starved out. Or a single volley, or a single charge by those grenadiers, would finish us."

"I know." Redmagne was quiet for a while, as was his friend. "I don't think Jack betrayed us," he said at last.

"It was Mr. Claxon who told Pannell. But Hopfius said he was feverish. His leg was broken in more than one place, apparently. I know what that can do to a man's mind. I won't say Mr. Claxon betrayed us."

"We must tell the men."

"If they don't already know." Skelly looked at Redmagne. "If we stay, John, you know this will be the end of us. We couldn't hold out. If you want to go, go now. There's Miss Morley in your future — and more long novels for you to write. But if you stay… "

"I'll stay, Augustus," said Redmagne. "But let me try to rescue Jack and Richard. Alone."

"And why would you want to rescue them? So they can share our fate?"

"No. To set them free."

"You don't know whether they're with the army down there or in Gwynnford. They could be anywhere, John. And wherever they are, they'll be under a strong guard."

"I know. I want to see if it's possible. That's all." Redmagne paused.

"Whether it is or not, I'll be back to stand with you and the rest."

"All right." Skelly closed his eyes, then opened them again. "Call a meeting."

Skelly stood at the head of the long table in the dining hall. He apprised his men of what had happened at Penlilly and of the peril. His speech was short, almost gruff, and he did not invite discussion. "I won't hold any of you here. You're free to go, as you always have been. Those who wish to leave, and who helped with today's run, will be paid, and without prejudice. God knows, there's a chance you may be able to start normal lives elsewhere. Those who choose to remain, do so with the knowledge that this is the end of the Skelly gang." He paused. "Think on your decision, gentlemen. Think hard. Then come to my quarters, each of you, when you've made up your minds. That's all." He turned without further word and left the hall.

An hour after the meeting, Charles Ambrose, the deserter, was the first to come to Skelly's quarters. Skelly was not surprised to see him. Ambrose left the Army because, as he explained to Skelly years ago, "I refuse to fight for foreign princes. It's as simple as that. Our own are bad enough. So why should an Englishman die for the right of some royal bugger to sit on a throne and diddle with his people and the folks next door? Presumptuous lot of snollygosters, our Crown, and I don't like being presumed."

Ambrose said now, as he stood not quite at attention in Skelly's quarters, "I'll stay, sir. You'll need someone to hold the line."

Skelly smiled. "Why, Mr. Ambrose?"

Ambrose smiled, then took Skelly's hand and shook it. "You're a prince among men, sir, and the only one I'd risk my prat for — excuse my language, sir."

"Thank you, Mr. Ambrose."

"I'll see to what we have in the way of weapons and powder." Ambrose turned to leave, but stopped. "I was thinking, sir. It's too bad we haven't any colors to fight under or mark our position. That Customs jack on the mess wall would do. It'd give Pannell pause for thought out there. Permission to hoist it, sir."

Skelly said, "But it bears the King's arms, Mr. Ambrose."

Ambrose chuckled. "I'll blot it out somehow. It's as much our flag as theirs."

"Permission granted." Skelly paused. "Mr. Ambrose, if there's a fight, are you certain you'd be able to fire on other Englishmen?"

Ambrose looked perplexed, as though the question contained the answer. "Sir, other Englishmen have been firing on me nigh on ten years now. That's the way I look at it."

There were only seventeen men left. Of these, four humbly informed Skelly that they would leave the caves. Skelly did not reprimand them, did not lecture them, and did not sneer at them. He questioned neither their fears nor their greediness to live, for they had lived in the caves with him for years. The men who came to him to say they had chosen to stay could not imagine living in any manner other than as free men. The one group he envied; the other group he cherished.

Close to midnight, Charles Ambrose and others were taking stock of the weapons they had at their disposal, when they felt more than heard a thud shake the caves' walls. Chester Plume came running down from the "crow's nest." "They're firing on us!" he said. "They've set up a gun on the Villers grounds — I saw the flash — and there's lights in the house!"

Skelly went up with Ambrose and the others to see. There were indeed lights in the Villers mansion. Skelly, holding a torch, took a turn around the top of the hill. Ambrose and the others trailed behind him. Below, all around the hill, they could see the flickers of dozens of flameaux and campfires. "They've surrounded the hill," he remarked. Ambrose spotted the cannon ball and a spread of shattered rock. He bent to examine it. "A six-pounder," he said.

They heard the report of another explosion, then the metallic crack of iron smashing into rock somewhere on the side of the hill. "Another six-pounder," said Ambrose, pointing to the west. "Set up in the Talbot fields." He shook his head. "They're getting their range right, that's all. They won't start the real business until daylight."

There was another report, but no ball came for what seemed like an eternity. Then they heard a massive thump that shook the ground under their feet. Stone disintegrated somewhere and slivers of it pelted them and stung their hands and faces. This was followed by a moan, which ceased before any of them could determine its source.

"The crow's nest," whispered Skelly. They hurried back to Chester Plume's post. One side of the box-like formation of limestone was gone, and lay scattered in pieces all around them. The sycamore trees that grew around it had been stripped of their bare limbs by the blast of the fragments. Beneath one of the larger chunks was Chester Plume, dead, his clothes and face disfigured.

"Lucky shot," remarked one of the other men. "Unlucky for Chester."

"Howitzer," said Ambrose ominously. "They can pound the roof down on us with it."

Redmagne did not hear the cannon. He left the caves an hour after the meeting, dressed in his finest silks, the suit he had worn to London in July. He rode straight to the main camp of the red-coats, and was challenged by a pair of young regulars. "What is your business here?" one of them demanded.

"I am Squire John Trigg," said Redmagne. "I have some land yonder" — he pointed vaguely with his riding crop to the north — "just beyond Marvel. I ride at night — don't you simply love it at this time of day, it's so peaceful and quiet! — and I heard the commotion you fellows were making, and I thought I'd see what was to do."

The men frowned and glanced at each other. The sergeant of the guard came from his tent and walked over. "What's the problem here?" he asked. He held up a flambeau to better see the stranger's face.

Redmagne introduced himself again. He finished, smiling innocently, "Thought I'd have a spot of tea with your commanding officer. This is the most excitement we've seen since the dragoons passed through here ages ago!"

The sergeant's mouth twisted wryly. The stranger's clothes, speech, mannerisms — and especially the large mole affixed to his left cheek — suggested that the man was no danger. This was a spoiled fop who probably had some strange personal habits. Still, he was a gentleman, and he could not be turned away. It would serve Major Leigh right, he thought, to sic the dandy on him. "Well, Mr. Trigg, the major may be busy, but his tent is right over there, the one with the drums stacked in front. Let him pass, privates."

Redmagne doffed his hat to the sergeant. "Thank you, sir. You're most kind." He rode directly to the tent, on the look-out for men in blue coats, and for a peasant's cart.

An hour later, seated at a campaign table with Major Leigh, and on his third cup of tea, he purred, "Most delicious leaf you carry with you, Major! Army life can't be the horror people make of it, if *this* is a sample of your emoluments!" He made a loud sipping sound on the rim of the cup, then gently set it down. "But, Major, have *you* seen action? I'll wager you have some exciting stories to tell."

"No," said the major, wishing Mr. Trigg would take his leave. The man was, like himself, a gentleman, and deserving of all the courtesies of a visit.

But he could not stand him. "I was assigned to the brigade when it returned from Flanders a few years ago. Most of the officers were killed there. I've simply been playing nursemaid to these ruffians, and trying to bring the regiment back up to strength."

Redmagne clucked his tongue. "Oh, I wouldn't worry about that, dear fellow! I'm sure the French will raise our hackles again, and then you'll be off to the Continent before you can buss your Lady Jane good-bye! Why, who knows? Someone may replace *you* when it's all over!" he added with a gay laugh.

Major Leigh's eyes narrowed, then glanced down at his pocket watch on the table. "If you'll excuse me, Mr. Trigg, I have duties to perform. We're positioning our ordnance around that hill, and I want to make sure the Commissioner and his men are not up to mischief, and that everything else is just so." His smile was thin and insulting as he rose. "Thank you for the story of the Villers estate and of your childhood escapades here. It was most entertaining."

"Why, thank you, Major, and best of luck to you," said Redmagne, rising. "I'm sure you'll score a glorious victory, though I still say there are no smugglers in this vicinity. Lud, you'll be assaulting that pretty little hill and frightening all the cuddly rabbitkins from their warrens!" He held out his hand.

Major Leigh shut his eyes briefly, then shook the man's hand. "Best of luck to you, Mr. Trigg, in your farming endeavors. It seems a pastime most suited to a gentleman of your, er, talents."

"Thank you, Major, for your hospitality, and good night." Redmagne gave the officer a broad, almost imbecilic grin, touched his hat, and left the tent.

Redmagne rode out of the camp with the knowledge, subtly extracted from the major's cautious but wearied mind, that Jack Frake and Richard Claxon were not there, but had been taken to Gwynnford.

Jack Frake was put on the cart with Richard Claxon and the bodies of their colleagues. The cart smelled of fish. The cart, Pannell and his six men followed the column of soldiers from Penlilly as far as a fork in the county road. Then Pannell assigned three of his men to take the cart into Gwynnford, while he and the other three accompanied the column on the road that led north to Marvel.

Jack Frake sat, cuffed as before, in a corner of the cart, near Richard Claxon's head, his sight locked on the bodies of the men that lay along the cartbed's length. Claxon clutched his Bible to his chest, and his lips moved in silent prayer. Jack Frake did not think his colleague knew where he was. With every jar of the cart wheels over a hole or a rock, Claxon's eyes would squeeze shut in pain. After a while, Jack Frake noticed that the Bible had slipped from Claxon's grip, and that his eyes stared steadily at the gray sky. The cart rolled over a bump, but the eyes did not blink, the face did not flinch. Jack Frake closed the eyes, then reached down and put the Bible back in the boy's dead hand.

In time, the road led into Trelowe. Jack Frake did not realize where he was until he began to recognize some of the fences, fields and trees they passed. The cart rumbled by his former home, which was now a tavern. A sign-board featuring the heads of three ewes swung gently in the breeze over the door. A sulky and two saddled mounts stood tethered to a post in front. He heard singing coming from the cottage, and laughter. A woman paused in the task of drawing water from the well to watch the cart and its escort pass by.

It was Huldah Leith.

Jack Frake recognized her, and she recognized the face in the retreating cart. The bucket rope slipped from her hands as they shot up to her face to muffle a scream. Then he saw her run back inside the cottage.

Jack Frake felt the beginnings of a terrible mixture of emotions rise inside him — regret, bitterness, and anger — but they subsided almost as quickly as he felt them. He was too exhausted to sort them out and wonder about them. He was looking to his left, to the Channel and the cliff, remembering his cubbyhole.

He did not notice the two receding figures that appeared on the road to watch the cart. They were his mother and Isham Leith.

Redmagne arrived in Gwynnford wearing a dark cloak over his silks. He had removed the mole from his cheek and discarded the white wig. He still looked like a gentleman, but a lesser one. There were people about on Jetty Street, but no one stopped to stare at him. He had two destinations in the town: the Sea Siren, and the jail behind Constable Jubel Skeats's house. He tethered his mount in the kitchen yard of the Sea Siren, and went through the back door. He told the cook to fetch Hiram Trott. The innkeeper came back and Redmagne led him outside. He told Trott what had happened at Penlilly, and what was to happen tomorrow near Marvel. "I don't know how much was told Pannell. You may be implicated, Mr. Trott. I wanted to give you warning."

Trott looked crestfallen, and his face was busy with confusion and anxiety. But part of Redmagne's information was not news to him. After a moment, he said, "They brought poor Jack in with the others, sir. Nobody's been talking about anything else all day."

"Any Revenue men inside?" asked Redmagne, nodding to the kitchen door.

"None of Pannell's crew. They don't come here anymore, anyway. They've been favoring the Saucy Maiden for some time now."

Redmagne frowned. "You said they brought in Jack. What about Mr. Claxon? His leg was smashed."

Trott shook his head. "He was dead, too, sir. They buried him with the others in a hole up in the fields." He wrung his hands in his apron. "You going to try for Jack?" Redmagne nodded. "Need help? You know I'm good with a cudgel."

Redmagne shook his head, then took the man's hand and shook it. "Take care, Mr. Trott. Get out if you can." Then he turned, mounted his horse, and was gone.

"What to do?" muttered Trott to himself. "What to do?"

The jail behind the constable's house was a short brick structure with a row of six cells, built primarily to detain drunken sailors. The cells had no windows. The doors were of iron-braced oak. A trap door on the bottom of each allowed the passage of meals. Redmagne left his mount tied to a post in the alley, scaled the wall that contained the jail, and went from door to door, calling after Jack Frake through the traps. No one answered. He strode to the back door of the house he knew so well, for it was in here that he had been interrogated by Pannell and Rear Admiral Harle years ago, and from the first cell by the door that he was rescued by Skelly and ten gang-members. He peered through the tiny window. Two Revenue men were in the kitchen, leaning back on chairs, their boots on the table, smoking their pipes. Mrs. Skeats, he assumed, had retired. There was a ring of keys on the table near one of the men.

Redmagne took two pistols from under his belt, twisted the barrels, stood back from the door, and was ready to cock the hammers and kick the door in, when he heard screeches of rusty hinges behind him.

"Drop the wedges, Mr. O'Such!" boomed a voice. "There are two on your back ready to talk!"

Redmagne lowered his hands and dropped the pistols. The two Revenue men inside came rushing out. He turned around and saw Constable

Jubel Skeats and the third Revenue man. Both had pistols leveled at his head. The two other Revenue men grabbed his arms and snapped cuffs on his wrists. Skeats stepped forward and grinned at Redmagne. "Pleased to make your acquaintance again, Mr. O'Such. We thought someone'd try to hijack the lad."

Mr. Fix waved a hand at the open door of the cell he and Skeats came from. "Welcome back, Mr. O'Such. Your cell awaits you, and you won't be leaving it this time!"

"Where's Jack Frake?" asked Redmagne.

"Sound asleep in the next cell, sir," said Skeats. "He's had a trying day, you know." He grinned. "I don't suppose you'll be leaving us a shilling for our trouble this time. But meals are six shillings a day, if you want anything better than soup."

Redmagne smiled graciously. "Then tell Mrs. Skeats to prepare a pair of her famous mincemeat pies, the ones I know she sells to the inns here, who pass them off as their own. One for me, and one for the boy. And coffee, with a dash of rum to keep the bones warm."

"She'll be pleased to hear it, sir," chuckled Skeats. "It ain't often we get a gentleman for a guest!"

Redmagne turned to Mr. Fix. "Before I'm locked up, may I see Mr. Frake?"

"All right, but just a look. He got roughed up at Penlilly today, but he's all right."

Chapter 24: The World Turned Upside Down

AT DAWN, SOLDIERS EMERGING FROM THEIR TENTS PAUSED IN THE CHILLY air to look up at the blue sky, and then at the hill, and saw a small banner floating on a staff on the eastern side of it. Major Leigh and Henoch Pannell, from the second floor of the Villers mansion, where they and their aides had spent the night, used the officer's spyglass to look at it. "It's one of ours," said the major. "What the deuce?"

"It's a Customs jack, Major, with His Majesty's arms removed by white paint. A provocative desecration, I must say!"

"Where did they get it?"

The Commissioner shrugged. "Damn them to blazes! I should like to know that myself!"

"But I never heard of a gang adopting colors, Mr. Pannell," said the major. He paused. "I'm not certain I could fire on that hill now."

Pannell glanced sharply at the officer. "It's merely a rag, Major. Don't let it deflect you from your duty. Those men up there have an elevated sense of themselves, it seems. But then all criminals do, don't they?" He paused. "I think you should begin firing on that hill."

Major Leigh put down his spyglass and drummed his fingers on the window sill. "No," he said at length. "We'll give them a chance to surrender to you first. There might be women and children up there."

"There aren't," snapped Pannell. "The boy said so. I *did* bother to ask.

I'm not the ogre you seem to think I am."

"I never said so," said the major too nonchalantly. "Still, it would look peculiar if we didn't give them a chance — given the number of them. Might save my men wear and tear, if they did surrender." Major Leigh turned and faced the Commissioner with a glacial expression. "You will accompany me under a white flag, Mr. Pannell." Then he turned and left the room. Pannell allowed himself a quiet curse.

Half an hour later the major, a lieutenant carrying a halberd to which was tied a strip of white muslin, and Pannell picked their way through the brush on horseback to the foot of the hill near the Customs flag. The flag served as a landmark, and without it they would have criss-crossed on the same paths, never coming any nearer their object. They saw that much of the brush had been used as camouflage, and had been cleared away. After returning from Portreach, Skelly had not bothered to have the entrances hidden again; the camouflage was intended to deter the occasional adventurer or the curious. He knew that it could not deter an army. Ten men stood waiting for them in a clearing before the entrance, each holding a weapon.

"Who's Skelly?" asked Pannell.

A tall man in a black tricorn and a black greatcoat stepped forward. "I'm Skelly," he said. "And you're Henoch Pannell." He paused to smile. "I recognize you, sir. I believe we shared the same table on one or two occasions in Gwynnford, for breakfast. You weren't very sociable." He turned and addressed the major. "And you, sir?"

"Major Leigh, of the Middlesex Brigade."

Pannell said, "We're here to give you a chance to surrender, Mr. Skelly. You and all your men. The choice is to stand trial, and take your chances with the courts, or to die here, miserably."

"Then there's no choice to make," said Skelly, "except in the manner of death we prefer."

"I should advise you that Mr. O'Such, or Mr. Smith, or whatever he calls himself, is in custody," said Pannell. "We received word early this morning that he tried to break into the Gwynnford jail. He succeeded. He is in it now."

"Who are you?" asked the major abruptly, pointing to a man dressed in the resplendent uniform of a senior sergeant of the Coldstream Guards. The man stood respectfully at a distance behind Skelly, and held a halberd.

"Charles Wilford Ambrose, sir," said the man. "Formerly of the Coldstream Guards. How are they, these days, sir?"

"A deserter!" spat the major.

"In appropriate company, Major," mused Pannell. "I don't know why you're so surprised." To Skelly, he said, "Let us not dawdle, Mr. Skelly. Will you and your men submit to arrest, or not?"

"Your breakfast is getting cold, Mr. Pannell."

Pannell snorted. "Not as cold as Warren Pumphrett's corpse," he said with a grin. "Remember him? A cousin of mine, for your information. And while it's quite incidental to me and the matter at hand — he was a bounder, wasn't he? and your wife wasn't the only one he dallied with — that piece of work of yours hasn't been forgotten. It will be up to the courts, of course, if you come out of this alive."

Skelly's face was expressionless. "By God and my country, let justice be done," he replied.

Pannell was disappointed that he got no argument from the man. But now that he had met Skelly face to face, he had a change of mind as he studied the figure in black. He saw no fear in the man's face, nor concern, nor regret. Nor even defiance. There was a priestly air about him, together with a vibrancy one did not associate with priests. The man exuded self-assurance of a kind Pannell had never encountered in other smugglers he had caught. The self-assurance had nothing to do, he was certain, with whether or not the man expected victory or defeat today. This was no wily criminal he was talking to, but someone more threatening. He was a rebel. And now Pannell wanted him alive. An idea was taking shape in his mind, a radical idea, though he did not realize it. He sighed. "Major, we have no further business here." He reined his mount around and moved away.

"One moment, Mr. Pannell," said the major. He pointed to the flag that fluttered over the cave entrance. "By what right do you… men… presume to display that?" he demanded of Skelly.

"The right of free Englishmen," said Skelly. "We have altered it to suit our republican sentiments, you may have noticed."

"You will kindly remove it!"

Skelly shook his head. "It's as much ours as yours, Major Leigh. Perhaps more ours than yours." He turned his head to address the man in scarlet behind him. "Thank you for the point, Mr. Ambrose. It was well taken."

"And ably parried, Mr. Skelly," replied Ambrose.

The major jerked his mount around and cantered back onto the path through the brush, followed by his lieutenant. Pannell turned once in his saddle, without looking at Skelly or his men, and with a desultory wave of his hand, said, "Good morning to you, gentlemen."

For two hours, Major Leigh's howitzer and two cannon pounded the hill. Residents of Marvel and neighboring villages came to watch, and were astounded by two things: that this was Skelly's hideout, and that it had been here for years; and the ferocity of the military action to destroy the gang. Some residents came to watch with sadness or grief; these were mostly women whose secret husbands or lovers were inside the caves. Most of the spectators were Whig families, who brought picnic baskets and parcels of food for the troops.

Inside the caves, dust and fine grains of stone fell intermittently from the caverns' ceilings. Skelly had recalled his men from outside for the duration of the bombardment. He sat peacefully in his quarters, a glass of burgundy at his side, reading *Hyperborea*. The other men waited in the main hall. Elmo Tuck, nervous but determined, fixed the men what he knew would be their last meal here, goose *a l'orange*, baked potatoes, and a dessert of *blanc mange*.

At nine o'clock, Jude Hockwell, a former goldsmith, ran in from his watch post at the sole western entrance to report that troops were forming up in the Talbot fields beyond the thicket on that side. A moment later the howitzer, also stationed in those fields, scored a hit directly over the portal. Rock and dirt collapsed over the entrance, and with a roar half of the passage leading from it caved in.

"Well, that leaves us just one flank to cover now," said Ambrose to Skelly. "They won't be climbing that hill on that side. It's too steep."

Skelly inspected the collapsed passage, and on his way back to his quarters stopped to accept a plate of Elmo Tuck's fare. "Mr. Tuck," he said, "you've made living in these caves an absolute delight."

"Well, Mr. Skelly," said the cook, "you see, it's a sort of Christmas dinner."

Skelly did not ask him why he chose to prepare such a holiday meal in November.

* * *

Major Leigh, astride his horse behind one of the busy gun crews, watched the cannonade for a long while, then lowered his spyglass. "All we're doing is raising dust, Mr. Pannell! That damned hill is solid rock! And there's not a man in sight! There's smoke, but it looks like chimney smoke!"

Pannell, watching through a glass borrowed from one of the major's aides, said, "I was hoping for a more spectacular consequence. The boy didn't say what the hill was made of. But your gun crews are superb. They hit the hill every time."

The major raised his glass again. "Pshaw! This is pointless, Mr. Pannell! We're beginning to play snooker with the ordnance we've already dropped up there!" He lowered his glass and said to an aide, "I'm ordering a cease-fire, Mr. Craddock. All guns. Tell Captain Massie and Captain Ramsome to prepare their companies to advance on the eastern flank, straight to that flag!"

The aide rode off.

"If you don't mind, Major," said Pannell, "my men and I will accompany your grenadiers. I want Skelly alive, if he isn't foolish enough to get himself killed first."

"I thought you hated the man, Mr. Pannell, and wanted him dead."

"I do. But he prefers one kind of death, and I prefer him to wait for another kind. He's tormented me for years. It's only fair."

Major Leigh gave Pannell a withering side-glance. He could not decide whether his dislike for this man stemmed from his reluctance to take orders from a civilian, or from being in the proximity of a species of malignity. "You may follow the companies in, Mr. Pannell, but not accompany them. Then you may salvage what you may."

* * *

At ten o'clock the muted thudding on the walls ceased. Skelly marked a page, and put his book in a pocket inside his coat. It was Redmagne's book. He had not given him a proper farewell. He wanted it with him. It *was* an enchanting story. He buckled on the sword he had taken from Warren Pumphrett, and took a last look at his painting of the Thames, which sat now on the easel in a corner. Then he joined the men who were threading their way past his door to the main east entrance. He paused to look at the inscription of Giles Kincaid.

Three cannon balls lay in the clearing outside the portal, among rocks, splinters of stone and pulverized vegetation that had fallen from above. The clearing itself was rock, once covered by a thin layer of earth that had been worn away by years of contraband traffic. The men looked up and saw that the Customs jack had not been hit, except by flying debris that had torn a few holes in it.

Skelly drew his sword, but let Charles Ambrose command the men, as they had agreed the night before. At Ambrose's word, the eleven men formed double ranks, first rank kneeling, the second standing behind it. They were armed with a miscellany of "firelocks," from 46-inch-long Service muskets with wooden ramrods, to shorter versions of these taken from Customs warehouse guards, to fowling pieces, to an ancient matchlock and blunderbuss. Two of the men, Elmo Tuck and John Greene, the cook and former highwayman, had a pair of pistols each.

Charles Ambrose stood to the right of the lines, his halberd in one hand, the fingers of his other worrying the knot of his crimson waist-sash. When he joined the Skelly gang years ago, his tattered uniform was all he possessed. Early this morning he dug it out from the bottom of a chest of the things he now owned, which included a box of one hundred golden guineas, on which he had hoped to retire some day.

Autumn had stripped the brush of most leaves, and they could see what was approaching, to the beat of a pair of drums, through the tangle of bare limbs. First it was a clot of red, then a stream of it following one of the paths. The morning sun flashed off white belts, cap plates, and fixed bayonets.

"Grenadiers, Mr. Skelly," said Ambrose. "There'll be no shooing them off. They'll give us a volley, then charge."

"How do you know that, Mr. Ambrose?"

"They can't reload with them stickers on the muzzle."

The grenadiers emerged quickly from the taller brush not fifty yards away. Two lieutenants on foot separated and marked the far ends of the line with their spontoons. Sergeants barked orders and hustled the privates into formation. A captain on horseback lingered in the background, overseeing the positioning. There was only enough clearance in the low brush between the two groups for a single field of fire. Skelly and his men saw another clot of red hovering in the brush behind the first.

"Two companies, Mr. Skelly," said Ambrose. "Tough-looking boys, too. Second company of regulars hanging back in reserve. Well, look at that!" he exclaimed. "Steel ramrods in their pieces! The Duke's been busy!"

"Excuse me, Mr. Ambrose?"

"Cumberland. George's favorite. He was made Captain-General a year after dear Jack joined us. He's been overhauling the army. Good idea, steel ramrods."

"Oh, yes," mused Skelly. "I read something about him." He sensed that Ambrose was not just making conversation. He noticed an unshed tear in the eye he was able to see from profile, but did not draw attention to it. The man was afraid. Curiously, he thought, his own eyes were dry, and he was unafraid. He patted the man on his shoulder. "Mr. Ambrose, this is your show. Thank you for everything."

Without waiting for a reply, he strode to the front of the two lines of his men. He doffed his hat to them, then turned to address the grenadiers. Pointing with his sword, he shouted, "We are all Skelly men! We, standing here, and you, out there! Those of us man enough to cherish our liberty!" Then Skelly stepped through the ranks to the rear, and pointed to the Customs jack above them. "Fire on us, if you dare!" He lowered his sword and held it, one hand on the hilt, the other on the end of the blade.

There was a moment of silence as the two lines faced each other. Skelly and his men scrutinized the faces of the men they could see fifty yards away. The grenadiers, standing "under arms," stared back at them with grim, closed expressions.

A calm, masculine voice said, "Cut them down, Lieutenant."

"Poise firelocks!" shouted the lieutenant. A sergeant repeated that order and every order which followed. The line of scarlet raised forty muskets in the air.

"Cock firelocks!" shouted the lieutenant. "Cock firelocks!" shouted Ambrose in unison with the grenadier sergeants. The Skelly men pulled back the cocks of their weapons.

"Present firelocks!" shouted the lieutenant. Forty muskets swung down with their gleaming bayonets. "*Aim* firelocks!" shouted Ambrose. The Skelly men brought their weapons to bear.

"Fire!" shouted the lieutenant. "Fire!" shouted Ambrose.

With an ear-splitting crackle of ignited powder, tongues of flame leapt from the two lines, punctuated by screams and gasps from both sides. The staccato musketry lasted only three seconds. There was little wind, and the acrid white smoke from fifty-two discharged guns did not drift away immediately, but clung to the lines like gloating entities savoring the carnage they hid.

When it was clear enough for each side to see through it, there were three vacancies in the line of scarlet. Five of Skelly's men were down. Elmo Tuck was dead, as were John Greene and Jude Hockwell. Rudolph Early, an instrument maker, took a ball in his collar bone and was knocked unconscious. Isaac Lightburn, a warehouseman, was hit in his right knee, and was struggling to prop himself up on the back of John Greene. He picked up one of the highwayman's pistols.

Charles Ambrose, the most conspicuous target, stood with his halberd, unscathed. Such was the erratic accuracy of eighteenth-century weaponry.

Skelly lay on the ground, a gash on his forehead. Ambrose shouted, "Close ranks, reload, and prepare to meet a charge!" He walked over to Skelly, and saw a hole in the chest of the greatcoat. But before he could stoop to determine whether the man was dead or alive, the lieutenant shouted, "Charge bayonets!" The line of grenadiers answered, "Huzzah!"

Ambrose rushed to stand at the end of the line of surviving Skelly men. "Cock firelocks!"

"Charge!" shouted the lieutenant, abandoning his spontoon and brandishing his sword. The drummer boys in the rear beat the charge.

"Aim firelocks!" shouted Ambrose. He waited until the advancing line of red was twenty yards away. "Fire!"

The Skelly men delivered a second volley. Two grenadiers stumbled in the brush and went down.

There could be no real contest between thirty-five veterans with bayonets, who had fought the French, and seven men with no bayonets, who had fought no one. The Skelly men managed to rush forward a few feet and use their weapons as clubs, but each was instantly cornered by two grenadiers and brought down. Other grenadiers bayoneted the men felled in the original volley, dead and wounded alike. It was the custom then. The fallen men were criminals, not soldiers.

Only Ambrose was able to keep the grenadiers at bay with his halberd. One of the sergeants dueled him staff to staff, and it was only when he had knocked the grenadier's halberd aside and struck his face with the end of his own, that two privates found the chance to run him through with their bayonets. The sergeant drew his sword and thrust it into the dying man's chest, for the impudence of wearing the King's scarlet.

"Search the caves, clean them out," ordered the captain, who had ridden in behind his men. He reprimanded the young lieutenant for leaving his spontoon behind, then rode up to the figure in the black greatcoat. The other lieutenant knelt and examined the man. "He's still breathing, sir."

The captain said, "That Revenue chap wanted him alive, if possible. Fix a stretcher. But first remove *that*." He raised a gloved hand and cocked a finger at the Customs jack hanging limply on the pole. "It is offensive to my eyes."

The second company of regulars swarmed in and was put to work scouring the hill in search of other smugglers. Pannell and his men rode up to the captain. "Fine work, Captain," said the Commissioner. "It's always a thrill to see our troops in action."

The captain regarded the Commissioner for a moment. "Thank you, Mr. Pannell. But I think your compliments do not suit the occasion. This was no fight at all."

Pannell was not certain by the captain's manner whether he was being advised or snubbed. He leaned over in his saddle and said quietly to one of his men, "Mr. Craun, everything inside is Crown evidence. You and the others see to it that none of it is… disturbed. Looting, you know." Craun and his colleagues dismounted and followed the grenadiers into the caves.

Pannell himself jumped down and leaned over Skelly. "Good. He's still alive. Not too much damage." He rose and laughed. "Behold a man who had an elevated sense of himself, Captain. And look at him now!" He waved a hand to indicate the other dead men. "Look at all of them!"

The captain asked, despite his reluctance to continue conversation with the Commissioner, "What did he mean by that? Being 'Skelly men,' I mean. Strangest ranting I've ever heard."

"It was just cheap rabble talk, Captain. Pay it no mind."

The lieutenant returned with the Customs jack on its staff and offered it to the captain. The captain's nostrils contracted and he nodded to Pannell. "It's the Commissioner's, Mr. Brown." The lieutenant handed the staff to Pannell.

Pannell held it for a moment. "See this, Captain? Soon I'll be able to trade this rag in for a great house and land with lackeys to work it for me. I shall call it Pannell Hall, and *this* will hang in my dining room! I invite you and Major Leigh to dine with me." He threw the staff down so that it draped over Skelly. "Thank you, Mr. Skelly!" Then he wandered away, laughing quietly to himself, kicking the bodies of the fallen gang-members.

The captain and lieutenant exchanged discreet glances. They thought the Commissioner was mad.

Chapter 25: The Prisoners

JACK FRAKE WAS DREAMING THAT HE WAS IN LONDON, IN THE FRONT ROW of the King's Theatre, and that Redmagne was appearing in an opera set in ancient Rome. Redmagne, he knew, had written the opera himself, and of course had cast himself in the hero's role. Skelly was in it, too, even though Jack Frake knew that the man could not sing. They played Roman noblemen who conspired to avenge the death of John Fineux, who had been murdered by henchmen of Emperor Nero, whose role was played by an actor who resembled Henoch Pannell, but was not the Commissioner himself. Fineux's body lay on the stage, in the incongruous garb of breeches, frock coat and cocked hat. When Nero gestured to his spear-bearing soldiers to slay the noblemen, Redmagne and Skelly drew their stage swords, and suddenly the whole gang appeared as if by magic behind them, some in Roman costume, others in English dress. Redmagne waited for the great orchestra in the pit to complete the overture, and then his tenor voice, in a heavy Scots brogue, pierced the hall with "The Death of Parcy Reed."

"They've stown the bridle off your steed,
And they've put water in your long gun!
They've fixed your sword within its sheath,
That out again it winna come!

"Awaken ye, waken ye, Parcy Reed,
Or by your enemies be taken!
For yonder are the twelve Cæsars,
And for your blood they're achin'!"

Skelly was about to answer with further altered stanzas from the ballad, which Redmagne once performed for the gang in the caves, when something alerted Jack Frake that he was not hearing it in his dream. He awoke with a start, rolled off the straw mattress and jumped to his feet. "Redmagne!" he called out in the darkness.

"Next cell, Jack," came a muted voice through the brick walls of the cell. "Use the trap door."

Jack Frake fell to his stomach and slid the iron plate aside. The moon was out and lit up the wall and the mire of the yard. Cold air shot through the open slit, and he could see his breath now. "Redmagne! How did you — Where are the others?"

"I'm alone. Thought I'd get you and Richard out of here," said Redmagne. "But they were waiting for me. And here I am."

"Richard died on the way here."

"I know." Redmagne paused. "How's your head, Jack? That fellow Fix said it got damaged."

"It still hurts a bit."

"Tell me what happened."

Jack Frake described the attack of the Revenue men at Penlilly. "I didn't tell Pannell a thing, Redmagne!" he said. "I swear!"

"I know you didn't. Hopfius said so. Well, Richard's gone to meet his maker, and that's done with."

"What about Skelly, and the caves?"

"Those soldiers were beginning to surround the hill when I left on this errand, Jack. I don't know what else has happened."

"Pannell's a brute!" exclaimed Jack Frake. "If Richard hadn't gone mad first, Pannell would've sat on his broken leg to get answers!"

"Nuns pray, and brutes slay."

They were quiet for a while. Then Jack Frake asked, "Why were you singing?"

"I was thinking of what I want to say in court, when the time comes. I'm not finished with surprising the law. I was singing to celebrate my argument. And to let you know I was here."

"What can you say in court?"

Redmagne told him.

Jack Frake was not sure of the significance of Redmagne's ploy. It sounded magnificent and unanswerable. But he said, "They won't listen."

"Perhaps not. But you and I will hear it said. That's all that matters, now — that the words are spoken, that we disturb the air with their sounds. Perhaps they will find a home in men's minds."

"I hope Skelly will hear them," said Jack Frake. "No! I hope he never hears them! I hope he's escaped!"

"I don't think he'll escape, Jack."

Jack Frake said nothing in answer. Then the power of the events of the day crushed his calm, and his head fell into the crook of his arm. He wept silently. Redmagne, who could hear an occasional groan and sob, did not need to ask what was wrong. He sat up in his cell and leaned against the damp wall, and thought about Millicent Morley.

The day passed. Constable Skeats brought the prisoners mincemeat pies and tankards of rum-laced coffee. Jack Frake ate. He was ravenous. He and Redmagne talked about London through the traps to pass the time. The boy told Redmagne about his dream, and Redmagne laughed. Then they both dozed off.

Jack Frake awoke again to the screech of a cell door. It was not his own. He heard many footsteps in the yard, and then Henoch Pannell say, "Good evening, Mr. O'Such. You have a visitor."

Jack Frake heard the clank of leg braces.

"Augustus!" exclaimed Redmagne.

"John," said Skelly.

"Your head's bandaged!"

"My hip might've been in worse shape, too, except that Drury Trantham stopped a ball. Had your book in my pocket… this morning."

"Which I've relieved him of," said Pannell. "He'll have to finish that novel some other time."

"Sorry, John, but I only had time to read up to Chapter thirty-six, where Drury is on the verge of seducing the high priestess of Apollo."

"Augustus," said Redmagne, "what about… the others?"

Jack Frake knew by the silence that Skelly answered with a shake of his head.

"All right," said Pannell, "that's enough of the pleasantries! Mr. Fix, put him in the last cell. You and the others set up a watch of three men outside these cells, at all times. God help you if anything happens to these scum."

Henoch Pannell also had an appetite that night, not for food, but for thought. He was having the only stroke of genius he was to have in his life. It did not animate him; it bothered him, and kept him from sleep and rest. He thought and mumbled to himself and paced the floor of his room until dawn. He would not let go of the idea until he had worked out all its nuances.

He gave himself credit for the notion, but was disinclined to examine it or trace its source, even though the contributing factors were fresh in his mind. He was not interested in how he arrived at the idea. He recognized it only in the image of Skelly. He had expected to encounter an ostentatious, flamboyant character whose mouth ran ahead of his discretion, the kind he had met before among smugglers and even common criminals, and on whom he placed little importance. Skelly, however, loomed large in his mind; in fact, towered over all the smugglers and criminals he had ever dealt with. Skelly, he knew, would remain unconquered even in defeat, or under torture, or on the gallows. When Major Leigh's surgeon had revived him and treated his head wound, Skelly was immediately cuffed hand and boot, and brought to Gwynnford on a cart. Yet, thought Pannell, the man bore himself like a king in chains. Which, reflected the Commissioner, was an ironic thing to think.

He was not just a rebel; he posed a bigger threat to the tranquillity of the Crown than had the Young Pretender, and especially to his, Henoch Pannell's, own tranquillity and his confidence in his place in the Crown's scheme of things. If the Pretender had succeeded in ousting King George, he thought, it would have been an easy thing to switch fealty and even one's church, once the dust of that magnitude of upheaval had settled and the blood spilled during it had congealed in men's memories. One king was as good as another. But Skelly represented something hideously worse, in Pannell's mind: no necessity for fealty at all, no lords, no privileges, no perquisites, no sinecures, no deference, no established *place* to work for. No special rewards in recognition of *service to the Crown*. In fact, no Crown.

No Crown! thought Pannell that night, as the draft of his pacing whipped the flames of his candles in the room. When he tried to imagine it, all he could conjure up was a great black hole into which he would be propelled by the erasure of everything he envied others for. The prospect was so frightening that his mind would not permit itself to give it another visual shape or form. But Skelly could exist without a Crown; he did not need to be a thread of its silken fabric, or be a strand of its velvet, or one of its jewels, to be Skelly. And though it was an impediment, he did not even bother to defy the Crown, as other rebels had. He opposed it — oh, how he had opposed it, when he could have easily escaped through the thickets surrounding those damned caves! — but the Crown meant less to him as a nemesis than did a reef or a rock on the Cornwall coast. Pannell did not need to be told this by Skelly or by anyone else. He simply fathomed the thing, without completely understanding it. Strange conception of a man, thought the Commissioner, the strangest he had ever observed! He knew that he must impress the court with the urgency of this phenomenon. You need not understand the anatomy of a shark to know that it can eat you.

At the same time that Pannell was churning these things in his mind, he was also working on a remedy, a solution, a means of plugging that great black hole. He knew too well in what esteem the people of Cornwall held Skelly and his gang. The affection granted these men by these people was more genuine than that granted the King in their toasts. The one affection was mere ritual and bravado; the other was heart-felt. He knew of a way to bring Skelly down in their eyes, and he had the means. All he needed to do now was to work out the details. And to be bold.

When dawn came, and men began to appear on Jetty Street below, Pannell had written four letters, two of them to go with the royal post-rider who would be stopping at the customs house today. One was to a friend of his in the Attorney-General's office in London. Another was to the Lord Chancellor himself, also in London. Another, to be carried by one of his own men, was to a colonel of dragoons in Saltash, who had provided him with mounted troops in the past, asking him to help secure and transport what had been found in Skelly's caves to the customs warehouse in Gwynnford. He already had three men guarding the caves now, to protect them from looters.

The fourth letter he set aside for personal delivery.

Isham Leith rode into Gwynnford with some trepidation. News of Skelly's capture near Marvel preceded the smuggler's arrival in town shackled to the bed of a cart. He was as stunned as everyone else, but less than most, for he had seen Jack Frake being taken to Gwynnford the day before, and realized that something was up. He wondered if the boy had talked, and if he had, whether he would now talk about Robert Parmley. Pannell could not have been referring to the boy that night when he claimed to have a witness. He could have known nothing about Jack Frake's role, unless the boy talked. But no one in the streets took notice of him. No one threw rocks at him, shouting, "There's the parson's murderer!" or "There's Skelly's informer!"

Huldah had succumbed to some odd hysterics after seeing her son, and for a fearful while he had expected her to ask him to do something for the boy. But she had quieted down, and did not plead with him. He was spared the necessity of having to slap her silly and remind her of their plan to sell Jack to the spirits. She remembered.

Anxiety drove him to Gwynnford, and curiosity, and hunger for news. His mind turned over all the possibilities and implications, but was able to resolve nothing. He left his mount tied to a post outside the Saucy Maiden, and wandered about town as though in a dream.

He found himself walking up and down Jetty Street past Constable Skeats's house. Like a hawk hovering over a field where it knows it has seen a rabbit, Leith knew that Jack Frake was in one of the cells in the back of the house. One half of his mind would not admit what the other half was doing, which was contriving a way of getting to the boy. To silence him. But he had heard that the cells were being guarded by Pannell's men, and that the Commissioner planned to take his prisoners to Falmouth on a coaster this afternoon.

Leith stepped into the Saucy Maiden to order a gill of whisky to calm his nerves. And there was Mr. Fix and a younger Revenue man, sitting at a table. Fix saw him come in, nodded, then raised his eyes and jerked his chin up. Leith gulped. Pannell wanted to see him.

Leith went back out and around to the inn stables, then stole up the stairs to Pannell's room. The Commissioner was there with two of his men. "Ah, Mr. Leith!" greeted Pannell. "You save me the bother of sending for you. Gentlemen, will you please excuse us?" The two Revenue men left.

"Well, Mr. Leith," said Pannell, who took a bottle and poured himself and his visitor brandy. "I wanted to express my thanks to you," he said, handing Leith a glass. "And to tell you that you won't be seeing much more of me." He walked away and sat down in his armchair. "Oh, I imagine I might return for the tedious but admittedly pleasant task of appraising the value of the contents of Skelly's hideout. There are my men to be paid, not to mention the Treasury — but other than that, I am done with Gwynnford." He paused and took an envelope from the side table he had been using as a desk, and fingered it as he spoke. "And you are here on what errand, Mr. Leith? More information for me, I gather?"

"No, sir." Leith had not touched the brandy, and did not know how to broach the subject. He said, "I stopped in downstairs for a bite to eat, and Mr. Fix said you wanted to see me. That's all."

"How fortunate that you stopped downstairs," remarked Pannell, who seemed to see through the transparent explanation. Then he sighed, put down his drink, and stood up. "Well, be that as it may, I have something for you." He held up the envelope. "I told you that your devotion would not be without its rewards, Mr. Leith. And here you are. This is a letter of claim to fifty guineas, made out in your name, for services in connection with the capture of Augustus Skelly." He smartly proffered the envelope.

Leith stared at the envelope, put his glass down, and then took it. He opened it and read the document inside. His eyes went back to Pannell, half in suspicion, half in disbelief. Pannell stood watching him with an enigmatic smile. He seemed pleased.

"Unfortunately, you must go to Falmouth to collect it from the Customs Bursar there. This is not my condition, but the Bursar's. Also, you will not be able to collect it until next month, when the Bursar has the funds to pay you and to meet his many other expenses. Again, that is not my arrangement, but the Treasury's. Naturally, all this will be done in close confidence. You will notice my signature, Mr. Leith. I may not be in Falmouth to assure the Bursar of the legitimacy of your claim, but that signature will allow you anything save an introduction to His Majesty."

"What about the… other matter?" asked Leith, not certain of his luck.

"The other matter? Oh! That!" said Pannell with a wave of his hand. He returned to his armchair. "Let us say that it is no matter at all. The chief witness is indisposed now. He is a felon, and felons are not acceptable as witnesses in our fine judicial system. The candlesticks? Why, it seems some gremlins *spirited* them away from my room here, and dropped them in the Godolphin, that sorry excuse for a river on whose banks this charming little town is built." The Commissioner finished his drink. "But, in all seriousness now, let us just say those pieces of silver have been misplaced, Mr. Leith — together with my recollection of them." Pannell looked at Leith with an expression warning him not to raise the subject again.

"What about Trott, and Rudge, and the others?" asked Leith timidly.

"I'm feeling generous, Mr. Leith. They may remain at liberty. When Skelly's gone, they'll get their just desserts. They'll just have to give the Crown its due." The Commissioner grinned. "That's all, Mr. Leith. I have a busy day ahead of me. Seems the constable and a riding officer in Styles have seized a sloop belonging to Mr. Skelly. The pilot and most of the crew escaped, but they were able to nab one of the mates. I've got to think of a way of impounding that vessel before too much time passes. Any ideas, Mr. Leith?"

"No, sir," replied Leith, blinking.

"Well, then, a very good day to you," said Pannell. "Thank you for coming."

"The boy?" ventured Leith, afraid even to say good day lest Pannell take the envelope from him. "Was he injured? I heard talk in town." He paused. "His mother might want to know."

"Master Frake?" chuckled Pannell. "Not permanently. But he'll dangle with the other two when the time comes. Very unfortunate business, that, but he is of age." He smiled pointedly.

Leith nodded his head, then took his leave. Outside, before he descended the steps, he tucked the envelope deep in his coat pocket, afraid that someone in town might see it and know what it was. He wondered now how to hide it from his wife.

* * *

Falmouth, situated in the crook of the Cornwall coast as it angled sharply to the south, was a larger version of Gwynnford. A "new" town, it occupied both sides of its arguably larger river, the Fal. A century before there were only a handful of sedate villages on its site, guarded by the wedding cake mass of Pendennis Castle, which sat at the end of the peninsula overlooking Falmouth Bay. In 1688 Falmouth became a Packet Service station, the first and last port of call for mail packets on their journeys between England and the North American colonies, and it had boomed. Its chief exports were granite, china clay, copper ore, rope, and fish. It had a customs house, a courthouse, and the King's Pipe, which was an ever-busy chimney in which seized contraband tobacco was burned.

Vessels entering the Fal from the harbor, said to be the finest natural harbor in the land, first passed the busy quay, then a collection of warehouses and commercial buildings, next a smoky graving dock holding boats of all sizes whose bottoms were being cleansed with fire, then the Chrysalis Academy for Boys, then a convent, and finally the mayor's palace. Across a neat square from the latter was the courthouse. On the square was a long, raised structure that looked like the frame of one side of a house under construction. This was the Falmouth gallows.

Skelly, Redmagne and Jack Frake were no strangers to the seaport. They were obliged to walk from the dock where the coaster that brought them here put in, as there happened to be no carts for hire at the hour. They were taken to the jail behind the courthouse, a fairly new building of green-painted brick with white granite Doric columns supporting a portico. The jail itself was a separate granite structure in the rear of the courthouse surrounded by a high wall. It had individual cells and a large area enclosed by iron bars in which as many as fifty prisoners could be kept. This pen was already noisily crowded with prisoners and their families; it was the practice then to allow a man's family to live with him while he awaited trial.

Pannell persuaded Humphrey Grynsmith, the Sheriff of Falmouth, to prevail upon the bailiff to remove prisoners from the cells to make room for his three prisoners. This was done. The cuffs were removed from the prisoners' wrists, but their legs remained in irons. Each was given a straw mat and a blanket. Usually a prisoner had to pay a jailer for these amenities. Pannell paid for them, as he did not want these particular prisoners to perish from the cold which swept through the iron-barred windows high above them. It was also the practice for prisoners to pay a jailer for food fit to eat. Pannell gave this man money to keep his prisoners well-fed. "I shall have these men checked regularly," he told the obsequious functionary. "If I do not see rose in their cheeks, I'll know that you're shorting them of victuals. Do not cheat me, sir, if you value your job." He asked the jailer to let him know if one of his prisoners wanted a woman, or asked for a letter to be posted, or expressed a wish for anything else. He instructed the jailer to let the prisoners stretch their limbs and partake of fresh air in the prison yard, but only under guard and without removal of their leg irons. He did not explain to the jailer or the bailiff why he wanted these things done. When he finished making these arrangements, he left with his men and took rooms in the Pennycomequick Inn three blocks away.

Neither Skelly nor Redmagne knew what to make of these arrangements, for Pannell had not spoken a word to them, neither in Gwynnford, nor on the coaster, nor in the Falmouth jail. The only personal attention the Commissioner paid them was when, outside the cell in which he was to be detained, he returned Skelly's bullet-damaged copy of *Hyperborea*, and said to Mr. Fix, "Remind me to get him some candles."

Four days later, Jack Frake was removed from the jail and installed in a cell of his own in the Falmouth Parish workhouse across the Fal River. He was not given a chance to talk to Skelly or Redmagne. Pannell gave him the suit of clothes he had worn to London in July, and made similarly thoughtful arrangements with the warden of the institution. "You're not to be worked here, Master Frake, as are the other poor devils in this place. The warden even has a library, and was pleased to learn that you can read. He's willing to lend you whatever you like."

"Why am I here?" demanded the boy.

"You are being considered for special treatment by the court, because of your age. For this reason, you will not be charged with the others. So you will not be incarcerated with them. They're doomed. You needn't be."

"Why?"

"That remains for you to see."

"I want to die with them!"

"With dignity?" chuckled Pannell. "There's nothing dignified in hanging from a gallows, Master Frake. Why, I'll even persuade Sheriff Grynsmith to let you watch, so you may judge for yourself."

"Take me back to my friends!"

Pannell shook his head. "Enjoy your stay here, Master Frake." He turned and walked out. An assistant warden swung the oaken door shut.

When Skelly and Redmagne learned that Jack Frake was not being returned to the jail, they demanded an explanation. The jailer delivered this demand to Pannell, who went to the jail and told the men, who had been strolling together around the prison yard, "The boy has a chance to live, if he cooperates on an altogether different matter. And he will cooperate. That is all I can tell you." He smiled. "Incidentally, Mr. Skelly, I have had your sloop, *The Hasty Hart*, impounded. Your pilot has eluded capture. You may take some consolation in that. But it is a fine vessel. As you were the only actual owner, you have forfeited title to it. The registered owner, a Mr. James Grier, I learned, was an alderman in Marvel who died some years ago, and who had never been to sea in his life." Pannell smiled. "I must compliment you on your sense of humor in that regard." Then he assumed his usual doleful look. "There are no other claimants to the property to be fined and punished. I will convince the Customs Board not to order its dismemberment, as is the current policy with seized vessels. It would make an excellent patrol craft and a valuable addition to our pitiful Customs fleet. I have recommended that it be renamed *The Spectre*." He paused. "Otherwise, sirs, how is Mr. Binns, the jailer, treating you?"

"We've no complaint but one," said Redmagne.

"I must insist on the leg-irons," said Pannell.

"No, the complaint is that you did not assault the caves two weeks earlier, on the 25th of October — St. Crispin's Day. We would have appreciated the honor and the irony."

Pannell squinted in bafflement.

Skelly said, "What he means, sir, is that you denied him the chance to deliver Henry the Fifth's speech to our late colleagues. It was a speech they well deserved to hear. Mine was a poor substitute."

Pannell screwed up his face in disgust. "Is nothing exempt from your mockery?"

"We are very much in earnest. You saw that in Marvel," said Redmagne. "But, as to complaints, were we emissaries of the King, we could not expect better treatment."

"Not 'our' King, Mr. Smith?"

"Not mine," quipped Redmagne. "Not anyone's, in fact. There are those, however, who feel the need of one. They have our compassion."

This answer caused Pannell to turn to Skelly and ask a question he had not wanted to ask. "You had opportunity to escape from those caves, Mr. Skelly. You and all those others. Why didn't you?"

Skelly answered with a deceptively serene smile. "The Crown robbed me once, with ease. It proposed to rob me again, and running suited neither me nor the others." Skelly paused. "I wanted to protect my property, that's all, Mr. Pannell."

Pannell involuntarily scoffed. "You knew what the outcome would be. You could be dead now, as the others are. What would have been the point of protecting anything then?"

"I've lived fully and freely as a man, sir. It was time I risked dying like one."

"That makes no sense," said Pannell with a superior air.

"What he means, sir," said Redmagne, "is that it is often preferable to die, and thus give one's life and possessions meaning, than to run, or submit, and render one's life and possessions meaningless." He paused, then mused, "To live free, or die."

"That would have made an appropriate motto for Ambrose's colors," remarked Skelly sadly, "where he had painted out the King's arms."

"Thank you. It could be taken in one of two ways: as a warning, or as a final, personal set of options."

The two prisoners wandered away from Pannell, talking. The Commissioner pursed his mouth contemptuously and watched them. He felt slighted by having been forgotten, but could not decide whether his sense of oblivion stemmed from the slight or the men's words. "Oh, you'll die, all right!" he muttered to himself. "You may be sure of that!" Then he turned and walked back into the prison.

Chapter 26: The Plea

A GRAND JURY WAS CONVENED IN DECEMBER ON THE ORDER OF JAMES Wicker, Justice of the Peace and chief magistrate of Cornwall, much to the consternation of the jurors, who were preoccupied with holiday concerns. The jury met in Falmouth, and Wicker presided. The accused were not present during the proceedings, at which evidence of the Portreach run was presented by Simon Haslam, the prosecutor, and closely examined. Redmagne and Skelly were brought into the courtroom only to hear that the grand jury had returned an indictment for smuggling, resisting arrest, and complicity in the deaths of deputized soldiery in the pursuit of their duties, and that the magistrate had endorsed the summary indictment as a true bill. There was the matter of the deaths of two Revenue officers during the raid on Skelly's hideout in Fowey in September 1740, but the magistrate set this aside until witnesses and evidence could be secured.

Skelly did not seek an attorney for the grand jury or the trial. He agreed to allow Redmagne to act as counsel. Redmagne, with some legal training in his past, claimed the right to represent himself and his fellow prisoner in court. This right was recognized by Wicker. When asked by the magistrate to answer the indictments, Redmagne stepped forward, the iron chain linking the braces around his legs clanking on the bare floor. He said, "We plead self-defense, milord."

The prosecutor, the clerks, the jurors, and the bailiffs all stopped what they were doing or thinking, and stared at Redmagne. Henoch Pannell, sitting alone in a spectators' gallery, gaped at Redmagne with astonishment. This was an unexpected ruse. He glanced anxiously at Wicker.

Wicker blinked, twice. "Excuse me?" he asked, not certain that he had heard the words. A plea of guilty would have resulted in immediate judgment and sentencing. A plea of not guilty would have meant a trial. Wicker had never before heard this particular plea in his thirty years on the bench.

"We plead self-defense. We were assaulted by agents of the Crown, and we resisted."

The prosecutor, his mouth open in near speechlessness, was outraged, and recovered from his shock enough to begin assailing Redmagne with some well-chosen, ungentlemanly epithets, but Wicker waved him down. "Even if the court recognized so ludicrous a plea, Mr. Smith," he said, "it would hardly apply to the smuggling charges."

"Begging your pardon, milord, but, yes, it would. The taxes which we sought to avoid violate our Constitutional rights to property and the freedom to trade that property without hindrance or penalty."

Wicker sat back and frowned in tentative amusement. "Explain that, please, Mr. Smith."

"All taxation is assault. It is merely a more efficient, insidious form of theft, but essentially the same as that practiced by highwaymen. We smuggled our goods past the thieves. The thieves, however, found us out, and assaulted us. We fought back, as is our right."

Wicker shook his head once, and wagged a finger. "'Tis *not* your right, sir, and the Constitution is not an issue here. You must answer the charges of the indictment. Guilty, or no?"

Redmagne glanced at Skelly, who stood behind a railing surrounded by bailiffs, then shook his head. "We do not recognize the legitimacy of the charges as they stand, milord. We have written *ignoramus* over that bill. Our Constitution is the only one in Europe which protects one's property and freedom to trade." He smiled with a wickedness that chilled Wicker to the core. "Either that means something in fact, or it is a cruel fiction amended at the caprice and convenience of the Crown." He stood and waited for the magistrate to reply.

Wicker asked again, looking past Redmagne at the man in the dock, "How do *you* plead, prisoner?"

Skelly said, "Counsel speaks my mind, milord." Redmagne smiled again, bowed, and stepped back to rejoin his friend.

Wicker would not recognize the plea, and at first thought of treating Redmagne and his co-defendant as standing "mute of malice," since Redmagne refused to answer now. In earlier times, within Wicker's own memory, a refusal by a defendant to answer an indictment was interpreted by the court as standing "mute of malice" or as "visitation of God," and the court would order an inquiry to determine which was the case. If a prisoner was found to have stood "visited of God," a trial was ordered. A finding of standing "mute of malice," however, resulted in the prisoner being compelled to undergo *peine forte et dure*, or ordeal by pain, to establish his innocence or guilt. But this was no longer the practice; that finding also meant trial by jury. It was a significant advance in jurisprudence.

Words had been spoken in answer to the charges; this Wicker could not deny. But he was under pressure to expedite the matter. And his mind, calcified by decades of passing judgment on formulary pleas, stratagems and arguments, could not find a hole in his legal knowledge in which to fit the peg of "self-defense." Wicker sweated under his wig. He was in a panic to block a dangerous appeal to the Constitution, one which he did not want to contemplate and did not want the responsibility of admitting. There was no precedent for it, and the issues the prisoner had raised foreshadowed wider matters which caused him to feel the first twinges of a paralyzing fear.

Still, the device of standing "mute of malice" was serviceable. After a long moment of thought, during which he felt every set of eyes in the courtroom on him, he spoke some words about the plea standing in nullity, and treated Redmagne's technical refusal to answer the charges as grounds for proceeding with a trial, resorting to the paradoxical fiction that Redmagne had both stood "mute of malice" and pleaded "not guilty" on behalf of himself and the other prisoner.

The prisoners were arraigned. Jack Frake's name was not spoken by the magistrate. Both Redmagne and Skelly thought that this was odd, but did not question the omission.

Following the indictments, Wicker scheduled a special assize in January, the day after Twelfth Night, for the joint trial of Osbert Augustus Magnus Skelly and John Smith. And in confidential letters to the Lord Chancellor and the Solicitor-General, to which he appended documents pertaining to the case together with a précis of the incident, he asked that a special magistrate be dispatched to the assize, as Skelly and his men were too popular, and the expected verdicts and subsequent executions might endanger his life, or at least render his continued tenure in Falmouth impracticable. He suggested the names of colleagues on the civil court circuit who had criminal trial backgrounds.

Henoch Pannell persuaded the Lord Lieutenant of Cornwall to furnish troops to guarantee the orderly conduct of the trial and of the expected executions. And he made further arrangements for a second trial, one which he hoped would be just as sensational as the first.

* * *

One morning after the grand jury indictments, at the end of the first week of December, Isham Leith bought passage on a coaster from Gwynnford to Falmouth. It was only a day's trip, and he told his wife, Huldah, that he had business there and would be back the evening of the next day.

In Falmouth, he strode up the street that paralleled the river and went directly to the Revenue Bursar's office in the mayor's palace. Here he told a clerk his business, and handed the man the letter of claim. There were other men waiting in the anteroom, but after a curious raising of his eyebrows, the clerk seemed to recognize his name on the document and rushed back into the Bursar's office. He emerged in a minute and asked Leith to wait on one of the benches in the anteroom. "It won't be more than a quarter hour, sir. There's so much work to do this time of year." Another clerk hurriedly passed through the anteroom and went out. Leith lit a pipe and waited, listening to the other visitors trading hearsay about Skelly and the indictments.

Twenty minutes later, a stocky, florid-faced man came into the room with two tipstaffs in tow, accompanied by the second clerk and, to Leith's surprise, Henoch Pannell. The Commissioner pointed to Leith, and the large man approached him. "Isham Leith, of Trelowe?"

Leith rose slowly. "Yes, sir."

The man produced a folded sheet of paper. "I have a warrant for your arrest for the murder of Reverend Robert Parmley, rector of St. Gwynn, in April of 1744. Submit to cuffs, and come along quietly." The tipstaffs had come behind him, and each laid a hand on his shoulders.

The pipe dropped from Leith's mouth. He shouted, pointing a finger at Pannell, "You great pile of sheep droppin's! You lied!"

Pannell smiled with a shrug. "May I introduce Mr. Humphrey Grynsmith, sheriff of Falmouth? You're in his custody now, not mine."

"Didn't my help count for nothin'?" wailed Leith.

"It counted for much, Mr. Leith. You will get your fifty guineas, if you don't first confess under interrogation, and I understand that Mr. Grynsmith is every bit as good in that art as his colleagues at Newgate. Or if you're not convicted."

"Why didn't you have me arrested in Gwynnford?"

"What?" chuckled Pannell, enjoying the man's predicament. "And embarrass you in front of your many friends there?" He shook his head. "I know it's been said of me that I lack merriment. But I do like to play my little jokes now and then." He paused. "Your real question, Mr. Leith, should have been: Why did I raise your hopes, why did I allow you to think you could commit a heinous crime and escape punishment? Well, it was my prerogative. You are a little man, but you will serve a large purpose."

* * *

Two weeks after the indictments, a day before Christmas Eve, several men met in the evening in the study of the chief magistrate's country house near Falmouth. They were James Wicker; Henoch Pannell; Fulke Treverlyn, a Crown prosecutor from London; and Lord Hugo Twycross, the designated presiding magistrate, who had been hastily drafted from his circuit court duties to handle the touchy case in response to Wicker's urgent letter.

Also present was the King's Proctor, Armiger Edgecombe, who suddenly appeared in Twycross's wake in a coach of his own. Edgecombe had yet to make the purpose of his visit known to his host, but Wicker dared not ask him his business. The King's Proctor, at that time, represented the sovereign when he wished to intervene in certain cases in which especial church matters were at issue, though his personal involvement would be seen as indelicate or controversial. Neither Treverlyn nor Wicker could imagine what interest the King could have in the Skelly case, though they both noted that Twycross and Pannell did not share their assumption that Edgecombe's presence was anomalous.

"It will be easy to dispose of the whole lot of these scum," said Treverlyn, standing before the fireplace, "but we want no complications. Mr. Pannell, you are certain that your witness will cooperate in this matter?"

"Yes, he'll cooperate," said Pannell, standing opposite him. He had been offered an armchair by Wicker, but he was too excited to sit. "He doesn't know it yet, but he'll cooperate."

"I've reviewed the evidence you have against this other party, and it looks fool-proof. An indictment is guaranteed. The local prosecutor may handle the Crown's case. Who would he be, milord?" asked Treverlyn, turning to Wicker.

"Simon Haslam," said the magistrate. "He presented the Crown's case to the grand jury. But, wait," said Wicker. "*I* am the chief justice here, and I would need to call a new grand jury to indict this person. I refuse to do it, at least not so hot on the heels of the Skelly matter. There are not so many qualified jurors for a grand jury or a trial in these parts that they wouldn't begin talking amongst themselves and see through it all. It would be a travesty of justice!"

"Well, then," said the King's Proctor, speaking up for the first time, "indict this witness with the rest of the accused, but neglect to include his name in the spoken, oral indictment. The accused do not receive a copy of the indictment, so neither this person, nor the accused, nor the jurors of the second trial would be the wiser. When the second trial is adjourned, put the witness in irons and read him his sentence — from the written indictment."

"Excellent suggestion," said Treverlyn with a chuckle, "but too late. That's already been done by Justice Wicker, at Mr. Pannell's suggestion."

Pannell took a sip from the glass of the Madeira in his hand. "The second trial will divert attention and passion from the first. It is a perfect opportunity. It cannot fail to achieve its purpose. My question to you, milord," he said, turning to Wicker, "is this: Will *you* preside over the second trial? It's absolutely essential that a man of your known character preside over it. You're practically one of the family in this lovely community."

The magistrate wavered. "I'm not entirely convinced of the necessity of my role in this ruse." He looked around at the expectant faces, then asked Pannell. "Where is this person? In custody?"

"Very much in custody," said Pannell, "and in very much of a frothy snit."

Wicker sat for a moment, thinking. "All right. I'll ask my associate justice, Mr. Ashton, to convene a *petit* grand jury for the day following Christmas. There'll be grumbling, but it shouldn't take more than an hour to secure an indictment, given what Mr. Pannell here has revealed."

"How do you think he'll answer the charges?" asked Twycross, an elderly gentleman seated across the fireplace from him.

Pannell's smile was faint but discernible. "He can be persuaded to plead guilty, or not guilty, if you like — just so long as he hangs. Expect no surprises from him."

Wicker turned to Treverlyn. "How long do you think I should, well, remain in *villegiatura*?" he asked.

Treverlyn laughed. "How *Italian* you are, in a venue so far removed from society as Falmouth!"

Wicker snorted in offense. "We are not all bumpkins here, I might remind you, sir," he said. "I am a premier member of the Silks Club of London, a most selective association of jurists."

"I did not mean to suggest that *you* were a bumpkin, milord," said Treverlyn with deference. He thought for a moment. "How long should you be away — ill, perhaps, incapacitated by some execrable malady? Well, I should say that if you took sun in Penzance, you may be tardy in convening the second trial. Even a brief sojourn in Wales to visit family would be too long."

"I do not have family in Wales," said Wicker, frowning.

"My apologies," said Treverlyn, startled at the justice's resentment. "I was merely making humor." He paused. "Now, I don't intend to dally at this trial. It's a pretty neat matter, all in all. The accused have no defense worth mentioning. I should think the trial would last no more than two days, at the most. And — *Prestissimo!* — immediately upon its conclusion, the second trial must begin, and also be brought to such a speedy conclusion that the accused of the second trial can be hanged with those of the first. I should like to speak with Justice Ashton and Mr. Haslam on the matter." Treverlyn strode over to the Commissioner and slapped his shoulder. "We owe much thanks to Mr. Pannell. He put his finger on the nub, milords. There is a point the Crown wishes to make in this matter."

"Which is?" asked Wicker.

"That there is no distinction to be made between *any* of the accused."

"Well, who makes such an unwarranted distinction now?"

"The people, milord."

"Oh… "

Treverlyn went on. "And before I forget, milord, may I compliment you on the reasoning you employed to deal with the prisoners' specious answer to the charges? A most unusual rebuttal to a grossly obscene plea, one which, I needn't stress, the King's Bench would not like to see encouraged."

Edgecombe leaned forward in his chair and said to Wicker with a wink, "A deftly dealt demurrer, milord, if I must say so myself!"

"Thank you, sirs," said Wicker. Then, unbidden, the fear he had felt that day as he tried to fathom the meaning of Redmagne's words came back to him. He exclaimed with an abruptness and a bitter petulance that startled the others, "Those men are a threat to the Crown! They must be exterminated as ruthlessly as Mr. Pannell assaulted their lair, as ruthlessly as the Duke punished those Scots rebels!"

"Milords," said Pannell, "can you imagine what would happen if all these smugglers and free-traders learned to use that trick in court? Or even on the floor of Parliament? Why, we would be poor in no time, and the King would need to return to Hanover for want of money. There would be anarchy, and chaos... And no Crown... " He looked earnestly from face to face. "There would be a revolution in law, and a fatal alteration in men's natural relationship to their sovereign. It could not be stopped... "

"We are all aware of the implications, Mr. Pannell," said Edgecombe. "There's no need for any *gentleman* to dwell on them. It's too horrifying even to joke about," he said with a shudder.

"We have endeavored *not* to imagine them, for the nonce," remarked Twycross. "Well, Walpole, God rest his soul, tried to scotch that kind of business back in '33, but no one wanted to listen to him." He turned to Wicker. "About your handling of that plea, Wicker. Well, it was a somewhat complex and confusing line of reasoning, I thought. It needs refinement. But, mind you, it did the job. We shouldn't complain."

"This Smith, or Redmagne, or whatever he calls himself," interjected Treverlyn, "do you think he'll make more trouble at the trial? Do you think he has another card up his sleeve?"

"That, I can't tell you," said Wicker. He waved a hand at Twycross. "That is now for Lord Twycross to worry about."

Pannell remarked, "Thank God he didn't pursue the law. We'd all be in a dither today. There mightn't be any advantage in pursuing a career!"

Twycross grinned over his glass of claret. "I do not expect this scribbler to surprise me, Treverlyn," he said. "Quite the contrary, I have a surprise or two in store for him." He turned and addressed Edgecombe. "Sir, would you be good enough to explain the thing to them?"

"My pleasure, your lordship," said the King's Proctor. He crossed his legs and looked at all the faces. "Have any of you ever read a book called *Hyperborea; or, The Adventures of Drury Trantham*?"

* * *

Isham Leith was accorded all the legal protection available to a man of his means, and then some. For his own protection — and for Pannell's purposes — he was put in a separate cell, and measures were taken to ensure that other prisoners could not get to him. The murder of a man of the cloth was regarded then as a particularly revolting crime, even in the minds of other murderers.

He smelled the muckish soup that was brought to him before he tasted it, expecting it to be doctored with poison. His ears pricked up when he thought he heard his name spoken by prisoners outside in the pen. His body jerked when he heard a footfall outside his cell door. He dreaded the return of Sheriff Grynsmith, who had promised to take him to the cellar of the prison for a "quiet interview." The shouts of other prisoners' children and the crying of infants played havoc with his nerves. Even the prison ordinary, a meek, almost dwarfish man with a limp and a cauterized eyelid, struck terror in him; the parson would sit across the cell from him and recite the most gruesome parts from the Old Testament, then ask Leith if he had any thoughts on remorse and vengeance.

On Christmas day, a local attorney, Oswald Frew, arrived at the prison and solicited Leith's custom. Leith, desperate, frightened, and still recovering from the shock of his arrest, listened intently to the man. Mr. Frew suggested that Leith plead guilty to the *petit* jury's certain finding the next day, on the chance that, having saved the Crown the time and expense of trying him, Justice Ashton would commute his certain death sentence to life imprisonment or to indentured servitude in Jamaica. "Justice Ashton is a fair-minded man, Mr. Leith," he assured his client, "and will take your circumstances into account. Why, I've represented other men who were found guilty of, well, far more barbarous crimes, and he sent them to Jamaica and even to the colonies, where, I have learned, they are doing quite well, and have even acquired property."

Leith exclaimed with exasperation, "I'm doin' well here! I already got property!"

"Do you, now?" remarked Mr. Frew. "Well, it's up to you, of course, how you answer the charges, but I know that the Crown has weighty evidence against you. If you force the prosecutor to present it, you will incur not only *his* added enmity, but that of the jury and magistrate."

Leith hedged on the matter of his plea. He could not think clearly. Mr. Frew, however, succeeded in having his client sign a document in which he surrendered most of the value of the letter of claim to the attorney in lieu of his fees. He tucked the document inside his folio and stood up to leave. "Think on your plea, Mr. Leith. You have all the particulars. I will see you in court tomorrow morning. Oh, and Merry Christmas to you." Then he turned and pounded on the cell door to be let out.

Jack Frake, on the same day, was visited in his cell in the workhouse by Simon Haslam and his secretary, and informed of his own arraignment, and also of the arrest of Leith. News of Leith took the boy's mind off of his separation from his friends. He was told by Haslam that his certain death sentence would be commuted to a seven-year term of imprisonment or to a like period of indentured servitude if he would act as a witness at Leith's trial. "You do want to see justice done, don't you?" asked the barrister, sitting on a stool in the cell opposite the boy, who sat on the edge of a crude frame bed.

"Yes," said Jack Frake. "The parson was a good man. He taught me so much. I think I was fond of him."

Haslam had not expected so frank an admission from the boy. "Yes," he said. "Well, to make certain that there is no room for error, you must tell me what happened that day."

The boy searched his memory and told the barrister everything, from overhearing his mother and Leith discuss the "spirits" to the moment he hurled the globe through the parson's study window.

"Hmm," mused Haslam. "But you did not actually see Leith enter the rectory?"

"No, sir," said the boy. "But I turned around once when I was running through the field in back, and I saw them standing at the window. Reverend Parmley and Leith."

Haslam suppressed a whoop of joy. "Jack," he said, " — may I call you 'Jack'? — can you write?"

"Of course."

Haslam clapped his hands together once. "This is perfect, Jack! Now, Leith will be arraigned tomorrow, but we're not sure how he will plead. And if there is a trial, you, for legal reasons I needn't explain to you now, will not be able to appear in person as a Crown witness. We will also leave your mother's role in this matter out of it, as she will be punished by God better than we mortals could ever contrive." He paused. "Have you any objection to either point, Jack?"

The boy shook his head. "None. God won't punish her, though," he said. "She will punish herself by marrying another man worse than Leith."

Again, Haslam was stunned by this frankness. "Well," he continued, "what I wish you to do is give me an affidavit, or a written statement of everything you've told me. It will serve a purpose whether or not Leith claims his right to a trial. It will be examined by the jury tomorrow. Would you do that?"

The boy nodded. The barrister turned to his secretary. "Give him your things," he said. The secretary opened his wooden case, took out quills, bottles of ink, and paper, then set the case on Jack Frake's lap, and laid the implements on top.

Minutes later, Haslam, reading the first page of the statement as the boy worked on the second, remarked, "You have a very fine hand, Jack, almost as fine as my secretary's. Also, you have a neat manner of composition. I have half a mind to persuade the court to indenture you to me as a clerk. Did Reverend Parmley instruct you in these arts?"

"Some," said the boy, pausing to look up. "But it was mostly Redmagne who taught me. I helped him copy out his book, *Hyperborea*. And he made me write summaries of all of Shakespeare's plays, and Jonson's and Marlowe's, too."

"I see," said the barrister. "Extraordinary man, this 'Redmagne.' He should have remained on the stage."

Jack Frake said, "But he never left it, sir. I mean, he brought the stage down to his own life." He paused. "Sir, would you be kind enough to tell him and Skelly that I'm all right... and that I miss them?"

Haslam turned away on the pretext of studying one of the cell walls. "No communication is permitted between you and them."

"I don't understand. I want to talk to them before we're... hanged."

Haslam faced the boy again. "Didn't you hear me, Jack? I told you I don't think you'll be hanged."

"Oh... I remember." The boy asked, "Did they plead self-defense?"

Haslam frowned. "Yes, they did. But that plea was trounced, as it should have been."

"I knew it would be. But I wanted to be there to hear the words."

Haslam studied the crestfallen look on the boy's face, then sighed. "Finish your statement, Jack," he said, "and I'll think about delivering a message to your friends."

* * *

Late the next morning, Leith was brought into the courtroom, in chains, accompanied by his attorney and two bailiffs. Magistrate Ashton, a cadaverous man, glanced down at the haggard, unshaven figure below, and wondered why the man looked so pathetic. He knew that the prisoner had not been pressed for a confession, that Justice Wicker and the prosecutor had requested that Sheriff Grynsmith not resort to his customary methods of forcing one from a prisoner. There was something special about this rogue, he sensed, some connection between this prisoner and the smugglers. But he had not been invited into the intrigue, except to be urged by Prosecutor Treverlyn to expedite this man's sentencing.

"Isham Leith, of Trelowe," he began, "damning evidence has been examined and you are charged with the murder of Reverend Robert Parmley, on the afternoon of the 16th of April, 1744, in the rectory of the parish of St. Gwynn-by-Godolphin. How do you answer this charge?"

Leith licked his lips and looked from the magistrate to Oswald Frew, who stood nearby. Mr. Frew nodded to his client with a smile of reassurance. Leith gulped, then turned and faced the magistrate. "Guilty, milord," he said hoarsely.

The magistrate seemed to sigh with relief. "The prisoner has entered a plea of guilty," he said to the recording clerk. "Therefore, I sentence you, Isham Leith, to hang by the neck until dead for this reprehensible crime. The sheriff will schedule your execution. May God have mercy on your wretched soul."

As Ashton brought down his gavel, Isham Leith fainted and fell with a crash to the floor.

Mr. Frew, disconcerted more by his client's fainting than by the sentence, glanced briefly at Leith, whom one of the bailiffs was trying to revive with smelling salts, then up at the magistrate. "Milord," he said, "I promised him a turn in Jamaica."

Magistrate Ashton replied in a bored tone. "Jamaica is but a parish of Hell, Mr. Frew, and Hell is where he is going."

Jack Frake was brought into the same courtroom not much later, escorted by Henoch Pannell and two of his men. He was informed, by Magistrate Wicker, of his *in absentia* indictment, and of his sentence. "As you were not in possession of a firearm upon your arrest," said Wicker, "and because of your value as a Crown witness in the matter of the murder of Reverend Parmley, this court mercifully commutes your sentence from death by hanging to another form of punishment. This court has taken the liberty of sentencing you to a term of seven years' servitude as a felon in one of His Majesty's colonies. Following the execution of your colleagues, you will be returned to the prison to await transportation." Wicker paused to look at Jack Frake. "Have you anything to say to the court, Mr. Frake?"

Jack Frake, denied the chance to stand with his friends in this same courtroom, glared at the magistrate, and replied, "The court has *taken* many liberties, milord. You will have reason to remember the theft, someday."

Magistrate Wicker bent his mouth in a placid, condescending smile. "You emulate the audacity of Mr. Smith, your colleague. How do you wish the court to understand your remark?"

"However it wishes." Jack Frake paused. "If the court is so merciful, perhaps it would permit me to see my friends."

"No communication is permitted between you and them," said Wicker. "If it so pleases the Commissioner, he may explain this prohibition to the prisoner."

Pannell stepped forward. "Further association of this youth with those criminals may have a deleterious effect on the prisoner's character, which I and others judge to be salvageable through the tonic of hard and honest labor. I have gone to great lengths to keep them separated as far as law and decency allow."

"I see," said the magistrate, studying Pannell with new interest. "The prisoner may be returned," he said, nodding to the two Revenue men. "A word with you, Mr. Pannell." When Jack Frake had been taken out of the courtroom, he asked, "Why do you wish to keep the boy parted from his friends? I ask this out of personal curiosity."

"To accomplish what has been accomplished, milord," answered Pannell. "This was explained to you."

"Yes, yes, so it was," concurred Wicker. "But there is something else to it, I'm certain."

Pannell shrugged. "Let us say it is a form of punishment for all of them," he said. "The boy and his friends offended me."

"They offend everyone, it seems." Wicker paused. "Well, when the rope is taut around their necks, and those men are kicking for their lives, we will have done a great service to the Crown, greater than His Majesty and the Privy Council may even realize." He smiled. "Come to my house tonight, Mr. Pannell, and join Lord Twycross and me for dinner. I heard him speak highly of you the other day, and he hinted that great things are in store for you."

Chapter 27: The Trial

TWELFTH NIGHT, THE LAST HOLIDAY BEFORE A DROUGHT OF HOLIDAYS THAT led to Shrove Tuesday and the beginning of Lent, was celebrated the first Monday twelve days after Christmas. It was a day of building bonfires, of wearing masks to dances, of staging plays, and of playing innocent games of forfeiture. It was a kind of post-New Year's carnival. Skelly and Redmagne, in the Falmouth prison, and Jack Frake in the workhouse, heard some of the revelry in the streets, but paid it little attention. There were more merry-makers in town than usual; great numbers of them had come to attend the trial. Someone brought Skelly and Redmagne a Twelfth Cake, an elaborately and exquisitely decorated confection in which was buried a golden guinea. Mr. Binns, when he presented the men with the cake, said that the donor did not wish his name to be known. "He said that he sends his compliments, sirs, and wishes you both well."

Redmagne persuaded Mr. Binns to allow him into the pen to sing songs and recite speeches from Shakespeare's "Twelfth Night." His enthusiasm was such that, for a while, all the prisoners, their families, and even Mr. Binns, forgot that they were in a prison. Only Skelly knew why his friend was so full of spirits; he had received a letter from Millicent Morley, in which she promised that, no matter what the consequences to herself or to her father, she would sail for Falmouth as soon as she could.

News of Skelly's arrest and indictment had reached London long ago.

Ladies and gentlemen of leisure had begun appearing in town days before. Respectable merchants and their wives, tradesmen, doctors, lawyers and men of dubious occupation were filling up the inns. Residents let rooms at a shilling a day. The boys in the Chrysalis Academy were promised a holiday from their studies and chores on the day of the trial, so that their schoolmasters and wardens could attend. A company of dragoons rode in and were billeted in an unused warehouse near the quay.

* * *

The trial itself was an anticlimax. Treverlyn spoke and conducted himself throughout it with an arrogance moderated by boredom and pity. It was neither pose nor theater; he knew that he had a clinched conviction and he assumed that he need not employ much lawyerly art. The verdict was a foregone conclusion in the minds of the magistrate, the jury, the prisoners, and the spectators. He knew that the jury was friendly to conviction; it was packed with "fair-traders," and in the impaneling of juries the defense then had no role. Treverlyn built his case for the Crown with proofs and sound logic. He may as well have been demonstrating the blackness of black, or the wetness of water.

He displayed samples of what had been unshipped in the Portreach run: Italian brierwood candlesticks, Prussian cobalt blue glassware, Flemish parchment and vellum paper, French West Indies sugar, sacks of Portuguese salt, and bolts of Dutch silk. "All of this is but a small portion of what was found stored in those caves, gentlemen." He noticed that jurors and spectators looked longingly at the objects he produced, so he ordered them removed and went quickly to his next point. He produced Skelly's account books, meticulously kept by Chester Plume, and showed that the Crown had been defrauded of at least a hundred thousand guineas in the course of the master smuggler's career. He painted a glorious picture of how the grenadiers had braved musket fire and fierce combat to overcome Skelly and his band of criminals. "Four stalwart men lost their lives in that fracas, and a fifth lost the sight of his left eye." He produced witnesses — Juno Waugh, a sailor who had worked on *The Hasty Hart*, now seized by the Customs Service, and an itinerant farmhand who had been hired by Skelly as an oarsman and to help unload contraband — who provided a wealth of particulars about the Portreach run. This testimony, everyone knew, was given in exchange for amnesty on all smuggling charges against the witnesses, plus a generous bounty of ten guineas per witness.

He produced two other witnesses, Revenue men who had participated in the Fowey raid years ago, who identified Skelly and Redmagne, having caught sight of them during the fight, in which two other Revenue men had been killed. Their testimony had little to do with the charges at hand, and the bench, prosecutor, and spectators expected Redmagne to object. He did not. Neither did Twycross.

Treverlyn also made much of the healthy condition of the prisoners. "While hard-working citizens of this county have been obliged to save farthings and pennies, and forsake many common necessities of life to keep their heads above the foul waters of these hard times," he paused to gesture at Skelly and Redmagne, "*these two* have lived lives of indolence and profligacy from the gains of their criminal careers! Why, they even had time to paint pictures and to write books! They are no less contemptible than the infamous Jonathan Wild, who lived a life of ease while robbing the good citizens of London who honored him." The prosecutor paused, and then permitted himself some theatrics. He walked slowly toward the prisoners, glowering at them. "Look at these prisoners! Do they appear in the least contrite? No? That is because they have even spurned the generous advice of the ordinary of the prison to make their peace with God. In fact, they have made themselves so obnoxious to that good man's office — and this is a man who has endured the insults and rude behavior of pirates and cutthroats — that he refuses ever again to enter their cells! Surely not the behavior of penitent men!" He gestured again to the prisoners. "Gentlemen of the jury! Behold the bane of England!"

Redmagne, on the other hand, had no witnesses and no countering evidence. He attempted no eloquence, and resorted to no clever stratagems. When Twycross at last asked him to present his case, he approached the bench and looked up at the bewigged authority. He said, calmly, "We are free Englishmen who have committed no crime. It is you who are about to commit one. If you punish us, you punish all free men." He turned to the jury. "You will punish yourselves. Your liberties will hang from rope as surely as will our bodies. " Then he turned and walked back to the bar and Skelly.

*　*　*

The jury returned a verdict of guilty on all charges, and recommended hanging. No one was surprised.

Magistrate Twycross said, addressing the two men, "As reward for your utterly flagitious lives, you are sentenced to hang by the neck until dead. The sheriff will schedule your executions at the earliest possible date, as neither the Crown nor this county wishes to bear the expense of your continued existence." He added, as a distasteful afterthought, "May God have mercy on your souls."

The spectators began to murmur, but Twycross banged his gavel. "The bench has not finished." He waited until the chamber was quiet, then reached for a sheaf of papers, adjusted his spectacles, and began to read. "Furthermore, John Smith, in addition to the jury's finding of your guilt in the matter of smuggling, and all other matters encompassed by this trial, I have other grave communications for you. You are the confessed author of a fictitious work, *Hyperborea, et cetera*, under the name of Romney Marsh. I have been instructed by the Lord Chancellor to reveal this action to you, in this court, regardless of the findings in these proceedings." Twycross paused, cleared his throat, and went on reading from his notes. "Said fictitious work has been discussed in Chancery, by the members of the King's Bench, and has been closely examined by the Lord Chamberlain and by the King's Proctor, and their various lordships have concluded that while *Hyperborea, et cetera* purports to be an entertainment of moral elevation and ingenious innovation, its righteous tone and feverish grammar, however, are of a disorderly and fractious nature, solicitous of anarchy, public discord, regicide, and treason; calumnious and offensive to the person and office of our gracious sovereign; libelous of Parliament and civil government and of the persons who sit in those august bodies; apostatical by omission of the least regard for the Almighty; suggestive of heresy in regard to accepted doctrines of the Christian faith of divers denominations; and impious in its repeated demonstration of disrespect for the established church of this country, for public morality, and for representatives of the Crown."

Redmagne stepped forward and said for all to hear, "Has my book been judged without the privilege of trial? Has the Lord Chancellor turned *critic*?"

Twycross did not rebuke him for the interruption. There was a look of satisfaction on his face, and he glanced once at Edgecombe in the gallery and smiled. The King's Proctor had written most of what he was to read.

"The Lord Chancellor has instructed me to inform the prisoner that while their various lordships can find no recent precedent for lawfully suppressing said work, they feel that said work is patently disruptive of the public peace, and their lordships, together with a committee of the Commons, view the work with the darkest countenance. It is their view that suppression may be accomplished *de facto*, by branding a stigma of criminality on its existence. The Lord Chancellor has granted leave to the presiding magistrate to devise an *ex officio* stigma — "

Redmagne struck the railing of the dock with his fist. "This is treason!" he shouted. "Treason against the people of this nation! Even a Stuart or a Cromwell would show more courage — " The bailiff behind him raised his staff, which was capped with an iron ball, and tapped Redmagne firmly on the back of his head. Redmagne collapsed in the box, but was immediately pulled up to his feet by the bailiff and his colleague.

" — to devise such a stigma," continued Twycross. "Therefore, this court, in accordance with the Lord Chancellor's instructions, orders that a copy of said work be consumed by flames on the occasion of, but not before, the execution of the author for other of his crimes. For this purpose, the prosecutor will release the handwritten copy of said work, which was found in the prisoner's former illegal domicile, to the sheriff, who will direct the hangman to tar it and light it, together with available printed copies of the work, before the eyes of the prisoner, and then to proceed with the sentence when the work has been reduced to ashes. The presiding magistrate will strongly recommend that a printed copy of said work be similarly stigmatized at the Royal Exchange in London." Twycross paused to adjust his spectacles. "However, in the spirit of these enlightened times, the prisoner will be spared the barbarous practice of relieving him of his right hand for this species of felony, as had once been the custom."

Another murmur ran through the courtroom. Spectators looked at Redmagne, expecting him to make another protest. Redmagne said nothing.

Twycross cleared his throat and continued. "I am further instructed to inform you, John Smith, that all extant booksellers' copies of said work have been bought or seized by agents of His Majesty's Revenue on evidence of irregularities relating to the payment of stamp duties by the printer, A. Dawson and Sons, of Pater-Noster Row, London, for other of his endeavors, and that, while an inquiry has exonerated him of the charge of knowingly entering into a transaction with a notorious felon, said printer has been constrained from making further copies of said work, pending resolution of those matters."

Redmagne said nothing.

"A final communication for the prisoners," said Twycross, who permitted himself a quick smile, "and perhaps one more welcome to them. The Attorney-General has apprised this court that the Crown would be disposed to be satisfied with the penalties handed the prisoners today on the matters of the chance-medley death of Geoffrey Hockaday, son of the late Marquis of Epping, at the hands of John Smith, in March of 1733, on the occasion of a rout at the late Marquis's residence in London, and of the murder in duel of Warren Pumphrett, by Osbert Augustus Magnus Skelly, in June of 1728, at the prisoner's former residence in London. There are ample surviving witnesses to both acts, adumbrated by the prisoners' state of *pro confesso* after the expiration of the recently published proclamations of their numerous subpoenas in the *London Gazette*, at the Royal Exchange, and in the parishes of the prisoners' last legal addresses. The Attorney-General avers, and this court agrees, that a trial of the prisoners on these old charges with the same likely convictions would add a redundant expense to the Crown to no avail, as the prisoners can only be punished once."

Redmagne glanced at Skelly beside him, then spoke again. "Are we to be presumed guilty without benefit of trial? Is this another form of your *ex officio* stigma? *I* did not do murder, and my esteemed colleague and dearest friend here was defending his home against the rapacious machinations of a Crown carbuncle!"

Twycross shrugged in pointed indifference. "When the executions have been accomplished, the prisoners' bodies shall be taken down and put in irons, and the sheriff will remove them to Clowance Castle, a ruin some miles south of the site of this assize, where he will cause them to be suspended from the prominence overlooking the Channel known as Tragedy Point, and will establish a guard to ensure that the prisoners' remains are not removed by relatives or sympathizers. The remains will be so displayed until such time as the civil authorities are satisfied that others tempted to emulate the prisoners' lives and crimes are discouraged." Twycross sighed and put aside his sheaf of papers. He removed his spectacles and looked directly at the prisoners. "Have the prisoners anything to say in answer to the court's findings?"

Skelly shook his head. "I am found guilty by laws which wish me to seem guilty, milord, but by my immortal soul I am guilty of nothing. That is all I have to say."

Redmagne stood his tallest and said, "You have turned justice to wormwood here, sir, and brought righteousness to the ground!" He paused to look the at Twycross, at Treverlyn, and at the jurors. "You trample on the poor, and take from them levies of grain to build yourselves houses of hewn stone and to plant yourselves pleasant vineyards — "

Twycross sat back as though he had been punched in the chest, his mouth pursed in shock. The jurors and spectators gasped. In the gallery, a parson turned to his wife and whispered, "He's twisting Amos, the sacred words of the prophet! What better proof of his reprobation!"

"What better proof, indeed!" muttered Edgecombe, who overheard the remark.

" — I know how great have been your sins here, in this room — you who afflict the righteous, who take a bribe! I have never kept prudent silence. This is an evil time, I have always said, and I say so again!"

Twycross leaned forward over his papers. "Your blasphemy suits you, sir!" he said. "Bailiff, remove these creatures!"

Chapter 28: The Conquering Hero

On Friday evening after the trial, Humphrey Grynsmith posted a schedule of the week's hangings on the door of his quarters, which was a block away from the prison. Then he went to the office of the weekly *Cornish Gazette* and gave a clerk a copy of the schedule, which appeared in the paper the next morning on the first page. That page reprinted details of the fight at Marvel, and of Redmagne's attempted rescue in Gwynnford of another prisoner, whose name was not revealed.

The hangings would begin at eleven o'clock Monday morning. In addition to Skelly, Redmagne and Leith, three other men and a woman were scheduled for the rope. One of the men had murdered his uncle in an argument over the possession of a horse. The other two had broken into the customs house and taken a quarter ton of East India tea. The woman was guilty of making lace and calling it "Irish"; imported Irish lace was taxed as heavily as were tea and liquor, and she had been selling her product for a mark-down price per yard only a little less than if it had been sold with the tax. The court not only found her guilty of fraud, but felt that she had cheated the Crown.

Under the column heading of "Guests of the Gallows" were reported the lives and crimes of the condemned. This column continued on page two, which it shared with items of Cornish and local interest. Page three featured news from the Continent and the colonies; page four carried shipping news, commodities prices, and advertisements.

At the end of the "Guests" column was a short, special item on Tragedy Point. It was so christened years ago when an alderman's daughter and the son of a local baron, whose marriage banns had just been published in the *Gazette*, drowned when their rowboat was swept against the rocks at its base. This was not news to Falmouth residents; the editor included it for the benefit of those coming to town from afar to witness the executions.

Two women arrived in Falmouth the evening before the scheduled executions. One had traveled by coach from London to Plymouth, and from there to Falmouth as a fare on a packet. The other, after a journey on a farmer's produce cart, boarded the packet in Fowey. They did not know each other, and did not exchange words on the boat trip. One was dressed in her Sunday clothes; the other wore a lady's traveling suit.

When the packet docked at the quay, both made their way through the dark streets to Falmouth Prison. The courthouse and prison were by now guarded by a cordon of dragoons, for the sheriff was concerned that some dramatic rescue of the convicted smugglers might be tried. In the prison office, each woman asked to see a prisoner. One was admitted to see her husband, as was her right. The other, claiming to be the fiancée of her man, was denied the privilege, and, in fact, told that he was not permitted visitors except immediate family. "Then would the prison chaplain agree to marry us?" asked the woman. No, she was told; the prison ordinary would sooner venture to baptize the Devil than to breathe the same air as the prisoner in question. The woman offered the jailer money, all that she had left. It was refused. "I'm sorry, milady," he said, "but it's a Crown matter. You'll have to settle for seeing him tomorrow, in the square." "Would you be kind enough to tell him that I am here?" asked the woman. The jailer relented and asked, "What name is it, milady?" "Millicent Morley." "All right, I'll tell him."

Millicent Morley left the prison and wandered the chilly streets until she found a great house with a sheltering portico. Here she sat down and, leaning against a granite pillar, quietly cried herself to sleep. She had been given the money to travel by her mistress, Madeline McRae, a French Huguenot. Her mistress had read *Hyperborea*, and found her governess reading it, and forced the story of her encounter and subsequent trysts with the author from her. She was pleased to learn that her employee had such a gallant as a lover; the English could otherwise be so common in their *amours*. She had even once espied the two together, entering a London coffeehouse. She approved of the man. She and her governess kept these things from Ian McRae, who, though a lukewarm Presbyterian, would not have approved, and in all likelihood would have dismissed Miss Morley, if he had learned. Madeline McRae invented a story about a sick relative to explain the governess's absence. Miss Morley was expected back in London in three days.

The other woman was Huldah Leith. She was not long on her visit. Leith was at first glad to see her, for neither his brother Peter nor his cousin, Jasper Dent, constable of Trelowe, had wished to see him or grant him an iota of succor. But once his wife learned that he had pleaded guilty to the murder charge, she was not so much shocked by the revelation that he had murdered a man as by the fact that his confession would now result in the forfeiture of all his property to the Crown. She would be left penniless and without even a home. Other men, she knew, had endured terrible tortures from efforts to wrest confessions from them, so that they could leave their families something after their passing. But her husband had lost everything without a finger having been laid on him. In the cell, she proceeded to abuse him with violent language, then physically assault him. He could not resist because he was shackled arm and leg to the cell wall. The commotion disturbed other prisoners and the jailer, who found it necessary to remove her from the cell and eject her from the prison. Huldah Leith stalked through the streets and found a tavern, in which she fortified her anger with gill after gill of gin. No thought of her son or of his fate even entered her mind. Two dragoons at liberty took a special interest in her story, and offered her the solace of their attentions, and eventually of their caresses.

* * *

Across the river, in the workhouse, Jack Frake fell into a fitful sleep on his straw cot, even though he had fought against it. He dreamed again. It was not a visual dream, this time, but an aural one. Redmagne's version of "The Death of Parcy Reed" resounded in contest with the workhouse choir singing "The Coventry Carol," which Jack Frake had heard the group practicing for three weeks. To this cacophony were added the words Skelly had spoken to him years ago: "This is not a lark... I killed a man!... You'll beg to be hanged!... We will submit to chains... but we none of us will submit to their paper and ink parents!... I envy you your future, Jack... "

And then the dream became a nightmare, for a horrible face suddenly appeared. He could not tell whose face it was — Skelly's or Redmagne's — because it was contorted in a pain that seemed to want to explode its features. Sounds came from the face's wreathing mouth, gagging sounds like those made by the highwayman he had shot. He saw a rope as thick as a man's wrist digging into the neck. As the rope grew bigger, the face grew green, then black...

Jack Frake awoke with a start and sat up. "No!" he shouted. He wiped a hand over his forehead and felt that it was wet. "No," he said again, quietly.

"No communication is permitted." No words could be exchanged, no words of encouragement, or of comfort, or of farewell. There was a reason for the arrangement, thought Jack Frake, other than the one Pannell had given to the magistrate. There was a malignity beneath his ostensibly civic purpose. He supposed it must be a kind of punishment. But he did not care what the man's purpose was.

We are strong men, he thought. We can defeat anyone's purpose. We have been hardened by life in the caves, by living out our own purposes. We could not have exiled ourselves for so long out of an act of mere disobedience. Skelly was right. But what moved us to live that way, and to accept an end such as that which the Crown has deemed proper for us?

The answer was within himself, thought Jack Frake. He could feel it. He slammed his fists on the cot mattress once in frustration, because he could feel the answer, but not give it a name. "Perhaps you will find the words, someday," Skelly had told him. Twice. If only he could find the words now, he thought, he could shout them to Skelly and Redmagne as they stood at the gallows, and he would consider it part payment for all they had given him.

The immediate purpose of hanging was twofold: to end the life of the condemned, and to end it as painfully as possible. But a crueler agony, he thought, would be to end one's life without knowing those words. There were tears in Jack Frake's eyes, but he did not feel them.

No communication between the prisoners was permitted. The boy answered this dictum with: None is necessary, but for those words. If I survive what has been awarded me, I will find the words that have eluded us. I am willing to die, but I am also willing to be punished and sentenced to be a slave. Should I live, he said to the images in his mind of Skelly and Redmagne, I will find the words, and dedicate the answer to you both. I will write it down and reclaim the liberties they have taken from us.

There, in the dark cell, deaf to the plaintive sounds that floated through the air of the children's prison, Jack Frake was hurled back in his mind to the afternoon he had learned about the globe. This was merged, not inexplicably, with the memory of the day he had run away, and faced a blank future, and had felt the thrill of expectation that the emptiness was his own to fill. The two memories became one. He sat on his cot for a long while, much as he had in his cubbyhole on the cliff long ago, in a state of immaculate self-possession.

Then the first light of dawn touched the iron bars of the window high above him. He looked up at the bars, and his first thought was: *They are strong men, and will not die easily. I never had a chance to save Skelly's life,* he thought. *But I can deny the Crown the pleasure of taking it.*

The lock on the oak door rattled, and a warden came in with bread and soup. Jack Frake ate every bit of it. He was hungry, and he would need his strength to do what he was resolved to do.

Two hours later, Henoch Pannell entered with two of his men and a warden. "You will put on your finery, Master Frake," said the Commissioner, pointing to the clothes which Jack Frake had not touched. "This is a special day, and you should be dressed for it." He grinned. "It's going to be a nippy but cloudless day. We even have a special place to view the moment, with the mayor and Lord Twycross."

"Then what?" asked the boy.

"Then what? Good news, of a sort, though you may have ambivalent feelings about it. Simon Haslam, the prosecutor, has prevailed upon the court to indenture you into his service. Later today he will exchange five guineas for your papers. Of course, you will be chained to the desk to which he assigns you — until you have accepted the fact of your servitude. The chain will be removed when you learn to treat the remainder of your sentence as a kind of apprenticeship." Pannell paused. "I made no serious objection to the proposal. It is past the season, but I was feeling, well, generous."

"I don't want your generosity."

"It was not entirely kindness that moved me to endorse the notion, Master Frake. You flouted the law for a very long time. Now it is time that you be made to serve it — for a very long time." Pannell picked up the cocked hat — the one Jack Frake had worn to London — and inspected it, then threw it back down on the pile of clothes he had guessed were the boy's and had ordered brought from the caves. "Accept Mr. Haslam's employment. Your fate could have been worse. But — one hint of misbehavior or disobedience from you this morning at the gallows, and I have the power to have you thrown into the felons' den to await your original sentence. You have no money or influence to make your stay there tolerable, and your incarceration could last for as long as a year. You could very easily die of some disease, or be murdered, or simply starve. Whichever way you look at it, Master Frake, your future is not sweet with 'dignity' — except, perhaps, at one of Mr. Haslam's desks."

* * *

People had begun assembling on Falmouth Square early in the morning. By ten o'clock, an hour before the seven condemned were to be marched out of the prison, the square was surrounded by a circle of dragoons and a deputized contingent of tipstaffs separating the crowd from the gallows. The dragoons were mounted and faced the gallows; they sat with sabers drawn and carbines primed. The cart was already in place beneath the gallows. The hangman and his assistant waited with a pile of noosed rope.

The condemned would be allowed to make a parting speech. At Tyburn in London, the prison ordinaries, acting as secretaries, would have printed the condemned's last thoughts on life and sold copies of them to touts, who would in turn sell them to the crowd as souvenirs; it was a way of augmenting the priests' meager income. In Falmouth, this practice was considered bad taste, and was not followed. When the condemned was finished with his speech, the hangman would step down, tap the horse's neck once with his whip, and the trained horse would move the cart away from beneath the gallows three or four feet. And the condemned would hang. The hangman would wait for a moment, then proceed to repeat the sequence with the next felon, and the next, until all the felons were dangling from rope or until there was no more room on the gallows. No College of Surgeons existed here to vie for the bodies, which would be stacked at the side until the public event was concluded. Then friends or relatives could claim the bodies for burial; if no one claimed them, they would be buried in a mass grave on the outskirts of town.

Three of the prisoners were notorious, or at least extraordinary, and few of the spectators had ever before seen a book burned. The crowd formed along the lines of rank, status and occupation. Ladies and gentlemen of leisure stood together. Tradesmen and men from other "genteel" professions such as physicians and schoolmasters and their families formed another clot. Maids, servants, seamen and laborers formed the biggest group. Some in the crowd came from sympathy for the condemned smugglers. They were not numerous. Of the latter, some came because Skelly and Redmagne had defied the tax, and their punishment was seen as disproportionate to the crime. And some came because everything they had ever heard about Skelly and Redmagne seemed to point to an answer to a great mystery about their country, about their neighbors, and about themselves.

At ten-thirty two constables, preceded by Sheriff Grynsmith, parted the crowd and lugged to the gallows an open iron box on legs. This was placed in front of the gallows. Next to it was put a jar of paraffin and a tinderbox. In the iron box Grynsmith laid a great mass of papers, and on this a printed copy of Redmagne's *Hyperborea*, taken from Skelly.

At ten-forty-five the crowd parted again to admit a special group of spectators: the mayor and his wife; several aldermen and their wives; Lord Twycross and the King's Proctor, who had postponed their return to London to see justice done; Henoch Pannell and two of his Revenue men; a warden from the parish workhouse; and a boy, almost a man, in green velvet breeches, a green silk coat, and a black velvet, gold-edged tricorn. Spectators wondered who the last personage was; he was surely a personage, to be dressed so richly and to carry himself with the assurance of a duke's son. But this personage's wrists were held together by handcuffs, and the two Revenue men each had a firm hand on the boy's shoulders.

At eleven o'clock, as Falmouth's church and town hall bells rang the hour, the crowd parted again to make way for the condemned. Their progress was slow. Each prisoner wore leg irons, and the cuffs linking their wrists behind their backs were linked by a chain to the cuffs of the next prisoner. The first prisoner was an old man, one of the pair who had broken into the customs warehouse, and he walked with difficulty. Each prisoner was flanked by a jail tipstaff. Sheriff Grynsmith led the procession mounted on a great bay. He carried a mahogany baton capped with a bronze and silver orb.

The top bar of the gallows was of iron with grooves at the top to better secure rope. The supporting poles were of white oak, and created eight spaces of irregular width along the length of the gallows; some spaces could accommodate one prisoner, others as many as three. The condemned were lined up along the gallows, one to a space, with a tipstaff standing behind each prisoner.

Skelly and Redmagne were dressed as they had been when captured. They both spotted Jack Frake in the special group of observers. The boy bit his tongue and held his hands up to reveal his handcuffs. Then he solemnly reached up and doffed his hat. The men smiled at him, and nodded. Redmagne's head turned and searched the crowd for Millicent Morley. He did not see her.

The last prisoner was Isham Leith. Someone in the crowd shouted, "Look! The parson killer!" Rocks suddenly sailed through the air at Leith. One hit him on an ear and caused it to bleed. But most of the missiles missed him to strike a dragoon's mount or spectators across the square. Leith hung his head, afraid to look up at the gallows or at the crowd. Nothing the crowd could do or say could surpass the treatment he had received at the hands of his wife the night before. His face bore the bruises and scratches of her fury.

At Tyburn Tree, prisoners debated among themselves and with the authorities about who had the right to hang first. In Falmouth, this practice was considered an abuse of the prisoners, and was prohibited. The sheriff assigned the order of hangings.

Grynsmith rode down the line of condemned and tapped the woman with his baton. She was unchained from the prisoners on her left and right, helped up to the cart once the hangman had positioned it, and a rope was slung over the iron bar and the noose fixed tightly around her neck. She was a handsome woman with reddish-brown hair. She wore a gown of white linen that resembled a long smock, and a mob cap.

"Speak, if you wish," said Grynsmith, "as is your right."

The woman looked around at the crowd, then said, "I am Nora McGillicutty. I am Irish, from Donegal. My husband, a chandler, died, and left me to make my own way. So I made lace, and so it was Irish lace. No purchaser of my lace had any complaint about it, for it was as fine and dainty as any that comes across the Irish Sea. And what was my crime? No one will tell me, except to fill my ears with laws. This is the way of England." She looked down then at the hangman, and nodded. "Send me to heaven, hangman."

The hangman shrugged, turned, and tapped the horse's neck with his whip. The horse rolled the cart away, then stopped. The woman gave a cry, choked, and her legs kicked. The body will fight for life independently of its owner's will to live or die. After twenty seconds, the body stopped jerking. The hangman did not bother to determine whether she died of strangulation or of a broken neck, for either was possible, and it made no difference to him.

Sheriff Grynsmith next tapped the shoulder of the old man. The hangman and his assistant hoisted him up onto the cart and affixed the noose. "Speak, if you wish," ordered the sheriff, "as is your right."

The old man looked around with a dazed, sorrowful expression. "I made my peace with God and my wife." Then he looked at the hangman and shook his head in question, as though there were nothing else that could possibly be said. The hangman nodded and tapped the shoulder of his horse.

The old man died instantly; everyone present heard the snap of his neck.

Sheriff Grynsmith rode down the line and tapped Redmagne on the shoulder. As the hangman removed the chain that connected him to Skelly on his right and to Isham Leith on his left, Redmagne addressed the sheriff. "Mr. Skelly and I wish to be hanged together."

Grynsmith frowned and glanced, not at Henoch Pannell, but at Lord Twycross. The magistrate nodded. Grynsmith took out a rolled sheet of paper from his coat and read it while the hangman made his preparations. "By order of His Majesty and the courts, the literary work authored by one John Smith — " he paused to point his baton at Redmagne " — called *Hyperborea*, has been deemed unfit for English eyes. It is to be so stigmatized." The sheriff rolled the paper up and put it back inside his coat. Then he nodded to the hangman.

The hangman took the jar of paraffin and poured the substance over the book and manuscript in the iron box. Then he lit a match from the tinderbox and held it against the manuscript paper.

Dirty smoke emanated from the box, then flames.

Redmagne watched the flames grow hotter and higher until the whole mass of paper was a glowing cube crowned with a flickering arabesque of fire. Anyone watching him who expected to see a look of anger, sorrow or anguish on his face was surprised to see a slight smile on his mouth. When ashes began to ascend and float in the breeze above the square, Redmagne glanced up at Grynsmith. "That is my soul burning there, sir. I will speak now, as is my right."

Grynsmith nodded. "Say nothing treasonous, or seditious, or blasphemous, or you will be gagged."

Redmagne closed his eyes, then raised his head and looked up at the sky and the smoke rising in the calm, chill air. He sang, and his tenor voice silenced the rustle of the crowd and carried his words clearly to the Fal.

"Sound the trumpet till around you make the listening shores resound!
Come, come ye sons of art, come, come away!
Tune all your voices and instruments to play,
To celebrate this triumphant day!"

Redmagne lowered his head to gaze again into the fire, then shut his eyes.

A woman's voice filled the shocked silence. "Redmagne! My cavalier! I will be with you always!" Redmagne opened his eyes in recognition of the voice. He saw Millicent Morley, her hair disheveled and her traveling suit in disarray, standing directly across the square from him. She had pushed and fought her way through the crowd and obstructing dragoons to see him.

No one recognized the melody, or the words. Most thought it a curious thing to do under the circumstances. But one very old gentleman remembered. He turned to a bystander, a stranger, and said, "The last time I heard that was when I was a tyke of ten, on Queen Mary's birthday. I was a page boy at court, then." Only three souls in that unholy congregation understood the intent of Redmagne's ode: Jack Frake, Skelly, and Millicent Morley. The sheriff was too startled to protest, and in any event would not have known on what grounds to protest. Lord Twycross blinked once. Edgecombe, the King's Proctor, searched his memory for the relevance of the lyrics. Henoch Pannell furrowed his brow in cynical confusion.

The hangman took his whip and with the handle poked the glowing cube of orange and yellow in the iron box. The cube collapsed in a brief fountain of sparks. He looked up at the sheriff. Grynsmith nodded. Redmagne was led to the cart and he stepped up into it. The hangman fixed a noose around his neck. Next came Skelly. When the two men were standing together, Grynsmith said to Skelly, "Speak, if you wish, as is your right." He paused to raise his baton and point it with emphasis at the man. "Say nothing treasonous, or seditious, or blasphemous, or you will be gagged."

Skelly did not look up at the sky. He turned his head as he spoke, and seemed to address each face in the crowd. There was no anger in his voice, nor rebuke for his listeners, nor fear of his predicament, nor regret for the actions that had put him in it. He spoke in a simple but penetrating tone.

"*I* haughty tyrants ne'er shall tame… All their attempts to bend *me* down… Will but arouse *my* generous flame… But work their woe and *my* renown… Rule, Britannia!" Skelly paused long enough for his glance to fix on Jack Frake. "This Briton will never be a slave."

Jack Frake felt a thrill of honor electrify his being when Skelly's eyes lighted on him, a mixed emotion of pride and justice.

Some spectators recognized the words, or thought they remembered them, and were struck by one or another paradox, neither of which they were able to resolve: That these were odd words for a criminal to utter, for they truly believed that Skelly was a bane of England and as evil as the court proclaimed, yet the poise of the man and the readiness of his words contradicted these assumptions, for as Skelly spoke, the aura of criminality vanished and he seemed to tower over them all, more a man than any of them; or that his words contradicted all their assumptions about their country, for the words he spoke were born of it, yet here was a man who knew them, on the gallows, and who spoke them as naturally and confidently as they now realized they themselves might have spoken them. Of those who remembered or responded to the words, the first group felt anger; the second felt shame.

Lord Twycross sniffed in recollection of the words, which he had last heard sung by a chorus, long ago, at a masque in the garden of the Prince of Wales, near London. Patriotic pap, he thought, beneath the serious sensibilities of a practical man, fit only for fools. Edgecombe remarked to the mayor of Falmouth, "No, that Briton will never be a slave. He will shortly be dead." Henoch Pannell muttered a curse under his breath, and gave the boy in front of him a brief look of disdain.

Redmagne turned to Skelly and said, "My friend, you have upstaged me. My compliments."

Skelly grinned. "My compliments to you, my friend. And — farewell."

"Farewell, Augustus." Redmagne turned to gaze at Miss Morley. In a whisper which not even Skelly could hear, he said, "Farewell, my Millicent."

Skelly looked down at the hangman, and nodded.

The hangman raised his whip and tapped the horse's shoulder. The cart moved away, and the men's boots dragged on the boards.

Jack Frake felt the grips on his shoulders loosening as the Revenue men on either side of him watched the two men begin to dangle, kick and twist on the ropes. He broke free and dashed to the gallows, his speed sweeping his tricorn from his head, and leapt and planted his feet on the chains that linked the men's legs. He landed as hard as he could, gripping the cloth of the men's nearly tangent shoulders for a hold. The three bodies swung on the gallows from the force of the boy's action. He jerked up and down with his legs, his eyes squeezed shut. "Die quickly!" he whispered. "Please die quickly!" The crowd gasped as one and now all roared, half in support of the boy's action, half in outrage at being cheated of the chance to see two famous criminals struggle for life. Jack Frake heard one neck snap, and then the other, before Sheriff Grynsmith struck him on the head with his baton.

He plunged backward to fall on the stones near the hooves of the sheriff's mount. He saw Isham Leith, cowering in terror of what he had just witnessed. As he rolled over to his hands and knees, he glimpsed Miss Morley standing in front of a dragoon, looking at him with an expression of gratitude and pity. Then a hand reached down and pulled him up by the collar of his coat. Henoch Pannell whirled him around and slapped him while clutching the boy's coat. "You little bastard!" he howled. "I told you what would happen if you interfered!"

Jack Frake tasted salt in his mouth from the blow. He balled his fists and struck up at the furious face with all his might, as well as the handcuffs on his wrists would allow. The blow connected and blood spurted from the Commissioner's nose, and the cuffs left a gash on one of his cheeks. The man's huge hands wrapped themselves around the boy's neck as the boy continued to pummel the man.

It took four men to pry the Commissioner from the boy, and two men to subdue Jack Frake.

Jack Frake was led away from the gallows to the prison. Sheriff Grynsmith continued with the hangings, selecting Isham Leith next. But the spectators were too excited and too talkative to watch his execution with more than idle interest. Few remembered what he had said, as was his right, or whether he said anything at all. A carpenter bet his apprentice a free day from his chores that it would take Leith ten minutes to die. He lost. It took him fifteen, and as he swung and kicked and choked, spectators pelted him with rocks and horse dung. A student from the Chrysalis Academy dashed past the dragoons and snatched up Jack Frake's tricorn.

* * *

Three bodies hung from the gallows, and by order of Sheriff Grynsmith were not to be removed until noon the next day. There was no one to claim them. Huldah Leith, drunk and on the arm of a tanner, came to the square after the crowds had dispersed, and spat up at the body of her husband. She had no money left to return to Trelowe; there was no longer a home for her to go to. She became the common law wife of the tanner, and an occasional prostitute when money was needed.

At noon the next day, the three bodies were cut down. Leith's was put on a cart and taken to the potter's field. The bodies of Skelly and Redmagne were stripped of all clothing, tarred entirely but for the heads, and put on another cart. Sheriff Grynsmith, on his bay, led a macabre procession of workmen, tipstaffs and carts across the Fal Bridge and south to Tragedy Point along the coast road.

Late in the afternoon, in a cold, driving rain, his workmen labored hurriedly to hammer spikes into an almost sheer rock of the cliff on the small tableland beneath Clowance Castle. Other workmen unloaded lumber from a cart and hastily erected a guard's shelter. And other workmen struggled to fit the bodies into iron gibbets that encased them from head to toe. With great difficulty, these were suspended on chains from the spikes. Ships entering and leaving Falmouth would pass the bodies, which were also visible for miles out at sea as black blots on the bare grey rock.

On their way back to Falmouth, the soaked procession passed a solitary figure walking in the direction of Tragedy Point. In the rain and growing darkness, no one wished to raise his head from his collar to see who the lone traveler might be.

In the guard's leaky shelter, the tipstaff, left behind to ensure that the bodies were not stolen or tampered with, was too concerned with keeping himself wrapped and warm in his cloak to investigate a sound he heard outside. It sounded like a footstep, but he dismissed it as rain patter.

It was in the brief moment between dusk and darkness that Millicent Morley, by lying on her stomach, was able to recognize Redmagne below, then reach down and touch his hair. "Because of you," she said softly, "I am more than I was, my love, and to try to live without you would mean being less than I am. That I could not endure." She allowed herself a serene smile. "My honor demands it. A lady can be cavalier in action, too." She brought up her hand and kissed it, because it had touched him.

When the moment had passed, and it was pitch black, she rose to look out over the cliff into the void that was the Channel beyond. She could see a single, tiny pinpoint of light in the invisible rain, the lantern of a faraway ship. She stepped over the edge to meet it, and, with a brief whisper of her skirts, the void swallowed her.

Epilogue: The Sparrowhawk

HENOCH PANNELL WAS SUMMONED TO LONDON BY THE CUSTOMS BOARD, congratulated on his fine work in Cornwall, and offered the Surveyor-General's post in Harwich, Suffolk. Quite to his surprise, he was made a gentleman of the King's Bedchamber, an office which demanded nothing of him except to appear at state functions and which came with an income of five thousand guineas per annum. He was presented to King George, who asked for his story of the capture and execution of Augustus Skelly. He was also awarded the baronetcy of a collection of villages near the Pannell home, and was given a warm welcome by the Pumphrett family, one of whose daughters he married. With the daughter came a great house in Suffolk and an estate of one thousand acres, complete with human chattel to work them. Eventually he was asked by a committee of election officials to stand for Parliament as the only candidate of a rotten borough — Skelly's former borough, as it transpired — and he accepted with indecently vengeful alacrity. It was the beginning of an illustrious political career. In Parliament, he voted for every measure that added to or strengthened the Crown's hold on England and its colonies. And over the fireplace in the dining hall of his Suffolk mansion, he placed the Skelly gang's Revenue jack. Everything was as it should have been, he reflected.

A year was added to Jack Frake's term of indenture, for striking an officer of the Crown. He was put into the prisoners' pen of Falmouth

Prison, and leg irons fixed to his ankles. With other prisoners, he was taken each morning from the prison to the King's Pipe to help unload contraband tobacco and burn it in the great furnace. On other days he was escorted to the yard in the rear of the customs house, where he was put to work destroying other seized contraband: French molasses, hats made in the colonies for illicit sale in England, and other proscribed wares. He would have recognized the goods taken from Skelly's caves, but these did not pass through his hands. Wherever he went, he was closely guarded.

His soul retreated into a kind of self-imposed numbness in which he refused to let himself feel despair or pain, hope or joy. It allowed him to survive the bland cruelties and crudities of prison life. He said little, and did what he was told. He noted, from the depths of his isolation, how most of his fellow prisoners adjusted to their captivity. But neither they nor his captors bothered him much, for there was in his expression and bearing a deceptive calm which they correctly assessed as a tension that could explode for any reason. He grew thinner, and sallow. He became as inured to the prison food as he was to the things he witnessed in the place. Captains of merchantmen and agents of men who bought and sold indentured felons came to pick men and women for transportation to the colonies. On these occasions, Jack Frake stared murderously at the men, behavior which made them conclude that the boy belonged in Bedlam, and so was never chosen for a voyage.

He was waiting for Captain Ramshaw.

* * *

Early in March, the *Sparrowhawk* dropped anchor in Falmouth Harbor. The frigate-sized ship, only a few years older than Jack Frake, was built in Portsmouth as a troop and supply ship, in anticipation of another war with France or Spain. But the war did not occur, and the Naval Board ordered it sold before construction of it was completed. A group of London merchants bought it, among them John Ramshaw, who was elected to be its captain. Like most merchantmen in those times, it was armed. It was one hundred and sixty-five feet long, with a beam of forty feet. Its bowsprit was sixty feet, and its main mast was one hundred and sixty feet high. Its sail area was eighteen thousand square feet; it displaced eleven hundred tons. It had two decks, and carried twenty 18-pound guns, plus ten "Quakers," which were painted lengths of oak fashioned to look like cannon and to give pirates and privateers second thoughts about attacking the ship. In addition, it carried two swivel guns, one fore and one aft. These were small cannon mounted on stanchions, which could be pivoted in any direction to fire at specific targets on an attacking vessel: sharpshooters in the rigging, the pilot at the wheel, or gun crews. The *Sparrowhawk* had been attacked twice in her career by French privateers, and had repelled both assaults. Its crew numbered eighty men; it could carry one hundred passengers when the cargo holds were not full.

Captain John Ramshaw came ashore to buy extra provisions for the trip back across the Atlantic to the colonies, to pick up mail, to hire some extra hands for the crew, and to see if it was true that there was a lone survivor of the Skelly gang, as he had heard in London. His vessel was loaded with cargo, paying passengers, redemptioners, several refugee Huguenot families, and a few felons whose indentures he bought in London. He held the indentures of the redemptioners and convicts alike, and would sell them to colonials. He also carried on board some Crown appointees, tax collectors for the ports of Savannah, Newport, and Charleston. In Southampton, where he stopped to purchase extra sailcloth and various ship's stores, a company of marines who were to join Admiral Knowles's fleet in the Caribbean was imposed on him at the last moment, and he was obliged to lay in extra supplies for them on the voyage. This delay caused the *Sparrowhawk* to miss joining a Navy-escorted convoy of merchantmen that rendezvoused near Land's End and departed.

Ramshaw was led into the prisoners' pen by Mr. Binns, with whom he had dealt before. Mr. Binns pointed out the good prisoners and the bad among the convicted felons. Ramshaw espied Jack Frake in a corner of the pen just as the boy saw him. Before the boy could open his mouth or show any kind of recognition, Ramshaw winked and shook his head imperceptibly. The captain followed the jailer around, listening to his patter. At length, he asked, pointing to the boy, "Who's that? I'll need an extra cabin boy for all the passengers I'm carrying, and he looks nimble enough."

"Him? He was with the Skelly gang. Would've been hung with Skelly and Smith, but he was mixed up in some other criminal matter, and so old Twycross gave him transportation."

"Seven years?"

"Eight," said Mr. Binns. "He bloodied the Revenue Commissioner's nose at the hanging. So Milord Wicker tacked an extra year to his sentence. Strange boy. Know what he did? He jumped on his mates' ropes and hanged them himself. Weren't no show to it then. Lots of folks felt put out by it. Traveled all that way to see Skelly run on air, and he dies like that!" said the jailer with a snap of his fingers. "And all 'cause of that Frake lad."

Ramshaw studied the jailer. "Maybe the lad was being merciful," he suggested.

Mr. Binns shook his head emphatically. "Weren't his business being merciful. That's the court's business."

"Well, I'll take him. The colonies are screaming for apprentices."

Jack Frake exchanged his leg-irons for jougs, a padlocked iron collar. The collar belonged to Ramshaw, and he was obliged to fasten the contraption around Jack Frake's neck before the bailiff surrendered custody of the prisoner. And in his cabin, Ramshaw told the boy, "You will have the run of the ship, but you must wear the jougs. There are Crown officials on board, and those marines. You're not likely to jump overboard and swim for it wearing that blasted collar. You'd drown. You'll be assigned deck duties, repairing sails and such, and train with one of my gun crews. I won't send you up in the rigging, of course, because of that collar. And I won't stow you with the other convicts, though you'll help feed the poor bastards. You'll quarter with the other boys. I won't need to tell them to spare you their initiation foolery. They'll be afraid of you, for a while. You're a piece of a legend, Jack, and they'll respect you for that. Now, I know some decent men in the colonies, particularly in Virginia, and I'll arrange to hand you over to one of them. It's the best I can do for you, son."

"I understand, sir."

"Now, have some chocolate and bread and cheese, and tell me everything that happened. Skelly was a great friend of mine… "

Ramshaw stood with Jack Frake on the deck as the *Sparrowhawk* got under way. When it passed Tragedy Point, passengers and crew pointed to the ruins of Clowance Castle — "Built by Sir Henry Clowance and his Royalists, but the Roundheads smashed it with artillery and slew every manjack inside, because none of them would surrender" — and to the two indistinct black figures that seemed to cling to the cliffside near the foot of the ruin. "That's Skelly and his henchman, O'Such," commented one of the officials standing near them. "I heard in town that even on the gallows they cursed the king."

"How?" asked another passenger.

"One sung Queen Mary's birthday song, and the other sung our anthem. What brazen effrontery! They got what they deserved."

Ramshaw turned to the official and said, "Sir, Mr. Skelly had more right to sing that anthem than you will ever have. He has my adulation, and you have my contempt." He smiled at the offended official. "And if you don't wish to find amusing things in your meals on this voyage, pray keep your mouth sealed on the matter of Skelly."

"Are you saying that you were a friend of his?" asked the official with sly smugness.

"I'm saying what I'm saying, sir. Skelly added happiness to men's lives. You and your ilk could never make that claim. Don't pursue the subject. I am not a patient man."

The surprised official sniffed and walked away to another part of the deck.

Jack Frake reached for his hat to remove it in a final salute, then remembered that he had no hat. He stood watching the cliffside until the black blots disappeared. He felt a great, tired sadness. He wondered if he would ever see England again, or ever want to see it again. It was the only land he knew; the colonies were an abstraction to him, an unknown realm. He knew their geography as well as had Skelly and Redmagne, but they were still an alien land to him. He was glad the ship was not close enough for him to see the features of the iron-gibbeted bodies; gibbeted criminals on posts dotted the land and it was not a pleasant sight. This was not how he wanted to remember his friends. The two figures on the receding cliffside marred his conception of what England was. His own servitude — the weight of the collar around his neck — was so personal an affront that to reflect on its injustice would be redundant.

He remembered the first time he had seen England from this vantage point, from the deck of the *Ariadne*, in the dead of night, long ago. For some reason he could not now explain, he felt a desire to shout "Huzza!" as he did then, but here in the daylight, to celebrate some bigger perspective. At the same time, he knew that he was not leaving something behind — something he had learned from the two figures on the cliffside — but taking it with him. In the next instant, he realized that he could measure the difference between what he was then, on the *Ariadne*, and what he was now. Then, he had celebrated the actual proof of the accuracy of some lines and colored shapes on a globe. Now, he could celebrate the actual proof of the shape of his own soul, a shape he was beginning to become aware of for the first time.

He did not shout "Huzza!" Instead, he placed a hand on his chest, near his heart, in possession of the greater thing he was, in a last salute to the men he knew once possessed themselves in the same precious manner, and in dedication to what was possible to himself.

A while later, as he roamed the deck to familiarize himself with what would be his home for two months, he heard a voice behind him. "Look, Mama! It's Jeremy Jeamer! He's Redmagne's friend! They saved us from the bad men!"

Jack Frake turned around and saw a man, a woman, and little Etain McRae. Too engrossed in his own thoughts, he smiled briefly at the girl, but noticed the woman looking at him with an interest that went beyond curiosity about his iron collar. She seemed to know why he was wearing it. He felt that she wanted to speak to him, but she glanced at her husband and turned away. He learned later that she was Madeline McRae, the girl's mother, and early in the voyage she managed to take him aside and ask about her governess. He told her what he knew, or rather, what he had heard from prisoners' talk in Falmouth Prison: that a woman's body was found floating in the Channel in the vicinity of Tragedy Point, and that it was said to be that of the woman who called to Redmagne at the gallows.

Madeline McRae dabbed an eye with a handkerchief. "I was afraid of that," she said in a French accent. "I knew it had to be that." She reached into her purse and gave Jack Frake a silver coin. "This is but a token of my thanks, Mr. Frake. I cannot repay you or your friend for what you did when my daughter was on the coach last summer. But you will be welcome at my house in Caxton any time."

* * *

But for two storms, it was an uneventful crossing. Early one morning, however, a month and a week into the voyage, the *Sparrowhawk* vanished into a vast fog bank which stretched from horizon to horizon, north to south. When it re-entered the sunlight, twenty minutes had passed when the lookout reported sails emerging from the phenomenon behind them. Ramshaw came up from his cabin and studied the distant ship with his spy-glass. He exclaimed to his sailing master and the lieutenant of marines, "It's the *L'Fléau*, blast it! Robichaux's following our wake! Full sails, Mr. Cutter! Tell the crew to take gun stations! Get the passengers down below, and give a gun to any one of them that's willing to fight!"

Out of the fog crept *L'Fléau*, a privateer commanded by Paul

Robichaux. *L'Fléau* was a full frigate with forty-five guns of comparable size to the *Sparrowhawk*'s, and a crew of three hundred composed of Frenchmen, Irishmen, Spanish and Dutchmen. Robichaux, who carried letters of marque from Louis, the King of France, had made a career of harrying English merchantmen, seizing their vessels and cargoes, and holding their crews for ransom. French jails were full of prisoners he had taken over a period of five years. Even though England was no longer an active belligerent in the War of the Austrian Succession, English shipping was fair game to French and Spanish privateers.

"She's giving chase," said Ramshaw. "She'll catch up with us soon." The privateer followed the merchantman for half an hour, each minute bringing it yards closer to the *Sparrowhawk*.

As *L'Fléau*'s sails came closer, Ramshaw called the Huguenots to his cabin and advised them that it was best that they stay below, and not take up arms. But the Huguenots would have none of that. "We are going to freedom," said the spokesman for the group. "It would be folly not to want to fight for it when it is so close."

"Consider this, sirs," replied Ramshaw. "If you people are taken under arms, your menfolk will be executed as traitors and your families sold into slavery in the French Indies or Barbary. But if you're taken as passengers, you'll be imprisoned with us, and ransom demands sent to your kin in France."

The Huguenot spokesman, a tall, balding educated-looking man, answered, "We are done with such options, Captain. We are prepared to accept the consequences of fighting our countrymen."

"So be it, gentlemen," said Ramshaw.

Jack Frake had trained to be a powder monkey for the aft swivel gun. It was his job to fetch powder and balls from the magazine and to help load the gun. Ramshaw's gun crews were as well trained and disciplined as any warship's; many of his men were Royal Navy deserters working for him for the better pay and under assumed names.

L'Fléau drew abreast of the *Sparrowhawk* and began to edge closer. The wind that drove the merchantman was blocked by the privateer now, allowing the frigate to use it to close in. Jack Frake watched with the others as the privateer's gun crews prepared for a broadside. Sharpshooters infested the French ship's rigging and fighting tops like starlings. A man ostentatiously garbed in a gold-laced greatcoat and ruffled cravat raised a trumpet and called over to the *Sparrowhawk*. "Captain of the good ship

Sparrowhawk! I am Paul Robichaux of the *Scourge*, and you know I do not repeat myself! You will be wise to surrender, or we will sink you or take you! What is your answer?"

Ramshaw, on the quarter deck, raised his own trumpet. "I am Captain John Ramshaw, and my compliments to you! We regret to say, 'Rule, Britannia!'" His men cheered at this reply, and he nodded to his master gunner to order a broadside.

Robichaux did the same, and both ships fired with thunderous roars that tilted them both in the water. Most of the cannon balls bounced off of the side of each vessel, but some did damage. A lucky shot from the *Sparrowhawk* shattered the gammoning of *L'Fléau*'s bowsprit, loosening the rigging to the foremast and rendering the privateer less manageable. Another severed a length of the mizzenmast's shrouds and a dozen sharpshooters tumbled to the deck or were forced to drop their muskets to hang on to the ropes. Shots from the privateer, in turn, crippled the merchantman's spanker, and struck one of the "Quakers" with such force that it was ripped from its carriage and flew against a sergeant of the marines, killing him.

While each vessel's gun crews rushed to swab and reload, the air crackled with musket fire. Men on both ships fell, and Jack Frake's crew tried to bring down the pilot or damage *L'Fléau*'s wheel or capstan. But it was difficult to hit anything as the two vessels rose and fell in the water. His swivel gun managed to fire its third shot by the time the two ships' main gun crews exchanged second broadsides. In the cool May air his hair and shirt were soaked with sweat.

It was an uneven battle, for while *L'Fléau* was able to bring to bear twenty-two of her guns, the *Sparrowhawk* could fire only ten. Soon, the privateer could fire twenty-one guns; the *Sparrowhawk*, just eight, for one of its guns had been blown off its carriage and the crew of another killed by sharpshooters. The marines, crew and Huguenot men kept up steady musket fire at the privateer, but even here the odds were in favor of Robichaux's men, and grew better as more and more men slumped down behind the railings and sandbags, dead or wounded.

The men of the *Sparrowhawk* heard the men on *L'Fléau* begin to laugh and shout cries of derision and victory. A shot from the privateer hit the lanyard of the merchantman's ensign, and the banner fell to trail in the water. Through the smoke, Jack Frake saw men on *L'Fléau* crowd at the railing with grappling hooks, and only twenty feet of water separated the two ships. Ramshaw gave an order, and boys and men rushed from below to pass out swords, cutlasses and pistols. The captain paced up and down the quarter deck, his sword under one arm, loading a pair of pistols. His tricorn had been shot away, and even as Jack Frake watched, a musket ball jerked one of the man's coat-tails. He wondered if Skelly had looked like that at the Marvel caves.

L'Fléau's sharpshooters fired a disciplined volley at the deck of the *Sparrowhawk*, and the privateer inched closer to boarding range. "There's Robichaux!" exclaimed one of the men at Jack Frake's gun. The gun was pointing to the sky, and Jack Frake dumped a small chest of powder into the muzzle, then hefted a cannon ball into it, and packed it all in with his ramrod. As the gunner brought the weapon down and around to aim at Robichaux, a hail of musket balls peppered the aft. The crewman with the linstock fell dead, and the gunner ran.

Jack Frake took up the linstock, then grasped one of the gun's handles and aimed it at the strutting, laughing figure on *L'Fléau*. He blew on the slow-match at the end of the linstock, and as another rain of balls whizzed around him, steadied his aim, waiting for the bobbing privateer to ascend to a particular point. Something struck his iron collar, and the impact seemed to turn his bones and muscles to jelly. But he applied the linstock to the gun's touch-hole, and an unholy halo of flame from the blast blinded him and obliterated all sight of *L'Fléau*.

He had put too much powder in the gun, and the force of the recoil snapped the oaken stanchion in two and the gun flew back at him and knocked him down. He was stunned for a moment, but recovered quickly and rolled the heavy, hot iron off of his chest. He ran down the main deck and picked up a fallen marine's musket. He could not see Robichaux.

But *L'Fléau* was drawing away now. Curses and cries of panic came from the privateer. The men of the *Sparrowhawk* delivered a volley of musket fire into the attacker, and the crews of the remaining six serviceable guns worked feverishly to reload. On the master gunner's command, they fired together and wrought havoc on *L'Fléau*, tearing open one of her foremast mainsails. One ball struck the mizzenmast, and though not powerful enough to topple it, cracked the timber so that it would be dangerous to use, for its sails were set to funnel wind to the sails of the main mast. The least attempt to move its spars to adjust the direction of the wind might lengthen the crack or even bring the mast down.

The *Sparrowhawk* and *L'Fléau* began to drift apart. When the ships were beyond effective firing range, Captain Ramshaw appeared behind Jack

Frake and touched his shoulder. "They'll leave off now, Jack, thanks to you! You blew off Robichaux's head, and killed his second in command! I saw it happen through my glass. They thought he was immortal." He paused, and added with a chuckle, "So did I, for years."

The *Sparrowhawk* caught the full wind again, and soon *L'Fléau* was a quarter mile away, dead in the water. It did not follow. Ramshaw's crew commenced with repairs, first clearing the decks of the dead and wounded.

That evening, in his cabin, Ramshaw took a key from his desk and unlocked the padlock of the jougs around Jack Frake's neck. He paused to inspect the collar, and saw two indentations where musket balls had struck it. He shook his head once in amazement, then dropped the collar on the floor. "You're a free man, Jack. At least, on this ship you are. Damn what the officials think! They owe you their lives."

"Will they make trouble for you?"

"They don't dare. None of them volunteered to handle a musket, you might have noticed." Ramshaw paused to drink some rum. "Well, they'll be talking about today's fight for a long time, in every tavern and inn on the Continent, from Stockholm to Bilboa. I heard a rumor that Louis was going to make Robichaux an admiral. He never lost a fight, you see. He was the toast of the privateers. Sailors used to murder each other just for a place on his ship. Now? Damn it all!" laughed the captain. "Every privateer on the Atlantic is going to mark my *Sparrowhawk* for extinction."

Ramshaw lit a pipe. "When we get to Yorktown, I'll hold you aside from the other convicts. It may take a few weeks to find the right man to buy your indenture, but we'll wait. Jack, you're going to a new world." The light from the lantern on his desk swayed with the ship and cast moving shadows over the boy's face. There were still some powder smudges on it, and these were deepened by the shifting light. It was an eager, expectant, innocent face, thought Ramshaw. But in the eyes he saw intelligence and a species of wisdom that he thought would be at home in the colonies. "Yes, Jack. A new world for you. I wonder how you'll do in it — after your eight years are finished."

Acknowledgments

I am indebted, first and foremost, to two individuals, no longer with us. One confirmed my approach to life, the other confirmed its direction: Ayn Rand, the novelist-philosopher, whose novels I discovered, when a teenager, in the vandalized library of a suburban Pittsburgh boys' home; and David Lean, the British director, whose *Lawrence of Arabia* I saw the same year, an event that cemented my ambition to become a novelist.

Special fond thanks go to Wayne Barrett, former editor of the *Colonial Williamsburg Journal*, who was certain this novel would see the light of day after having read the first page long ago; and to the BookPress in Williamsburg, whose partners, John Ballinger and John Curtis, also encouraged me and allowed me to rummage through their valuable stock on the track of ideas and materials.

Further debts of thanks are owed to the staff and past and current directors of the John D. Rockefeller, Jr. Library at Colonial Williamsburg for their assistance; to many of Colonial Williamsburg's costumed "interpreters," too numerous to name here, for the passion, lore, and information they imparted; and to the staff of the Earl Gregg Swem Library at the College of William & Mary, Williamsburg.

Pat Walsh, editor, together with Robert Tindall and John Gray, have my gratitude for their incisive suggestions and innumerable corrections, and for sharing my confidence that this novel will find a large and appreciative readership.

Lastly, I owe a debt of thanks to the Founders for having given me something worth writing about, and a country in which to write it.